KOSTYA

(Her Russian Protector #7)

Roxie Rivera

Night Works Books
College Station, Texas

Copyright © 2019 Roxie Rivera
Print Edition

All rights reserved. No part of this publication may be reproduced, distributed or transmitted in any form or by any means, including photocopying, recording, or other electronic or mechanical methods, without the prior written permission of the publisher, except in the case of brief quotations embodied in critical reviews and certain other noncommercial uses permitted by copyright law. For permission requests, write to the publisher, addressed "Attention: Permissions Coordinator," at the address below.

Night Works Books
3515-B Longmire Drive #103
College Station, Texas 77845
www.roxierivera.com

Publisher's Note: This is a work of fiction. Names, characters, places, and incidents are a product of the author's imagination. Locales and public names are sometimes used for atmospheric purposes. Any resemblance to actual people, living or dead, or to businesses, companies, events, institutions, or locales is completely coincidental.

ISBN: 978-1-63042-044-4

Kostya/Roxie Rivera—1st ed.

CHAPTER ONE

NOTHING BROUGHT A smile to my face faster than the soft chatter of happy clients and cheerful stylists. As I swirled a brush through the demi-permanent formula I had just blended together, I glanced away from my guest seated at the color bar and leaned to the left to get a better view of the cutting floor. Four clients sat in chairs, smiling and talking as their stylists snipped and combed.

"So, you want to start the arch of your eyebrow right about here," Savannah explained, holding a spoolie brush at an angle against a woman's face. "I like to follow the natural shape of the brow and pluck as little as possible after trimming."

"Can I get you another a drink?" Billie, our guest relations manager, glided from station to station, checking in on clients and offering refreshments. She gathered up the occasional damp towel or empty water bottle as she made her round of the stations. The fishtail braid cascading down her back looked fantastic and had been incredibly popular on our salon's Instagram account today.

Pleased by the smiles and gossipy chit-chat, I returned my attention to the carefully mixed chemicals I had prepared for another stylist to apply. Nisha, the most popular stylist in our salon, was finishing up a haircut so I had pitched in to keep her on track with her appointments. Even though I had mixed color multiple times a day, I always checked and rechecked my formulas before painting even one strand of hair on a patron's head.

A bad bathroom dye job during the summer between my freshman and sophomore years of high school had taught me that painful and embarrassing lesson. Sometimes I couldn't quite believe the girl who had turned her hair violet and then a sickly shade of green before running to a salon with her tail tucked between her legs was now the most successful color specialist in the city.

I placed the small bowl of product on the rolling cart with the other supplies and pushed it toward Nisha's waiting client. Hannah was close to my mother's age, but the years hadn't been very kind to her. Stress had eaten away at her self-confidence and left behind the tell-tale signs around the corners of her mouth and eyes. She smiled timidly at me, almost as if she feared doing or saying the wrong thing, and I ached for her.

Like all the women in our salon this Sunday afternoon, Hannah had come here as part of an outreach program we offered through a handful of domestic violence and homeless shelters. Bianca Bradshaw and her mother hosted a gently-used clothing boutique at their church's fellowship hall that provided these women with basic pieces for starting over as well as work attire. We provided hair coloring, cuts, styling and basic spa services like eyebrow shaping for women who needed a little confidence boosting pick-me-up or a fresh look to get them ready for job hunting and the new lives they were trying to build. They left with a gift bag of supplies and vouchers for two years of free services.

A day of beauty wasn't going to solve their problems or heal the wounds violence and homelessness had inflicted, but I liked to think the short escape we provided offered a brief reprieve and a little happiness. For the women who were searching for employment after years of being homeless or under the thumbs of controlling spouses, I hoped it gave them newfound self-assurance. I wanted these women to know they were beautiful and worthy and had every right to go after the futures they deserved.

"Would you like another cup of tea before I start on your color?"

Hannah tugged at the neckline of her cape and shook her head. "I'm fine."

"Is this too tight?" I touched the cape. "I can adjust it."

"No, it's fine." Her hands immediately dropped to her lap.

"Let's take a peek, just in case." I could tell the cape was bothering her, but she wasn't about to tell me that she was uncomfortable. I didn't even want to imagine what hell she had endured that left her feeling as if she shouldn't even voice something as simple as her discomfort. "Sometimes these capes get a little frayed on the edges and scratch the skin."

When I unclipped the cape, I spotted a gnarly, thick scar running along her neck, just above the collar of her T-shirt. It was an old wound that hadn't healed well and looked angry and red. I had a terrible feeling she had doctored the injury herself, probably to keep the abuse she had suffered a secret. Not wanting to draw attention to something that had obviously made her uncomfortable, I lied. "Yep! It's a frayed cape. Let me get you a different one, okay?"

I swept away the cape she was wearing and switched it out for a different one from the drawer at the color bar. I grabbed a small towel too and tucked it along the cape's neckline as a liner. "How's that?"

"Much better." She managed another smile. "Thank you."

"No problem." With her comfort assured, I slipped on a pair of black disposable gloves, grabbed a comb and began to section off her hair for color application. Not wanting her to feel pressured to speak, I filled the time by talking about my mother's recent adventures with decorating the townhouse she had recently purchased. "We're going to take a little trip down to Round Top for the antique festival next month. Mom's on the hunt for a hutch and credenza and some light fixtures."

"What does your daddy think of all that renovating and antique buying?" Hannah seemed genuinely curious and maybe even a little worried. "It sounds awfully expensive."

"I don't have a daddy." It was an admission I found easy to make now, but there had been a time when I had burned with shame and embarrassment at having no father to give me a name or claim me as his own.

Hannah glanced back at me and frowned. "Everyone has a father."

"I mean, sure, *technically*, I have a father out there somewhere, but I don't know him, and I doubt he knows me."

"That must have been hard for your mother."

"It wasn't easy, but she found a way to balance her career and being a mom. She always put me first though, even if it meant she had to go in late at night after I was in bed to get caught up on work."

"She sounds tenacious."

I laughed as I considered my spitfire mother. "That's Mom all right."

"It's good that you had a role model like that," Hannah quietly remarked. "My daughters…"

When her voice trailed off, I didn't know whether I should ask about them or let it go. Thankfully, Nisha saved me from having to make that decision by appearing at the color station we were using and bumping me with her hip. Tall and curvy, Nisha displayed her killer fashion sense with a knockout black dress paired with a silver belt and lots of big, chunky turquoise jewelry.

I so envied her luscious dark curls and her fuller figure. Nisha made looking that damn sexy so effortless. Our clients loved her, and her book was six weeks deep with appointments. Without Nisha, Savannah and I never would have been able to make Allure what it was today. I couldn't wait to see Nisha's face on Christmas morning when we surprised her with a piece of the salon as our third partner. She had more than earned it.

"Thanks for pitching in to help me stay on schedule," Nisha said while pulling on a pair of gloves. "I can take it from here so you can help our last client."

I carefully handed her the brush I had been using and peeled off my gloves. I made sure to let her know when I had started the application of color before breaking away from the color bar to the waiting area where our final appointment of the day waited.

A young woman sat in the lobby with her hands clamped between her knees. She wore an ill-fitting ikat print dress with a too-big navy cardigan that looked as if it had been dug out of a donations box. It didn't escape my notice that she had chosen a seat that gave her a clear view of the front door and let her keep a wall against her back. She seemed nervous and afraid so I decided to move slowly and give her some space.

"Hello." I shifted aside a few magazines and sat down on the round white leather ottoman in front of her. "I'm Holly Phillips, and I'm going to be your stylist today."

She lifted her gaze from the hands clamped between her knees—and I was taken aback. We looked so similar! Same eyes, similar noses and mouths. Her hair was longer than mine and showed the tell-tale signs of a botched home bleaching attempt. We would definitely have to correct that during our appointment.

As if seeing the uncanny resemblance between us, she grinned. When she spoke, the words were foreign to me. *Russian*, I realized. It was a language I was hearing more and more around the salon. Our client base had shifted a bit after Erin Markovic introduced Vivian Kalasnikov to our services. Everyone in their husbands' social circles wanted an appointment here now.

"I'm so sorry. I don't speak Russian," I apologized. "Our massage therapist who does isn't here today either." Realizing she probably didn't understand a word I was saying, I stopped talking. How the heck was I supposed to style her hair if we couldn't communicate?

"My name…," she said haltingly and with emphasis on each word, as if she were trying them out for the first time, "is Lana."

"It's nice to meet you, Lana." I shook her hand and got a glimpse of her manicure. It was clean and neat and the soft coral shade looked fun and fresh. Someone had painted an intricate design in the palest shell pink on them. "Your nails look fantastic!"

She understood that, it seemed, and perked up a bit. 'Thank you. I do it with...um..." She seemed to be searching for the right word. "Toothpick!"

"Really?" I examined them more closely and fell in love with the lace-like design she had created. "Look, um, can you just sit tight for a second? I need to make a quick phone call." I gestured for her to stay seated and crossed the waiting area to the reception desk. "Hey, Billie, will you keep an eye on my client for a second? I need to pop into my office."

Billie nodded. "Sure."

Glancing over the styling products she had pulled from the retail shelves, I asked, "Is this the last of the clearance?"

"It is." She picked up two bottles of a discontinued lotion fragrance from our spa's preferred line and quickly applied bright red clearance labels. "If you want me to stay late, I can tackle the new shampoo and conditioner display tonight."

"You can take care of it in the morning. You didn't take a single day off this week, Billie. When we're done tonight, head home and enjoy your night off."

She quirked a smile. "Whatever you say, boss."

I left the reception desk, glided along the perimeter of the salon to the employee door and ducked into my office. We had a zero-tolerance policy for cell phones on the salon floor. I hated to break a rule, even on a day when the salon was technically closed to the public, but I didn't know what else to do.

I didn't have to roll very far through my mental Rolodex

of contacts to come up with some names that might be able to help. Vivian was my first thought. She was a faithful client of the salon and someone I had come to consider a good friend. As the wife of one of Houston's richest Russian émigrés, she seemed to be one of the leading ladies of the city's small but very tight-knit Russian community.

But I hesitated to call her on a Sunday—especially *this* Sunday. Last night, most of the people in our overlapping social circles had been at the wedding of Bianca Bradshaw and Sergei Sakharov. Vivian had been the maid of honor, and I could only imagine how tired she was today, especially since she was pregnant. The last thing she needed was me bothering her when she was probably resting.

Kostya.

The moment the name of my mercurial and mysterious Russian neighbor registered in my mind, I felt instantly calmed. Was he in Houston this week? He worked in the private security field and traveled quite a bit, almost as much as my mother. I hadn't seen him at the wedding yesterday, but it was worth a try.

I quickly swiped the screen of my iPhone with my thumb, punched in my passcode and tapped in the number of the only man I trusted to come running if I asked for help.

Sometimes he came running even before I asked for help…

As I waited for Kostya to answer, I toyed with the delicate gold and jade bracelet he had given me for Christmas. The memory of that night still made my heart race. After fighting off the worst blind date of my life, I had been shoved out of a car onto my front lawn and hit with my own clutch. It had been humiliating and terrifying—until Kostya had emerged from the shadows like some kind of dark knight. He had defended and protected me from that jerk before tending my injuries with such tenderness.

"Holly?" The rasp of his deep voice sent a shiver of pure delight right down to the feminine core of me.

"Hey, Kostya." I drummed my fingertips on my desk. "Um...are you busy?"

"You know that I'm never too busy for you." His answer left me grinning like a fool. "Is everything all right?" He went straight into alpha over-protective mode, just as he did every time I called. "Are you okay?"

"I'm fine, but thank you for asking. Actually, I sort of need a favor."

"Of course. You know that you can ask me for anything."

When he said *anything*, I got the feeling that he meant just that. I wasn't sure if I should find that flattering or terrifying. "You know how we offer special services for the women's shelter on the first Sunday of the month?"

"*Da.*"

I slowly made my way out of my office. "So, there's a young woman here who doesn't speak much English—"

"She speaks Russian?"

"Yes."

"And you want me to help translate?"

I stopped on the edge of the cutting floor and bit my lower lip. "Would you mind?"

"Not at all," he assured me.

"Thank you so much." I walked to the waiting area of the salon and sat down on the ottoman again. Lana now had a bottle of water in one hand and flipped the pages of a magazine opened across her lap. The cuffs of the too-large cardigan she wore had ridden up a little and revealed nasty bruises on her wrists. I could see the imprints of fingertips and long, thin lines that might have come from cords or ties.

Sweet Jesus! What had this poor girl survived?

She must have felt my stare because she self-consciously tugged down the sleeves of her cardigan and swallowed nervously.

I caught her eye and smiled, hoping to set her at ease. Tapping my phone screen, I activated the speaker and held it between us. "Can you hear us, Kostya? I have you on speaker."

"Yes." Kostya introduced himself to Lana who perked right up when she heard someone speaking her language. I noticed the way she relaxed right before my eyes and actually smiled when answering Kostya's questions. She touched the ends of her hair while she talked as if describing a shorter cut.

"Holly?" Kostya addressed me. "Are you there?"

"Yep. Right here." I leaned toward the phone, just in case the background noise of blow dryers and music was too loud.

"Lana says that she likes your hair color and the style of your haircut. She would like to do that if you think it will work."

"I think they'll look great on her, but can you ask her what products she's used on her hair? It looks as if she tried to do a home bleaching kit and then changed her mind and put ash blonde over it. I just want to make sure I know what's on her hair before I start her color session."

Kostya chatted with Lana for a few moments and then gave me a quick rundown of the products she had put in her hair over the last few weeks. "She says that she understands English very well. If you stick to yes or no questions, you'll be fine. If you need my help, call or text me. I'll be around all evening."

"All right. Thanks again, Kostya."

"Anytime, Holly."

As I ended the call and slipped my phone into the back pocket of my black skinny jeans, I noticed Lana's curious look. "He's my neighbor," I explained. "We're friends."

Her blue eyes glinted with skepticism. She didn't believe me anymore than I believed myself. Friends? Sure. We were friends—but I wanted so much more with him.

And it drove me crazy that Kostya seemed completely oblivious. I'd finally discovered the one man I couldn't charm with my Texas sass and flirty smile. It didn't seem fair that he lived next door, tempting and taunting and frustrating me all at once.

Catching myself toying with the bracelet again, I forced my fingers to go still and focused all of my attention on Lana. "I'm going to make sure you have a wonderful experience in my salon. Okay?"

"Okay."

"Great." I motioned toward the color bar. "Let's get started."

While she headed for the closest chair, I bent down to grab a cape from the basket under the counter. When I turned around, I had to stifle the shocked gasp that threatened to escape my throat. Lana had taken off her cardigan, probably to keep it free from any of the bleach that might drip down her neck during the rinsing process. The spaghetti straps of her dress revealed bare shoulders and a neck mottled with bruises in varying stages of healing. The bones in her arms and shoulders were so prominent, and I could only wonder at how many nights she had gone to bed hungry or been beaten. Refusing to make her uncomfortable, I schooled my features and draped the cape around her shoulders. I figured she had probably had enough of people digging into her business and asking her uncomfortable questions. For the few hours that she was in my salon, I wanted her to be able to escape the awful memories of what she had survived.

I was careful not to touch her or move quickly as I evaluated her hair and formulated a plan to give her the shiniest, iciest platinum white possible. Typically, I made sure my clients understood that going so pale meant a lot of upkeep and expense but I had already decided that this girl was getting whatever she wanted and on my dime.

As I worked on her hair, I was close enough to notice just how young she seemed. More and more, I worried that she might be *too* young. A sick feeling invaded my stomach. What if this poor girl hadn't willingly come to Houston? There had been so many trafficking busts in Houston and the surrounding counties over the last couple of years. A lot of those women came from Southeast Asia, but I had seen a recent news report about girls from Eastern Europe and Russia being at a high risk for trafficking.

But how in the world did I approach a subject so sensitive? Would Lana even tell me if I could figure out a way to talk to her? What could be done if my suspicions were proven true? She was in a safe place now—but was she safe enough? Shelters had security, but the kind of people who would traffic a young woman were the kind of people who wouldn't let a couple of rent-a-cops slow them down.

Kostya was the obvious choice here. Not only was he someone who shared her background and language, but he made a living as a very successful security systems consultant. His business was keeping people safe. Surely, he could figure out a way to keep Lana out of harm's way if she needed help.

Besides, more than once, I had heard rumors that he was *the* man in Houston to approach if someone needed information of a sensitive nature or needed help getting out of trouble. I tried not to pay attention to the *other* rumors I'd heard about him, but it was difficult not to worry about him when I heard dark things about his friendship with Nikolai Kalasnikov.

People whispered words like *mafia* and *mobster* and *gangster* about that small group of men. I wasn't sure what to believe. From the outside, Kostya and his friends—Nikolai Kalasnikov, Ivan Markovic, Sergei Sakharov, Besian Beciraj, Alexei Sarnov—seemed like upstanding, successful members of the community. But I had heard things. Things that made me bite my lip with concern. Things that made me wonder if I really knew my neighbor that well...

"I like very much," Lana remarked with a grin as she checked out her feisty white-blonde hair in the mirror. It was still damp from a final rinse but it looked fantastic.

"Just wait 'til we get it cut and styled!" I finished squeezing the last bit of excess water from her hair before spritzing her strands with a styling product that worked well with her new ultra-blonde color. I slowly worked my way through her hair with a comb and then used a few clips to hold up short twists of hair. I gently manipulated her head into the right position. "Can you look down please?"

She did as asked while I picked up my cutting comb and shears. The haircut was a simple one to achieve. I had been wearing my hair styled in a long bob with messy, loose waves and curls for the last few weeks and loved it. I had a feeling Lana was going to enjoy the versatility of the cut and the ease of styling.

While I was cross-checking my cut, Billie wandered over with a broom and dustpan to sweep up the floor. I caught her eye for a second. "Hey, Billie, can you grab my cell phone out of my pocket and send a quick text to my friend?"

"Sure." She picked my phone out of my back pocket and typed in the text as I dictated it to her. I needed Kostya to translate the hair upkeep instructions for Lana in an email that Billie could print. She made a big production of tapping my screen before tucking my phone back in my pocket. "Sent. Anything else?"

"Go to the front and grab my favorite hair products. Shampoo, conditioner, toning shampoo, hair mask, blonde-friendly styling products…"

"Will do." She finished sweeping up the last bits of hair from the floor before heading off to complete her task.

My cut complete, I dabbed a little more styling product on Lana's hair and reached up on tiptoes to grab the blow dryer dangling over my station. I finger combed her hair as I blasted it with some heat to dry away the lingering moisture. She paid close attention as I worked with a small straightener to achieve the right look, pulling down and curling just a tiny bit at the end to develop an easy, loose curl.

After putting away my tools, I unclipped the cape and offered her a mirror so she could see the back of her hair. The happiness lighting up her face convinced me I had given her exactly what she wanted. We had found a common language—fashion and beauty—and no longer needed a translator.

"Beautiful." Lana primped happily. "I like very much."

"You look fantastic." I folded up the cape and draped it over the chair. "This is a good look for you." I gestured for her to follow me. "Let's go play at the makeup counter."

Like two little girls sneaking around in our mother's makeup stash, we dug through the colorful drawers and displays until we found the perfect shades of blush, eyeshadow and lipstick. As I watched her apply makeup, I confirmed my earlier suspicion. If this girl was a day over eighteen, I would do cartwheels in the parking lot. She was a kid, just barely this side of childhood, and it pained me to think of the misery and suffering she had known. It wasn't right, and she deserved better.

As our appointment drew to its close, I started thinking of ways to keep in touch with Lana. Women at the shelter were known to disappear, either returning home to their abusive partners or running away in fear. My instincts screamed Lana was still in trouble. She needed people she could trust. She needed a safe place that wasn't the shelter.

I caught sight of her beautiful manicure and an idea struck—but I'd need some time to pull it off. "Listen, Lana," I stopped her before we reached the reception counter, "how would you like to come work for me?"

Her face reflected comprehension and then surprise. "Work?" She gestured around the salon. "Here?"

"Yes. Here."

She winced. "My English…"

I cut her off before she could sell herself short. "We'll figure something out."

She started to protest but the ear-piercing squawk of the security system interrupted her. We both jumped, and I scowled at the ceiling. This was the fourth time in the last two weeks this frustrating thing had just randomly blasted us during business hours.

"Lana," I touched her arm to get her attention and had to shout over the siren, "come see me tomorrow." I glanced at the reception desk where Billie stood with her hands clapped over her ears to drown out the siren. "Billie, make sure Lana gets her bag and the instructions for upkeep."

Billie shot me a thumbs up and then answered the ringing phone. "Security guys," she mouthed while pointing at the phone.

"Tell them to shut this thing off!" I quickly turned on my heel and sprinted to the back of the salon where I found Savannah smacking and cursing at the box mounted on the wall there. "What set it off this time?"

"Hell if I know!" She slapped the keypad twice and growled. "I was looking over our notes for the Monday morning staff meeting, and this thing just flipped out and started screeching. Now I can't get it to take our code."

Figuring she was about two seconds from ripping it off the wall, I gently shouldered her aside. "Let me try."

"It's all yours!" She threw her hands up in the air and stormed away in a huff.

I fished my phone out of my pocket and quickly dialed the

security company's support line while trying to reset the system manually. If Billie couldn't get them to shut it off, I wanted to be already on the line with a representative. I was still waiting on hold when I managed to get the system to accept our override code. I stayed on the line for another twenty-seven minutes troubleshooting the ongoing issues with the representative who answered.

When the representative couldn't offer an explanation for why our system was on the fritz, I hung up in frustration. Using a nationwide company was proving to be a pain in my ass. More and more, I wondered if choosing a local security company wasn't the better choice. Conveniently enough, I had an expert in security living right next door.

Speaking of doors...

I noticed the double doors to our main supply closet were open and walked over to close it. Savannah must not have seen it when she was back here beating on the security system keypad. If she had, my phone would be vibrating with a new email alert because she would have sent out a company-wide email reminding everyone to close doors, turn off electronics and flip light switches. As the salon's money maven, she watched our utility bills like a hawk and was fanatical about conserving energy.

Standing alone in the back hall near the rear entrance, I suddenly had the strangest sensation of not being alone. It was an odd flutter in my stomach that spread into my chest. Hand on the supply closet door, I held my breath and listened for...well. I wasn't sure what I was listening for actually.

Quit being such a baby! There's nothing in there but shampoo and towels.

When I heard nothing, I rolled my eyes and shut the door. Feeling silly for letting my imagination run wild, I headed back to the salon's main floor. Lana had disappeared along with the last few straggler clients. Billie was shutting down our registers and books for the night while Savannah wiped down the makeup counter. Nisha glanced up at me and smiled as she straightened up her station. I went to my own and went through my usual end of night routine so I could start my morning off right.

By sunset, only Savannah and I remained at the salon. I wandered back to my office and kicked off my heels before sinking into my desk chair to tackle the backlog of paperwork waiting for my attention. There were vacation requests to sort, new stylist applications to pick through and vendor literature piling up to be read.

"Hey, Holly?" Savannah called out to me as she stepped into my office. "You busy?"

"No." I swiveled around in my desk chair and discovered Savannah leaning against the door frame. I grinned at the sight of the mannequin head clamped under her arm. "Is Nisha starting her Halloween pranks a few weeks early?"

Laughing at the reminder of Nisha's ghoulish pranks, she gave the male mannequin a little shake. "No, I found Harry in the conference room and thought he looked lonely." She sauntered across my office and plunked the practice manne-quin down onto my desk. With a saucy wink, she flashed her whiskey brown eyes at me and said, "I'm embracing my inner matchmaker. I think Harry is the perfect guy for you."

I snorted softly. "How's that, Savvy?"

"For one, he doesn't talk back. And look!" She gestured to

him. "He doesn't have hands so we don't have to worry about him getting grabby or overstepping the line, right? Plus, he has fabulous hair." She ran her fingers though Harry's wavy dark locks. "See? You love a man with thick, wavy hair, right?"

I shook my head at her silliness. "I love you, Savvy. Don't ever change."

"I'm too stubborn for that." She leaned back against my desk and crossed her arms. My envious gaze settled on her ample bust and killer curves. Even dressed in simple skinny jeans and a flirty high ponytail, she was a knockout. "You, on the other hand, could use a little change in your life."

I rolled my eyes and sagged in my chair. "Not this again."

"Yes. *This.* Again." She nudged my leg with the toe of her red ballet flat. "We missed you last night at the wedding reception. You should have come."

"You know I don't like receptions."

"It's not about liking or not liking them. This was about networking and building our business and being a good friend to Bianca. She and her mother own the most successful bridal boutique in this city. They see a lot of brides and recommend our salon to those bridal parties. We see a lot of word-of-mouth business because of them."

The financial and marketing brains behind the salon, Savannah framed the issue in a way that hit home for me. Chagrined, I nodded contritely. "You're right. I should have gone and pulled my weight as an owner of the salon."

"It's more than that, Holly. Bianca and her mother have been clients at this salon since we opened our doors. We're all friends and colleagues. You even came in on your day off to help with the bridal party's hair and makeup. I thought for sure you would stick around after the ceremony, but when we got to the reception, I looked everywhere and couldn't find you."

I shifted uncomfortably beneath her perturbed stare. "I didn't have a date."

"So?"

"So, I hate being the single girl at the wedding."

Savannah rolled her eyes. "There were plenty of ladies there without a plus-one, and there were so many great single guys there last night. *Hot* single guys," she added with a saucy smile. "All those big, delicious, sexy fighters from Sergei's gym were there." She fanned herself. "You missed a hell of a party!"

"Apparently," I said giving her an appraising glance. "And which one of those fighters did you take home?"

"Now, now," she replied rather primly, "you know me. I'm a good Catholic girl."

I leveled a look her way. "Mmmhmm."

"Hush." She playfully chastised. Then, more serious, she said, "Holly, you're one of the prettiest women in this whole city. You're sweet, smart and funny. You own the most popular salon and spa in Houston. Men are *tripping* over their feet to get in front of you so you'll notice them. If you weren't so dang picky, you could have any man in Houston."

"I don't want just any man in Houston," I replied rather indignantly.

She narrowed her eyes in suspicion. "Is this about *him*?"

"Him?" A nervous burst of energy rippled through my belly. "Who?"

She saw right through my act. "You know damned well I mean that Russian fox who lives next door to you." She exhaled in frustration. "You're still pining after Kostya Antonovich."

I huffed at her. "I'm not pining."

She gave me a look. "Oh really?"

"It's not pining," I insisted defensively. "Pining is what happens after a break-up. I haven't even gotten as much as a date with him!"

"And whose fault is that?"

"What?"

"You heard me." She hitched her shoulders up as if itching to argue. "I'm going to ask you something, and I want your honest answer."

"All right." I had a feeling I wasn't going to like what I heard next.

"Do you really want *this* man, Holly?"

I narrowed my eyes at her. "What does that mean?"

"It means that I've heard things about Kostya. Things that make me nervous for you," she added with concern.

"What things?"

"Holly..."

"Savannah." I sat up straighter and held her gaze. "What things? If it's those mob rumors, I've heard them and they're all nonsense."

"I'm pretty sure it's *not* nonsense. Come on, Holly! Open your eyes. What the heck was that attack that happened last year? The one where Vivian was dragged out of a car and Nikolai was beaten half to death? Doesn't that sound a little mobbed-up to you?"

"The paper said it was because of her dad. You saw the news coverage when he got away from those US Marshals."

She rolled her eyes at me. "Okay. We'll chalk that one up to dear old dad, but don't you think it's a little suspicious that Vivian's husband is *that* rich just from owning a restaurant and some other small businesses?"

"Maybe he came here with a little money in his pocket and made some good investments," I offered. "There was a lot of money to be made in Russia. Look at Yuri Novakovsky and some of the other oligarchs. It's plausible that Nikolai got his hands on some of that money."

"Fine. I'll give you that one, too. But what about Erin Markovic's husband? The guy was a straight-up brawler, Holly. I've heard he even used to beat people up to collect money and fought underground in cage matches! And have you seen the tattoos on his hands?" Her eyes widened with something very close to fear. "When Erin was in here for her mani-pedi, he dropped her off and came in to wait for her. He paid her bill, and I got a good look at the ink on his hands. Those tattoos scared the shit out of me. That ink means something, Holly. It means something *bad*."

I didn't want to dig into the dark and complicated history of Erin's husband. Ivan was a big, scary guy, and I had no problem believing he had done some less than savory things. Even so, he had never shown me anything but kindness and respect. I believed in second chances, and he seemed to have earned his. Turning the conversation, I insisted, "Kostya doesn't have those tattoos."

"Maybe not on his hands or arms but who knows what's under his shirt?"

"Well I haven't seen him naked yet so I wouldn't know," I replied rather testily.

"It's not just the mob rumors, Holly. There are some not-so-nice things about Kostya that are facts."

"Like?" Even as I asked for information, I feared what she would say. Savannah was the biggest gossip in the salon and had an uncanny knack for getting people to divulge their secrets.

"He owns strip clubs."

I blinked at that unexpected revelation. "How do you know that?"

"Nisha recognized him outside the church at Bianca's wedding. She told me that he co-owns a bunch of clubs around town with some gangster loan shark guy."

"How does she know that?"

"Her uncle, Nicky," Savannah said. "You know he's into all that shady stuff. Her ex is in the pen for same kinds of awful shit so when Nisha tells me that someone is trouble, I believe her."

I swallowed hard. Honestly, I didn't know how to feel about the discovery that Kostya made money from strip clubs. It was a dirty, exploitative business. "I don't know what you expect me to say, Savvy."

She stared at me for a long moment before exhaling slowly. "I expect you to say that you have your eyes wide open and you understand that Kostya has a complicated history. He's probably done some bad things, Holly. Maybe he's doing bad things right now. I need to know that you've thought long and hard about that before you go chasing after him."

"I'm not chasing after him."

"Not yet," she retorted, "but you will. If you want him, you're going to have to go and get him. Quit waiting for him to make the first move and make it yourself."

"This isn't high school, Savvy. It's not that simple."

"You're right. It's not high school so stop acting like a scared teenager whose never been kissed and act like a grown ass woman who knows what she wants and what she needs."

Hating that she was right to call me out for being so ridiculous but unwilling to concede defeat so quickly, I frowned up at her. "Well, aren't you just Miss Bossy today!"

"I'm too tired for my usual grace and charm. I had to get up super early to grab a spot in the confessional before Mass this morning." Smilingly mischievously, she admitted, "After the fun I had last night, I deserved every single one of those Hail Marys."

Her nearly blasphemous remark made me twitter with nervous laughter. "You are *horrible*."

"Oh, please." She tipped her nose up in the air. "You know you're jealous."

"I am. Completely." Poking her with my pen, I said, "You know I want the details of all that fun you had, right?"

"Tomorrow," she promised. "Right now, I have a dinner date at Goodnight Charlie's with the Katies."

The Katies were three of our sorority sisters who sat on the charity gala planning committee that Savvy chaired. The Houston alumni for our sorority hosted a huge, ritzy New Year's Eve dinner and dance to raise money for sick children. Every year, Savvy said she would never chair the committee again. Yet, every year, her hand was the first to go up when volunteers were sought.

"What are we donating? I asked, certain she had figured out the max gift the salon could offer.

"More than last year," she said, checking her watch. "We've set a very aggressive goal for the overall fundraising of the gala so you may need to shakedown all of your mother's super rich friends."

"Can't wait," I replied sarcastically.

"Are you sure you don't want to come? Be my backup against the Katies?"

"I'm good." I gestured to my desk. "I need to deal with all the things I've been putting off for the last week."

"Fair enough." She shoved off my desk and headed for my door, leaving Harry behind to keep me company. "Don't stay too late. We have a staff meeting tomorrow."

"I won't."

"Follow me out and lock up behind me?"

"Okay."

"Oh!" She hovered in the doorway of my office. "What did the alarm folks say?"

"Nothing helpful! I think we may need to find a new company."

"I'd offer to call around for bids but something tells me you're looking for a reason to go knock on Kostya's door. Far be it from me to deny you the chance to get your flirt on…"

"Get out of here," I said while dramatically shooing her away from my office. Her laughter echoed down the hallway as I followed her to the rear exit. After a quick hug and goodbye, I made sure the shop was locked tight behind her and detoured into the employee kitchen to grab a can of soda from the fridge. I cracked the tab, took a sip of the fizzy lemon-lime sweetness and returned to my office.

I had just started sorting through vacation requests when I

heard the first shrill chirp. *Oh, no.* I recognized the sound instantly as the low battery alarm for a smoke detector. Flopping back in my desk chair, I pinched the bridge of my nose and exhaled roughly. Every few seconds, the smoke alarm chirped.

Shoving out of my chair, I walked out of my office and down the hall to the maintenance closet for a step ladder and battery. I hefted the ladder around the salon, working my way from the back of the building to the front in search of the chirping alarm. Standing in the reception area, I waited patiently for that annoying beep but heard nothing. I waited and waited but there was only silence.

What the hell? I couldn't shake the feeling that someone was screwing with me. More and more, I became convinced that someone had hacked our system or something. *This isn't normal*, I thought as I dragged the ladder back to the closet and tucked away the battery.

Back in my office, I sat at my desk and picked up my soda. As I took a long drink, I tried to piece together the timeline of strange occurrences around the shop. Either the security company wasn't telling me the truth about all the issues we were having—or someone was maliciously targeting our business.

Unfortunately, the latter possibility wasn't too far-fetched, not for Houston at least. Not that long ago, one of our clients had nearly lost her life when a greedy developer had hired arsonists to force her out of her bakery building. This town had a dark, seedy underbelly that encouraged terrible deeds in the name of money.

But who in the world would want to attack my business?

The building was owned outright by my mother so we didn't have landlord problems. Savannah and I had a good relationship with the businesses on either side of us, a little coffee shop-slash-café and a clothing boutique. We'd never had any issues with salons in the area so it definitely wasn't a professional jealousy thing, and we hadn't fired an employee since our first year of being open.

I took another sip, making a face at how flat the soda tasted, and then tapped at my keyboard. Thinking about the security system, I wondered if the easiest option would be to simply replace the entire system and switch providers. If that didn't solve our strange issues, well, then I would start to worry.

Yawning loudly, I rubbed at my tired eyes. The words and numbers on my computer screen seemed so blurry. I blinked and picked up my can of soda, hoping the jolt of sugar would give me the energy I needed to get through this last bit of paperwork before calling it quits and heading home. *I should have grabbed something with caffeine...*

Focusing on my bright computer screen, I tried to make sense of what I was reading but there was a weird disconnect between my eyes and my brain. Suddenly, my eyelids felt heavy, so very heavy, and I felt my body starting to relax. Whether I wanted to or not, I was going to fall asleep. My sluggish brain urged me to give in and accept the drowsiness. A nap now was better than falling asleep while driving, right?

As I leaned forward and rested my head on my arms, I thought maybe, just maybe, I had detected a hint of movement reflected in the computer screen. *Shadows,* I convinced myself. *It's all just shadows and dust...*

CHAPTER TWO

A CURL OF cigarette smoke drifted on the night air as Kostya stood on the roof of the high-rise and watched the city slowly slide into darkness. He felt the heat moving ever closer to his fingers as the unsmoked cigarette burned from the tip to the filter.

He'd lit and wasted four so far. Still not in the mood for a smoke, he dropped the fifth and crushed it with the toe of his boot. He bent down, picked up the butt and slipped it into his pocket to dispose of later. There wasn't much chance of anyone discovering his stakeout spot or combing the rooftop for evidence but old habits like these were ingrained.

There must never be a trace of evidence left behind. Ever.

Clean it.

Burn it.

Destroy it.

He projected cool disinterest, but the pit of his stomach was a mess of knots and tangles. His mind raced with the bits and pieces of intelligence and recon that his little spiders had been gathering and reporting back to him all day. He checked his watch. Ninety-four minutes—and the whole damn city would erupt in chaos and violence.

His stomach pitched violently as a streak of anger and

despair zipped through him. All that work! All those years of planning and scheming and setting up his intel network! All that money spent and all those favors traded to turn snitches inside the Guzman organization had been wasted.

Tonight, Hector Salas would lead a bloody coup, taking out the power players standing between him and the cartel throne. Come sunrise, a new man would be in charge south of the border—and that intricate web his spiders crawled would have to be redesigned and woven all over again.

Blowing out a resigned breath, Kostya wiped a hand down his face. This wasn't the first time he'd been forced to start over from scratch. His entire life seemed to be an endless cycle of hastily wiped slates and new starts. When the dust settled, he would have to take stock of which informants had survived the power shift and begin the tedious process of rebuilding his network.

His personal cell phone in the front pocket of his jeans started to vibrate. It was a number only a handful of people had—one of them Holly. Worried she might be calling, he unzipped the dirty overalls and retrieved it. The phone number wasn't Holly's. It was Liam, the Irish gunrunner he had worked with for many years. Despite the bad timing, he had to take the call.

"Yeah?" he answered gruffly.

"I'm sure you're busy," Liam replied quickly, "so I'll cut right to it. Can you do some freelance work for me?"

"Depends." Freelance work for Liam could mean anything from old school wetwork to acting as a broker or go-between.

"I need help getting one of my Russian contacts a green card. He needs to get into the US as quickly as possible, and he needs to be able to stay there. It's a life or death matter."

"It always is. Does he have any ties to Houston?"

"Yes. He's got an aunt and uncle there. One of them works in your boss's restaurant. He's traveled there a few times for me on business."

"How's he set up for money?"

"He's good."

Good meant millions in their world. Gun running had its perks, apparently. "And his record?"

"It's clean. No arrests. No time served. Not even a fucking parking ticket."

"Interpol?"

"He had a blue notice thirteen or fourteen years ago. He was just a kid then."

"Watchlists?"

"I can't be sure. It's not likely."

"I'll see what I can do. Whatever solution I find won't be cheap or easy." He was already thinking that it would probably include a marriage of convenience and a large payment to a suitable woman who could keep a secret.

"These things never are. That's why I go to the best."

"Anything else?"

"No. That's it."

"Send the information about your colleague via my courier. I'll sort out the details on my end."

As soon as he had secured his personal phone, the burner tucked into the back pocket of his dirty overalls vibrated. One of the knots in his stomach relaxed and unwound as he read the message from Fox.

It's time.

He tapped out his short one-word reply—*coming*—and slipped his phone back into his pocket.

Adrenaline surged through his system as he pulled on the baseball cap emblazoned with a plumbing company's logo. He hopped behind the wheel of the van he had borrowed to satisfy a gambling debt owed by the proprietor. After a quick glance in the rear-view mirror to check the fake moustache he'd applied earlier, he pushed a pair of thick-rimmed glasses into place. Nobody paid attention to tradesmen, especially not the ones who looked like someone's creepy fucking uncle, and that was the way he liked it.

As he left the parking garage, he ran through the plans in place for the night. Nikolai wouldn't let Vivian out of his sight, as usual. The boss had ensured that all his captains knew to keep their soldiers in public tonight. They would be seen in bars and restaurants and clubs. Everyone needed a solid alibi. There wasn't to be a whisper of Russian involvement in the violence that was going down tonight.

Certain the rest of the family would be safe, he was focused solely on protecting Holly. It hadn't been that hard to convince one of the coffee shop baristas working next door to Holly's salon to sabotage the plumbing in exchange for the promise of a new car and a fat envelope of cash.

Fox, one of the street kids he had saved years earlier and now employed, had been hacking into the salon's security system repeatedly. It was imperative that Holly grow so frustrated with her current security service that she come to him for help. After tonight, he needed to have his eyes on her at all times. Setting off the alarm randomly during the day and having Fox hijack the security tech support phone line would push Holly over the edge and force her to look for outside help. *From me.*

Guilt soured his gut when he thought of all the ways he was manipulating Holly's life. He was doing it to keep her alive but that didn't lessen the uneasy feeling twisting his stomach. Their friendship had been the truest of his life, and now he was abusing it and gaslighting her in ways that would have made his instructors back at the Centre so very proud.

From a very young age, he had been conditioned and trained by his parents, both covert Soviet operatives based out of East Germany, not to feel guilt. He'd been taught never to get involved, to build walls, to never trust. He had taken those lessons to heart, especially after his mother and father had been betrayed and murdered. Their deaths had taught him the most painful lesson of all, and he'd promised himself that someday he would revenge their deaths.

Someday? *Blyat.* Never.

All these years later and he was no closer to solving the mystery of his parents' gruesome deaths. It had been an inside job. Of that, he was certain. The KGB had been in turmoil at the time his parents had been killed. As members of the inner circle, they had been high value targets. Their deaths had signaled the end of an era and the beginning of a newer, leaner and even more corrupt intelligence agency.

Kostya had wasted no time in pledging himself to the FSB, the KGB's successor agency. He had been just a boy, but he'd been determined to prove himself. It hadn't taken him any time at all to get out into the field where he had excelled in a specific kind of covert work. *Mokroye delo.* Wet work. Assassinations. Cleanings.

But he'd never been good at playing the kinds of games that were necessary to stay alive inside the agency. He didn't like politics, and he sure as shit wasn't going to lick boots to climb the ranks and move from the field into a cushy foreign post on an official diplomatic mission.

So, when the rumor of his impending demise had reached his ears, Kostya had quickly pivoted and sought employment with Maksim. Moscow's most ruthless criminal godfather had been in need of a man with Kostya's skillset. Once hired by Maksim, he had jumped at the chance to leave the country and leave it fast.

A clean identity and a fresh start in the United States.

He had made a good life for himself here in Houston. But he had a gnawing ache in the pit of his stomach that wouldn't go away. It was a foreboding sensation he couldn't escape. He had a bad, bad feeling that his good days in Houston were numbered.

And the countdown was starting tonight.

For weeks, there had been rumors circling the Houston underworld of a retaliatory cartel hit planned for someone close to Nikolai. Kostya had feared the hit might be meant for Vivian, now pregnant with the boss's heir, but the truth had been even more earth shattering for him.

The intended target for tonight's hit was Holly Phillips.

His fingers tightened around the steering wheel.

His jaw clenched.

My Holly.

He wasn't an easily surprised man, not after all that he had seen, but his knees had gone weak and his stomach had lurched painfully when he had read the information in the file

Finn Connolly had handed him during their earlier rendez-vous.

The middle Connolly brother was neck deep in hot water after taking out a cartel hitman with a perfectly placed sniper shot during a shootout earlier in the summer. Now Finn was being blackmailed into helping the cartel with their Russian problem. Someone out there had informed the cartel that Holly and Nikolai shared the same father. Now the cartel wanted to send a message to Nikolai and the big boss back in Moscow by killing her: No one is safe.

If what the file said was true, if Holly and Nikolai were half-siblings, her life was about to get very complicated. She had grown up in a tangle of secrets and lies. Once the truth came out—and it would—she would be devastated.

The thought of hurting Holly made his chest ache. He rubbed at his sternum and tried to play out all the different angles, but he couldn't find an outcome that saved her from pain and heartache.

And you're part of those lies...

Still loathing himself for adding to the pain and betrayal she would someday experience, Kostya pulled up to the coffee shop and backed into the space closest to the door. He surveyed the surrounding area while pretending to start a work order. He quickly noted the locations of the various vehicles in the mostly empty parking lot and then glanced at the darkened storefronts surrounding Holly's salon.

Metal clipboard in hand, he exited the van and moved around to the rear doors. Hidden from view, he tucked an almost invisible ear bud into place and cleared his throat to make sure the tiny microphone embedded in the ID tag clipped onto his uniform overalls picked up the sound. Two short clicks echoed in his ear. Fox, his tech goddess, signaled that she could read him loud and clear from the van she had parked in a nearby big box store lot. She was handling all the surveillance for tonight.

Carrying a toolbox, Kostya entered the coffee shop and found the employee Sunny, another of his spiders, had bribed earlier that morning. The shift manager led him to the rear of the building where a pair of clogged kitchen sinks were overflowing and spilling murky water all over the tile floor. He cast a cursory glance at the problem. It would be easy enough to clear the sabotaged drain after he had taken care of his more illicit business.

He plunked down the toolbox on the stainless steel counter, opened it and lifted up the expandable top tray to reveal the inner compartment. He placed his left hand on the pistol with a silencer attached and used the right to grab the five fat envelopes stuffed with hundred-dollar bills. He tossed the money at the shift manager. The envelopes hit the counter with a loud *thwap*.

The younger man swallowed hard and stared at all that money. He reached into his pocket with slightly shaking fingers and withdrew the keys to the shop. He placed them on the counter. "I've closed up the registers and done all the paperwork for the night."

"I'll lock up when I'm done."

The man nodded and reached for the money. "This is more than I was expecting."

"Consider it an incentive to get the hell out of this city. Tomorrow," Kostya added with a steel edge to his voice.

"Tomorrow?" He hesitated before taking the money. "That wasn't the deal the girl offered me. She told me I'd get a new car and some cash. I can't just leave like that."

Kostya wrapped his fingers around the handgun but didn't bring it out of the toolbox just yet. Holding the manager's gaze, he intoned levelly, "I can just as easily clean up two bodies tonight."

The manager paled and licked his lips. "How long should I be gone?"

"A week should be enough."

"I'll be out of here before sunrise."

"Good decision." Kostya kept his grip on the Grach pistol and watched the manager take the money—all fifty grand of it from his personal stash—and leave the shop.

Alone in the building, he walked to the front door and hopped up into the back of the plumbing van to get the tools he would need to fix the clogged drain. If anyone had eyes on the building—and he was sure the cartel hitman did—they would see him doing his job and nothing else. Back in the kitchen, he left the plumbing tools on the floor next to the sink before closing up the toolbox and taking it with him to the supply room that shared a wall with Holly's salon. He found the small closet housing the breaker box and security alarm and located a drywall panel with a small access door already cut into it. It was going to be a tight squeeze but it was the only way into the salon without using the front or rear entrance.

After pulling on a pair of black leather gloves, he opened the access panel and flicked on his flashlight. The panel on the other side of the wall had already been removed. He saw a blur of movement before a familiar face peered back at him. Brown eyes, dark hair and that young, innocent face—Lobo.

For a brief moment, he felt another stab of guilt when he considered what a girl of her age should be doing right now. Hanging out with her friends? Finishing up homework? Watching some sappy teenage shit while painting her toenails? *But not this*, he thought, *definitely not this*.

Lobo slipped into the tunnel and reached out to him. "Give me your toolbox."

He pushed the toolbox through to her and shimmied through the access tunnel between shops. On the other side, he climbed to his feet and scanned the supply closet they were standing in now. The space was lit by their flashlights and a few glow sticks, all easily extinguished light sources. He noticed that Lobo had put together a small pallet of towels along one wall.

"Black Swan is working in the front of the salon. Her outfit isn't a perfect match for Odette's, but it's close enough. No one watching her sweep or stock shelves through the windows will be able to tell the difference between them, not with the lights dimmed. Fox has control of the cameras. We can see everything happening inside and outside the salon. Sunny is tailing Jarhead. He hasn't left the hospital yet."

Black Swan. Lana.

Odette. Holly.

Jarhead. Finn Connolly.

A perfect little protégé, Lobo had complete control of the job. He would do the dangerous work tonight, but she was running this show. It was time for Lobo to prove herself capable of the work he had been teaching and training her to do. It was time for her to get real-life experience. Tonight, they would both learn whether she had the stomach for wetwork.

As much as it pained him, Kostya believed she would excel tonight. She would do her job and she would do it well. After tonight, there would be no turning back for her.

All the times he'd offered to get her a new identity, to set her up in a private school and pay for her college, to give her a normal life, she had politely declined. Inside, she was just as broken and busted up as he was. Maybe she understood as he had at a similar age that there was no other course for her life but to live in the shadows and do these terrible deeds.

In every way she had been the ideal student since the night he had discovered her chained to a wooden post in that shithole brothel in Ciudad Acuña. Scrawny, filthy and damn near mute, she had somehow escaped the horrors of sexual abuse that were rampant elsewhere in the house. But the bruises mottling her skin had been proof enough of the hell she had endured there.

He had been in the border city on a side job at the time and having a witness to his crimes that night was not a good thing. Putting a bullet between her eyes and ending her suffering probably would have been a kindness, but he had dismissed the thought as quickly as it had entered his brain. Something about her had called to him. He hadn't been able to leave her behind. So, he had broken those chains, wrapped her up in a blanket and taken her.

He cast a quick glance at Lobo as she started placing pieces of medical equipment from her own backpack next to the little pallet. Had it really been seven years since he'd found her?

Seven years since he had offered her that choice—to be dropped off at the first police station he reached in Texas or to come with him and learn how to avenge her family's deaths.

Seven years since he had christened her Lobo, wiping away the identity and childhood she couldn't remember, and giving her a new life as a ghost who didn't exist.

Seven years that he had been keeping her a secret from Nikolai and Ivan and everyone else who thought they knew him. *Even from Holly...*

Seven years that he had been training and molding her into the perfect covert operative.

He left the supply room without saying a word. Lobo didn't need him standing over her to get things done. He moved quietly and quickly through the back hallway, keeping tight to the wall on the way to Holly's office. Lana appeared briefly in his view, and his feet stuttered beneath him. Fuck, she looked so much like Holly with her hair bleached ice white and cut short. The similarities unsettled him.

Not even a week ago, one of his underworld contacts—the Liquidator—had called him with a strange request for a middle of the night rendezvous. Kostya had expected to be given interesting information or first dibs on virgin steel or maybe even the chance to pick up a little side work to earn some money for his retirement fund. Instead, he'd been led to a hotel room where Lana, bruised and battered and rail thin, had been waiting for him. She had been clutching a note from the Liquidator explaining that he had found the young woman in the home of a target he had just neutralized. After hearing her speak Russian, the Liquidator had decided to hand her off to someone else.

It hadn't taken Kostya long to work out that she had been trafficked from her home in Belgorod after answering one of those popular models wanted ads. She had been through hell in the last year, and eventually he would find the men who had done this to her and hurt them even worse.

Nikolai would have to be told about her soon—tomorrow, even. The boss would go fucking ballistic when he found out there was trafficking going on right under his nose. He didn't draw many lines in the sand when it came to the illicit businesses other bosses ran but trafficking was punishable by death. Nikolai wouldn't stand for it.

Kostya made a sweeping motion at Lana, silently telling her to get back to work. She had one purpose tonight. He wanted her to play the role of decoy to keep the cartel hitman busy here. In exchange for taking on this dangerous role and risking her life, he would give her an apartment, a car, living expenses and a clean identity. He was a bastard for putting her in this position, especially after the ways she'd been abused and manipulated and debased, but keeping Holly safe was a goal he would achieve no matter the cost to himself or anyone else.

When he finally entered Holly's office, he hesitated. Disgust grabbed hold of him and twisted up his insides at the sight of her slumped back in her desk chair. She wore a nonrebreather mask, and the low hiss of oxygen was easy enough to hear.

Fucking monster, he silently berated. *Take a good fucking look and remember this the next time you get stupid ideas about having this woman.*

He moved toward Holly and checked her pulse. It beat steadily and strongly beneath his fingertips. Under his orders, Lobo had slipped into the salon earlier, purposely setting off the alarm so Fox could take control of the system and get a good recording of Holly's voice. He had given Lobo a precise dose of a hypnotic sedative to add to whatever Holly was drinking—usually soda or sweet tea—and demanded that she put Holly on supplemental oxygen as soon as she was out, just in case.

The medical files he had stolen spoke of no contraindications to the drugs he'd just forced on her, but he wasn't taking any chances. The pulse oximeter clipped to her finger assured him that she was breathing adequately, but he would feel better once she was safely locked away in the supply room with Lobo playing nurse and bodyguard.

If anything happened to her tonight, he would have to follow her right into the grave. Holly had scratched away the protective armor he wore and had wrapped those beautifully manicured fingers around his heart. He had never allowed her to see what she meant to him. He couldn't risk alerting anyone to that vulnerability because of the danger it would pose to her. But she was it. She was the one—the *only* one.

And you can never have her. Never.

Very carefully, he placed the lightweight oxygen tank on Holly's lap and then gently lifted her from the chair. He cradled her fragile neck against the curve of his arm and carried her out of the office. The scent of her perfume and shampoo teased his nose. The feel of her in his arms, of her slight weight and her heat, was a cruel reminder of all the things he would never experience with her.

This was probably as close as he would ever get to Holly—and she would never remember any of it.

But that was a good thing. He didn't want her to see or

hear any of the violence that was about to happen here. He didn't want to break her heart or shatter her sense of reality by revealing all the secrets he knew about her.

What would he say?

Your father is a ruthless fucking mob boss?

Your mother is a liar?

If she even is your mother...

Kostya had his doubts that the woman Holly knew as her mother was her actual flesh and blood. Maksim had a type and a notorious penchant for criminally young blondes, but Frances Phillips had been at least forty when she'd supposedly become pregnant by the most powerful and dangerous man in the Moscow. It didn't make sense to Kostya.

"You brought the DNA kit?" Kostya asked as he placed Holly on the pallet of towels and arranged the oxygen tank on the floor next to her shoulder.

"Right here." Lobo placed it on the pallet before picking up an automatic blood pressure cuff. "Max said to get hair and saliva."

"Get it done. Quickly," he added before digging through his toolbox for the items he needed. Platinum blonde wig. Two pistols with silencers attached. Garrote wire as a backup option for a quick, stealth death. Small portable speaker.

"Do you think he'll do it?" Lobo pulled aside the oxygen mask long enough to swab the inside of Holly's cheek.

Kosyta didn't have to ask which he she meant. Finn Connolly was supposed to come here tonight to kill Holly. There would be a cartel hitman following Finn to snip any loose ends and make sure the job was done. They would probably try to plant evidence to spark a war between the Russians and the

Albanians or the Russians and the Hermanos crew to muddy the waters.

But he would kill the *sicario* first and anyone who came with him. If he somehow failed, Lobo would be the one to finish the job. He placed the second pistol next to her knee and caught her gaze for a moment. She glanced down at the weapon she knew how to handle with almost expert marksmanship and nodded.

Answering her question, he said, "Finn will do it."

Lobo didn't ask him how he could be so sure. She tucked the swab into the protective tube and sealed it tight. As he watched her pluck a few strands of hair from Holly's head and stuff them into a small envelope, he thought of the contingency plan in place tonight. It was a plan he hadn't mentioned to Lobo because she would give him that look, the one that made his chest tighten with something suspiciously akin to shame. He didn't have time for that shit tonight.

As soon as she finished with the DNA samples, Lobo checked Holly's blood pressure with the automatic cuff and read out the number to him. Reassured that she was stable despite the drugs, he reached into his toolbox and withdrew the syringe pre-loaded with a precise dose of a fast-acting sedative. "If she wakes, you hit her with this."

"She won't wake." Nevertheless, Lobo took the syringe and set it aside.

"Don't let her see your face."

"I won't."

"Once I leave this room and Lana returns, no one opens this door again except for me. You put two bullets in the first chest you see. Understand?"

"Yes." She held his gaze and calmly gave her answer. "I won't fail you."

A fatherly pride warmed him right to the core. Lobo was of an age that she could be his daughter. Their relationship over the last seven years mimicked that of a father and his daughter—if the father was a notorious killer and the daughter had a thirst for vengeance.

Casting one final glance at Holly, he took the tools he needed and left the supply closet, securing the door firmly behind him and leaving the two women alone in the dark except for the glow sticks and flashlight. He was three steps from Holly's office when two clicks echoed in his ear. He perked up to the warning of an incoming communication.

A moment later, Fox came across the airwaves. "Clone system is up and running."

After her multiple infiltrations and tests, she had duplicated the salon's security system, creating a clone dummy that the cartel hitman could set off without alerting the police or the security company. It was one that she fully controlled and could manipulate if the hitman managed to hack it. She would allow them to see real-time video of the salon's floor where Lana pretended to be Holly, but they would see stock recorded loops of the hallways where he or Lobo might be seen. "And Jarhead is nine minutes out."

"Received." That part of the update provided a bit of relief. He no longer had to worry about ordering Artyom to do something truly unspeakable to force Finn to follow through with the plan.

Aware of the time crunch, he entered Holly's office to set up the speaker, dim the lights and set the scene. He flicked the switch on the speaker. "I'm go for the recording."

"I'm queued up and ready. Standby."

After a quick glance around the office to ascertain whether the lights were dim enough, he pulled on the wig, removed the fake glasses and dropped into Holly's chair. He smacked the spacebar on the keyboard to wake up her sleeping desktop and typed in the passcode Fox had temporarily placed on all the computers logged into the salon network.

Appreciating how seamless she made all this technological bullshit, he decided to pay her a little bonus on her birthday. She was so damn good that she made everything look so easy, but he had seen her in action and knew how hard she was working to make this operation a success.

Sitting there, waiting for the hit squad to set off the alarm to draw Holly—*Lana*—to her office where the instructions left for Finn had promised she would be, he thought of all the ways his plans could go to shit tonight.

If Finn made one misstep, he could catch a bullet. A wounded veteran with a very rich and very well-connected girlfriend was going to be a big fucking problem.

If the cartel hit squad was larger than he had anticipated, Lobo and Holly could be badly hurt.

If the hit squad noticed Sunny trailing Finn or Fox's van parked not far from here, they could be identified and marked for retribution.

"It's time," Fox calmly warned.

All those troubling what-ifs fled his mind. He steadied his breaths and waited for it all to start. When the alarm blared, he swallowed slowly and adjusted his grip on the clean Grach he'd picked up for this job. He heard footsteps—Lana's footsteps—that paused in the hallway near the security system keypad. She banged on the box a few times and then punched in the passcode that Lobo had helped her memorize.

The phone on Holly's desk started to ring, the signal that would call Lana into the room. It would be Fox on the other end, of course. Lana jogged into the office, playing the role of Holly superbly, and slipped into the small closet on the left. He picked up the phone but said nothing as Fox played the recorded conversation from earlier. Her portion of the fake call that had aggravated Holly so much played over the phone line while Holly's replies came through the speaker.

The earbud crackled against his eardrum. "Jarhead is on site."

It wouldn't be long now. Sixty seconds? Seventy? One or two nicely placed shots—and it would all be done. He controlled his breathing and listened intently, waiting for the whisper of a footstep or the creak of a door.

There! Finally.

The office door opened slowly. He held his breath now, straining to hear over the recordings. The fine hair along the back of his neck stood on end. He glanced away from the computer screen to stare at the darkened corner of the room to give his eyes time to adjust before he had to make a good, clean shot.

A hand gripped the back of his chair and spun it around with a quick burst of force. Finn Connolly dropped down to one knee, moving out of the line of fire. Kostya spotted the dark figure in the doorway and centered his muzzle on the target. He squeezed off two quick shots and the man in the doorway, the *sicario* who had been sent to trail and kill Finn—

and Holly if Finn failed—fell forward.

Kostya shoved out of the chair, sidestepped Finn and rushed the doorway. He kicked away the gun still held in the cartel hit man's hand and then crouched down to check the man's pulse. He found only the erratic pumps of a dying heart and exhaled a pent-up breath. *It's done.*

"Is he dead?" His gun pointed safely at the ground, Finn rose to his feet with only the slightest wobble before quickly finding his balance on that prosthetic leg.

"Yes." He picked through the hitman's pockets but found nothing interesting or useful. The dead man was a professional and had nothing on him that could identity him or tie him back to the cartel.

Finn moved closer—and then stopped suddenly, his entire body going rigid. Kostya lifted his head just as Finn tapped his shoulder, the silent signal alerting him to the sounds of another person approaching.

Shit.

Even before Kostya could react, Finn displayed those finely honed Marine instincts and grabbed the possible assailant the moment he appeared in the doorway. Finn slammed the man into the wall and pressed his forearm across the man's throat.

"Hey! Hey!" Hector Salas lifted his hands while croaking the words.

Finn spotted the gun in Hector's hand and stripped him of it before pointing his own weapon on the cartel's new boss. "You have three seconds to tell me why you're here."

Fuck. The last thing Finn needed was to make an enemy of Hector Salas, a man secretly related to Finn's new girlfriend,

Hadley. Whether Finn was aware of that connection or not, Kostya couldn't say.

Trying to head off a disaster, he tapped Finn's hand. "Lower your weapon."

As if realizing he didn't know the full score, Finn frowned and did as instructed.

Kostya glared at Hector. "You're late.

"It's been a busy night."

He could only imagine. "Did you get it done?"

"It's finished." Hector slashed his hand through the air. "It's over."

He harrumphed and nudged the dead man with the toe of his boot. "What do you want to do with this one?"

"That's your specialty, not mine," Hector replied easily.

"That's right," Kostya answered dryly. "Betrayal and treachery are yours."

Hector flipped him off, but Kostya ignored it. He noticed that pensive expression on Finn's face and decided it was time to get the injured vet out of there before he started piecing things together. The less he knew the better.

As if sharing his thoughts, Hector gestured toward the door. "You should go, Finn. This isn't the sort of night you want to be without an alibi. Get back to the hospital. Hadley needs you. This is done. You're free of whatever obligation you had to the cartel."

"Wait." Kostya reached into his pocket for one of his special cards. He handed it to Finn. "Consider it your insurance policy. Whatever you need, you call me. I owe you a debt."

Finn took the card and tucked it into his back pocket. He glanced at the dead body on the ground, shook his head and left the building without saying another word. Kostya hoped it was the last he ever saw of him.

Alone with Hector, Kostya glanced at the usurper who had led tonight's coup. "You should get out of here, too."

"I only came to make sure you didn't put a bullet in my *prima's* new boyfriend." Hector's gaze drifted down to the dead man bleeding out on the tile floor. The whitish blue light from the computer screen illuminated his confused expression. "There were supposed to be two of them. So, he either lied to my face or this one killed the other one before the job started to keep the money." He paused and grimaced. "Or we're missing a man."

His pulse pounding now, Kostya tilted his head down toward the ID badge dangling from the front of his coveralls and rushed out of the office. "Did we miss someone?"

"Jarhead was trailed by one man." Fox answered him quickly amid the tap of keyboard keys. "Sunny didn't see anyone else. I haven't picked up anything in the salon or at the rear or front entrances."

Fuck.

Fuck.

Fuck.

Fox mentioned the entrances, and he realized he had forgotten to lock the front door of the coffee shop or set the alarm. "Do we have eyes in the coffee shop?"

"There's no video link there. It's just straight security with motion sensors." *Tap. Tap. Tap.* "There's a traffic cam with a view of the coffee shop. Let me see if I can—hell! It's been knocked off line."

Shit.

Fearing the worst, Kostya reached the door of the supply closet and rapidly knocked five times to make sure Lobo wouldn't put a bullet in him the second he opened it. He twisted the handle and pushed the door open.

The scent of blood and worse hit him right in the face.

An invisible fist twisted his gut. He slapped at the wall to find the light and blinked away the momentary blindness from the sudden blast of brightness.

When his eyes focused on the bloody, messy scene before him, Kostya expelled an agonized breath. *Fuck.*

It seemed Lobo had a stomach for wet work, after all.

CHAPTER THREE

D ETERMINED TO KEEP Lobo a secret, Kostya slammed the door shut and spun around on Hector. The other man eyed him with suspicion and confusion. Kostya put a hand on Hector's chest and gave him a slight shove. "You need to go." He pointed toward the exit. "I work alone. Leave. Now."

Hector looked as if he wanted to argue but didn't. Maybe he was glad he hadn't seen anything inside the room. The man had enough secrets of his own to keep and didn't need another one. Backing away slowly, Hector said, "Good luck."

Kostya followed Hector to the rear exit and locked it behind him. He ducked into the office and opened the closet where Lana had hidden earlier. She had tucked herself away in the corner, her knees folded demurely and her feet curled up beneath her. The position couldn't have been comfortable, but she seemed almost serene and completely closed off in her own head. Her bony little legs looked so sad and pathetic. He'd have to make sure this girl was eating well now that she was under his care.

"Come with me."

She nodded and rose to her feet with effortless grace, her movements lithe and practiced. He didn't have to ask where she had learned to move like that. He'd been inside enough private sex clubs to know that some men liked their submissive women to learn certain positions for kneeling and sitting and even more rules for how to stand or bend. Even if he had never seen the horrible bruises marking Lana's body, her quiet feminine grace and her rush to please would have been enough to make him suspicious.

Following close behind, Lana trailed him to the supply closet. He glanced back at her and frowned. "I hope you have a strong stomach."

Her pale eyes glinted with a flinty hardness. She hadn't lost that spark of strength he'd always admired in Russian women. Replying in their shared language, she lifted her chin and demanded, "Show me what needs to be done."

Kostya stepped aside and opened the door to reveal Lobo, her face battered and her hands slick and red hurriedly wiping up the puddle of blood that had pooled next to the dead body. Moving closer, he put together the clues to form an idea of what had happened. The man had obviously come through the same access tunnel he had used earlier. Shampoo and conditioner bottles had tumbled off the shelves while Lobo fought the man. Lobo had put herself between the cartel's man and Holly's sleeping body. Something had happened—a kick or a slap—that had knocked her gun away before she could fire. Or, maybe she had hesitated to fire because she didn't want to spook the other hitman in the salon.

Whatever had happened, it was clear Lobo and the assassin had battled to the death before she had stabbed him repeatedly with the green handled screwdriver from his toolbox. Her face was a fucking mess, and she moved slower than usual and favored her left side. She needed to get those ribs checked.

Lobo finally looked up at him. She wiped her bloody nose with the back of her hand. "Sorry about your screwdriver."

The sound that escaped his throat came out as a strangled, rough laugh. "I don't give a shit about that screwdriver." Crouching down in front of his protégé, he cupped her face and forced her to meet his inquiring gaze. "Are you all right?"

She reached up with a trembling hand and jerked his gloved fingers off her face. "Not now," she all but ordered. "Don't be nice to me now."

He understood what she meant. She needed him to keep her in the mission mindset, to keep her running on those adrenaline fumes. Later, when she was alone, she could fall apart. And she would fall apart. A first kill? It was always the hardest.

Kostya rose to his full height. It was too much to ask of her, but he had no other choice. "Get this body wrapped, and clean up this fucking mess." He looked back at Lana. "Get in here and help her."

Leaving the two young women to work, he walked over to Holly and knelt down at her side. He checked her pulse and studied her face. She was still out cold. Glancing at his watch, he figured they had a two- or three-hour window to get everything cleaned up before she started to stir.

He moved away from Holly and plucked a pair of surgical booties from Lobo's backpack that he quickly slipped over his boots. Grabbing the wipes and disinfecting spray he preferred, he said, "I'm going back to the office."

"Here." Lobo handed him a neatly packaged tarp and a roll of duct tape from her backpack.

He took the tarp and tape and headed for the office. With the practiced efficiency of a cleaner, he wrapped the body in the plastic and sealed it tight. When he was done, he began spraying down the office. The fluid degraded DNA but didn't leave any residue or scents. He followed the same methodical routine. From the ceiling to the floor, he cleaned every surface before finely detailing the room. It was mindless work, the kind he had completed so often he could do it on reflex.

What would happen tomorrow? South of the border, the war would just be kicking off come sunrise. Hector had come here to take out the power players north of the border. Back home in Mexico, he had a bigger, messier and more dangerous war to win. It wouldn't be easy, and the cost would be high in lives, bribes and product.

Kostya doubted all that carnage would stay in Mexico. Everyone in the underworld would know that Nikolai had given permission for Hector to turn the streets of Houston red with cartel blood. Knocking down the head of the biggest drug cartel? It wouldn't be popular among the other families in Houston.

Besian and his Albanian crews would fall in line because Nikolai had given them a heads-up and the offer of a little taste of that drug money. Nickel Jackson would have to be given a small piece of the action from Hector or else he'd find another supplier or make trouble with the Hermanos street gang tied in with the cartel. Mr. Lu and the Asian syndicate wouldn't like this new development at all, and any solution offered by them would be expensive. Mueller would be easier to push into line—for now. He was the new face in town and hadn't been able to find an ally for any power plays. Eventually he would figure out the game. Kostya needed to make sure he had the intel Nikolai would need to stay five steps ahead of Mueller.

Finished with the office, he dragged the wrapped package out into the hall and left it next to the rear exit. He returned to the supply closet and found Lana sitting quietly next to Holly. Seeing them side by side, he was even more shocked at the resemblance. As much as the old man fucked around, he probably had children spread across Russia, from Sokol to Novorossiysk.

Maybe I should take her DNA for testing, too.

"Where is Lobo?"

Lana pointed at the open access panel.

He crossed the supply room and knelt down in front of the panel. With a short whistle, he called for her. She didn't come immediately. When she did appear on the other side of the access panel, she had a wet shirt and a wrench in her hand. He realized she was clearing out that clogged drain. "Do you need help?"

She shook her head. "I'm done. It was just a washrag stuffed down near that bendy part of the drain. Give me ten minutes. I'll get this cleaned up and then move the van around back."

He nodded and replaced the access panel. There was a lightweight shelf that usually sat in front of it so he dragged it into place. Taking a moment to check the room, he found it damn near sterile. The girls had gathered up a bag of trash that would need to be burned.

"They might notice the missing towels," Lana said quietly. "Some of them were sprayed with blood."

"They might," he agreed, but there was nothing to be done about it now.

Turning back to Holly and Lana, he started removing the medical equipment they had placed on her. She was tolerating the sedative well and would be metabolizing the last of it very quickly. He handed off the equipment to Lana who hurriedly packed it away in Lobo's bag.

"She offered me a job," Lana said, her voice carrying surprise. "She doesn't even know me, but she offered me a job."

Kostya's expression softened as he gazed down at Holly. "She's a good person."

He couldn't imagine what task Holly would assign Lana, but he supposed having Lana here would be a good thing. She would be a full-time set of eyes on Holly. "You need a job. This is as good a place as any to work." Casting a sideways glance at Lana, he warned, "You'll have to work on your English. It's terrible."

Her hopeful expression deflated, and she shrank inside herself. "Yes, sir."

Blin. Hating himself for being such an asshole, he was glad Holly hadn't heard him just now and that she couldn't understand Russian, even if she had. Her disappointment would be harder to bear than her anger.

With the most encouraging smile he could manage in such grim settings, he said, "Working here is a good way to practice. I'm sure you'll learn quickly."

Her bruised feelings didn't recover quickly, but what else could he expect after what she had suffered since being trafficked? She was used to being told she was stupid and worthless. Knowing he wasn't any different than the bastards who had hurt and used her didn't sit well with him, but somehow, he couldn't make himself apologize for hurting her feelings. He had been raised to sniff out weaknesses and prey on them, after all.

"Are we ready?" Lobo appeared in the doorway behind them. "I've got the van all the way up against the back doors."

Shit. He hadn't even heard her come back into the building or open the doors he had locked. As if reading his mind, she waved the key she'd had made earlier that morning. She was getting good.

Maybe too good, he worried with a bit of paranoia. Someday the student would overtake the master and then what?

"Watch Holly while we get the packages taken out to the van," he instructed Lana. "When we're done, you'll have to go with Lobo."

Putting on Lobo's backpack, Lana glanced back at the dead man and shrugged. "I'm not afraid of dead men." She turned her attention back to Holly. "Dead men can't hurt me."

Kostya ignored the little twinge in his chest at that remark and grabbed the heavy end of the tightly rolled package. Lobo lifted the feet, and they carted the first body out to the van. She hopped up into the van's cargo area and guided the corpse into the right spot before jumping out and following him to the second body. This one was heavier than the first, but she didn't complain or make him carry more weight. It seemed the cardio and weight lifting regimens she followed were working.

When they were done, he peeled out of his coveralls and booties and tossed them in the trash bag. While Lana climbed into the back of the van, he pulled Lobo aside in the hallway. He settled a fatherly hand on her shoulder and gave it a squeeze. "You did well tonight. I'm very proud of you."

Lobo stood a little straighter, but her eyes betrayed the shock starting to take hold of her. "It was harder than I thought it would be."

"I know. We practice and practice and practice so that we react on reflex when the shit hits the fan—but it doesn't make washing the blood off our hands any easier." He lightly chucked her chin, lifting her battered face and forcing eye contact. "If you wake up tomorrow and decide this was too much, you just say the word, and I'll help you start over in a new place. It's all right if you discover this work isn't for you."

She shook her head slowly. "That's not what has me scared. I think—I mean—*God*." She closed her eyes and her expression turned dark with self-loathing. "I think I liked it too much. All of this—the planning, the sneaking in, the hiding, the drugging, the wetwork. It felt *good*. It felt *right*."

His chest tightened painfully. All these years, he had been training her for this moment. He had known it was coming. This was the inevitable outcome of turning her into his little shadow, but it twisted him up inside.

Was this how his parents had felt when they had first recognized the spark of enjoyment in his eyes? Was this how his mentors and teachers had felt the first time he had taken out a mark? Proud but conflicted?

"You had your whole family taken from you. You had your childhood ripped away. What you're feeling now—the power and the control over life and death—it's intoxicating," he added knowingly. "But it's also dangerous. You can get drunk on this kind of power over other people. You can become addicted to the adrenaline. You can start to see everyone—even your friends—as disposable bags of meat and bones instead of flesh and blood people with souls."

She nodded at his warning. "I understand."

Dropping his hand from her shoulder, he gestured to the double doors. "Take these two to the funeral home. *Krikun* will be waiting for you. Run them through the furnace yourself. He can be trusted, but he's an old man who needs his sleep. Wash the van and detail it before you drop it off. Fox will be following you all night. She's going to kill any traffic cameras you pass and help you avoid any police checkpoints."

"I know the drill, Big K. Stay off the toll roads. Stay away from busy areas that have multiple security cams. Use the back roads when possible and keep my head down."

"Keep your eyes open. The city is going to be a dangerous place tonight."

"Did you leave your gun in my backpack?"

"Yes."

"I'll make sure it's cleaned and dumped on the black market before sunrise. I know someone looking to move some steel to Mexico."

He frowned at her. "I'm sure you do."

She rolled her eyes. "I've told you a dozen times. It's not like that with him. He's just a friend. And not the kind of 'just a friend' you are with Holly," she needled.

She had him there. "Be careful with that boy. Someday he'll want more than you can give him, and he'll start to ask too many questions."

"You mean like Holly does with you?"

Irritation flared within him. "Don't be a smartass, Lobo." He pointed at the door. "Go. Get this shit done."

She mockingly saluted him and spun on her heel to leave the salon. After watching the van leave, he returned to the supply room and gently gathered Holly up in his arms. He carried her into the office and placed her in the chair. He made a quick trip to the supply closet to move the towels used for the pallet back onto the shelves and completed a final walk-through of the salon to make sure everything was just right.

"Time to sign off," he instructed Fox via their comms. "We're done here."

"I sent Sunny packing an hour ago. I'll keep eyes on our girls to make sure they get through the city without any harassment." Her fingertips could be heard clacking against a keyboard. "The city really needs to work on the firewalls protecting these traffic cameras. I mean, any miscreant with a keyboard and a WiFi signal could hijack them for her own nefarious purposes..."

"Try not to get arrested," he suggested dryly.

She snorted with laughter. "These wannabe white-hats working for HPD wish they could track down a girl like me."

"Goodnight, Fox."

"Night, boss."

Done with the job, he peeled off the fake moustache and stuck it in his pocket before wiping away the sticky residue clinging to his upper lip. He tugged the earbud free from his ear and slipped it into the back pocket of his jeans along with the fake ID embedded with a radio transceiver. From the other pocket, he withdrew a capped syringe, wrapped carefully for safekeeping, and the alcohol swab taped to it.

Kneeling down next to Holly's chair, he considered her small body for a moment. She had the petite, thin frame of a gymnast or ballerina. The anti-sedative he wanted to use on her needed to be injected into a muscle with a bit of padding over it. He also needed to put it in a place she wouldn't have an easy time seeing, just in case she bruised. A little soreness along her hip or bottom wouldn't rouse suspicion. She could have easily bumped into something here at the salon and would think nothing of it.

Feeling like the worst pervert in the world, he shifted her in the chair and braced her body against his before tugging down the top of her pants and underwear to reveal a suitable injection site. He swabbed her skin and uncapped the syringe but hesitated a few seconds before stabbing the needle into her. He hated the thought of causing her pain and loathed himself for invading her privacy and touching her unconscious body.

There was a word for men who did things like this, and it sickened him to think he had crossed that line all in the name of saving her.

After administering the drug, he guided Holly back into a sitting position and tucked the capped syringe back into his pocket. He backed away slowly to the doorway of the office and waited for her to wake fully. It wouldn't be long now. Ten minutes, maybe fifteen if her body was slow to react to the medication.

As he waited for Holly to rouse, he made a mental note to ask Zec to bring him another shipment of medications. The Albanian transporter had a global network that moved illicit contraband and legal goods. He was the only man Kostya trusted to get him the specific drugs he wanted from secret Russian stockpiles and not dangerous or ineffective counterfeits.

This specific drug he'd used on Holly he had also given to Lobo a few weeks earlier to help her understand the effects and how to use them to her advantage. Too little of the drug and a person would remember bits and pieces of what they'd witnessed or overheard while slipping in and out of a drowsy sleep-like state. Too much—and—well, it would be time to take a trip to the funeral home to use the furnace again.

Holly made a soft whimpering sound. Holding his breath, he watched from the shadows of the doorway as she came awake so slowly. When she started to stretch her arms high overhead, wiggling her fingers toward the ceiling, he backed away from the office until he stood at the rear doors of the salon. Reaching back, he opened and closed the doors with a loud *bang*.

"Holly?" He called her name loudly. "Holly, are you here?"

"In my office," she called back in a sleepy, slightly confused voice.

He strode down the hallway to her office and stepped inside. Facing the doorway, she leaned back in her chair and rubbed her temples. Looking at him in complete bewilderment, she asked, "What are you doing here?"

"I was out with a friend. We drove by, and I noticed your car was still parked here. I asked him to drop me off. I was worried about you." Not all of that was a lie. Not the most important part.

She inhaled a deep breath and glanced around her office. "I must have fallen asleep after Savvy left." She yawned loudly and then made an embarrassed face. "Sorry! That wasn't much of a cat nap, I guess. Not if I'm still this sleepy…"

"Let me drive you home. Whatever you're working on can wait until tomorrow," he gently ordered. With some of the sedative still circulating in her system, she was open to suggestion and easily manipulated. He wanted to walk a straight line here and reminded himself again and again to be very careful. "You need some sleep."

Holly looked around her office and then nodded. "I think you're right. I don't feel safe driving." She smiled up at him, her loopy expression betraying just how much of the drug still surged through her veins. "You're the best neighbor ever."

He returned her smile but inside he felt pure disgust with himself. The best neighbor ever? *Hardly*, he thought as he helped her close up the salon and get into the passenger seat of her sporty luxury coupe. He had actually been the one to suggest Alexei's dealership earlier in the summer and had even helped her haggle down the price on the dream car she wanted.

"Tango red with gray leather," she'd said again and again to the salesman. It was the only package she wanted, and she had been so proud of herself for scoring her dream car for such a good deal.

Of course, she had no idea that he had paid for that discount the next time he'd played cards with Alexei...

"I'm pretty sure I locked the door after Savvy left," she murmured drowsily from the passenger seat as they flew down the highway toward their West U neighborhood.

"You gave me a key." He easily covered his mistake. "You were telling me about the security system problems last week and gave me an extra key when I offered to check on it."

"Oh? Right," she replied uncertainly. Rubbing her forehead, she sighed. "I really have to stop working these long hours. My brain is turning to total mush."

You're a fucking bastard. A real piece of shit. He had done some really terrible things in his life but slipping those drugs into Holly's drink ranked right up there as the worst of the worst. He wasn't used to the feeling of guilt eating away at him and didn't like it one bit.

"You just need some rest." He guided her car off the highway and down a side street.

"Maybe I need a vacation." She slowly rolled her head to stare at him. "Maybe we should go on a cruise."

"We?" He glanced at her. "Me and you?"

"Sure. Why not?"

The image of Holly sunbathing in a tiny bikini on a cruise ship deck made his stomach leap wildly. He cleared his throat and shifted in his seat. "I'm not really a cruise kind of guy."

She rolled her eyes and scoffed. "You're not a cruise guy. You're not a dog guy. You're not a dates-your-neighbor guy. What kind of guy are you?"

He winced. She was loose-lipped because of the drug and seemed to have a bone to pick with him.

You're not a dates-your-neighbor guy.

Where the hell did that come from?

"I told you why I haven't cashed in the gift certificate to the shelter. I travel too much, Holly. I'm not dog owner material right now." He couldn't tell her that dogs barked and were nosy and liked to dig things up that he might like to keep buried.

"So, leave the dog with me when you're out of town," she offered helpfully. "We can be co-owners!"

The thought of owning a dog with Holly did something strange to his chest. He wasn't sure what that emotion burning him up was. *Hope?* "We'll talk it about tomorrow, okay?"

Grinning triumphantly, she poked his arm. "You big softie!"

"Holly." He shot her an irritated look, but she just mimicked his expression in an exaggerated way before bursting into laughter. "You're a mess," he remarked, unable to keep a straight face as she giggled next to him. *And it's all my fault...*

She leaned her head back against the seat and exhaled loudly. He pulled into the driveway of her house and pressed the garage door opener clipped to the visor. While she drew lazy shapes on the window, he checked out the garage interior and then used her house key to take a quick tour of the house, opening up closet doors and even checking the backyard. A third or fourth assassin was always a possibility.

He returned to the garage and opened her car door. "Come on," he reached over to unlock her safety belt. "Let's get you into bed."

She yawned again and climbed out of the car with his help. He followed her into the house and coaxed her to eat something—a glass of lemonade from a carton in her refrigerator and a banana—before walking her back to her bedroom. It was exactly the kind of space he had always imagined for her. With the white metal bed frame and fluffy comforter, the dove gray room looked like something he'd see on the cover of *Country Living* while waiting in line at H-E-B.

She didn't seem nearly as loopy, but she was still a bit unstable on her feet as she entered her bathroom. He leaned against the wall closest to her bedroom door and checked his cell phone for messages and updates from his spiders. When Holly exited the bathroom in a pair of long pajama bottoms and a loose tee, he watched her movements and tried to gauge whether she was safe to sleep alone or if he should drag a chair in here, just in case.

When she wobbled a bit, he crossed the space between them in four quick strides and slipped his arm around her waist. She sagged against him and dropped her forehead to his chest. "Sorry. I'm feeling a little dizzy."

"I can see that." Silently berating himself for not being more conservative with the sedative dose, Kostya carefully walked her to the bed and bent down to draw back the duvet and top sheet. He helped her into bed and then turned to switch on the lamp. "I'm going to leave this on in case you get up later."

"Kostya?" She said his name in that soft, breathy voice that made his dick stand at attention. When she threaded her fingers around his and clasped his hand, his heart started to pound. "Will you stay with me?"

He gulped. "I'm going to crash on your couch."

"No." She gave his hand a tug before rolling onto her side facing the window, dragging his arm with her. "Stay here with me."

"Holly, I don't think—"

"I need you," she cut him off with the three words guaranteed to keep him right there. She had him twisted around her little finger and wasn't about to let go. Her voice muffled by a pillow, she implored, "Stay."

"All right. I'll stay." He gently pulled his hand free and sat on the edge of her bed. He unzipped his boots and toed them off before reaching back to free his favorite handgun from the waistband of his jeans. He placed it on the nightstand and then ran his fingers through his hair, scratching at his scalp and blowing out a noisy breath.

Leaving his jeans on, he stripped out of his shirt and socks and slipped into bed with her. *This sure as fuck isn't the way I've always imagined this happening...*

Careful not to touch her, he hugged the edge of the bed and kept four or five inches between them. He listened to her breathing and could tell she wasn't asleep yet. What was she thinking? Was she remembering things she had heard tonight? Was she wondering why she had fallen asleep so quickly? Or trying to remember a conversation about that key and the security system that had never taken place?

Feeling like the lowest scum, he swallowed anxiously and wiped a hand down his face. Long undercover missions had never twisted him up like this, not even when he'd been ordered to seduce his marks or coax them into relationships to get his hands on sensitive information. But lying to Holly was slowly eating him up inside like a cancer. It was gnawing on his marrow and leaving him hollow and aching.

"Are you okay?" She whispered the question, as if afraid of the answer.

"I'm fine," he lied. Turning his head so he could stare at her back, he asked, "Are you okay?"

"I'm cold," she admitted. Already burrowed deep under her comforter, she trembled. He was about to ask her if she wanted another blanket when she rolled over and searched his face with her questioning gaze. "Will you hold me?"

As if he could say no! He opened his arms to her and Holly squirmed into them, resting her head on his chest and curling an arm across his stomach. She let loose a contented sigh and then cuddled in closer. "You're warm," she said in a happy, sleepy voice. "And you smell really good!"

He bit back a laugh and brushed his fingers down the back of her head, reveling in the softness of her pale white hair. He was breaking the rules right now by holding her like this and touching her hair and caressing her back—but he didn't care. He didn't give a shit anymore.

I killed for you tonight.

What would Holly say if he confessed his sins? Would she love him for what he had done to protect her or would she run away in horror? What would she say when he told her that he'd asked another young woman to kill in her name?

Someday soon, the truth about the monster he was and all his lies would be forced into the open and Holly would revile him. She would curse the very sight of him and wish him dead.

So tonight? Tonight, he was going to hold the woman of his dreams, the woman he could never have, and he was going to enjoy every fucking second of it. He would breathe in her tantalizing scent and imprint it on his brain so he would never forget it. He would memorize the gentle curve of her spine and burn the heat of her right into his fingertips.

Mine, he thought possessively. *Tonight, she's mine.*

"I don't care what Savvy says," she murmured unexpectedly. "You're a good man, Konstantin."

His heart stuttered in his chest. He couldn't even remember the last time someone had used his full name. Thirty years ago? Before he walked into FSB headquarters and pledged himself to the cause? The night his mother had kissed him goodbye before sending him away to spend time with friends in the German countryside in a dangerous bid to save his life?

As Holly drifted off to sleep, he closed his eyes and swept his fingers through her hair. A good man? No. Never.

But tonight?

Tonight, he could pretend that he was all the things Holly deserved.

CHAPTER FOUR

I WOKE TO the oddest buzzing sensation against my hip. Awash in confusion, it took me a few seconds to realize it was a vibrating cellphone. Even more strange? I could hear the unfamiliar and unexpected sound of a low, thudding heartbeat beneath my ear.

Bewildered, I blinked a few times. The sensation of warm skin under my fingertips and cheek surprised me. I lifted my head and glanced bleary-eyed around my bedroom. My brain was a jumble of memories but a few were clearer than the rest.

Kostya standing in the doorway of my office. Kostya driving me home. Kostya climbing into bed with me after I asked him to stay. Kostya holding me when I said I was cold.

Holy. Shit.

Had I really asked him to sleep with me?

Heat flared in my face and spread down my neck. We were in bed together, and I was snuggled up against him with one leg hooked over his. I worked up the courage to look at him—and my heart stuttered wildly. I'd never been this close to him. I could see the faint lines around his eyes and the stubble darkening his cheeks and chin and smell the lingering hints of eucalyptus from his aftershave.

Trailing my gaze down his handsome face, I finally noticed the incredible amount of ink covering his lower neck, shoulders and torso. All these years we'd lived side by side and I had never seen him without a shirt. Now I understood why.

A tattooed dagger pierced the skin of his lower neck. Blood dripped from the pointy end. Lower down on his chest were spider webs crawling with black widows. Scorpions crept across his clavicles. A snarling devil and a fanged cat wearing an ostentatious hat decorated his biceps. There were Russian words I couldn't read and other symbols I couldn't quite make out in the dim morning light.

Savannah's warning from last night rang loud and clear in my mind. What had she said about Erin's husband's tattoos? They meant bad things, right? But what bad things?

"You can ask." Kostya's gravelly voice startled me. Embarrassed to have been caught ogling his hard body and those interesting tattoos, I cast a sheepish glance at his face. He had one eye open and followed my movements with it.

Not sure I wanted to hear the answers he might have for the tattoos, I said, "I was going to ask if you wanted me to cook breakfast."

His other eye opened with surprise. He lifted his head off the pillow and gazed down at me. "You don't have to cook for me."

I rolled my eyes. "I know that, but I want to." I pushed up on my elbow and bravely traced the outline of the dagger on his neck. I felt his shuddery breath on my arm as he exhaled shakily. *Did I do that? Is it my touch?* "You're here. I'm here. I'm hungry. You're probably hungry. So…"

I could feel his throat move as he swallowed. His voice still thick with sleep, he said, "I am hungry."

"Good." Feeling rather brazen, I crawled over him and right out of the bed. As I stood up, the tactical style pistol on my nightstand caught my attention. He must have seen me looking at it because he quickly said, "The safety is on."

"I can see that." I opened the top drawer of my nightstand to reveal my pistol rack. Because I never had kids in my house, I had gone with something easy to access over a more secure lockbox. "I'd prefer you stow it here when you're staying over." Realizing what I'd said, I hurriedly added, "I mean, you know, if you're here again for whatever reason."

Cringing at the way I'd stumbled over that invite to sleep with me again, I waited for him to say something. Kostya's smile set me at ease. "I understand what you mean." He slipped his SIG Sauer into the slot next to my Walther. Seemingly impressed, he said, "I never figured you for the gun-next-to-the-bed kind of girl."

"Then you're going to be really surprised when you peek inside my Tory Burch and see that little .38 Special hanging out in my purse holster."

He seemed to relax right at the mention of my concealed carry weapon. "You're armed always?"

"Mom demanded it. The world is full of sickos, you know?"

"Yes, I do." He sounded sad as he confirmed that. Considering his line of work, I could only imagine what kind of crazies he came across when setting up security systems for his clients. "We should go to the range sometime."

"Only if you promise not to pout when I beat you at target practice," I warned.

Kostya laughed and crossed his heart with his fingertip.

"I'll be on my best behavior."

Deciding I liked the sight of him in my bed with that big grin, I headed for my bathroom. I paused in the doorway and looked back at him. He'd rolled onto his side, propping his head up on his hand, and watched me with the same intensity of a predator scouting prey. A frisson of wild delight burned through my belly and into my chest.

"You can use the guest bathroom across the hall." I didn't know what was happening between us right now, but it felt a little too intense and rushed so I pumped the brakes. "There are extra toiletries in the top drawer of the vanity. Oh! And your phone was ringing."

"Was it?" He frowned and patted the pocket of his jeans. "Sorry that it woke you."

"I have to get into the salon soon anyway so it's no big deal."

"Do you need me to drive you this morning?" He narrowed his eyes and scrutinized me. "You were dizzy last night. How do you feel now?"

"I feel great." I shrugged. "I have no idea what happened last night. I think I've got to start being a bit kinder to myself and put a stop to those late nights."

"That sounds like a good idea." He sat up, and I marveled at the way his lean stomach rippled with movement. I had always suspected he was seriously cut underneath his clothing, but this was ridiculous. I could actually count the ridges of his abdominal muscles. "Holly?" The amused expression on his face told me he knew exactly what I'd been doing. "Was there something else?"

"Nope." I quickly ducked inside the bathroom and shut

the door. Leaning back against it, I inhaled a steadying breath and tried to stop smiling. Suddenly, I was fifteen-years-old again and on the verge of an excited giggle fit because Dean Chavez, the hottest high school quarterback in Houston, had invited me to a homecoming dance.

Not that my mother had allowed me to go, I remembered with a scowl. She had been aghast and had subjected me to a two-hour talk about the evils of older boys and how it was important to be a strong woman with an established career before adding the complications a man would bring.

At the time, I had been so mad at her for killing my chances with the cutest boy in town. Now, of course, I understood what she had been trying to help me understand. Everything I had accomplished so early in life was due to my mother's support and guidance. Even when we butted heads and went after it like angry hens, I always knew deep down inside that she was trying to help me reach my full potential.

Climbing into the shower, I couldn't help but wonder what she would think of this development with Kostya. She had only met him once, briefly, and I had immediately sensed that she didn't like him. Knowing how her own Russian affair had gone so badly, she wouldn't be very enthused about me dipping my toes in that poisoned water.

We had never spoken about my father or why he had left her to raise a child on her own. Sometimes I worried she was keeping a dark secret from me. What if my father had another family? A wife and children? Or maybe he was a corrupt politician she'd met through her oil and gas connections? Or— heaven forbid—a criminal?

As I stood at my vanity blow drying and styling my hair, I

couldn't stop thinking about the tattoos on Kostya's body. I applied some makeup, nothing too heavy and just enough to highlight to my eyes and mouth, and decided I would just ask him. If he got cagey or weird, I would have my answer.

I plucked a black shift with a deep V neckline from the side of my closet where I kept all my work apparel and slipped it on over my underthings. I settled on one of my favorite pairs of Manolos and picked turquoise jewelry to complement the all-black outfit. After tidying up the bathroom, I made my bed and scooted out of my bedroom.

Kostya stood in my living room with a cup of coffee in one hand and his cell phone in the other. He was tapping away at the screen with his thumb while watching the morning news. I noticed his lingering gaze as I stepped up beside him to catch the latest updates around Houston.

"They're forecasting rain this evening." His gaze drifted down to my high heels. "You might want to throw your wild pink rain boots in your car so you aren't wading through your parking lot tonight in those thousand-dollar shoes."

He had a point. Knowing I would forget, I segued to shoe rack by the door to the garage, grabbed my rain boots and put them in my car. When I came back inside, Kostya's mouth quirked with a smile as he leaned back a little to ogle my backside. "I've never understood how you can wear those for twelve hours a day but I do appreciate the effort."

"Pervert," I said, smacking his arm lightly. Before I could continue flirting, my attention was snagged by the horrible news flashing across the television screen. There had been some kind of cartel murder spree during the night. The screen was a blur of images—yellow police tape, police cruisers with flashing lights, state troopers in their Stetsons, crime scene techs and bloodied sidewalks.

"What in the hell is happening to this city?" I cast a look of sheer disbelief at Kostya as he calmly sipped his coffee. "It's a good thing we were just minding our own business and hanging around my salon last night! At least we were safe there."

Nodding, he slowly sipped his coffee before turning his gaze to me. "Do you want help with breakfast?"

"I've got it." I headed into the kitchen. "I hope you like pancakes because that's my specialty."

"I like pancakes." He followed me and took a seat at the island on one of the counter height stools. "I grabbed the paper from your driveway. You want me to read the front page to you?"

I made a face. "No, it's probably just violence and mayhem. Just toss it in my recycling bin when you're done."

As I pulled the necessary ingredients from my pantry and refrigerator, he read quietly at the counter. "Your new ad is nice." He flashed the half-page above-the-fold spot at me. "I've seen a few of your new billboards around town, too."

"That's all Savannah." I cracked the eggs into a bowl and tossed the shells in the compost container under the sink. "She's the brains behind all the promo and marketing we do."

"It must work."

"I think word of mouth has grown our business more than any flashy advertising, honestly." I splashed some milk into the bowl and popped the egg yolks with a fork. "Frankly, Lena Cruz bringing Vivian and Erin into the salon has led to our biggest business boom ever. We used to get most of our word of mouth business through Bianca and her brides, but these days most of our new bookings are from ladies who know Vivian or Erin."

"I can only imagine how many new faces that brings into the salon." He turned the page and scanned the next set of headlines. "Those two have never met a stranger."

I smiled at the way he described the two friends. Figuring this was a good opening to ask about the tattoos, I said, "You know Erin's husband, right?"

"Yes."

"From Russia?"

He lowered his paper. "Are you asking me if I know that her husband is Russian or if I knew him back in Russia?"

I huffed at him. "Obviously, I'm asking if you knew him back in Russia."

He smiled before raising the paper again. "Yes, I knew him back then."

When he didn't offer any further comment, I wondered why he was being deliberately vague. I measured out some pancake mix and dumped it into the bowl. He kept reading his paper while I heated a pan and dropped the first scoop of batter onto the hot surface. I prodded the pancake with the tip of the spatula and decided to be bold. Standing sideways at my gas cooktop, I could keep an eye on our breakfast and him. "Kostya?"

"Yes?" His gaze was glued to the newspaper in front of him.

"Your tattoos…" My voice trailed off as I tried to think of how to ask without being, well, rude. "They look a lot like the ones Erin's husband has on his hands."

He slowly raised his head and put down the paper. I couldn't read his impassive expression. He smoothed his fingers over the newsprint. With a steady gaze, he didn't blink or glance away. It was almost as if he wanted to assure me that he wasn't lying when he said, "They look a lot like Ivan's because we got them for the same reasons."

Unsure what to do with this opening he'd allowed, I flipped the pancake. Kostya stood up and walked to the cabinet where I kept the plates. He selected a pair of them and held them out for me so I could place the cooked pancake onto one of them. Our gazes clashed. It was almost as if he were daring me to ask.

So I did.

"Are you in the Russian mob?"

"Yes." Standing this close to him, I could see the tension fade in his jaw and neck. He looked relieved to confirm my suspicion. "Do you want eggs?"

His question threw me, and I frowned at him. "I ask you if you're in the mob, and you ask me if I want some eggs?"

"I like eggs with my pancakes," he said matter-of-factly.

Unsure if this was his way of changing the subject or his way of trying to buy some time to decide how much to tell me, I pointed at the pot rack over the island. "You know where the pans and eggs are if you want them."

"Fair enough."

While I finished the pancakes, he scrambled some eggs, offering me some as I gathered butter and syrup and silverware. I poured a glass of almond milk and refilled his coffee cup before joining him at the island.

"Is that all you wanted to know?" he asked before digging

into his breakfast.

"What am I allowed to know?" I stabbed my fork into the eggs. This was new and—frankly—frightening territory for me. I wasn't sure what I *could* or *should* ask.

"I think you probably already know more than I'd like," he said in between bites. "I think you've wondered about Vivian and Erin, about their husbands and their tattoos and if the rumors about how they make their money is true. I think you know exactly what Nisha Jackson's uncle does, and I'm sure you know all about her ex-husband doing his stretch in the pen for drugs and guns. I think you've probably heard things about me that confuse you."

I sipped my almond milk confessing, "Savvy told me that you own strip clubs."

"Yes, I do." He smeared some butter on his stack of pancakes. "Does that bother you?"

"Of course, it does!"

He made a strange face. "Why?"

"Really?" I didn't for one second believe he was that dense. "You have to ask why I think it's skeevy that you own clubs where women take their clothes off for money?"

"No one forces them to dance. They're independent contractors, and most of them—the ones who understand their craft and take advantage of their natural assets—are compensated very well."

"Konstantin!"

He seemed taken aback by the strident tone I'd used. His eyes flashed wide. "That's the second time you've called me by my full name in the last eight hours."

"And?"

"And I like it," he admitted in a rough voice.

A bright thrill arced through my chest at his heated gaze. Pointing my fork at him, I warned, "Stop trying to distract me with your Russian hotness. I'm not done with this nasty strip club business."

He grinned and acknowledged that I was onto his game with a slight nod. "Have you ever been inside a strip club? A high-end one," he clarified. "A real gentlemen's club."

"No!"

"Would you like to visit one?"

Something wild and wicked flared inside me. The taboo of a strip club was one I had never dared to indulge. The idea of going to a strip joint with Kostya, of seeing a lap dance up close or going into one of those VIP booths alone with him, had me clenching my thighs together.

"You don't have to decide today." He cut a neat triangle of pancakes with his fork. "The invitation stands."

We ate in silence for a few moments. Eventually, I asked, "Why strip clubs? Doesn't your security business make good money?" My stomach clenched as another thought struck me. "Your security business is real, isn't it?"

"It's real, and yes, it's very profitable."

"But?"

"But strip clubs make it easier to launder money," he stated.

I regarded him with surprise and a little bit of suspicion. "You're being awfully candid today."

"Maybe it's time we had a little honesty in our relationship," he grumbled.

I didn't like the sound of that. "I've never lied to you, Kostya."

"I meant me," he said, his tone filled with loathing.

"Well, I mean, I assume the mafia thing only works if you keep secrets, right?"

"That's generally true, yes." We shared a look that made my chest ache. "You understand that everything I've told you this morning has to be *our* secret now. If anyone thinks that you know more than you should, you'll be in danger. If you tell your friends, you put them at risk, too."

"I understand." The weight of his admission was heavy on my shoulders. Savannah would never ask, but she would *know*. She had a way of reading me just like my mother.

My mother...

Oh, hell.

She was going to be furious if she found out that I was getting involved with a man tied to the Russian mafia. Whenever she spoke of her time in Russia—and that was rare—it was to warn me about how dangerous and corrupt the country was and how the mafia controlled every level of it.

Kostya finished his breakfast, grabbed an orange from the bowl on the counter and produced a terrifyingly sharp knife from his pocket. He sliced the top and bottom off the orange and cut out a slice before unfolding it to reveal perfectly sectioned wedges. Seeing his neat work and the easy way he handled the knife, I started to wonder just what exactly he did for the Russian mob.

"Is money laundering your specialty?"

"Not even close," he replied while wiping clean his knife and folding it closed. Catching my eye, he warned, "You can ask questions, but I won't always answer them. It's not that I don't trust you to keep quiet. I simply don't think you need to be burdened with the reality of what I do."

His ominous tone scared me. I gripped a napkin as it occurred to me that maybe he'd used that knife to cut into something other than oranges. I wanted to ask him. The question was right there on the tip of my tongue, but I couldn't make my lips move.

Was this what it was like for Vivian Kalasnikov? If the rumors were to be believed, her husband was the boss of the family Kostya served. Did she sit at home wondering what her husband was up to all day? Did she worry about the risk of arrest and prison? Did she worry that someone might put a hit out on her man or even her?

"What are you thinking now?" He studied me closely while peeling free another orange wedge.

"Honestly? I'm thinking about the tattoo on the back of Vivian's neck." I touched the same spot on my skin. "It wasn't there the first time I cut her hair, right before her wedding. When I noticed it a few haircuts later, I thought it was just a pretty piece, but now?" I gestured to the base of his throat where I'd seen that dagger tattoo. "Now I'm thinking maybe that crown on her neck means something to people in your world."

"It means that she belongs to Nikolai." He held out an orange section and offered it to me. "It means she's under his protection."

When I reached for it, Kostya stunned me by gently capturing my hand and pulling me closer. He fed me the orange, pressing the juicy bit of fruit against my lip and teasingly swiping it over my skin. Holding my gaze, he said, "It means that Nikolai will kill any man who touches her because she is his queen."

There was a wild flutter in my stomach as the sweet citrus taste burst on my tongue. Kostya dragged his thumb along my lower lip, gathering up the sticky juice lingering on my skin. He slowly licked the residue from his thumb, and my toes curled as I felt that lick in the pulsing feminine core of me.

Still holding my hand, he interlaced our fingers and reached up with his other hand to wind some of my hair around his forefinger. "We've had an interesting night and very nice morning."

"But?" I knew what was coming. He had finally given me a taste of what we could have together, but he seemed almost afraid to believe it could be permanent.

"But," he said with a heavy sigh, "my life is very complicated right now. I can't—I won't—do that to you."

"And what if I don't care about your complicated, messy life?"

He gave my hair a playful tug. "I just told you that I'm mobbed up, and you're arguing with me when I'm trying to protect you."

"I'm a big girl, Kostya. I know how to protect myself."

He regarded me for a few moments. "Four weeks."

I frowned with confusion. "I don't understand."

"I want you to really think about what I've told you this morning. I want you to understand what it means to be with someone like me. All that shit you saw on the news this morning? That's my life, Holly."

It suddenly occurred to me that his visit to the salon last night hadn't been coincidence at all. "Did you come for me last night? Did you know that the cartel was in town? Did you come to the salon to protect me?"

"Yes." His hand moved from my hair to my cheek with a tender touch. "To all three questions. It's no secret that we're friends. Hurting you would hurt me."

I might not wear a tattoo like Vivian's, but it seemed I was under this man's protection. There was something intoxicating about the idea of belonging to him, even though he hadn't branded me as his—yet.

Cupping my face and holding my hand, he started to lean forward. He searched my gaze as if hoping to find permission. I made sure he found it. Closing my eyes, I held my breath and waited for that first perfect kiss...

The sudden snap of Warren Zevon belting out *Werewolves of London* startled me. My eyes flew open just in time to catch Kostya casting a murderous glare at his phone. Making a snarling noise, he snatched his phone from the counter and hastily answered it in rapid-fire Russian. I couldn't understand any of the conversation, but I could tell from his tone that it wasn't good.

When he finished the call, he tucked the phone into his back pocket and then placed his hand along the back of my neck. "I'm sorry." His thumb brushed up and down my nape, eliciting a dizzying wave of excitement. "I have to go."

"Mob business?" I hazarded a guess.

He didn't lie to me. "Yes."

"Then I won't ask anything else." For now, I could handle being in the dark. I didn't have any claim over him or how he spent his time. But I wasn't sure whether I could handle this huge secret life of his long-term.

Which was exactly why he was insisting I take some time to think this through before leaping into a relationship with him. He wanted me to take a step back and consider what a future with him might look like. The romantic, hopeful side of me wanted to believe that I could make him love me enough to walk away from this life, but the realistic side of me accepted that there might not be a way to walk away from his ties to the Russian mafia.

Blood in.

Blood out.

Even if he loved me with every fiber of his being, I could never ask him to risk his life in that way. I would rather have him alive and neck deep in the murky waters of the mafia than free of those criminal chains and six feet underground.

Even if that meant we could never be together.

Kostya saved me from that sobering thought by reaching back to grab his wallet from the pocket of his jeans. "When you have some time today, I want you to call or email my friend, Fox. She operates a comprehensive security service here in Houston that specializes in banks, tech companies and hospitals, but she also offers more streamlined security services for small businesses owned by women. She can help you get the problems at your salon sorted."

Had I mentioned the security system problems to him last night? My memories were fuzzy, but it seemed like the kind of thing I would have done. I took the card from him and glanced at the information on it. I smirked at the cartoon fox trying to pick the lock on a chicken coop. "Hen House Security, huh?"

"Fox is quite a character." He shoved his wallet back into his pocket. "I should warn you that she can be a bit abrasive, but she's very good at her job."

"Thanks for the lead." I set aside the card. "But why can't I hire you?"

"Because I don't ever want you tangled up in the illegal shit I do." His hand found its way back to my neck and he drew me in close. When he kissed my temple, I melted into him. It wasn't the lip lock I wanted, but it was more than enough to be embraced. "Fox will keep you safe when you're at work." He pressed his lips to my forehead. "And I'll make sure you're safe when you're home."

I wanted to tell him he was being overprotective but I thought of all the horrible things we had seen on the news this morning. "Maybe it wouldn't be such a bad idea to see if Fox can take a look at my home system."

"I think that's a very good idea." He seemed reluctant to leave me as he gathered up our dishes and carried them to the sink. "That girl? Lana?" The one you asked me to translate for?"

"What about her?" I finished off my almond milk and handed over the glass.

"She seemed very young on the phone."

"She's maybe eighteen." Sadness engulfed me as I thought of her bruises. "I think something really horrible happened to her. I didn't feel right letting her go back to the women's shelter without being able to help her so I offered her a job."

"I'll do some digging and see what I can find out about her. It shouldn't be too difficult to find out where she came from and if she has any family."

"She seems like a really sweet girl. She deserves a fresh start. I kind of think I should try to find her a safe place to live so she can get out of the shelter."

"I have some friends who own apartment complexes around town. I'll what I can find that's close to the salon."

"She'll need to be in walking distance or bus distance to a grocery store and things like that. I doubt she can get a driver's license yet. Try to cap the rent at one thousand. I'm not sure my budget can fit more than that."

"I'll handle it."

"But—m"

"I'll handle it, Holly," he repeated, his voice firm but kind.

"Fine, but don't put yourself into a financial bind. We can even go half on the rent."

He looked as if he wanted to argue, but instead, he just nodded. "All right. I'll get some options together, and we'll go half."

"Thank you."

He hesitated. "I really have to go."

"But?"

"I don't want to," he admitted.

"I don't want you to go either."

"But?" he asked, parroting me.

"I have to get to the salon for our Monday morning meeting." Anxious, I drummed my fingers on the counter. "I know I have to wait a month before you'll agree to date me, but will I see you around?"

"Yes." He hesitated one last time. "Are you sure you're safe to drive? You're not still sleepy or dizzy like you were last night?"

"I'm fine, but thank you."

Nodding, he backed away slowly. "Call me if you need anything."

"I will." Watching him leave was harder than I had expected. After that tiny glimpse of what was possible between us, the thought of calling a four week time-out was excruciating. But Kostya had trusted me with his secret for a reason. Like Savannah, he was urging me to make my decision with eyes wide open.

As I gathered up my things and left the house, I realized that I didn't need four weeks. I had already made my decision.

I wanted Kostya.

All of him.

The good.

The bad.

The ugly.

I just wanted him to be mine.

CHAPTER FIVE

REELING FROM HIS surreal morning with Holly, Kostya ducked into his house for a quick shower and a change of clothes. Coming clean to her about his mafia connections had never been a part of his plan, but he hadn't been able to stomach lying to her anymore. He couldn't tell her the whole truth, not the facts about his early years in FSB or the covert work he had done for his country and certainly not about her connection to Maksim and Nikolai, but it felt good to tell her *something* truthful.

It was like an anchor point in their relationship. This was one bit of truth that she would always know he had entrusted to her. Someday, perhaps, he would tell her all the rest. He could only hope that when that day came, she would listen and try to understand why he had kept the other details, the ones most fatal, a secret.

Four weeks, he thought as he pulled two DNA collection kits from a drawer and slipped them into the back pocket of his jeans. It was too much time and not enough time. His stomach knotted up with the likely outcome of the break he had insisted upon. Given a day or two, Holly would surely weigh the risks of pursuing any kind of relationship with him and insist he never visit her again.

At least now Fox would have her eyes on Holly round the clock. With Lana working at the salon, he would have a constant feed of information on Holly, even if she shut him out of her life completely. It wasn't a perfection solution, but it would keep her safe. That was all that mattered.

As he waited for the stream of scalding hot coffee to fill his cup, the doorbell rang. Setting the cup in the sink, he pulled his pistol from the back of his jeans and left the kitchen. He checked the peep hole before opening the door to frown at the FedEx driver on his doorstep. "Yes?"

"Mr. Antonovich?" The driver didn't look up from the device he held.

"Yes." Kostya's hand tightened around the grip of his pistol.

The driver scanned the barcode and handed it over to him. "Have a nice day, sir."

"Thank you." Kostya took the thin, stiff envelope and shut the door, locking it behind the driver who had unknowingly had a brush with death. He watched through the closest window, peeking behind the wooden blinds, to make sure the driver went on his way.

When the van rumbled along, Kostya glanced at the address label and didn't recognize the Kazakh address. Wary of receiving strange pieces of mail from his old neighborhood, he regarded it with suspicion. An envelope this size couldn't hold enough explosives to kill him. Powdered poison on the other hand? Exactly the right size for a lethal dose of anthrax or worse. He recoiled from the envelope as thoughts of polonium-210 and the gruesome death of former KGB agent Litvinenko entered his mind.

Holding it carefully, he walked down the hall to his office. Opening a desk drawer, he retrieved a pair of gloves and a surgical mask. He slipped both on before taking a Geiger counter from the bottom drawer. It was unlikely that anyone would be brazen—or stupid—enough to send a highly radioactive piece of mail but the world had gone crazy. The old ways of doing things, the unwritten rules for covert agents and burned spies, had been cast aside. There was a long fucking line of people who wanted to hurt him and a seemingly harmless piece of mail was a perfect way to do it.

Sweeping the probe over the envelope, he watched the Geiger counter for the first hint of an alarm. When nothing happened, he tossed aside the machine, opened another drawer and pulled out a simple dissection kit. He dropped the envelope on top of a clean sheet of paper and kicked back his desk chair so he could sit. Picking up the scalpel, he used it to slit the top edge of the envelope. Carefully, he gave the envelope a shake.

A few bent photographs fell out first. A slip of paper, yellowed with age and ripped margins, fell out next. Setting aside the empty envelope, he picked up the first slip of paper and studied it. Old and stained, it was a record of some kind. Names. Dates of birth. Dates of intake.

It was a page torn from a prison logbook.

He tried to make sense of the smudged and untidy handwriting as he scanned the front and back of the page, looking for some clue as to which prison it had come from and when. His gaze slid down the column of convictions, the crimes that had brought each prisoner there. Murder. Child molestation. A serial killer. A cannibal.

There was only one prison in all of Russia that came to mind for housing prisoners like these. Penal Colony 6. The Black Dolphin.

It was a place where the worst of the very worst were sent to disappear. None of the prisoners who passed through the front gates ever left it.

But why would someone send me a page from the logbook?

In his time working for the Russian government, he had put his fair share of prisoners there. But this logbook page was from before his time as an agent. If anything, the dates corresponded more closely with the deaths of his parents. Was that the clue? Was there a name on this list that had ties to his mother and father? To some operation they had worked two or three decades ago?

Setting aside the logbook page, he picked up the first photograph and unfolded it, flattening the faded image with his fingertips. His throat seized, and his heart stuttered when he realized what he was seeing. There in black and white was the lifeless body of his mother. Shot. Dead. Splayed on the wet, cold street.

Dread washed over him as he picked up the second photo. It was a crime scene photo of his father's brutal murder. Gutted. Blood pooling around his contorted and broken body. His face forever frozen in a grimace of pain and suffering.

What the fuck?

Memories long suppressed rushed to the front of his mind. The hurt and fear and grief of his childhood overwhelmed him. He tried to push it aside, to focus on the contents of this strange package, but it was impossible to ignore it. The anguish tried to strangle him, wrapping tight around his throat and squeezing the breath right out of him.

The murders of his parents had irrevocably broken him. It had taken away the future he'd once dreamed of and set him on a tormented and difficult path that he had never been able to leave. Here he was, all these years later, the product of all that bloodshed and death. Still fucked up. Still the scared kid feeling out of place, without a home, lost.

He dropped back in his chair and stared at the photos and the logbook page. What did all of this mean? Was it a warning? Was someone trying to help him? Was it someone from his past? Someone still on the inside? Or was it something else? A threat?

What he did know without any question was that this was a complication and a distraction he didn't have time for right now. There were still loose ends from last night. There were still problems to be solved and messes to be cleaned. He couldn't get drawn into this mysterious package and what it meant. He had to focus on the most pressing issues at hand.

Gathering up the strange contents of the envelope, he pushed out of his chair, knelt and lifted up the chair mat under his desk to reveal the hidden drop safe. After unlocking and opening it, he stared at the envelope for a lingering moment, allowing himself to remember the smiling faces of his parents, of the safety and security and love he had known as a child. When that hauntingly sad moment passed, he shook off those unwanted feelings of sadness and grief and dropped the envelope inside the safe.

Standing there in his office, thinking about the strange photos and the logbook page, he considered grabbing his bug-out bag and leaving Houston immediately. If there was a target on his back, everyone he cared about was at risk. Would they be safer if he left? Or would they be in more danger? Would they be used as pawns to draw him back into the open? Would they be picked off one by one to hurt him?

The thought of Holly being hurt or any of his little spiders was too much to bear. He had to stay. His girls were all counting on him for protection.

Feeling skittish as he left the house a short while later, he checked beneath the hood and undercarriage of his A8 for explosives. It was a far-fetched possibility, but he looked nonetheless. He climbed a stepladder to give the garage door opener a closer study, just to be sure. Satisfied he wasn't wired to blow up half the neighborhood, he got into his car and left.

The drive to Nikolai's grand manor in River Oaks wasn't a long one. He pulled into the driveway and followed it to the converted carriage house in the rear where Nikolai had given him a permanent space. When he stepped out and locked his car, he cast a casual glance to the left and right but saw nothing to arouse suspicion. He was halfway up the sidewalk when Boychenko exited the house in his running clothes, ready to accompany Vivian on her morning run.

"Boy, keep an eye out today, yeah? It's quiet this morning, but we can't be too careful, not with her."

"I'll keep her safe," the kid promised. He had that puffed-up bravado that was so prevalent in young men who hadn't yet had a real taste of violence. Maybe Ivan needed to bang this kid around a little harder in the cage...

As he entered the house, he glanced back at the kid and wondered if Boychenko might be a little too attached to Vivian. They were closer in age than Nikolai and his wife, and sometimes young men got stupid ideas about the women they guarded. Vivian only had eyes for Nikolai, but that might not stop another man from falling for her.

"Good morning, Kostya," Vivian greeted him with a smile. Dressed in black compression tights and a loose long-sleeve shirt with reflective stripes, she was finishing up a simple breakfast of juice and toast slathered with peanut butter. She gestured toward the platter heaped with delicious looking Mexican pastries on the counter. "Dimitri stopped by a little while ago," she explained. "Help yourself if you're hungry."

He shook his head. "I've eaten."

"Kolya is in his office." She touched his arm as he tried to pass, stopping him before he could leave the kitchen. She leveled a cautious look his way. "He's in one of his dark moods"

Appreciating the heads up, he nodded and wished her well on her run. Ilya entered the kitchen, grabbed a pink-iced pastry and a bottle of water from the refrigerator and hurried after Vivian. He would be riding escort while Vivian and Boychenko ran.

Kostya found Nikolai, seeming lost in thought, standing at the bay window in his office that overlooked the front yard.

"Shut the door." Nikolai gave the order without glancing back.

Although he'd always chafed at taking orders, he did what Nikolai asked. There was something in the air that warned him not to push this morning. It was a static crackle of warning, a swirling bite of energy that pulsed from Nikolai. The boss might have mellowed in the last few years, but Kostya had been around long enough to know that calm exterior could hide a hurricane of rage.

Not saying a word, he sat in one of the comfortable chairs near the fireplace and studied the chess game in progress. By the looks of the pieces and their positions, Vivian was a terrible player. He decided to give her some help and quickly nudged a few of her pieces into better positions. If Nikolai noticed when they sat down to resume their game, he wouldn't say a word. He would let Vivian win just to see her smile.

"Ten's P.O. tossed his room this morning," Nikolai said finally. "They forced their way inside Vanya's house and tore up the place looking for an infraction to pull his parole."

"Shit."

"Vanya is furious. He was already on thin ice with Erin about Ten living there. Having the police in his house? Having his wife bothered like that? He's going to be a fucking bear about it."

"What about Ten?"

"His P.O. ordered a piss test, but he conveniently didn't have one in his kit. They dragged him into the office for testing." Nikolai glanced back, frowning. "And to sweat him, I'm sure."

"Ten is the mostly loyal soldier you have." He wasn't worried about the enforcer-turned-bodyguard talking. "He's already done six years in the pen for you. He's been living under his parole terms since May and hasn't put a toe out of line. He'll go back inside before he says a word against the family."

"That's what concerns me." Nikolai blew out a noisy breath and raked his fingers through his hair. "You and I both know why they dragged him in this morning. They know he's one of my pressure points. We all have alibis for what went down last night, and we're in the clear. The police want answers. They'll never be able to prove it, but they know I sanctioned Hector's bloodbath. Threatening to put Ten back inside is an easy way to force my hand." He turned around and crossed his arms in front of his chest. "We may need to give them some of Hector's men to relieve the pressure."

Kostya groaned. "Hector won't like it."

"Hector is a big boy now. If he's going to sit at the table with the rest of the adults, he'll have to learn that sometimes we have to make painful sacrifices."

What Nikolai said was true, but Hector was on shaky ground right now. He would need weeks, maybe months, to solidify his hold on the cartel and cement himself as the new boss. Judging by the tension radiating from Nikolai as he lowered his arms to his sides and left the window, he knew that. Nikolai dropped into the open chair on the other side of the chess board, picked up the white queen and rolled it between his tattooed fingers.

The wheels in Kostya's head began to turn as he looked for ways to take the heat off the family. "I'll go see Diego Reyes. He'll know if any of Hector's triggermen had bad blood with any of their targets. If there's prior history, we can give the police a nudge in the right direction without it coming back on us. There's a new detective working homicide. He's hungry to prove himself. He's a soft target. I can work him."

"Be careful." Nikolai's mouth settled into a flat line. "Eric will be all over this. I won't have him upsetting Vivian. I don't want our fingerprints on any of this." He seemed to think about it for a moment. "Use Ilya. *Blat*? It's his specialty."

Ilya had become their unofficial *tolkash*, a pusher who dealt in favors. More and more, they relied on Ilya to smooth out little problems and maintain relationships with the other families in town.

"Speaking of Ilya, I may need his help with some freelance work Liam sent my way."

"What kind of work?" Nikolai made a gun sign and crooked his finger as if firing it.

"No, not that kind of work. He needs to get one of his boys into the US. Permanently," he added.

"A green card marriage?"

"That was my thought."

"It will have to be someone we can trust. We don't need a bad marriage blowing up in our faces three or four years down the line. It's too risky."

"That's why I wanted to use Ilya to pick the right woman to approach as a possible bride. He's better at reading women than I am."

Nikolai laughed roughly with agreement and then tapped the chess piece on his knee. He had that irritated gleam in his eye as he asked, "When were you going to tell me about sending Artyom to the hospital to watch over Hadley?"

He sat back in his chair and shrugged. "I wasn't."

Nikolai's jaw tightened. "You weren't going to tell me that you sent my best captain into that fucking hospital to kill a girl who is dying of heart problems?"

"The plan was never to kill her." Annoyed, he exhaled in a huff. "This is why I didn't tell you about sending him."

Nikolai glared at him. "Are you out of your fucking mind sending someone to threaten Hadley? She's one of Vivian's friends and a colleague. Not to mention, her father has connections that could bury us."

"No one threatened her." Technically, he was right. He'd threatened Finn. "Artyom was just there to keep an eye on things."

"Don't bullshit me, Kostya. We both know why he was there." He pointed an angry finger. "Don't use Artyom like that again. He's done enough for this family. He's finally found someone who makes him happy and—"

Nikolai stopped abruptly as Kostya lifted his head with interest. "Artyom found someone? Who?"

Nikolai seemed hesitant to answer. "It's Chess."

Stunned, he insisted, "You're not serious."

"I am."

They shared a look that silently communicated the ugly truth about Adrian, the street soldier who had been part of Artyom's crew and the father of Chess's almost seven-year-old daughter. It was Adrian's fault Ten had gone to prison, and the rest of the family had never forgiven him.

"I didn't realize they were that close," Kostya admitted, simultaneously irritated that he had missed a connection to the family's top captain and impressed that Artyom had managed to keep a secret from him.

"I didn't either," Nikolai replied. "Not until Vee told me about the house," he added.

"What house?

"That new build—the Mediterranean one with the red tile roof—across from Vanya and Erin," he clarified. "Erin told Vee that she saw Artyom with Chess looking at the house. I asked him about it. He told me that Chess put in an offer and got the house."

He tried to follow the chain of information that had flowed from woman to woman. "How the hell can that girl afford a house in Vanya's neighborhood? She was fucking homeless and pregnant a few years ago."

"She was, but now she's loaded."

"How? Doing what?"

"She owns a babywearing company."

"The fuck is babywearing?" he interrupted with confusion.

"It's a fabric harness," Nikolai tried to explain as he gestured at his chest. "Vee has decided she's wearing our baby instead of putting him in a stroller." He made a face, and Kostya smartly decided not to ask why. "She was showing me some of the designs that Chess sells, and I got curious when I realized it was Adrian's Chess."

"And?"

"And she's made millions selling her slings, clothes and nursery things."

"Millions?" he asked skeptically. Was there really that much money in baby gear?

"It's the fabric designs, I think. She draws them herself and uses organic whatever," he said with a wave of his hand. "She also has cloth diapers and furniture and clothes. Vee showed me her Instagram. The girl has millions of followers. Target is going to start carrying some of her goods."

"Did Artyom give her money?" he wondered. "Is that how she got started?"

"Yes. He told me that he felt responsible for her after everything that happened with Adrian. He looked after her and the baby."

"And now what? They're a couple?"

"He said no. That they're just friends." At his look of disbelief, Nikolai raised his hands. "That's what he said. I didn't push."

"But?"

"But he had that look in his eye."

Knowing the hell Artyom had survived back in Russia—losing his woman and his baby—Kostya wasn't at all surprised that Artyom would gravitate toward a single mother. But there was a huge fucking complication with his choice of this girl and her baby.

"I know what you're thinking," Nikolai interjected, as if reading his mind. "Adrian."

Not another word had to be said. They both seemed to be sharing the same thought about what had really happened to Adrian and all the players involved in the coverup.

"It could get messy," Kostya said matter-of-factly. "It might even be the sort of mess I can't clean."

"Then we'll have to make sure that Artyom understands that before he makes any promises to Chess," Nikolai decided. Still toying with the white queen, he admitted, "I think he's going to end up marrying her. When he talked about her and tried to defend their friendship, it gave me fucking flashbacks to all of my excuses about Vivian. It's not about paying the debt he owed her as Adrian's captain. It's something more than friendship and protection."

"She's a ready-made family," he said somewhat unkindly. "After what he lost…"

"I don't think it's that simple, Kostya." Nikolai exhaled and stretched out his legs. "You know the little girl has autism?"

He shook his head. "I didn't."

"Well, she does. It takes a special kind of man to want to step into the big shoes that little girl's father needs. This isn't about replacing what he lost. He could have married and had kids with Lidia or a dozen other single moms that he's fucked around with over the years. No," he said firmly. "Chess is different."

"So?" he asked, certain Nikolai was about to lay down an order.

"So," Nikolai interjected pointedly, "you want to play spy games? You want to pull shit like you did with Hadley last night? You send someone expendable."

"I don't trust the expendable ones. We can't afford any mistakes."

Nikolai squeezed the bridge of his nose and muttered rudely. It was clear the stress of the last few months was gnawing away at him. "Kostya…"

"Look, I didn't tell you about Artyom because I knew that it was going to eat you up inside if I had to pull that trigger. You've never been good when it comes to applying pressure on families, on women and kids."

"There's a line, Kostya," Nikolai insisted roughly.

"Only because you drew it!" Irritated, he said, "This is what I'm good at. Just let me do my job."

Nikolai shook his head. "Maybe you shouldn't be doing the ugly things either. Maybe it's time we found different ways to get things done."

"It's a dream," he replied coldly. "A fantasy. These are the rules of our world. We have to play by them—or we have to get out of the game."

Nikolai's gaze hardened. "Don't lecture me. This was my world long before it was yours."

The boss had him there. Kostya touched his chest in a signal of apology, and Nikolai nodded in acceptance and continued playing with the white queen. Clearly wanting to change the subject, he asked, "How is Holly?"

"She's fine." He wasn't about to tell Nikolai he'd spent the night with Holly. Lifting up in his seat, he reached back and withdrew the boxed DNA swab and the rolled-up plastic hair collection bag from his pocket. He tossed them onto Nikolai's lap. "I need your DNA."

Nikolai's lip curled with distaste. With reluctance, he set aside his queen and opened the swab first. After vigorously rubbing the inside of his cheek, he slipped it into the box and then tugged free a few strands of hair for the bag. After they were both sealed, he threw them back at Kostya. "When will we know?"

"Soon."

"You'll only confirm that Holly is my sister and Maksim is our father. You can't prove anything about her mother."

"Not yet, but I'm working on it."

Nikolai didn't ask how. "Is there anything else I need to know?"

He didn't think it was time to tell him about the strange package he'd received earlier that morning. Instead, he pulled his phone from his pocket and found the photo he needed. "You'll want to know about this gift the Liquidator left me."

"What kind of gift?" he asked guardedly.

"This kind." Kostya showed Nikolai the snapshot of Lana

he'd taken at the motel.

The boss's reaction was instant—and furious. "What the fuck?"

Before he got the wrong idea, he quickly explained, "They found her in a mark's house. The contract didn't include her—alive or dead—so he decided to give her to me. He doesn't deal with trafficked girls."

"He gave her to you? As a gift? For what?" Nikolai shot him a murderous glare, and Kostya had to fight the urge to recoil.

"Not like that! He wanted me to find her family or help her go back home."

"You can't send her back home! You know what will happen to her or her family if you do. Even if the traffickers didn't come back for her, the shame of it would ruin her life." He slashed his hand through the air. "She stays here where we can keep her safe."

Nikolai's gaze returned to the phone. It was clear that he was having the same thoughts as Kostya when he'd discovered her in that rundown motel. "She looks so much like Holly." The boss glanced at him. "You don't think…?"

"I don't know," Kostya admitted. "I used her as a decoy last night at the salon. I had her pose as a client from the women's shelter so she could get a free haircut and dye job like Holly's and then sneak away and hide in a closet until it was time."

Nikolai huffed as if amused. "Free? Hardly. Vee shook me down like a loan shark to get every penny she could as a donation to help Holly fund that program." Returning his attention to Lana, he asked, "What did you promise this girl in exchange for her help last night?'

"An apartment, living expenses and a clean ID."

"She'll need a job."

"She has one."

"How?"

"Holly offered her one."

Nikolai laughed softly. "She's as soft-hearted as Vee."

"Is that a bad thing?"

"It makes them vulnerable and easy to hurt." Nikolai rose from his chair and walked to his desk where he grabbed his suit jacket. As he slipped into it, he said, "I want a meeting with the Liquidator. I need to know who this mark was so we can figure out how Lana was trafficked into Houston."

Kostya tucked his phone into his jeans as he stood. "You know he doesn't do face-to-face."

"Then a phone call," he insisted. "You'll figure it out."

And he would. Somehow.

Nikolai flicked his fingers in a gesture for Kostya to walk with him. As they left the office, he explained, "I'm making a trip to see a dog breeder and then I'll be back in town. I put Boychenko and Ilya with Vivian. Danny will provide additional cover until Ten gets cut loose."

"Are you taking Artyom with you?"

Nikolai nodded. "Where will you be today?"

"Around," he replied vaguely. "I have some work to do."

Nikolai eyed him warily. "I don't want to know."

Kostya smiled. "I'm sure that you don't."

CHAPTER SIX

HE LEFT NIKOLAI'S home but didn't drive straight to the hub where his spiders liked to congregate. Always concerned about a tail, he switched up his route and kept an eye on his rear-view mirror. Eventually, he pulled into the parking lot of a busy shopping center and went inside a bookstore chain. He walked through the store and ducked into the stockroom where he snatched a baseball cap and jacket from a locker he paid the manager to use.

With the cap pulled low and the jacket changing his appearance just slightly, he emerged from the rear of the store and headed straight for the closest bus stop. It was a short 7-minute wait for the next bus and a quick ride to the next stop where he kept an old Dodge Neon in a parking garage.

It was imperative that he never be traced back to the building his little spiders had dubbed their lair. The commercial building on McKinney was a few blocks from Minute Maid Park and in a well-trafficked area. It didn't fit the normal specs for a hideout which had made it so attractive to him.

He pulled into a parking space along Ruiz Street and nonchalantly checked his surroundings before leaving the car. He entered the building through the employee door of Sunrise Sunset Delivery Service, the legitimate courier service that

Sunny operated from the warehouse. He covered his finger with the sleeve of his jacket and punched in the code to unlock the rear door. Bypassing the break room and employee lockers, he unlocked another door that led to a cramped hallway with a dark stairwell at the end. He took the stairs two at a time to the upper floor.

When he entered the warehouse space on the top floor, he spotted Max scowling from her perch on one of the long stainless-steel worktables. Suddenly, he regretted coming here. Her dark hair fanned around her face like angry flames, her blue eyes and bright red lipstick giving her a fierceness he wasn't at all prepared to face this morning. Her pale skin seemed even whiter against the black tight-fitting skirt and blouse and the dangerously red high heels she wore.

Shutting the door, he surveyed the rest of the room quickly and noticed Sunny eating a cup of yogurt while balanced cross-legged on a swiveling barstool. She'd staked out a seat that gave her a perfect view of the argument that was about to erupt. The wild pink tint to her short mohawk and the piercings in her face and ears glinted in the sunlight streaming in through the oversized windows behind her. Holding his gaze, she mouthed silently, "You're fucked."

Sighing, he leaned back against the door and crossed his arms. "Go ahead, Max."

Her eyes blazed as she asked, "What the *fuck* were you thinking taking Lobo on your job last night? How fucking dare you put her at risk like that! She's just a baby, K. She's *our* baby," she gestured toward Sunny, "and you almost got her killed! Did you see her face? Did you see what that asshole did to her? What the fuck do you have to say for yourself?"

A stab of guilt tore through his chest. She was right, of course. About all of it. Years earlier, he had entrusted Lobo's care to Max's mother, a dancer at one of the clubs he co-owned with Besian. A few faked papers, and the little girl was officially part of their small family. When Tracy died, Max had taken over as her guardian, working and going to college full-time and still finding the time to play mother.

"I didn't expect her to get hurt. She was just supposed to babysit, Holly. That's it."

"Yeah, well, that didn't work out so well, did it?" Jaw clenched with anger, she snarled, "She could have been killed, Kostya!"

"I know," he said gravely.

"*I know*," she mimicked. "Seriously? That's all you have to say?"

"What the hell do you want me to say, Maxine? Huh?" he shouted as he shoved off the door. "What the fuck more do you want me to do?"

Max hopped off the table and stormed toward him, smacking him hard in the chest with both fists. The impact knocked him back a step. "I want you to stop using her like this. She's a child, Kostya. She's not a fucking assassin. She's not FSB or GRU. She's not a soldier or an operative. She's just a kid."

His chest was on fire, probably marked with an imprint of her knuckles. Staring down at her, he said, "Lobo made her choice. She wants to learn. She wants—"

"She doesn't fucking know what she wants! She's just a kid!"

"She's old enough to make her own decisions, Max. You

need to stop coddling her!"

"That's my job! *You* made it my job when you gave her to my mom. She's my baby sister, and I love her. I do not want her going down the same fucked up path that you've lived. She deserves better!"

Stung by her words, he was about to unleash a torrent of mean words that he would probably regret when the door behind them swung open and Fox burst inside the room. Panting from exertion, she apologized loudly, "Sorry! Sorry, I'm late." Slamming the door and sagging against it, she asked, "So, did I miss all of the fireworks? Did you make him cry yet?"

"I don't fucking cry," Kostya growled.

"I would cry if Max yelled at me," Fox replied. "She's got that disappointed mom glare thing that makes me feel like I'm five again."

"Fox, I've seen you cry at commercials," Sunny interjected before licking her spoon clean.

Fox rolled her eyes. "One time! And I was flying on those edibles Nate gave me."

"Can we get back to the issue at hand?" Max asked, her voice filled with irritation.

"You were just telling K what a monstrous fuck up he is," Sunny reminded ever so helpfully.

"Thank you, Sunny," he intoned drily. Not breaking his stare off with Max, he said, "I made a mistake bringing Lobo on the job. I own that fuck up."

"And?" Max asked, her brow arched as she waited for him to say something more meaningful.

"And that's it," he said matter-of-factly. "I'm not going to stop training Lobo if she wants to learn."

"You're making a mistake." Max held his gaze, her face hardened with that disappointed look that Fox had just described. She was right. He *did* feel like a five-year-old kid again. "I think that someday you're going to regret all of this shit." Exhaling sadly, she said, "I can't stop her from doing work for you, not when you've got me and Sunny and Fox wrapped up in your web. But," she poked him right in the chest, her sharp stiletto nail digging into him, "I don't want her doing anything else on this case. She's *done* with this shit. You can use Fox, Sunny, me or the new girl for this Holly mess, but you leave Lobo alone."

"Fine," he agreed sharply. "I'll keep her out of the loop on this."

Max didn't miss the qualifier he had added to his agreement. As if sensing he might be wounded from her earlier verbal slash about his fucked-up life, she went right for the kill. "Can you please act like the father she seems to think you are?"

Sunny's sharp intake of breath echoed in the room. Fox was still in his line of sight, and she tensed, her nervous gaze darting between him and Max. He wanted to slash back at Max, to say something shitty about her own deadbeat father, but he didn't. Deep down inside, down where it was painfully raw, he knew that she was right.

"I don't know how to be a father, Max," he admitted finally. "I don't know what the fuck I'm doing half the time. When it comes to you girls, I'm just stumbling along, hoping I do the right thing and if I don't, that I don't screw you up for life. And…," he exhaled loudly, "and when it comes to Lobo, I'm trying to give her the skills she's going to need someday." He hesitated before confessing, "There are things about Lobo that none of you know. About her parents," he clarified. "Someday, that's all going to catch up to her, and she needs to know how to protect herself."

"Well, she's not going to need to know how to protect herself as an adult if you get her killed when she's just a kid," Max retorted angrily.

Certain this fight would go on for hours if he didn't surrender, he said, "You're right, Max."

She narrowed her eyes. "You're just saying that so I'll leave."

"Is it working?"

She checked her watch and grimaced. "Only because I have to get to a class that I'm covering for Vuong."

"Take this," he said, stopping her as he reached into his jacket and withdrew the labeled DNA kits he'd collected. "I need them done as soon as possible."

Frowning, Max took them. "I'm super busy this week with lecturing and lab work and my research. I don't have time to rush this for you."

"You'll find time if you want your expenses covered," he warned. "That's our quid pro quo."

She rolled her eyes. "A better quid pro quo would be you getting me a meeting with some of those wealthy Russians you have in your pockets."

"You don't want money from any of those men." He had told her this a thousand times, but it didn't stop her from asking. "There are better ways—safer ways—to get the funds you need to get your work noticed."

"Yeah, well, I'm running out of time to get noticed and

find that easy money." Heading for the door, she paused and glanced back at Sunny. "Don't forget to pick up groceries. It's your turn this week."

"Yes, Mommy," Sunny answered with a roll of her eyes.

Ignoring Sunny, Max turned to Fox. "Did you schedule your visit with your asthma doc yet?"

Fox made a face. "I forgot."

"You're almost out of your nebulizer meds and your inhaler is on its last refill. Ragweed is supposed to be a bitch this weekend, and you know how bad you get when it's high. I'm not waking up at four in the morning to drive you to the ER for a breathing treatment because you forgot to make a phone call."

"I'm calling now," Fox said, waving her phone to prove it.

Her mothering done, Max left, and Fox walked off to a corner of the room to call her doctor's office.

After the door closed, Sunny eyed him carefully. "You know she's not going to stop asking for an intro to those loaded Russians, right?"

"I know." He strode toward the whiteboards covered in Sunny's scribbling and hastily slapped up photos. She had been working some leads for him, tracking down various members of the cartel and the Albanian syndicate he wanted to keep tabs on at all times. Glancing at the box on the worktable nearest him, he asked, "What's this?"

"A gift," she said, finishing off her snack and shooting the empty cup into the trashcan with ease.

He opened the flaps on the dented box and stared at the surprise inside. "Where the hell did you get these?"

"Sorry," she said, rising to her feet and walking to the table. "The first thing you ever taught me about informants and contacts is to never share them with anyone, not even you."

He carefully reached inside and sifted through the sealed evidence bags. They held spent rounds and shell casings, discarded weapons and blood-stained clothing. "What made you think I'd want any of this evidence from last night?"

"Call it a hunch. I figured we might need to apply some pressure in the future, maybe blackmail some of the shooters last night."

"It was a good hunch." He smiled at her. "You're always two steps ahead of me."

Ego stroked, she grinned right back at him. "Since the day we met."

The memories of that night were still crystal clear. He had been outside Racks, one of the strip clubs he owned with Besian, smoking a cigarette in the shadows, when he'd spotted her slipping along the perimeter of the parking lot, moving like a jungle cat stalking prey. At first, he'd figured her for a thief about to roll a drunk for his wallet and watch, but then he had zeroed in on the asp baton in her hand. With one quick flick of her wrist, she had a fully expanded weapon capable of causing serious damage.

He probably should have stopped her as she crept up on the customer who had just left the club and was standing next to his car. At the time, he hadn't known if her mark was innocent or guilty. But he'd remained rooted to the spot and had watched from the shadows as she had applied a beating unlike any he had ever witnessed. It had been quick and fierce, her blows perfectly placed to cause serious damage, and surprisingly quiet.

Only when she was done, when she stood over the bleeding, dying man, did Kostya realize she was so shocked by the violence she had committed that she couldn't move. He had acted on impulse then, rushing out to grab her and the weapon and dragging her to his vehicle. It hadn't taken him long to get the full story from her.

After her young niece had been sexually assaulted and left for dead by a pedophile neighbor, Sunny had traced the bastard from New Orleans to Biloxi, Biloxi to Mobile, Mobile to Memphis, Memphis to Tulsa, Tulsa to Dallas and finally Dallas all the way to Houston. She'd caught up with him in the parking lot of Racks. At the time, Kostya had marveled at the way she had so easily tracked the man across seven states when the police hadn't been able to locate or arrest him.

He'd seen something in her. A gift for skip tracing. Something useful that he could nurture and use. So, he'd offered her a choice: stay in Houston and learn a new skill or take an envelope of cash and disappear. Four years later, she was still here, learning and practicing and quietly working in the city's shadows.

As for the man she had beaten? Before he could regain consciousness in the hospital, Kostya had taken care of the problem on the man's first night in the ICU. He and Sunny never spoke about what he'd done, but the truth had been acknowledged with a single look when the news of that pig's death had hit the papers. If anything, he had forever secured her loyalty with that one act of protection—and vengeance.

"I've got to jet," Sunny said, grabbing up her backpack and a package. "I promised to get this delivered for Zec before lunch."

Kostya decided the less he knew about the package's contents the better. The Albanian had a soft spot for Sunny and often sent business her way. She had proven herself trustworthy enough that even the Professionals used her as their main courier. He worried about her getting into trouble acting as the middle man for those types of illicit transactions, but at some point, he had to let his little spiders leave his web and spin their own.

"Can you get a message to the Liquidator?" he asked.

"Sure," she said, sliding her arms through the straps of her backpack. "What message?"

"Nikolai wants a meeting. Not for a contract, but to get some information about Lana."

She made a little face. "I'll pass along the message, but I wouldn't get his hopes up. You know what they're like. I've run courier jobs for them for years, and I've never once seen their faces."

"Ask. If he declines, Nikolai will have to deal."

When Sunny was gone, he closed the box of stolen evidence and reached for a roll of packing tape from a shelf underneath the table. As he ripped off a long strip of tape, Fox finished her phone call and slipped her phone into her pocket. Joining him at the table, she said, "You know I have."

"You have what?"

"Seen their faces. The Professionals," she clarified. "Well, one of them."

He couldn't believe the way she said it so nonchalantly, mentioning it as if she'd seen the most ordinary thing in the world. "How? When?"

"A few months ago." She walked over to the whiteboard

and studied it. "I was meeting Nate for a drink. You know, just sitting at the bar, waiting. I heard this voice." She glanced at him. "It was like an electric shock right up my spine. I've heard that voice only once before, on a phone call when you needed me to farm out some work. I knew who it was immediately. It was *him.* The Cleaner."

He didn't doubt what she had seen or heard. Fox had always had a strange knack for remembering things—faces, voices, obscenely long strings of numbers and data. "Did you make eye contact with him?"

"Do I look fucking stupid?"

"He didn't see you at all?"

She shook her head. "I took a selfie and managed to get enough of him in it to piece together an image later."

"And?"

"I have it somewhere safe. Encrypted. Do you want it?"

"Yes. Did you tell Nate? Or anyone else about it?"

"No. You're the only one who knows."

"Keep it that way," he warned. "Those guys have stayed anonymous for a reason."

"I know." She reached for the dry erase board and gave it a little push, flipping the board upside down to reveal the back. There were diagrams and family trees mapping out the various syndicates in town and how they were all connected to each other. "Sunny had Lobo work on this last night. She was trying to calm her down, I think. Get her out of that fucked up head space she was in after…well…you know."

"I know," he murmured guiltily. "Where is she today?"

"She was playing video games in my room when I left the house. I promised I'd bring her some tacos when I get back."

"How is she handling it all?"

Fox looked at him as if he might be the stupidest man she'd ever seen. "She's fucked up, K. Honestly, you're lucky Max didn't kill you this morning. For your own safety, I wouldn't eat or drink anything she gives you for at least the next twelve months. She's probably cooking up an undetectable poison in her lab right now."

Not wanting to get into that argument again, he nodded. "I'll take that under advisement."

"You need to talk to her. Lobo," she clarified. "Sunny talked to her last night. You know, about how it feels to kill someone and what it's like after it happens. I think it helped a little, but you should sit down with her. Talk it through. Be the good dad Lobo needs."

"I will." He hesitated before asking, "What about you? Did you tell her about your experience?"

Fox's shoulders stiffened. Voice tight and clipped, she said, "No."

He didn't push. It had been seven years since the night she stabbed Cory to death. Seven years since she called him for help, answering her door covered in blood, her body bruised from Cory's fist and teeth. Seven years since she had discovered her longtime boyfriend was a serial rapist who had been terrorizing Houston for more than a year...

Fox turned away and headed for the backpack she'd hastily dropped near the door earlier. Hefting it up, she brought it over the worktable and opened it. She pulled out the thick dossier given to Vivian by her cousin, Eric Santos. Eric, a Houston detective, had received the file from an unknown Russian female not long after Vivian had been shot.

"I went through this like you asked. Scanned everything so I can start breaking it down for you."

"Be careful with it." The file was filled with detailed information about Nikolai, Ivan, Artyom and a few other captains in the family. They'd immigrated with scrubbed backgrounds and clean records, but that dossier included all the secrets they had tried to leave behind.

"I'm always careful with these types of things." She turned around and faced the white board. Picking up a green dry erase marker, she uncapped it and drew a rectangle. Inside, she scribbled *krisha*.

Krisha. Roof. It was the word used to describe the protection paid for by rich Russian businessmen, politicians and mobsters.

"What about *krisha*?" He wondered where she was going with this.

"The shit in this file is the kind of stuff you pay your roof to protect you from, right? It's the kind of shit someone in that line of work would have at their fingertips, yeah?"

"And maybe this dossier came from someone inside Maksim's house," he said, piecing together her theory. "Maybe I should be looking inside—under the roof—instead of outside."

"Maybe," she replied. "It still doesn't explain how the dossier got to Eric. Who was the woman he met? How is she connected to all of it? Who paid her? Who pulled her strings?"

For a split-second, he debated whether to tell her or not. Knowing she could keep a secret and needing her help, he said, "I got a package this morning."

"What kind of package?"

He gestured toward the dossier. "Similar to this. It might have come from the same place for all I know."

"Do you have it with you? We could have Max run it for trace before I go through it."

"I'll get it to you later. Do you still have a way to access prison records?"

"Over there? Or here?"

"There."

She grimaced. "I can get into the electronic ones without a problem, but it depends on the years you need. Some of them have to be pulled by hand from old, moldy-as-fuck files in some dank ass storage room in the middle of Nowhere, Russia."

"I want whatever you can get on the Black Dolphin from '85 to now."

"That could take a while, K. I'll have to find someone on the ground that we can trust."

"You still have contact with Denis?"

"Your Moscow shadow?" she asked with a smile. "Yeah, I've got his number."

"Talk to him. Don't tell him why we're looking. Just ask for the files."

"I doubt he'll ask why I want them. Like he needs anymore secrets to keep?"

The door opened behind them. His hand went to the pistol holstered under his jacket while Fox slid her hand under the table where the girls kept a P30 suspended by a large magnet for easy use. At the sight of Lobo walking through the door, they both relaxed.

"You're supposed to be at home," Fox remarked. "I'm going to tell Mom on you."

Lobo removed her sunglasses, rolling her eyes at that. "Snitch."

Fox laughed, and then as if noticing the tension in the room, cleared her throat and said, "I think I'm going to grab those tacos I promised you. I'll be back in, like, an hour to take you home."

After Fox left, Lobo joined him at the worktable, leaning back against it. He surveyed the damage to her face. The bruising wasn't nearly as bad as he'd expected. Her nose wasn't broken, but she had some ugly splotches that would take some time to heal and fade. It was a damn good thing she was homeschooled. She'd have CPS and a school counselor all over her if she was in one of the public schools.

"How are your ribs?" She didn't seem to be guarding them anymore, but he wanted to be sure. "Do you need to see a doctor? We can get one of them on our payroll to come see you."

She shook her head. "I think it was just a muscle cramp last night, actually. I didn't take a real hit or anything, but I was doing a lot of twisting and kicking." She lifted the side of her shirt and showed him the slightly reddened area there. "I must have banged it on the shelves or something."

Not sure how to talk to her about what had happened last night, he decided to be honest with her. "I should have come back here to check on you. I shouldn't have left it to the girls to care for you."

Lobo shrugged. "You needed to be with Holly. She's important to you."

He nudged her shoulder with his own. "You're important

to me."

Lobo made a face. "Let's not get all mushy and talk about feelings, okay?"

"Sometimes we need to talk about our feelings. Other times, we need to box them away."

"Is today one of those days where I need to talk about it?"

"Probably."

"And what am I supposed to say?"

"Whatever you're feeling. Anything you want."

She didn't speak for a long moment. When she did, she admitted, "I had a nightmare last night, but it wasn't about what happened at the salon. It was about Mexico. It was about my mom."

Kostya was surprised to hear her mention her mother. It happened so rarely that he was inclined to believe this mention had been spurred by the trauma of last night. The knowledge that she had been alone all night, hurting inside and confused, stabbed him in the gut and twisted like a knife. His morning with Holly had been something truly special, but it had come at the cost of Lobo's welfare. Max was right. He was a total piece of shit father.

"We were in this hotel room," she continued. "It was nice. Clean. Not like a roach motel or anything. High end. Maybe a resort? I don't know." She hesitated. "My mom hugged me, and she was crying. She kept telling me she loved me…and then these gloved hands dragged her away from me. Someone behind me put something on my face. A hood maybe? And then I smelled something funny…and that was it."

"It was probably ether. Not my first choice for knocking someone out," he said, "but it has its place."

She snorted. "You weirdo. I'm over here telling you about my nightmare, and you're using it as a teaching moment."

"Sorry." He shrugged. "I'm not good at this, okay? I'm trying." A second later, he said, "I have dreams about my parents, too."

She looked up at him, surprised. "Nightmares?"

"Yes, but not the way you're thinking. I dream about happy things. My parents taking me to the park or teaching me to ice skate or play hockey. My mom singing me to sleep at night." His voice was soft, vulnerable as he admitted, "I wake up crying sometimes."

"We are so fucked up. You. Me. Sunny. Fox. Max. We're all broken inside. I don't think there's enough therapy in the world to put us back together again."

He shook his head. "There's not. It makes us stronger in some ways and weaker in others."

"Max wants me to stop all of this. She wants me to leave Houston. Go away to a private school and then college and forget any of this ever happened."

"Is that what you want? If it is, I'll make it happen."

"No, that's not what I want. I'm not sure where I'm going to end up or how I'm going to get there, but I feel like this," she gestured around the room, "is where I'm supposed to be right now. I feel like there's something out there waiting for me. Something big and scary and dangerous." She looked at him, her gaze far too serious for the child she was. "I need to be here. I need to prepare."

Awkwardly, he reached over and wrapped his arm around her shoulders for a quick hug. "But not today. Today, you should rest. Go home with Fox. She'll keep you entertained."

"Oh God," Lobo groaned. "Her idea of entertainment is telling me about her whacko conspiracy theories about false flag operations and the deep state and the Illuminati."

"Well, she's probably not wrong about some of her conspiracies."

Lobo rolled her eyes. "Please don't encourage her."

"I don't think she needs any encouragement." He walked over to the white board and began erasing it, wiping away any evidence that could be seen by the wrong eyes. If only it were this easy to wipe away memories...

CHAPTER SEVEN

WITH THE PULSE of upbeat pop music marking each step, I left my office and stepped onto the main floor of the salon. It was a busy Wednesday morning and nearly every station was in use. I had a break between clients, so I decided to make the rounds and get in some face time with our guests.

"Miss Candace is here for her first color appointment," Nisha explained to her newest associate, a recent cosmetology school grad she'd handpicked from our hiring pool. "So, Mallory, I want you to take a minute to examine her hair and create your plan for covering the sparkles."

They were discussing the amount of grey—sparkles as we called them in our salon—and how to give their new client the best color experience. When Mallory started to discuss glosses and glazes with the client, I moved along to the next station. Clearly Nisha's new girl knew her stuff.

I drifted along the aisles, stopping here and there to smile and make small talk or to discuss services like Brazilian blowouts with curious clients. Using those waitressing skills from college, I also picked up empty mimosa glasses and soda cans and kept track of the client requests.

After I had handed out the beverages or snacks, I noticed Andy motion me over with a frantic wave of her hand. I hurried to her side and found myself taking her shears and comb in hand and finishing the haircut she had started.

"Is she okay?" the client asked with concern.

"Just a little tummy trouble," I lied, knowing that Andy wasn't sharing her pregnancy news yet. Seven of our stylists were moms so morning sickness was something we all had experience with around here, but Andy seemed to be having a harder time of it than most. Savannah had already offered to give her a week or two off or let her slide to half days, but Andy seemed determined to stay at the salon until right before she left on maternity leave. I suspected money was an issue and began to think of ways we could offer her work in the back of house until she felt better.

I had just started the blow dry for her client when Andy returned and resumed her duties. As I stepped away from her station, I caught sight of Lana carrying a stack of clean towels to the wash stations. The moment she had the cabinet restocked, she grabbed a broom and dustpan and began gathering up the clippings at the haircutting stations nearest her. Her work ethic never failed to impress. From the moment she walked through the door to the moment she left, she was busy.

Sometimes I worried that she liked to keep busy because it kept her from having time to think about the horrible abuse she had survived. She still hadn't confided in any of us about how she had come to be in the women's shelter or even how she had come to this country. All her paperwork checked out so she was here legally, but I couldn't help but wonder.

Billie had taken to her immediately. Nisha had an affinity for her. Even Savannah, who had been less than enthusiastic about my decision to hire her, couldn't say enough good things about her now. Just this morning, Savvy had dropped the application for the spring semester of cosmetology school in Lana's locker. It was the only program in town with an ESL component that encouraged the students to improve their English skills and their marketability.

I wasn't quite sure that Lana wanted a career in cosmetology. She clearly had a flair for nail art and a love of all things related to beauty, especially makeup, but I wasn't sure it was her passion. After seeing her playing with a client's two kids, I had a feeling she might be better suited to nannying or teaching.

For now, though, I hoped she stayed with us. She needed support. In the month Lana had been with us, she had been welcomed into our salon family. We were like sisters here, each of us guarding the others.

Not a month, I silently amended. *Four weeks and one day.*

I had been keeping track of Lana's time at the salon because it was an easy way for me to keep track of how long it had been since my breakfast with Kostya.

Four weeks.

One day.

And not a word from him about our arrangement.

We had exchanged a few text messages, and a couple of awkward waves in our driveways, but that was it. I couldn't understand when and why it had all gone sideways. I had thought for sure that things would progress quickly and heatedly, but it was as if Kostya had tossed cold water on the fire between us. We had fizzled out—and I wasn't sure how to spark that fire again.

Raucous laughter drew me toward the reception area of the salon. Even if I hadn't glanced at the books this morning, I would have recognized those familiar laughs and voices as belonging to Vivian, Erin, Benny and Bianca. The four close friends were at the salon for their monthly massages and mani-pedis. I had seen Lena's name on Nisha's books for a color and cut, but I didn't hear her distinctive laugh. Knowing her schedule, Lena was probably hopping off a plane and rushing to the salon via private car right now.

When I walked into the reception area, I found Erin regaling her girlfriends with a story about her great big bear of a husband. By the look on Vivian's red face, I had a feeling Erin's tale was rather bawdy. The other girls were laughing so hard. Head thrown back, Benny wiped at her eyes while Bianca looked as if she might fall off the couch.

Together, the group presented such a pretty picture. Vivian and Bianca, both pregnant, preferred more classic styles. Vivian wore a simple dress in a deep wine shade that she had paired with gold jewelry. Bianca's dress was cut with a similar high waist from a vibrant coral fabric. She also wore gold bangles and large gold hoops to match the gold medallion dangling from her neck. Erin looked similarly elegant in her wispy champagne pink peasant dress and strappy gold sandals.

Benny looked more casual in denim chinos and a silky blouse. Unlike the others, she seemed a bit tired and didn't have that well-rested spark in her eyes. But she had a young baby at home and a bakery that opened at four in the morning! I couldn't even imagine trying to run a business with a small baby and a husband. I had a hard time handling myself and the salon.

Of course, from what I little I knew of Benny's husband, he seemed to be a very hands-on father. More than once, I had seen Dimitri at the grocery store handling the shopping and the baby with ease. Benny seemed to have chosen well when she had picked Dimitri to be her partner in life.

"Sorry, sorry, sorry," Lena exclaimed as she hurried into the reception area, a mimosa already in hand and an outrageously expensive handbag dangling from her arm. I had to smile at the way she so easily paired her designer shoes and accessories with a pair of black leggings and an oversized University of Houston baseball tee. "My flight from Moscow was delayed and then we hit traffic coming from the airport."

Erin was the first to jump up and hug her best friend. Lena moved down the line, hugging and smiling. As the group of friends finished up their reunion, Billie gathered them up and led them back to spa area for their mani-pedis.

When they left, I noticed the heavily tattooed giant sitting in the corner of the waiting area. There was an iPad on his lap and an earbud firmly stuck in his left ear but the right was empty, probably so he could hear Vivian if she needed him. She called her bodyguard Ten, and wherever she went, he was right there beside her.

Like Bianca and Erin's husbands, Ten towered over everyone else. He had tattoos on his hands, arms and peeking out the top of his fitted black T-shirt. The snarling Siberian tiger on his arm was one of the nicest pieces I had ever seen. Not that I would tell him that.

As I made my way to the reception desk to check my appointment book, I watched the way Ten couldn't take his eyes off Nisha as she came into the waiting area for her next client.

It wasn't the first time I had seen him looking at her like that. His intense focus on her every move betrayed his interest.

It was misplaced interest, unfortunately. Nisha had sworn off men for good. She had gotten married straight out of high school—like two days after graduating—to her sweetheart who turned out to be a violent monster. He regularly beat her so badly he put her in the hospital. Luckily, he had screwed up a drug deal and ended up going away to prison. Not long after he was locked up, she had him served with divorce papers and never looked back.

But something about Ten made me wonder if he might be the man who changed her mind about relationships.

"Your client had to cancel and reschedule," Billie said as she returned to reception desk where I clicked through the appointment book on one of the computers there. "She was held over in a closing and had another house with two offers that she needed to negotiate."

"Oh, well did you find a day to work Susan back into my schedule?" My books were nearly as tight as Nisha's, but for a client like Susan who had been with me since the day I opened, I would come in early or stay late.

"You had a slot tomorrow morning, but you'll have to duck out of a vendor meeting ten minutes early."

"That's fine. Savvy makes the final decisions anyway."

"When I was taking the girls back, Benny mentioned that she needed to book a trim and Vivian needs a haircut. I thought maybe we could work Benny in with Peyton and then slide Vivian into the second half of Susan's empty slot?"

"Works for me." I clicked out of the appointment book screen. "I'll be walking the floor if you need me."

Before I left the reception area, I grabbed a cold bottle of water from the beverage cooler and walked over to Ten. He glanced up as I approached him and tugged the lone earbud from his ear. I handed him the water. "Are you on the salon's free Wi-Fi? No reason to burn through your data while you're waiting for Vivian."

"I am." He accepted the water bottle from me. "Thank you."

"Vivian is going to stay after her spa appointment for a haircut with me." I glanced at his iPad. "If you get low on battery, ask Billie for a charger. We keep a few different ones in the drawers at the reception desk."

After making sure Ten was comfortable, I made my way across the salon, stopping at the color bar, at the shampoo basins and at each cutting station to chat with guests. Noticing the hampers for capes and towels were getting full, I carefully maneuvered the rolling bins out of the shampoo area toward the staff hallway.

When I passed the guest bathrooms, I heard crying and slowed down to see if someone needed help. Almost immediately, I began to worry that one of our guests hated her haircut or the color. I tried so hard to make sure my crew knew to communicate and be conservative when it came to big changes or new clients, but sometimes we missed the mark and missed it by a lot.

"I feel like shit for being jealous and for not being enthusiastic about their showers. Like I know it's my job as Vivian's friend to throw her baby shower but I start thinking about me and Ivan and how long we've been together and how we still haven't gotten a positive test. Starting my period this morning and then having to hear about the nursery plans and the baby names—I just couldn't keep it inside. But what kind of friend am I to be jealous about stuff like this?"

"You're a good friend, Erin, and I know that if Vivian or Bianca knew that you were going through this they would do anything to make you feel better." Lena tried to be the voice of reason to her distraught friend. "Hell, knowing Vivian, she would be on the phone to every single fertility specialist in the city demanding they fit you in today for a checkup. She and Bianca would never begrudge you feeling jealous or sad or whatever it is that you feel when you see their big baby bumps."

It wasn't uncommon to hear things like this at the salon. Sometimes I felt more like a therapist than a stylist, to be honest. But I didn't know that Erin and Ivan were having problems getting pregnant. They hadn't even been married a full year yet, but maybe they had been trying since their engagement?

"What if I'm like my mom and Ruby? What if I have endometriosis? What if I can't have kids? Ivan wants to be a dad so badly, and I want to be a mom and have lots of babies. What if I can't have them?"

"Then I'll have your babies for you," Lena said matter-of-factly.

"What?" Erin asked, her voice thick from crying.

"Girl, I was built to have babies. Look at these hips! Look at my backside and these tits! After Yuri and I have had a baby, I'll be your surrogate."

My eyes widened at the very calm and confident way Lena made her offer. She could have been talking about loaning

Erin her car instead of her uterus.

"You're serious," Erin said a moment later. "You would really be our surrogate if it comes to that?"

"Of course, I would! You're like my sister, and I love you. We're family, Erin. I would do anything for my family."

"Even carry a giant Ivan-sized baby?"

"Well, it will have to be a C-section!"

The two friends started laughing and giggling, and I took that as my cue to hurriedly push the two hampers to the laundry room. A short time later, after starting a load of laundry, I peeked out of the room just in time to see Erin and Lena emerge from the bathroom with arms linked.

"You need a massage," Lena decided. "We'll see if one of the therapists can work you in, okay? And when we're done here, we'll raid Yuri's wine cellar for something stupidly expensive, order something totally unhealthy and binge Netflix ..."

When the hall was clear, I left the laundry room. What I had heard, I would never repeat. Like a lawyer, I believed in the stylist-client privilege.

Back in the spa, I found Bianca giving Benny and Vivian hugs as she rushed off to a bridal appointment at her boutique. It seemed that Lena had already moved on to her appointment with Nisha, and Erin had been taken back to a massage room. Only Vivian and Benny were left as they finished their manicures.

"I think it's good that you and Nikolai are talking about it," Benny was saying as she admired the soft peach shade on her nails. "When I couldn't stop crying and couldn't sleep and had all that anxiety, Dimitri and I didn't know what was wrong. I felt like a horrible mother, and he felt like a terrible father and husband. He thought all the problems were his fault because he was working too much or wasn't getting up enough with Sofia at night, but that wasn't the case. It was just hormones and the chemicals in my brain that needed an adjustment."

"But you feel okay on the medicine now?" Vivian asked, her worry clear by the tone of her voice as she slipped back into her rings and bracelets.

"The difference was night and day once the medication kicked in," Benny assured her. "I only needed a low dose, and it was safe for breastfeeding. If you need it, you'll be fine, and the baby will do great because his mommy is healthy and happy."

His? That was the first I had heard of Vivian having a boy. I would have to make a note for Savannah. She loved buying baby gifts for our clients and making sure they had their complimentary prenatal and postnatal massages and pedicures booked.

I waited until there was a lull in the conversation between them to walk over and smile and ask them if they were ready for their haircuts. I gathered up their handbags and phones so they wouldn't have to worry about dinging their manicures or getting lotion and hand serum stains on the leather. While Vivian made a quick beeline for the restroom, I led Benny to her stylist. When I was done, I found Lana walking Vivian to my styling station. They were chattering away in Russian, and I was glad to see that Vivian had taken an interest in Lana.

"How was your spa appointment?" I asked as Vivian settled into the chair at my station.

"Very good." She flashed her fresh manicure at me. "What do you think?"

"Rock Royalty?" I guessed, pretty sure I had nailed the deep purple shade.

"Yes." She held out her hand and wiggled her fingers. "I wanted something fun and different this time."

"And do you want to do something fun and different with your hair?" I combed my fingers through her long, dark waves.

She laughed. "Definitely not. Nikolai would have a stroke if I walked into the house with shorter hair." She touched the ends, winding them around her finger, and a look flitted across her face. It must have been a good memory because a wicked little smile lifted the corners of her mouth. "No, let's just trim the ends and a blowout if you have time."

"I have time." I touched her shoulder and met her smile in the mirror. "Let's get you to one of the sinks for a shampoo."

We took the corner sink, and I draped and fixed a cape around her neck before helping her lean back in the chair. I adjusted the footrest for her, hoping to ease the strain on her lower back. Remembering that she was more tender-headed, I kept the water temp warm but not too hot. "Is this okay?"

"Feels fine," she said, smiling up at me.

We made small talk as I lathered, conditioned and rinsed her hair. When we moved back to my station, we kept talking about her latest art projects, a gala she was co-hosting in November and how hard it was to find elegant evening wear in maternity styles.

"And it doesn't help that I seem to be growing every day," she added, rubbing her stomach. "If I buy a dress this week, it might not fit me next month."

"I'm sure someone at Bianca's boutique could alter your dress," I suggested as I trimmed and tapered. "She's probably going to have the same problem."

"Only worse since she is having twins," Vivian replied. "She finally gave up the high heels this week. Well," she laughed, "I should say that Sergei went through her closet and boxed them all up and brought them to my house for safe-keeping. He was convinced she's going to lose her balance and get hurt all in the name of fashion."

"She does love her high heels." I cross-checked my cut. "I'm surprised that shoe collection of hers isn't under lock and key. It must have cost her a fortune, all those Jimmy Choos and Manolos and Louboutins."

"She went ballistic when she got home and her closet was empty. He came by the house later that night to load them all back into his SUV and take them home. Had his tail tucked right between his legs," she added with a laugh.

"My God, can you imagine how hard she must have made him grovel?"

"Oh, I'm sure he thought of something to make her forget how frustrated she was with him."

The mischievous gleam in Vivian's eyes made me blush. Sergei was alpha to the core, and it was obvious to anyone who saw him with Bianca that he loved her and thought she was the sexiest woman alive. My face got hot as I imagined what a man like that was like in bed. "I'm sure he did."

"Speaking of men and frustration..."

At first, I thought she was talking about me, but then I noticed her gaze had drifted to Ten. Her giant bodyguard was coming out of the hallway, probably after making a trip to the bathroom, and had his gaze fixed on Nisha as she styled Lena's hair. I could practically feel the heat of his desire from here.

"I think he's going to stay frustrated," I gently warned. "Nisha isn't really in the market for a man right now."

"Ten is tenacious. He won't let that stop him, not if he thinks there's even a snowball's chance in hell of her returning his interest."

"Is that why they call him Ten?" I opened a drawer at my station and removed a round brush. "Because he's tenacious?"

"No."

I had the feeling that this was one of those gray areas of her life so I didn't ask for any further explanation. Rising on tiptoes, I grabbed the blow dryer dangling from the ceiling and began to dry her hair. As I worked, I thought of Kostya and all the gray areas of his life that would become the gray areas of mine if I went after him.

"Are you okay?" Vivian asked while I pulled a straightener down her glossy strands. "You got quiet."

"I'm just thinking."

"About?"

It finally occurred to me that Vivian was the only person I could trust to talk about something like this. I glanced around and noticed we were alone. Even so, I kept my voice low and asked, "When did you know that you wanted your husband even with all of his…baggage?"

Vivian waited until I had cleared the straightener from the ends of her hair to turn in the chair for a better look at me. She seemed to be looking deep inside me, as if trying to decide whether I could be trusted. She must have seen something that convinced her of my trustworthiness. "It was never a question for me. I love him. All of him," she added. "Even the shadowy parts."

The shadowy parts? That was a nice way to describe all the dark and dangerous things the men we cared about did.

"Is the man with baggage someone I might know?"

Certain I could trust her, I confessed, "It's Kostya."

"Kostya?" She seemed utterly shocked. "How did—?"

"We're neighbors. We have been for the last couple of years. We aren't dating. Like officially or anything," I added hastily. "We've been dancing around it for a while. A month ago, we had this perfect breakfast and morning together—"

"And then he pulled back and away from you?"

I nodded. "Basically."

"Kostya is like Nikolai in a lot of ways. They're quiet men. They're private. They're also very complicated and stubborn." She touched the bracelet on my arm as if seeing it for the first time. "This is one of Zoya's pieces. I know her work, and I also know that Kostya must have given it to you."

"For Christmas," I confirmed.

"What did you give him? I mean, if that's not too personal a question to ask, of course."

"A certificate to the animal shelter."

Vivian smiled. "That is the sweetest gift idea."

"I don't think he was very excited about it. He still hasn't used it."

"They've been very busy," Vivian said carefully. "It's been a difficult year so far. Lots of expansion and growth and turnover," she added, prudently choosing her language. "It really hasn't been a good time to add a dog to his life."

"I told him we could adopt one together and share responsibilities."

"What did he think about that?"

"I don't know."

"And what does he think about you two dating?"

I shrugged a bit sadly. "He told me to take four weeks to think about whether I really wanted to get involved with him."

"Has it been four weeks?"

"Yesterday."

"And?"

"And I haven't seen him," I said, stepping back behind her to finish styling her hair.

"Do you want him?" She held my gaze in the mirror. "Do you want him and all of the shadowy parts? Do you want to be part of his complicated life? Do you want to make *your* life more complicated?"

"Yes." I didn't think. I didn't question. I simply answered truthfully. "I do want him in my life."

"Then you have to tell him," Vivian replied matter-of-factly. "Be forceful, if necessary. Sometimes these men of ours can be hardheaded."

These men of ours...

As I finished Vivian's hair, I caught sight of the crown tattoo on the back of her neck. If things with Kostya progressed the way I wanted I might someday be part of *her* family. There was something strangely alluring about the idea of belonging to something so powerful and yet so very secret.

When I was finished with Vivian's haircut and style, I swept the cape away and carried it to the hamper tucked away in a nearby cabinet while she snapped a selfie. That mischievous smile of hers was back as she typed in a quick message and sent her photo.

Taking her guest folio from my top drawer, I asked, "Do you want to schedule another trim for six or eight weeks?"

"Let's do six." She walked next to me to the reception desk where I handed off her guest folio and told Billie to book her for another trim. Before I left to tidy up my station, Vivian touched my arm. "If you ever want to talk, I'm always around for a chat."

"Thank you. I really appreciate that offer."

"Just come by the house or find me at Samovar. I'm usually there for the lunch rush."

"I will."

When I returned to my station, I discovered one of Vivian's gold bracelets on the counter where her handbag had been. Picking it up, I started to call out to her, hoping to catch her before she left, but then I spotted the appointment card tucked under the bracelet and the note she had scribbled onto it.

I'll send Kostya to pick this up. Good luck!

I pocketed the delicate bracelet for safekeeping and tried to stop grinning. Apparently, the queen of Houston's underworld had decided to make some luck for me.

CHAPTER EIGHT

"I DON'T KNOW what to do. She doesn't listen to me anymore. She thinks he loves her, but she's just a child. She doesn't know what love is."

Kostya stood back, leaning against the kitchen doorway as the tired, crying mother poured out her problems to Nikolai. Seated at the round table in Rada's neatly kept home, the boss listened intently as the older woman told him what everyone on the street already knew—her sixteen-year-old daughter had run off with one of Lalo's street slingers.

"He hits her," she cried with despair. "Not just the time Ilya took care of it. Another time, just a few days ago. She had marks on her arms. Purple marks, big and angry."

Assaulting Tiffany, Rada's only child, was as serious to Nikolai as if it had been his own blood. Rada's late husband had worked for the family back in Moscow. When she had emigrated to Houston with her sister and brother-in-law, they had all found work and protection under Nikolai. Rada had worked at Samovar since before its opening day, first as a line cook and now in the back of the house as the day-to-day operations manager. She ran the restaurant like a mother, being tough when necessary and always encouraging and kind. She was a good woman, and no one had a bad thing to say about her.

And to see her weeping over her wayward daughter, crying so hard she sounded as if she might make herself sick, tugged at something deep inside Kostya. Marco and the girl had vanished, but they wouldn't be missing long. Not if he had anything to do with it.

"We took care of this before," Nikolai reminded her, not unkindly but sternly. "Ilya made sure that Marco got the message not to touch her again and to leave her alone, but she went back to him and now…"

After Tiffany had been found with Marco that first time, Nikolai had sent Ilya to straighten Marco out and put an end to his dalliance with an underage girl under their protection. Ilya had given him a message—with fists and boots. By the time his crew had been done with Marco, he'd ended up in the hospital, limping and pissing blood.

But it wasn't enough to break up the two illicit lovers. Before long, Tiffany had gone right back to sneaking around with the older dope slinger. Lalo had been told to get his man in line, but he clearly didn't have any control over his crews. And now here they all were with a teenage girl missing and the very real chance the police would get involved. If the police found him first and put him in an interrogation room, Marco would break—and then what?

"I don't know what to do," Rada repeated, sobbing so hard that Kostya worried she might choke. This was a mother who had clearly reached the end of her fucking rope.

Nikolai pulled a monogrammed handkerchief from his pocket and gently pressed it into Rada's hand. "You don't need to worry about this anymore."

Nikolai didn't need to say anything else. Rada understood what he meant. Tiffany would be found and returned. Marco would be dealt with and Lalo would pay whatever reparations Rada demanded. The police would be kept out of a family problem and that would be that.

He stayed behind to assign two men to watch the house, just in case Tiffany or Marco decided to come back. By the time he caught up with Nikolai, the crew shadowing them had already loaded up and were waiting for their instructions. His hand on the passenger door handle, Nikolai asked, "Do we know where Marco is?"

"I sent Danny to chase him down. He sent a message to let me know that Lalo is playing games and won't tell him anything about Marco."

Once they were safe inside the car, Nikolai exhaled roughly and jerked on his seatbelt. "Letting Hector put Lalo in charge of Houston was the biggest fucking mistake I've ever made."

"I wouldn't call it the biggest mistake you've ever made," he replied, thinking of at least two other times Nikolai had royally fucked things up.

Nikolai nailed him with a warning glare before remarking, "I should have let Besian and Alexei finish Lalo off when they had the chance ten years ago. That prick is dangerous to all of us. He's flashy and stupid. He doesn't respect the code. He can't even control his men."

"Well, maybe you'll get lucky and someone will do you a favor." Kostya made a slashing motion at his throat as his phone buzzed in his pocket. "Lalo has enemies everywhere." He retrieved his phone and glanced at the screen. "Speaking of favors…"

"What now?" Nikolai asked tiredly, probably expecting another heavy cost in either coin or men.

"Besian," he said, tapping the screen and opening the message. It was coded but easily decipherable. "No leads yet. They'll keep looking."

"What did you tell him to do with Marco if he finds him?"

"Take him off the streets. Get the girl back to her mother."

"I want to talk to her first. This can't happen again." Nikolai drummed his fingers on the dashboard. "What about Diego?"

"Diego?" Why would Nikolai want the leader of the Hermanos? They were the street level enforcement for the cartel, but there was bad blood between Lalo and Diego. Bad blood that went back at least ten years, back to when they were kids in high school, back when Gabe, Diego's older brother, started a feud. "Lalo will go ballistic if he finds out we went behind his back to get Marco, especially if he finds out we're using his own people."

"They aren't *his* people," Nikolai muttered. "The ties between the Hermanos and the cartel are thin and stretched to the breaking point. Lalo has fucked over Diego and his boys too many times. He doesn't understand loyalty. He's only looking at the next back he can step on to climb higher."

Despite his concern for the way this would turn out, he nevertheless asked, "Do you want me to talk to Diego?"

"No, I'll talk to him." Nikolai rolled down the window and whistled to get the attention of Ilya's crew. One of them jogged over to get the order for a meetup. "Tell the king of Coronado Street that I want to meet." He glanced at his watch. "Noon.

Catholic Cemetery."

The soldier nodded and ran off to make the necessary calls. Diego would be wise not to miss the meeting set for half an hour from now, even if he had to run every red light in town.

As they drove to the cemetery, Kostya thought about the kind of deal Nikolai would probably offer Diego. It would be something that set the wheels in motion for another regime change that would benefit Nikolai's long-term interests. Lalo had always been a placeholder in their minds. They needed a stronger partner, someone they could trust and someone who was trusted by the men who served him.

They arrived at the meeting spot early, giving Kostya plenty of time to scout the area. He sent the usual guard vehicles to specific spots on the perimeter and then got back in the car to wait. Keeping quiet, he ran through his own mental list of tasks and problems he still needed to tackle before the end of the day.

"It's the Wives and Widows Tour tomorrow," Nikolai said, breaking into his thoughts.

He cracked a smile at the name they had given the monthly circuit of visits that had to be made. Each crew paid a tax to cover the family support payments for their brothers-in-arms serving time, or the widows and families left behind when a soldier died—naturally or in the line of duty, so to speak. Nikolai also extended help to families who had worked with the family or paid a protection tax for their businesses. It was all about rewarding loyalty.

A few weeks after they had married, Vivian had taken over a duty that Nikolai had never quite felt comfortable doing.

Frankly, she was better at this kind of thing than her husband. He was cold and scared the shit out of people, especially the wives and girlfriends of soldiers who were locked-up in the pen. Those women were never quite sure where they stood or just how safe they or their men were.

Until Vivian came along.

She genuinely cared about people and their problems. She made them feel as if they mattered and were important to her. She listened, and she was compassionate and kind. She was also smart enough to understand the rules of the game. Vivian seemed to understand that keeping those other families happy protected *her* family.

The men doing time for misdeeds they'd committed under Nikolai's order needed to know their wives and families were being looked after properly. Men who thought their wives and kids had been forgotten were a snitch risk. They were vulnerable and weak and easily manipulated into talking to the wrong people about the wrong things.

Cash envelopes to pay for groceries and rent and medical bills were delivered the first week of every month to the families they had left behind. It used to be a straightforward drop-off situation, but Vivian had changed all of that. She always brought something nice to the family she was visiting, usually a box of pastries and desserts from Samovar, and then stayed for a while to chat. She made sure that the wives and girlfriends had help with daycare bills, school clothes and extracurricular fees and tried to find them work if they needed or wanted it.

Nikolai hadn't been pleased at first by what he saw as her meddling, especially when it cost him more money out of his pocket, but Vivian had neatly put him in his place by reminding him that it was cheaper to pay for field trip fees and daycare for a few families than it would be for the lawyers if a RICO case was ever built.

Remembering that tense conversation he'd overheard still brought a smile to his face. More and more, Vivian pushed back against Nikolai. He suspected that deep down inside the boss *liked* it when his wife refused to back down.

A black Chevy truck rolled into the cemetery. It came alone because Diego wasn't flashy like Lalo. Diego had more men under his control and was personally responsible for holding all of the territory Lalo claimed as his own, but he didn't flaunt it. There had been some trouble a few years earlier with Benny's kid brother, but Diego had learned his lesson and got his shit straight after that. Considering all he had accomplished at such a young age, he had earned the right to be cocky, but he was quiet, a real old school throwback and street king.

Diego and his younger brother, Nate, got out of the truck. Kostya sized up the youngest Reyes boy. The kid was a natural born fighter. If the stories Fox had told him were to be believed, Nate had been brawling since they were in kindergarten together, often taking on boys three or four years older than him. He had lost most of those early fights, but they had ignited a fire inside him that couldn't be doused. Now he was one of the best fighters on the underground circuit and was poised to kill the long winning streak of Nikolai's fighters.

"We're fucked if that kid keeps getting better in the ring," Nikolai grumbled and reached for the door handle.

"If that kid wasn't Diego's little brother, I'd take care of him," he remarked. "Just the knee. Nothing too damaging."

Nikolai laughed as got out of the car. "This won't take long."

Kostya slipped out of his seat and glanced around the cemetery, his honed gaze looking for any signs of trouble. Because Diego kept the streets of his neighborhood secure and quiet, Kostya wasn't that worried about this meeting. Safe in this territory, there was only the slightest chance that something might kick off.

While Diego and Nikolai took a walk along a line of graves, Nate Reyes wandered over and came to stand next to Kostya. He leaned back against the car and nonchalantly reached into the back pocket of his jeans to retrieve his wallet. "My brother wanted me to give you this."

Kostya glanced at the card Nate had pulled out of his wallet. "Let me guess. Diego got you a fight manager?"

Nate laughed. "Wrong brother, man."

Kostya didn't try to hide his surprise at the mention of the eldest Reyes brother. Gabe hadn't been seen this side of the border in over ten years. There was a price on his head and a warrant for his arrest waiting for him if he ever tried to cross back into the US. As far as Kostya knew, Gabe had been making quite a good living—seven figures a year—doing wetwork for high-paying anonymous contracts.

Wondering what Gabe wanted, he took the card offered to him and turned it over to see the email address scrawled on the back. It was an address using an infamous and extremely secure darknet provider. "What am I supposed to do with this?"

Nate shrugged. "I don't ask him questions."

Certain whatever the eldest Reyes brother had to tell him was dangerous yet important, he slipped the card into his wallet. His gaze moved back to Nikolai and Diego who were already walking back toward the vehicles. As the two men drew closer, he noted the stiffness in Nikolai's jaw and the harsh steps that brought him back to the car. Interest piqued, he waited until they were safely in their car and Diego and Nate were driving away to ask, "Well?"

"We need to find Marco. I don't want the police getting to that bastard first."

Kostya kept his foot on the brake. "You think he's going to talk?"

Nikolai twisted his wedding band around his finger. "Diego thinks he's been talking for a while now."

Stomach churning, he asked, "He's a fucking informant?"

"Diego has suspected it for a while, especially after last week."

"That thing in Longview? With the undercover cop?" he interjected. "The Hermanos boys are still in jail, yeah?"

"Yes."

"What does that have to do with Marco?"

"Marco set up that drop."

He let that sink in for a moment. "It's possible that possible Marco didn't know he was setting them up with a cop." Nikolai glared at him. "What?" he shot back defensively. "It happens."

"In movies, maybe. This is real fucking life, Kostya."

"What did Diego do about it? Has he talked to Lalo?"

"He tried. Lalo wouldn't listen to him."

"He could be in on it with Marco."

Nikolai blanched. "We are fucked if that's true. For all we know, this is about building a RICO case. If we've been exposed...? If someone has talked...?"

"If someone has talked, they won't have a tongue much longer," Kostya promised. Lifting his foot from the brake, he drove away from the cemetery. His mind raced as he thought of all the ways this could hurt them. If the snitch angle checked out, Marco could have talked about all the recent power plays and hits.

There was a lot of blood on the streets. Kostya had done all he could to place strategic sandbags that would keep it from flowing back to the boss's door. There wasn't a Russian or an Albanian in town who would speak a word to the police. The bonds of their criminal brotherhoods were built on loyalty and honor.

But the other families?

Kostya didn't trust a fucking one of them.

"We have to stop using all phones. Right now." He had trained the captains and their soldiers not to use their personal phones for sensitive information. They used burners when on jobs and destroyed them immediately after use. They talked only in code or kept their messages short. All of the heavy shit was discussed face to face.

But there was always a chance someone was being careless.

He reached for his work cell and called Ilya who picked up on the second ring. "I found a better deal on our wireless contracts. Meet me at the car wash."

"On my way." Within in moments of ending the call, Ilya would be dialing the next captain on the list to give out the message. One by one, each captain would learn that they may have been compromised. Phones would be destroyed. Cars would be checked and rechecked and checked a third time for bugs or GPS devices. Hangouts and businesses would be cleared and checked down to the baseboards and studs. There wouldn't be an inch of duct work or piping that wasn't searched.

They would close ranks and stay away from the other organizations. Business transactions would temporarily halt. There would be no protection tax pickups, no gun shipments moved or sold and there would be no new deals of any kind. Nikolai always kept enough cash in reserves hidden away to float payroll and cover hush money for six months or until the all-clear was sounded.

Kostya powered off his phone and tossed it into the cup holder. "You still only use your phone for personal calls?"

"Always."

Nikolai hated using his iPhone and only kept it because it was necessary for his legitimate businesses and personal life. There were burners at his house for late night emergencies, and even then, he only gave short messages.

Meet me.

I need to see you.

We have a problem.

"No apps? Not even the ones Vivian uses with her friends?"

Nikolai shook his head. "No."

"We'll need to search her phone."

Nikolai cursed under his breath. "I'll deal with it."

"I'll get the captains together and try to trace back all the interactions we've had with Marco."

"There shouldn't be many. We don't have a piece of that business." Nikolai tapped his nose to indicate the cocaine the cartel sold.

"Unless one of the younger boys is stepping out of line and trying to make some quick cash off a side hustle," Kostya warned. "We might be more exposed than we know."

"If one of our younger boys is selling coke?" Nikolai jabbed two fingers toward his neck. It wasn't an empty threat. There were rules, and there were consequences.

As he drove, Kostya worried about the small and improbable chance there was a RICO case in the works. The cartel violence south of the border was still hot, and Lalo clearly had zero control over his men and their mouths.

"Even if Diego is wrong—and I fucking doubt it because he's solid—the police could still use this shit with Tiffany—knocking the shit out of her and kidnapping her—as leverage to get Marco to talk. He'll flip if they give him the chance. We have to find him."

"I gave Diego an incentive to find Marco and bring him to you."

"How much?"

"Enough." It was said with a meaningful look, one that said the incentive was about more than money.

Ready to get to work, he asked, "Do you want me to take you back to Samovar?"

"Drop me at Benny's bakery. I'll have Danny come get me. We still need to have our talk."

"What the fuck has the kid done now?"

"It's that thing with the neighbors."

"The neighbors? At his apartment?"

"That deadbeat who is deep in the red to Besian."

"Shit," he swore. "I thought Artyom told him to stay in his own fucking lane?"

"He did. He told him not to intervene, that the man owes what he owes and needs to pay."

"But?"

"But there's a girl involved."

"For fuck's sake," he swore even more roughly.

"Seems there's always a girl involved lately," Nikolai muttered. A moment later, he added, "She's *young*."

Not missing the emphasis, he asked, "How young?"

"Seventeen? Eighteen maybe."

Kostya decided the less he knew about *that* the better. Still, he felt the need to defend Artyom's nephew. "Danny's only a couple of years older than her. He's a good kid. He's always been a standup man. The crews respect him. He's loyal. He's smart. He's always followed orders—until now."

"That's what worries me," Nikolai admitted. "If his loyalty to that girl puts him in Besian's crossfire, we're going to have problems. I've already exhausted my stockpile of favors with Besian. The next one will be full price."

He tried not to think about how badly Besian's crew would fuck Danila up if they got their hands on him. Artyom would be dragged into it because of their shared blood and then what? It would be messy, bloody and costly.

"You're sure you want me to drop you here?" He flipped on his turn signal and waited at the intersection for a chance to make his left turn. "I have time to drive you somewhere else."

"I need to stop here." Nikolai's mouth slanted with a lopsided and guilty smile. "I ate all of those little Mexican wedding cookies Vee loves. She'll banish me to the couch if she doesn't have a new box to satisfy her late-night cravings."

His gaze shifted to Nikolai's finger sliding over his wedding band, the movement one that seemed to reassure and soothe him. Was he thinking of the way he could so easily compartmentalize his life? For most of the morning, they had been talking about getting rid of Marco and other messy parts of their business. Now he was talking about buying cookies for his pregnant wife as a sweet gesture.

For Kostya, it was another reminder of all the reasons he couldn't pursue Holly. He had given her a month to think about things. Yesterday, he had sat outside the salon for an hour trying to convince himself to go inside and talk to her. Brave as he was, he had been afraid to hear her decision. It was humiliating to admit that even to himself, but it was the truth. He still wasn't sure what answer he wanted to hear. Either way, he was going to complicate—or even ruin—her life.

When they pulled into the bakery parking lot, Nikolai unbuckled his seatbelt. "I'll see you at Samovar or the warehouse."

"I'll chase down some leads and report back as soon as possible."

Nikolai hesitated, his hand on the door latch but not moving. "Be careful, Kostya. If Diego is right about Marco, Lalo might panic and do something stupid to cover it up."

"And if he does?"

Nikolai made a quick slashing gesture with his thumb. "Take care of it. I'll clean up the fallout."

He hoped it wouldn't go that far. The city couldn't stand

to be destabilized again, not with Mueller moving in and trying to gain more ground. Nickel Jackson and his enterprise already felt threatened by the growth of Besian's crew. There were daily scuffles as the soldiers on both sides fought for each street and the right to do their business there. If Lalo fell and there was no plan in place to quickly prop up another kingpin, mayhem would erupt as the Albanians and Jackson's crews tried to rush in and fill the void. But if the word got out that Lalo had a mole in his organization? The streets would burn.

Determined to prevent either of those outcomes, he waited until Nikolai was safely inside the bakery to leave. As if on cue, Danila and Artyom arrived, both leaving their vehicles to follow the boss inside, tailing and protecting him. The soldiers from their crews stayed outside, keeping a watchful eye.

Checking his rearview mirror, Kostya kept track of the vehicles on the street behind him as he drove away from the bakery. The idea that he might be under surveillance even right now annoyed him, but he was better than any bullshit Houston police detail. If anything, it might be fun to play cat and mouse.

He pulled into a rundown food mart, ducked inside and waved at the elderly owner who allowed him to use the phone. He kept trouble away from the store and paid the old man's protection tax to the Asian syndicate. Making sure the door to the office was closed, he picked up the phone and dialed Fox's private business line.

"Hen House Security. You've reached the Fox."

"Fox, pull up everything you know about Marco Villarreal. Go deep. Arrests. Bank accounts. Cell records. Landlines. Vehicle registrations. Property taxes. Liens. All of it."

"Hang on," she said, her voice fading away as if she were reaching for something. "Okay. Marco Villarreal," she muttered. "What else, Big Papa?"

Frowning at the nickname, he quickly listed off the other pieces of information he needed. "Look into the girl he's run off with and her parents," he added, wanting to make sure all his bases were covered. "The girl might try to get money from their accounts if Marco runs short."

"How quickly do you need this?"

"Yesterday," he said before hanging up and dialing the number of the tire rental joint where Lobo worked part-time. He was the silent backer in the string of franchises that former loan shark John Hagen had started years earlier as part of his legitimate retirement plan. Lobo worked there under a clean ID they were using to build her "legend." It was important that she have a solid life history—a diploma from homeschool, a work history for Social Security, 1040s filed with the IRS, medical and vaccine records, a good passport. Someday, she might want to get out of the underworld and clean record would help her.

"EZ Rental Tires and Rims. This is Emily. How may I help you?" Lobo answered in a cheerful tone.

"Emily, I'm looking for a set of new tires for my 2014 Chevy Tahoe." Using her fake name felt strange to him even after all the years they had been using it in public. "I have chrome wheels with gold spokes and royal purple detail. Custom," he added, describing the vehicle Marco was known to drive. "Do you have tires to fit that?"

"You'll have to bring in your vehicle for measurement, sir. My shift ends in half an hour, but one of my other associates would be happy to assist you."

"I need the job done by tonight. It's important."

"We have a satisfaction guarantee, sir. Should I schedule you in for an appointment?"

"Yes." He hung up, dropped five crisp hundred-dollar bills on the desk for the store owner and left without making eye contact with the handful of patrons. When Lobo finished her shift at the tire shop, she would find Sunny and together they would track down Marco. His little spiders were crafty and would find Marco before anyone else. He was sure of that.

CHAPTER NINE

"W E'RE CHASING DOWN a lead," Lobo informed him later that evening. "Sunny's wagging her tail like a bloodhound."

He smiled at Lobo's description of her partner-in-crime. Once she got a whiff of a target's scent, she wasn't coming back without her prey clamped between her jaws. "Update me in one hour."

"Will do."

He pulled into the parking lot of Ivan's warehouse. He noticed the small changes Erin was making on the exterior of the gym. The building was still a rundown looking wreck from the outside, but there was a new sign with the logo she had commissioned. Markovic MMA also had a newly paved parking lot with actual slots marked by crisp white lines. Gone were the days of Erin stealing car keys from lockers to move trucks and cars that were double parked, blocking fire lanes or making it impossible for deliveries to be made.

Inside, the gym looked the same as it had always been except for updated equipment and mats. Ivan allowed Erin to do whatever she thought was necessary for promotion and marketing and keeping the books clean, but the gym itself was his domain. Judging by the way their business was expanding, their arrangement was working well. Ivan had never liked handling the money and business side of things; Erin was an accountant by trade and a party planner as a side hustle. She liked to plan and crunch numbers and boss people around the place.

But most importantly, in Kostya's estimation at least, Erin had developed a mothering instinct looking out for her junkie sister and her close-knit group of friends. This warehouse was Ivan's den, and she had embraced her role as the den mother. She knew which fighters were having problems at home and which fighters were running short on cash. At the first sight of a limp or a wince, she had ice and bandages and ibuprofen at the ready and the direct scheduling lines for doctors and physical therapists.

Crossing the narrow pathway between mats, he spotted Ivan and Nikolai standing outside a cage. They were watching Kir working with one of the new fighters Ivan hoped would be able to take Sergei's place in the underground fights. By the looks of it, this kid wasn't going to work either. More and more, Kostya wondered if their days of fielding powerhouse fighters and dominating the underground tournaments were done.

Stepping up to the cage, he caught Nikolai's eye. With a slight shake of his head, he answered the boss's silent question about Marco. Nikolai's mouth settled into an irritated line, but he didn't say anything.

Ivan had a smile for him and a handshake. "Are you here to scope out the new fighters?"

"Can any of them take Nate Reyes?"

"If he's drunk? If he's sick? If he has two broken arms?

Sure."

Laughing, Kostya glanced at the cage and delivered his verdict with a frown, "He's not you, and he's definitely not Sergei."

"The only chance we have of finding another Sergei is pulling his brother in to fight for us when he gets here or bringing in some new blood from somewhere else."

"Bianca will burn this warehouse to the ground before she lets Sergei or his brother get dragged back into fighting underground," Kostya warned. He wasn't exaggerating. That woman had gone to great lengths to save Sergei. She had only recently married the man she loved and word on the street was that they were expecting twins. Bianca would savage them like a mama bear if anyone tried to tear apart the family she was building.

"Then we need to start a recruiting drive," Ivan suggested, only half-joking.

"Brighton Beach," Nikolai cut in, his gaze never leaving the cage. "I'm drafting some new soldiers."

Kostya eyed Nikolai with barely contained surprise. This was the first he had heard of such an idea. The order must have come down from Moscow and very recently. There had to be some weight behind the order, a threat or a bribe. There was no other reason Nikolai would agree to bringing in fresh blood. He liked to handpick his men. Everyone one here in the Houston syndicate shared the bonds of childhood friendships or prison time together or blood relations. Taking these castoffs from New York was a risk. They were likely to be dead weight, idiots and fuck-ups.

"This kid is okay, but he needs a lot of work." Nikolai

shook his head and turned his attention to Ivan. "What about Boychenko? How is he coming along?"

"He's good, but he doesn't have the power or the size to fight underground. If he was legit?" Ivan shrugged. "The kid could be competitive in the right weight class."

It was Ivan's subtle way of asking permission. For some reason, the ex-enforcer had developed a seemingly paternal affection for Boychenko. Ilya had complained that Ivan was trying to talk Boychenko into leaving his crew.

"That's up to him," Nikolai replied. "He can do whatever he wants with his life. He can stay with us—or he can leave."

Kostya shared a look with Ivan that said everything. Boychenko had never been arrested. He was as white as snow and had options that men who had been in the family longer had forfeited. He hadn't even gotten his first tattoo yet. He could leave and make a life for himself doing anything else.

But he wouldn't. He had gotten a taste of their illicit life, of the shadowy world and the strong brotherhood that held them all together.

Nikolai's phone rang, and he reached into his suit pocket to retrieve it. He stepped away to answer it, but Kostya could hear most of the boss's side of the conversation. It was quickly apparent that it was Vivian on the other end of the line.

"Yes, he's here with me. Why? Is there a problem at the house?" He paused. "Your bracelet? I can get it for you." As he listened to whatever she had to say, he cast a strange look Kostya's way. "I see. Well, I don't think..." He pinched the bridge of his nose and closed his eyes. "Yes, yes, you were right about that, but..." He exhaled a long, slow breath as if trying to remind himself that his wife was pregnant and prone to mood swings. "Fine. *Yes.* I'll do it. No, no, I won't be late. I'm having dinner with Ivan and Yuri and then I'll be home." He went quiet again. "I always am, and I love you, too."

When Nikolai walked back to the cage, Kostya asked, "Is everything okay?"

He nodded stiffly. "We need to talk."

Not taking his eyes off the fighters in the cage, Ivan gestured to the suite of newly renovated offices at the rear of the warehouse. "You can use my office or Erin's if you need privacy."

He followed Nikolai into Ivan's office and shut the door behind him. Nikolai leaned back against the desk and leveled a hard stare. "What the fuck is going on between you and Holly?"

Taken aback, he said, "What I do on my private time doesn't concern you."

"It concerns me when it's my sister," Nikolai hissed, his voice low and dangerous. "You told me there was nothing but friendship there. That she was only a neighbor—"

"She was when we had this conversation before, but—"

"But?" Nikolai leaned forward, as if ready to launch toward him.

"But things have changed," he confessed, fully expecting to be punched at any moment. "I spent the night with Holly after all that shit went down in her salon. The next morning, I told her about me and this." He gestured between them. "She knows I'm in the mafia."

Nikolai gripped the edge of the desk, narrowing his eyes in that menacing way that made other men squirm. "Are you in love with her?"

That was a question that made him swallow nervously. "I'm not sure."

"Don't fucking lie to me," Nikolai shot back. "I can see it in your face, and if I can see it, other people can see it, too. You know what that means."

"It means that I've put her in the same position that you put Vivian in," he replied with an edge to his voice. "You don't get to stand there and lecture me on putting Holly in danger when you did the same thing to Vivian."

Nikolai didn't have an argument for that point. Better than anyone, he understood what it meant to drag an innocent woman into the life they had chosen years earlier, before thoughts of love and family had ever entered their heads. Eventually, Nikolai exhaled noisily and said, "The old man is going to lose his shit if he finds out you're with Holly."

"Maksim is the least of our worries when it comes to Holly." It was a fact that he worried about constantly. Someone out there knew that she was Maksim's biological daughter and wasn't above using that information to hurt her.

"You destroyed the tests?"

"I burned them myself." As soon as Max's tests had confirmed Nikolai and Holly as half-siblings with the same father, he had destroyed the evidence. "I'm still working on getting her mother's DNA. She's been traveling, and when she is in town, she's very careful. Too careful," he added with a knowing look.

"You're still convinced she's like you?"

Like you. Not a mobster, but a spy. A covert operative. Probably old school KGB. "She's too clean. Her legend is flawless. Both parents? Dead. Homebirth? The doctor who signed her birth certificate? Dead. Her high school diploma? Lost in a school fire. Until she showed up at college, there is no trace of her. No photos in papers. No birth announcement. No obituaries for her parents. There are no loose ends for anyone to dig up."

"That doesn't mean that she's some kind of operative, Kostya. She could have just been unlucky. You are paranoid as fuck."

"For good reason," he shot back. "You don't know the things I know. My parents were involved in heavy shit. The whole reason I was born in Dresden was to help my parents build my identity so that I could work for foreign governments without the barriers my Russian nationality would have caused. There were dozens of us, Nikolai. And not just in East Germany. Here, in America, and in England and France and Canada."

"So what? You think Holly's mother came here like your parents and brought Holly back from Russia to—what? Become a successful hair stylist? How is that helpful to the Russian state? It's ridiculous, Kostya. This whole thing is ridiculous."

"What if Holly's mother came here as a teenager? What if she's working here without cover or protection? She has the perfect job. She can travel to places in the Middle East and Russia and China without rousing too much suspicion. She is directly involved in US energy policy now that she's on an advisory council to the president. She's acted as a conduit between her Russian oil and gas contacts and the State Department here."

Nikolai didn't want to hear it. "Even if what you say is

true, we don't need to get involved in it. *You* need to stay out of it. You were burned, Kostya. You have no protection on that level anymore. If Holly's mother is what you say she is, she could hurt you and she could hurt us." He slashed his hand through the air. "Leave it alone, Kostya. Whoever she is and whatever she might be, Maksim trusted her to raise and protect Holly. I don't think she's a risk to us if we just leave her alone."

Kostya wasn't so sure. People in his line of business always had an ulterior motive.

"You said you told Holly about the mafia. What *exactly* have you told her?"

"I only confirmed what she asked. She wanted to know if I was in the mob. She had heard rumors about you and Ivan. She put two and two together. I told her the truth. Mostly."

"And?"

"And I told her that she should take some time to think about what getting involved with me would mean," he answered matter-of-factly.

"Apparently, she's done thinking." Nikolai shoved off the desk and crossed the space between them. "Vivian conveniently left her bracelet at the salon today. She wants you to go pick it up. She also said you need a haircut."

Kostya touched the long ends of his shoulder length hair. It was getting scruffy, and he had been entertaining the idea of a change. Knowing Vivian had pulled a similar stunt with Sergei, pickpocketing Bianca's phone and sending Sergei to take it back to her friend, he warned, "Your wife is devious."

"I'm not sure whether I should be proud or afraid," Nikolai admitted with a smile. His smile faded, and he turned serious. Taking a step closer, Nikolai invaded his personal space. "If I find out that you dishonor my sister, I'll cut your fucking throat myself."

From anyone else, it would have been a bombastic and empty threat. From Nikolai, it was a promise. The boss had softened some after marrying Vivian, but he was still an extraordinarily dangerous man. He didn't have a relationship with Holly, but she was family. He was a man who do anything for his family. To make them happy, there was no limit to his generosity. To keep them safe, there was no limit to the violence he was willing to perpetrate.

"I don't want to hurt her."

"You will," Nikolai said sadly. "We always hurt the ones we love."

And he would know best. His love for Vivian had put her in danger, had gotten her kidnapped and almost trafficked. He had hurt her in other ways, too. But he had made his amends, and she had forgiven him.

Would Holly be so generous when she learned the whole truth about him? *Probably not*, he silently acknowledged as Nikolai left the office. Holly didn't have the sort of life experiences that mirrored Vivian's. She had grown up privileged and protected and knew nothing of heartbreak and sadness and pain.

Troubled by his thoughts, Kostya drove to the salon and parked in the back. It had been closed for an hour, and there was only one vehicle—hers—left in the salon's marked spaces. He stepped out of his car, locked the doors and retrieved his personal cell phone from his pocket. It was the phone he used only for legitimate business contacts and friends. He dialed

Holly's number as he walked across the parking lot and waited for her answer.

"Hello?" she answered breathlessly. "Kostya?"

The sound of her panting voice did wild things to him. He tried to shake the images the sound inspired from his head as he asked, "Holly, are you okay?"

"Sorry, I had to run from the stockroom to my office to grab my phone. I recognized your ringtone and didn't want to miss your call."

He couldn't ignore the heavy beat of his heart at her mention of a special ringtone. It was a simple, silly thing and he didn't want to read so far into it, but he couldn't stop himself. "I'm at the back door. Can you let me in?"

"You're here?" She seemed excited. "Sure. See you in a bit." She hung up, and a few moments later unlocked the back door. She greeted him with a beautiful but shy smile. "Hi."

"Hi," he echoed, suddenly at a loss for words.

Still shy, she asked, "Are you here for Vivian's bracelet?"

"She asked me to come get it." Remembering Vivian's other instruction, he reached up and touched the ends of his hair. "I know you're closed and it's late, but do you have time to cut my hair?"

Holly seemed surprised by his request. "You want me to cut your hair?"

"I can come back in the morning if that's better," he offered, all the while hoping she would tell him to stay.

"I have time for you now," she said, stepping aside. He walked into the salon and waited for her to lock the door before following her out of the employee areas at the rear of the salon onto the cutting floor. She led him to her station and motioned for him to sit. "Vivian's bracelet is locked in the safe in my office. Remind me to get it for you when we're done."

"I will."

"Let's see what we've got to work with…" She began to examine his hair, using her fingers to separate the strands. He experienced a wicked thrill of pleasure that settled right in his groin as Holly combed her fingers through his hair.

She tilted her head to the side as she studied him in the mirror and dragged her fingers through the dark strands that ended at his shoulders. "You have really nice hair." She tugged lightly on the ends, and a strangely pleasurable tingle shot through his scalp. "The ends definitely need a trim. How short do you want to go? Do you want something that you have to style?"

"I'm a simple guy, Holly. I want to shower and go."

"I like it kind of long and messy," she admitted, her fingers still driving him crazy as she combed through his hair. "Let's clean it up and give it some shape. I won't go too short."

He held her gaze in the mirror. "I trust you."

Her hand fell from his hair to his shoulder and gave it a squeeze. "Let's go to the shampoo station."

In no time at all, he was on his back, his head resting comfortably along the lip of a sink and a cape draped around his upper body. She wet his hair with soothingly warm water. The peppermint scent of the shampoo and the incredible sensation of her fingers massaging his scalp helped him relax.

Even in this vulnerable position and even with her hands so close to his neck and eyes, the places he had been trained since childhood to protect from attack, he experienced no anxiety or fear. No woman had ever touched him like this. He simply hadn't allowed it. His interactions with them were almost transactional. Drinks. Fucking. A quick goodbye. He didn't like kissing or long foreplay. He just wanted to get off and go. No strings. No feelings.

He understood now what he had been missing as Holly's soft, gentle hands sent shivers of heat and need through him. When she began to massage the back of his neck, he felt some of the tension that always plagued him begin to disappear.

"You need to book a massage. Your neck is so tight," she murmured with concern. "This kind of stress isn't healthy."

He bit back a laugh. *If she only knew…* "I'll think about it."

"If you won't let one of our therapists do it, I can," she offered as she began to rinse his hair. "I'm not a trained masseuse, obviously, but I know the basics."

The thought of Holly running her hands along his naked body made his dick throb. Just having her fingers combing through his hair and massaging his scalp was enough to make his heart race. If she touched him all over, he would be reduced to a melted, worthless heap of man.

"You really need to add a good conditioner to your hair-care routine," she gently admonished. "What kind of products are you using?"

"Whatever is cheapest at Target."

She clicked her teeth as she worked the conditioner into his hair. "Well, not anymore. I'm sending you home with some handpicked products."

He wanted to argue that he wouldn't use them and he didn't have time for so many steps, but that would be a lie. He would use them because it would make her happy. "All right."

Holly rinsed the conditioner from his hair and then

squeezed out the excess water before reaching for a towel. She stepped in front of the sink, her hip against his shoulder, and carefully towel-dried his hair. Their gazes clashed as she worked, and he swallowed hard, his body reacting in the expected way at her closeness.

One of her hands moved from his hair to his forehead and then trailed long and slow along the curve of his cheek and jaw. The bracelet he had given her glinted in the bright light coming from overhead. She wore it every day, the act one of silent but steady commitment.

He had been a fool to ever doubt her affection for him. She had been trying to tell him every day since he had given her that Christmas gift. He just had just been too blind to see it. "Holly..."

"I've made my decision." She touched his lips, quieting him for a moment. "I want you."

He carefully dragged her hand away from his mouth. "I'll hurt you, Holly. Not physically," he clarified. "But I'll break your heart someday."

"Probably," she said a bit sadly, "but I know what I'm risking."

He was a selfish bastard, but he couldn't stop himself. It was a terrible idea, and it would all end in tears, but he didn't care. He was done denying himself these brief moments of happiness. Holly was a grown woman, and she had made her decision with eyes wide open. If she wanted him, he was going to let her have him.

Sliding his hand to the back of her neck, he tugged her down for a kiss. It was an explosive moment when their lips finally met. A burst of anticipation and need rocked him. With a hand on her hip and the other at her nape, he sat up and stabbed his tongue against hers, desperate to taste her. She grabbed the cape and yanked it free before tossing it aside.

To keep her balance, Holly put her hands on his shoulders as their tongues tangled, but as their kisses grew more passionate and almost desperate, she used her hand position for leverage. Slinging a leg over his, she pushed up on the reclined shampoo chair and climbed on top of him. The chair was a tight fit, and she wiggled her hips until she straddled his left leg.

"Fuck, Holly," he groaned against her mouth at the feel of her hot body pressed against the denim along his thigh. Her greedy hands slid under the thin fabric of his shirt and glided over his stomach and up toward his chest. He was taken aback by how quickly she had assumed the role of aggressor, taking control and reveling in it. All his life, he had been the one who chased. It was a novel experience to be on the other end of that equation. All he could do now was lean back and let her have her way with him.

"Touch me," she begged, her lips still ghosting across his. "I need your hands on me."

"Holly," he whispered in between kisses. "If I start touching you, I won't be able stop."

She nipped at his lower lip, that sharp sting of pain going straight to his dick. "So, don't stop."

Burning up with lust, he rocked his hard cock against her body, aching for stimulation to ease the throbbing, and slipped his hands under skirt. His fingers trembled with the shot of adrenaline that saturated his bloodstream. He pushed the stretchy fabric of her pencil skirt up her thighs until it was bunched around her trim waist. He discovered the tiniest little black thong on her body and had to bite back a groan.

Cupping her bare bottom, he shifted her toward him and met her ravenous kisses with equal fervor. A small voice in the back of his mind told him to put on the brakes and slow this down. She deserved something better and classier than a quick, rough fuck on a chair. "Holly, we should stop."

"Why?" She was already tugging on his belt buckle. "I don't want to stop. Do you?"

Quickly losing control, he admitted, "No, I don't."

She unbuttoned and lowered the fly of his jeans. Her small hand brushed against the hard ridge of his erection, and he saw fucking stars. "Don't make me wait any longer."

"This chair is too small for us this way," he stated the obvious. "You'll sprain something trying to ride me like this."

She grinned "Then I'll ride you tomorrow night."

Blown away by this sexy, confident woman grinding atop him, Kostya let those animal instincts overtake him. He helped her slide off his lap and stood. Without warning, he grabbed her by the waist and deposited her on the chair so that she was in the perfect hands and knees position. Glancing over her shoulder at him, she wiggled her bottom in an enticing way, and he gave each cheek a good slap before jerking down the tiny scrap of underwear guarding the place he most wanted to see and taste. Her pale skin was flushed with excitement and desire, and the light smacks he had landed left rosy imprints on her bottom.

Wanting to shock her, he bent down and swiped her already wet slit with his tongue. Holly inhaled a sharp breath and squealed with surprise before trying to wriggle away from him. He gripped her thighs and held her in place, teasing her clitoris with the pointed tip of his tongue for a few good flicks before grazing his teeth along the curve of her perky little ass.

He pushed down the front of his jeans and freed his cock. Running his hand up and down the stiff length of it, he used the fingers of the other hand to trace the seam of Holly's pussy. She was soaking wet, so hot and slick and ready for him. He guided the ruddy head of his shaft into place and pressed into her on one slow, easy thrust. Holly let loose a sound that was a mixture of a laugh and whimper before pushing back against him, urging him to slide deep and right to the hilt.

Taking a handful of her hair, he lifted her onto her knees, forcing her back to his chest, and noisily kissed her neck. He had been waiting so long for this moment, had been fantasizing about it and more for months, and now he wasn't sure how long he would last. He hadn't been with a woman in almost a year, and he was operating on a hair trigger.

Wanting this to be good for her, he slid one arm around her waist, resting his forearm between her breasts and lightly gripping her neck. His other hand snaked down to the spot where their bodies were joined. He framed her clitoris between two fingers and began to massage it.

Holly shuddered at his touch and reached back to grip his hip, her perfectly manicured nails scratching and marking his skin. He pumped into her pussy, his thrusts shallow and quick while he listened to her breathing and paid attention to the clench of her slick walls around his cock. She was close. He nipped at her earlobe and kissed her neck again and kept fucking up into her, faster and deeper, while rubbing her clit in the way that she seemed to like.

"Konstantin!" She shouted his name, her voice echoing throughout the empty salon as she came. His tenuous control snapped at the sound of his name and the feel of her pussy squeezing him in rhythmic bursts. His hands moved to her hips, gripping them tightly as she fell forward onto her hands and knees. He took her hard and fast now, chasing his own release and relishing the way she shoved back to meet each thrust. "Kostya! Kostya!"

That familiar buzz started low in his belly and spread along his spine and down his legs. He started to pull out, but Holly shocked him by pushing back until her perfect ass was flat against his pelvis. With his cock sheathed in her wet heat, she pleaded, "Come inside me. I want to feel it."

"Holly," he growled, his voice rough and low. She controlled him in that moment, ordering him to give her what she wanted and not allowing him to refuse her demand. She rocked back against him, milking him for each drop and then lowered her forehead to the chair. Shaking and shuddering, she panted just as hard as he did.

Trying to catch his breath and feeling lightheaded, Kostya bent forward and pushed up her shirt. He kissed a meandering line along her spine before ending at the curve of her neck. Standing up straight, he snatched up the damp towel that was hanging precariously along the edge of the sink. He tidied them both up before tugging her thong back into place and pulling down the hem of her skirt.

Turning her around, he cupped her face in both hands and kissed her. His kisses drifted along her cheek to her neck and back to her mouth. He couldn't ignore the guilt that gripped him as he thought of the way he had just ravished his best friend's sister on a salon chair.

"I don't regret it," she said, as if reading his mind. "I don't need romance and candles and music for our first time together. This was perfect."

"It was rough and dirty, and I should treat you with more respect."

She rolled her eyes. "Sometimes a girl wants rough and dirty, Kostya." Rising up on tiptoes, she kissed him again. Smiling impishly, she said, "Tomorrow you can treat me with respect all night long, okay?"

"Holly." He laughed softly and shook his head at her silly come-on. Brushing hair behind her ear, he tried to figure out how this incredible woman was still single. He couldn't understand it. She was smart and sexy, talented and funny, kind and patient. There wasn't a man in Houston who wouldn't jump at the chance to be *her* man.

She's been waiting for me.

It was a heavy realization, and one that made him reconsider so many things he had accepted as inevitable. What if he didn't break her heart? What if he told her the truth about him—about everything—but in small, easily digested pieces? She already accepted that he was part of a shadowy underworld. Would she accept what he did? Could she still care for him if she knew that he was a cleaner? What would she think of his little spiders and of Lobo, in particular?

Could she learn to accept his past? To understand his old life as a covert operative? Would she understand the need for secrecy and accept the possibility that all the terrible, dark things he had done in his past might hurt him? Hurt *them*?

"Are you okay?" she asked quietly. Seeming uncertain, she

wondered, "Are you second-guessing this? Us?"

"Never," he answered truthfully and stridently. "The only thing I regret is making us wait so long for this." He traced her full lower lip with his thumb. "This feels right. It feels *good*."

"I know that it's going to be complicated, but I want to try, Kostya. I want to see if we can make this work."

"And if we can't?" he asked, more worried for himself than her. Holly would never have a problem finding a better man, someone who could offer her the world, but she was his only chance at this kind of happiness. Now that he finally had this chance in his hands, he experienced a possessive and overwhelming need to hold tight and never let it go. He wanted to keep her in his life forever, no matter the cost.

"Then you'll have to sell your house and move," she deadpanned. "Because, obviously, Savannah and Nisha will make your life a living hell if you break my heart," she laughed. "They'll run you out of town if you make me cry."

"I would deserve it." He kissed her again, taking his time and enjoying the sweet heat of her mouth. *Please let me figure out how to make this work.*

"You're never going to get your haircut if we keep this up," she teased playfully while touching the still wet ends of his hair.

Back at her station, she sprayed his head with some concoction in a chrome bottle and took a comb from one of her many drawers. "Are you tender headed?"

"Am I what?"

"Is your scalp tender? Like when you're combing?"

"Oh. No. It doesn't hurt."

Even though he denied any pain, she combed gently, holding the strands of hair in her hand before tugging the teeth through the tangles that had accumulated during their wild ride in that salon chair. When she was done, she set aside the comb and dragged her fingers through his hair and tilted his head left and right. Once she had decided on a plan of attack, she opened another drawer and removed a straight razor with a menacingly sharp blade.

He warily eyed the fatal instrument. "Holly...?"

She touched his shoulder. "Trust me. It will look better this way."

He did trust her, but he was still nervous about having a gleaming razor that close to his face. She worked quickly and with such skill, flicking and slicing. Cutting hair was more of an art form than he had understood. He had always just assumed this was a straightforward technical skill that anyone could master, but as he watched Holly work, he could see that it was a creative endeavor.

"There. See?" She set aside the razor and dragged her fingers through his still damp hair. "Look at how natural this looks."

He nodded even though he couldn't really tell the difference in using scissors versus a razor. She was pleased with it and that was all that really mattered. She stepped away to a wall of products and came back with a tube and a bottle. She spritzed his hair and then applied some kind of serum. "I took a little of the weight out with the razor."

"I can tell." That was the first thing he had noticed about the haircut. The shape and length were fine, but it was nice to have some of that extra weight off his neck.

She raised up on tiptoes to grab the blow dryer dangling

from a cord and made quick work of drying his hair. When she was finished, she tousled his shorter hair and smiled at him in the mirror. "Well?"

"I like it."

"Only like?" she pouted dramatically.

"I love it," he amended.

"That's a better answer." She unfastened the cape and brushed off his shoulders. "We're all done."

They weren't done. They weren't even close to being done.

When he stood up and turned to stand in front of her, she placed her hands on his chest. As she gazed up at him, he wanted nothing more than to take her home and spend the night doing wicked, dirty things to her. Her dilated pupils and deeper breaths told him she wanted the same thing. Sliding his hand along the curve of her waist, he pulled her close and captured her mouth.

Just as things began to get interesting, the pocket of his jeans started to vibrate. He silently cursed the cell phone tucked away there. The call ended before he stopped kissing Holly. Five seconds later, the vibration started again. After two rings, it stopped. Five seconds later, the pattern began again.

"That sounds important," Holly murmured against his lips. "Maybe you should answer it."

"I don't need to answer it. I already know what she wants." He tried to kiss her again, but she leaned back and stared up at him with confusion.

"She?"

He might have been imagining it, but he thought he detected a hint of jealousy in her voice. "Not like that, Holly," he assured her. "She's one of my little spiders."

"Your little *what*?"

"My spiders," he repeated. "They crawl all around Houston and gather up information or do little jobs for me."

"Like?"

"Like tracking people down," he said.

"Like a skiptracer?"

Surprised she knew that word, he asked, "What do you know about skiptracers?"

"I dated a bail recovery agent when I was in college. He schooled me on all sorts of interesting things."

"*You* dated a bounty hunter?"

"He was hot and interesting and a little dangerous." She traced the collar of his shirt. "I guess I've always had a thing for men like you."

"There aren't many men like me, Holly," he warned carefully. "If you think a bounty hunter is dangerous—"

"I know it's a different kind of danger with you," she interrupted. "I know."

She had the most honest and open eyes. She hadn't been taught to hide her feelings or emotions. He could see it written plainly on her face. She understood what he was, even if she didn't have all the gory details.

"I need to answer that call." He hated to do it, but he had to ask. "May I use your phone?"

"You can't use yours?"

He swept his fingertips down her cheek before tucking one of her pale blonde waves behind her ear. "It's better if I don't."

"Oh," she said quietly. Taking a short step back, she patted his chest. "I need to get Vivian's bracelet out of the safe anyway. You can use the phone in there."

He followed her back to her office and picked up the phone while she unlocked the safe hidden there. He dialed Sunny's courier line and waited to punch in the right extension. When he reached the voicemail box of that extension, he keyed in the passcode and listened to the coded message Sunny had left for him. He committed the GPS coordinates to memory before erasing the message and hanging up the phone. Sunny would call the same number in a few moments, check the voicemail box and find it empty. That would be her signal that the message was received.

"Here." Holly presented one of Vivian's delicate gold bracelets on her palm. "She left this after her appointment."

"On purpose," he said, taking and pocketing it. "She's done this before with Bianca and Sergei," he explained. "She stole Bianca's phone at a wedding and then sent Sergei to return it to Bianca. You know how that story ends."

"She is so sneaky!" Holly laughed. "But I guess I owe her now."

"She doesn't operate that way." He was certain this wasn't the time to educate her on the language of favors and debts that ruled the mafia. Someday, when she learned that Nikolai was her brother and Maksim was her father, she would be taught that lesson. *Not tonight*, he thought sadly. *Not tonight.*

"When will I see you again?" Uncertainty filled her voice.

He wanted to promise her tonight and tomorrow morning and all the rest of the days that followed. "I'm in the middle of something important. I'll try to see you tomorrow night."

She grasped his hand and rubbed her thumb along the side of his. "Business?"

"The kind we can't talk about," he reminded her.

"I understand."

She did now, but in a few weeks or months, her patience with his secrecy would wane and then what?

Leaning down, he kissed her, letting his lips linger against hers. He didn't want to leave, but he didn't want to lose Marco if Sunny had picked up his trail. Sliding his arms around her waist, he tightly embraced her and kissed the side of her neck. "I'm sorry I have to run like this. I wish—"

"It's all right." She kissed his jaw. "You know where to find me."

Not for the first time, he hated himself for the decisions he had made in his past. Holly shouldn't have to wait around for him to have time for her. She should have been the center of his fucking universe, but instead he was running off to capture, interrogate and possibly disappear someone.

Loathing the way he was leaving her after this incredible shift in their relationship, Kostya pressed a final kiss to her temple. He didn't look back as he practically fled the salon. He wasn't sure he had the willpower to keep walking if he saw her sad face.

CHAPTER TEN

O UT IN THE cool but humid October night, he unlocked his car and slid behind the wheel. He didn't have to punch the GPS coordinates into the navigation screen. Sunny's coded message directed him to a storage facility he owned across town. He kept this one a secret from everyone except his little spiders and made sure there were about a dozen layers of protection between his name and the owner of the facility. It was located in an underdeveloped area so privacy wasn't an issue. There was no manager or security at night, and Fox had the ability to remotely wipe the security cameras, if necessary.

When he was on the property, he slipped on his favorite pair of black leather gloves and typed in the access code at the gate. He drove to the back row of storage units and pulled up next to Sunny's sleek black Ducati. He got out of his car, locked it and walked over to the door of the unit. He knocked twice before entering the brightly lit and air-conditioned space.

"You're late," Sunny announced, already shoving out of the banged up old folding chair and stalking across the unit to meet him. "We have places we need to be."

He raised an eyebrow at her, but let it go when she slapped an address scribbled on a piece of paper against his chest. He took the paper from her and glanced at the address. He wasn't thrilled by the idea of driving that far tonight. "College Station? You're sure he's there?"

"It's the best lead you're going to get," she answered matter-of-factly. "We chased down all the loose ends here in town. They were all bullshit. Between Diego, Ilya and Lalo, those hideouts and hangouts had all been trampled and searched. He's not in Houston."

"What makes you think he's in College Station?"

"You know that rundown roach hole that Lalo and Marco call their club?"

"Sure."

"There's a little grocery store about a block away from it where Marco likes to walk over and pick up his cigarettes every afternoon. I decided to check in and see if they would talk to me. The old lady who runs it doesn't like him. Called him a *pendejo*," she added with a smile. "She told me he comes in once a month and sends money via Western Union to some girl in College Station. She told me the woman's name, and I ran it."

"And?"

"And eight years ago, he guaranteed a bail bond for a woman who was picked up for hot checks. She was pregnant at the time she was booked and had a little boy seven months later." She paused as if to let him do the math. "The kid has another man's name, but Marco sends her at least two grand every month. He also had a vehicle registered at that address in College Station until two weeks ago."

"What happened two weeks ago?"

"The car was registered under her name in Phoenix."

"Arizona?" He said curiously. "Why?"

She shrugged. "No idea. The place she was living in was a rental. I called the landlord and found out she still has seven months on the lease and the rent is paid in full. Guess the name of her co-signer?"

"Marco."

"Yep. That address is the same address he uses for one credit card with a very large amount of unused credit and five different phones."

"Does anyone else know about this connection?"

"I don't know. Probably not." She zipped up the front of her jacket. "So are we taking your car or my bike?"

"We'll get one of my decoy cars."

Sunny slid into the passenger seat and buckled up. She began spouting off all the intel work she'd done, telling him about the routes in and out of the mobile home park and giving an estimate of the police response time to a 9-1-1 call. "I doubt anyone would call," she remarked. "You know how a lot of these trailer parks are. No one wants to be nosy or start drama by calling the police."

"Usually," he agreed.

"I scoped out a few places we can use for interrogation if you don't want to drag Marco all the way back to Houston."

"I have a place outside of College Station. It's quiet and secluded."

She twisted in her seat and eyed him with interest. "How many properties do you own?"

"Me personally? Just my house and some of the clubs."

He could practically feel her rolling her eyes before she asked, "How many properties do other people own for you?"

"Thirty-seven."

"How do you keep track of it all?"

"Very carefully," he said, pulling into a nearby convenience store with a payphone outside. "Can you run in and grab some coffee?"

"Sure."

While Sunny shopped, he called Nikolai to let him know that he was going out of town and then called Artyom. He spoke three words to the captain, their secret code to be used whenever Kostya was going to be out of town, before hanging up and returning to the idling car where Sunny waited with two cups of black coffee.

He drove to the parking garage where he kept an extra car registered in the name of an exotic dancer who worked for him. He kept vehicles like these stored in parking garages, storage units and apartment complex parking lots all around the city. He had placed them strategically, making sure they were close to major highways. Each one had a duffel bag packed with necessary gear and money in the trunk. After taking the bag out of the trunk, he checked the contents. It was a redundant move considering he had packed the bag himself, but he always had to be sure, just in case.

"You want me to drive?"

"I've seen the way you drive." He gestured to the passenger seat before closing the trunk. After he finished swapping vehicles, they drove out of the city, avoiding toll roads and red-light cameras.

Sunny didn't seem particularly interested in talking. She stared out the window, her mind obviously occupied with something that she wasn't comfortable sharing with him yet.

He let his thoughts wander as he drove the speed limit, checking his mirrors often. A dark, foreboding sense of dread plagued him. He hadn't been able to shake that strange, aching feeling since receiving the package. His insomnia was back, and he had been spending hours at night digging through old coded notebooks. He'd been poring over his old life, his mind running through the seemingly endless number of bodies and lies he had left behind as he tried to find the missing connection. He was stuck in a tangled web he couldn't escape.

Sooner or later, it would all catch up to him. All that cleaning and wetwork put the people he cared about at risk. Long ago, he accepted that he would die a violent death, but he had never wanted that for people close to him. His stomach churned painfully at the thought of Holly being hurt because of things he had done twenty years ago.

Of course, when he had made the decision to follow in his dead parents' footsteps and become a covert operative, he hadn't had any friends or family. He had been an angry teenager hungry for vengeance and determined to prove himself as the son of two of the most dedicated agents the KGB had ever spawned. Things like feelings and affection were weaknesses he had purged from his system.

Until Nikolai had shown him friendship and Lobo had looked to him for paternal comfort and guidance and Holly had smiled so sweetly at him...

Trying not to think about Holly's smile or any other part of her, he navigated the dark streets of the sleeping city according to Sunny's prompts from passenger seat.

"Left up here," Sunny said, "and then it's the last mobile home on the right. The white one with the red shutters."

He killed the lights as he pulled into the neighborhood. This wasn't the kind of place he would have chosen as a hideout or bolt hole. "I can't believe he was able to keep this woman and her son a secret."

"His son," Sunny corrected. "And I can believe it. What I want to know is what's in Phoenix? Why did he send his ex and kid there? What did he know was coming?"

"Something that's probably going to hurt us badly." He rolled to a stop, using a large dumpster for cover. His trained gaze scanned their surroundings. Most of the windows were dark up and down the street, but there was a dim glow behind a broken blind a few houses down. There was no movement on either side of the street, but there was always the chance someone would step out for a late-night smoke or leave for a late shift.

So far, the neighborhood had been quiet, but there were probably more than a few dogs locked away behind chain link fences. He didn't see anyone standing outside in any of the yards or on the porches, but there was always the chance someone would sneak outside for a midnight smoke or leave for a late shift and spot him.

"I see something," Sunny said, looking behind them. "Shit. It's a car."

They both slid down into their seats, hiding below their windows as the flash of headlights turned onto the street behind them. In the next moment, the headlights went dark.

"Honda," she said. "Late model. Do you recognize it? I can't see the plate."

"No, I don't recognize it. Don't waste your time with the plate." There was no point in getting the license plate. The car would be chopped and farmed out to junkyards before sunrise.

He lifted his head just enough to see the sedan slow to a stop in front of the double wide where Marco was supposed to be hiding. The driver's side door opened, but the interior lights didn't turn on which meant they'd been disabled by someone who wanted to stay hidden. He caught a glimpse of a man-shaped shadow get out of the car.

Watching the man walk up to the mobile home with purposeful strides, Kostya reached into the back seat and grabbed the bulletproof vest that was part of his gear. He draped it over Sunny and pressed her down toward the floorboard to make sure she was as protected as possible. Reassured that she was safe, he kept his gaze glued on the man moving quickly across the yard and up onto the porch.

There was a brief flash of light as the man opened the front door—but it was all Kostya needed to identify the assailant. The outline of his jaw was familiar, but it was that long braid that gave him away. Spider. The president of the outlaw motorcycle club that Vivian's father had founded and handed over to him.

What the fuck is happening here?

"Stay here. If you hear anything—"

"Get into the driver's seat," she answered. "I know the drill."

He slipped out of the car and moved with stealth through the shadows. He unholstered his weapon, keeping it low against his hip, ready to lift and fire in a heartbeat. With the other, he retrieved the ultra-bright flashlight from his pocket. Taking care with the rickety front steps, he opened the door with his leather-clad hand and stepped into the dimly lit house.

Immediately, he lifted his weapon and the flashlight, training both on Spider where he stood in the kitchen. The biker shut his eyes and grimaced, flinching away from the painfully bright light. Before Kostya had even uttered a command, the stench of blood, fresh and hot and metallic hit his nose. Someone was dead or dying.

"Put your hands up," Kostya ordered. "Don't make me ask twice."

"Jesus Christ, Kostya!" Spider hissed, careful not to raise his voice and alert the neighbors. "I damn near pissed myself! Get that fucking light out of my face!"

"Put your hands up!"

"Fuck you!" Spider snarled but did as he'd been asked, lifting his hands and showing that he wasn't a threat. "Satisfied?"

Wordlessly, he lowered the flashlight beam and swept it across the open living space. There was a shotgun propped next to the sofa to his left and pistol and extra magazine on the kitchen counter. A can of beer on the kitchen table had been knocked over and liquid still dripped off the edge of the table. There was a box of pizza in the puddle of beer, the cardboard crumpled in one corner as if it had been stepped on and smashed.

As the beam moved to the other side of the table, he spotted Marco slumped against the island, his chin touching his chest and his body slack. Blood, thick and dark, soaked his shirt and jeans. The gash in the side of his neck and the stab wounds in his chest and stomach explained everything. Marco's panicked heart had pumped out his blood in rapid bursts, spraying the floor and wall and chairs.

He shined the beam over the pool of blood, along the arterial spray and then followed a mess of bloody foot and hand prints on the cheap linoleum. It led him to the awkwardly huddled lump wedged between a chest freezer and a cabinet on the far wall.

A flash of blonde hair. Shaking shoulders. Small feet.

Tiffany.

Turning his attention back to Spider, he asked, "What the fuck are you doing here?"

Spider glanced at the girl. "I don't think this is a good time to talk about that."

Kostya lowered his weapon and turned toward the window behind him. He flicked the flashlight on and off twice to signal Sunny that he needed her help.

Looking back at Marco and then Tiffany, he tried to piece together what had happened. Knowing the history between the two, Marco had probably started smacking the girl around and she had finally snapped. Dealing with the body and the scene would be a problem, but at least Marco wasn't a threat anymore.

"Holy shit," Sunny said as she came into the trailer and surveyed the scene with her own flashlight. She dropped the duffel bag she'd brought from the car onto the sofa and unzipped it. She tossed him a pair of disposable gloves and put a pair on herself. Without a word, she grabbed a set of surgical booties for each of them and then pulled together what she needed for Tiffany.

Careful not to step on any blood, she crossed the living room and kitchen and crouched down in front of Tiffany. He couldn't hear what Sunny said but the girl stopped crying and let Sunny pull her into a standing position. It took her less than a minute to get Tiffany into disposable booties and scrubs over her bloody clothing. Catching his eye, Sunny said, "I'm getting her out of here."

"Go. We'll catch up later."

"You need anything out of the car?" she asked, guiding Tiffany around the mess.

"No. Ditch it when you're done."

With a silent nod, Sunny grabbed a jacket from the couch near the door and draped it around Tiffany, hiding her face. As soon as they were gone, Kostya turned on Spider. "Don't touch anything."

"Not a problem." Spider waited a moment before adding, "I didn't come here to kill him."

"I don't have time for this right now. You can explain why you were here later." Careful not to disturb the growing pool of still warm blood, he crouched down to search Marco's pockets. There was nothing in them so he stepped over the body and retrieved the dead man's phone. It needed Marco's fingerprint to unlock the screen so he carefully picked up Marco's hand and tried the right thumb. It unlocked the phone.

"Get an evidence bag and the pruning shears out of the duffel," he ordered, glancing back at Spider.

A few seconds later, Spider returned with the items requested. With a quick snap of the shears, Kostya removed the thumb he needed. Behind him, Spider swore at the gruesome act. Ignoring him, he cleaned the shears and handed them back to Spider. "Put these away."

He wrapped the thumb in a bit of gauze and sealed it in

the evidence bag. He stowed the bag and phone in his jacket pocket before rising to search the rest of the house. He found a pale purple Jansport backpack on a chair in the bedroom. He glanced through it and saw only the normal paraphernalia he would expect in a teenage girl's bag. In the bathroom, he gathered up the few things that seemed to belong to Tiffany and stuffed them into the backpack. He didn't want to leave anything connected to her if he could help it. She would need a clean alibi to keep her off the police radar.

Taking the backpack, he finished checking drawers and shelves and cabinets and closets in the rest of the bedrooms and the other bathroom. Most of the house had been cleaned out prior to the Arizona move, it seemed, so there wasn't much to dig through anymore. Finding nothing that seemed useful, he gathered up the weapons Marco had left.

As he passed a mirrored cabinet in the kitchen, he caught sight of his noticeably shorter hair and swore.

"What?" Spider asked, his voice tight with worry.

"My fucking hair," he snapped back. "I got a haircut earlier. I'm dropping hair everywhere."

"We could vacuum?" Spider suggested, clearly out of his depth.

"We don't have that long." Glancing around the kitchen, he thought about how much evidence he had unknowingly scattered around the place. There was only one option now. Wincing at the thought of how much collateral damage a fire in a crowded mobile home park could create, he nevertheless said, "Find some fuel."

Spider hesitated. "A fire? You ever seen a fire tear through a trailer house?"

"That's the point."

"Fuck!" Spider made a rough and hard sound before stomping across the living room and the kitchen toward the back door. "There's probably a grill or lawnmower out back. I'll see what I can find."

Spider wasn't gone long. He came back with a box crammed full of flammable things. "You can tell there was a boy living here," he said, handing over a gas can and bottles of lighter fluid. "Found some camping stuff," Spider tilted the box to reveal the stack of camping stove canisters, "and fireworks."

"I can work with this." Kostya started parceling out Spider's finds and formed a plan of attack. He had been building bombs by the time he was fourteen. Starting a raging fire out of all this would be like child's play. "Did you see any propane tanks?"

"No, I checked the grill. It's charcoal. I looked for a gas meter and didn't find one. The whole neighborhood seems to be electric."

"I sure as shit hope so." He didn't want a massive explosion on his conscience. He didn't need the hassle of the investigation either. Glancing at Spider, he asked, "Have you done this before?"

"How the hell do you think I know how fast a trailer burns? You're not the only one who's done horrible shit for your boss."

He handed Spider the bottles of lighter fluid. "Master bedroom and bathroom first. Then the other rooms. Pop all the smoke detectors."

They worked quickly. All the long years of working in the

shadows, doing terrible deeds for money, lent themselves to moments like this. The skills they possessed weren't particularly glamourous, but they could be useful in terrible ways.

By the time Spider came back from the bedroom, Kostya was spreading the last of the combustible fuel gel on Marco's skin. "Get out of here. Take your car and wait for me."

"The streets in this park are laid out parallel to the main road. To Graham," Spider clarified. "I can wait for you at the mailboxes by the second entrance. When you leave here, run four streets to the right and I'll be there."

"You fucking better be."

Spider left quietly. Kostya didn't even hear the car start or drive away. He got busy finishing his work, packing all the trash he'd created in a garbage bag he found in the cabinet under the sink after washing his hands. Glancing around the kitchen, he took a moment to go through his mental checklist, running through every step he needed to follow to make sure this scene was clean.

Satisfied he'd done his best, he started soaking dish rags and towels with the lighter fluid he'd reserved. Starting at the rear of the house, he began lighting and dropping them. The flames flickered before exploding as they followed the zigzags of fuel Spider had carefully placed through the house, a wandering path of destruction from one end to the other. Back in the kitchen, he dropped burning rags on the body he needed to destroy. Stepping back, he winced at the blast of heat that hit him in the face and the horrible stench of burning hair.

All around him, the fire burned fast and hot. The reputation mobile homes had for being fiery death traps was too real.

The flames crackled louder and louder, almost a roar now, and he backed out of the burning house, taking every last trace of his presence with him. He left the door open behind him, giving the fire plenty of oxygen.

Head down, he moved with stealth, hopping a fence and keeping to the shadows of the dark streets. The burned out street lights were his saving grace tonight. It was so dark he couldn't even see what was in front of him as he cautiously hurried along. A barking dog drew a whispered curse from him, but he moved at the same speed, wary but quick.

When he spotted Spider's car idling, he hastened his pace. He opened the back door and tossed everything he'd brought out of the trailer onto the seat there. Sliding into the front seat, he put on his seatbelt and nodded at his driver. "Let's go."

A police scanner chirped from the console. Spider gestured toward it and said, "Nothing yet."

"It won't be long. The smell of smoke is starting to reach this far." Glancing back through the rear window, he could just see the faint glow of fire in the sky. Soon, the whole neighborhood would be awake.

Not another word was spoken as they sped away from the scene of the arson they had just committed. The static and chirp of the police scanner filled the void. His mind was racing forward, compiling a list of tasks that had to be completed before sunrise.

"I need you to drop me off."

Spider eased to a stop at an intersection. "Where?"

"Alexei Sarnov has a buy-here-pay-here lot in town."

"Yeah. I know it." Spider switched lanes. "You don't want me to drive you back to Houston?"

"If we get picked up together, we're fucked, and our bosses are fucked."

Spider agreed with a nod. "We still need to talk about tonight."

"Later," he replied with a sigh. "Find me tomorrow."

When they reached the car lot, he got out of the car and took his things from the back seat. Spider left as soon as he was out of the car, clearly wanting to get the hell out of town before trouble caught up to them. Kostya made quick work of opening the gate and shutting down the security alarm before entering the small office building for a set of keys to a gold sedan.

Leaving the car lot as he had found it, Kostya pulled onto the street and drove out of town. A few miles outside of the city, he texted Max and asked her to meet him. She would be pissed off to be summoned this late at night, but he needed her help. Everything had gone to shit tonight, and he had to figure out why.

CHAPTER ELEVEN

I N A BLISSED stupor, I leaned against the wall of the salon and stared into space after Kostya left the salon. I had never had an encounter like the one we had just shared. Wild. Hot. Fast. Hard.

And good. So damn good.

My knees were still a little wobbly as I pushed off the wall. I returned to my station and tidied up the clipped ends of his hair before disinfecting the shampoo basin and drying it. One by one, I turned off the lights heading back to my office.

Standing at my desk, I stared at the phone Kostya had just used and tried to ignore the voice that told me to hit redial. A louder voice told me to leave it alone, but I didn't listen. Curiosity got the best of me.

After two rings, an automatic answering service clicked on the line. A pleasant female voice said, "You've reached Sunrise Sunset Delivery Services. We're away from the office at the moment. To check the status of a delivery, press…"

I ended the call. *Sunrise Sunset*? I had never heard of them. Picking up my iPhone, I opened the Google app and searched for the courier service. There was no website or any other social media presence. Odd for a delivery company, but maybe they were a specialty type of courier service.

Or a front for something dark and illicit.

It was a possibility I couldn't dismiss. Wasn't that how the mafia operated? Shell companies and fake businesses? Was this one of his companies? Was this how he laundered money? What *exactly* was he doing for Nikolai tonight?

I jumped as the phone started to ring in my hand. Glad to have a reason not to think about all the bad things Kostya was probably up to right now, I glanced at the screen and smiled as I answered. "Hey, Mom!"

"Holly! Are you home?"

"No. I'm at the salon? Did you just get back?"

"We landed about half an hour ago. I just cleared customs and got my bags. Are you busy tonight?"

"I'm not busy. I was just about to lock up and leave." Missing my mother after not seeing her for almost two weeks, I asked, "Do you want to meet for dinner?"

"Come to the house. I'll make you something."

"Mom, you just stepped off a ten-hour flight!"

"Fourteen, but who is counting?" she laughed in that carefree way of hers. "Holly, let me cook for you. We hardly see each other anymore."

Certain my mother was feeling homesick, I agreed. "All right. I'm leaving now. I'll meet you at the house."

"Drive carefully."

"I will." Hanging up, I grabbed my handbag and coat and shut off the last lights. I set the alarm before stepping out of the building and kept my hand inside my purse, right on top of my craftily hidden holster. This wasn't a dangerous area by any stretch of the imagination, but I'd woken up the last few mornings with this strange, aching pit of worry in my stomach.

I couldn't discount that feeling. The last time it had hit me, I was fourteen and on vacation with my mother in Providenciales. I had woken up from a nightmare with a sick feeling in my stomach and had told her that I thought something was going to happen. She had given me a hug and promised that she would always keep me safe and not to worry. But, sure enough, our hotel room had been broken into and ransacked while we enjoyed the beach that day. Ever since then, I had listened to my gut.

The drive to Mom's new townhouse on San Felipe didn't take long. We arrived at her house almost exactly together, with her pulling into the garage only moments after me. As soon as I stepped out of the car, she engulfed me in a bear hug and squeezed me so tight I could hardly breathe. My mother had never been like other mothers. There wasn't much soft about her. Even now, in her sixties, she had the physique and strength of a woman half her age.

Mom pulled back suddenly and gave me a strange look. Nervous, I asked, "What?"

"You smell like a man." There was a slight accusatory tone to her voice. "I can smell his aftershave all over you."

"And?" We had always had an open relationship when it came to men and sex. I wasn't going to lie to her. "I'm not allowed to have a little fun on a work night?"

"Well, that depends on the man, I suppose." She narrowed her eyes. "Do I know him?"

"You've met him." Leaving it at that, I reached for her rolling luggage. "How was Qatar?"

She was onto my game but didn't press for information.

"Hot. Dry. The shopping isn't nearly as nice as Dubai, but I found a few small things for the girls at my office."

"And how was your flight?"

"Long, but those new first-class cabins on Emirates are wonderful. The next time we go abroad, we'll fly with them."

As we entered the house, I was struck by how empty and cold it felt. There weren't any memories here, not like our old house. No memories of tearing through wrapping paper on Christmas mornings and snuggling on the couch with hot cocoa while we watched movies in our pajamas. No memories of giddy excitement as I got ready for homecoming or prom.

Although she'd been living here in this outrageously expensive townhouse for almost a year, it still didn't feel like home to me. I understood why she had sold our old house, especially now that she had taken the leap from the C-suite to consulting internationally and flying all over the world, but it had been an unexpectedly hard adjustment for me. I hid my feelings, threw myself into helping her decorate her new place and had even hosted her housewarming party.

"On the flight, I read an article about the world's best beaches. I thought we might go somewhere warm for our winter trip."

"You know I'm always up for a beach trip. I have to be back before or leave after the Denim and Diamonds gala."

"Let me know what I need to donate to help your chapter hit their goals. I have some colleagues I can hit up for donations, as well."

"Savvy is already hustling," I said with a small frown. "I'm going to get dragged onto a committee. I can feel it."

My mother laughed. "You love this gala!"

"I like dressing up and drinking champagne," I countered. "The gala is just the price I have to pay to get those things."

"Well, it's a worthy price," she said. "You know, I was also thinking about going to Amsterdam in the spring. Just a short trip," she added. Smiling gently, she asked, "Do you remember how much you loved the tulips when we were there?"

"Yes." *But only barely.* I didn't tell her that. From her wistful expression, she seemed to be having a sentimental moment, and I didn't want to ruin it.

"I can still see you in that pretty little pink dress at Keukenhof." She took a bottle of white wine from the cooler built into the island. As she reached for the wine bottle opener, she admitted, "I still have that dress upstairs. I kept it all these years thinking that someday your daughter might wear it."

It was the first time my mother had ever talked to me about grandchildren. I was taken aback by it and wondered what in the world had brought on this strange conversation. "Did something happen on your trip?"

Her gaze was unnaturally focused on the wine bottle. "No, of course not."

A terrifying thought struck me. "Are you sick?"

She laughed hard at that. "Oh, Holly, I haven't even had a cold in three years!"

"Then what's with the trip down memory lane and the grandbaby talk?"

She popped the cork and glanced at me. "I'm sixty-six years old, Holly. My doomsday clock is ticking just as loudly as your biological clock."

I rolled my eyes. "My biological clock is not ticking. I have plenty of time to make babies."

"But I may not have plenty of years left to enjoy them," she replied soberly. "I started my motherhood journey late."

"You had your reasons, and they were good ones."

"I suppose they were." She poured wine into two glasses and pushed one toward me. After a long drink, she exhaled and said, "Well—tell me about this man of yours."

"I don't think he's the fatherhood type," I warned carefully before she got her hopes up. Saying that aloud made my stomach feel funny. It was a sharp, painful stab that surprised me. Someday I wanted a family. I wanted kids, pets and a noisy, messy house, but I had a hard time picturing that future with Kostya, who wouldn't even adopt a damn dog.

"It's good that you see that from the beginning," she decided. "It's fine to have a good time with those types of men— and they can be awfully fun—but you should be looking for a man who wants to build a future with you." She raised her wine glass to her lips but lowered it before taking a drink. "You still have your IUD?"

"Yes, Mother," I answered with a roll of my eyes and a long drink. I didn't tell her the part about Kostya not using a condom. She would have gone ballistic about that—and rightly so. He was my friend, but I had absolutely no idea what his health situation was.

"You said I've met him?"

"I did."

"The football player? The big, sexy one that comes for his buzz cut?" There was no mistaking her excitement at the thought of me getting together with an athlete who had a bright future.

"No, it's not Levi."

She nursed her glass of wine while thinking. Her lips thinned as a thought occurred to her. "It's your neighbor isn't it? You're sleeping with that Russian?"

I might have imagined it, but I thought there was a bit of a sneer to her question. Straightening my back and lifting my shoulders, I held her gaze. "Yes."

She sighed and poured more wine into her glass. "Do you remember what I told you about Russian men?"

She had given me this lecture a hundred times. I really wasn't interested in hearing it tonight. "Not this again."

"Yes, this again."

"Mom, I really don't think it's fair to judge an entire country of men based on whatever horrible crap went down between you and my dad."

She slugged half her glass before setting it down rather sharply. Her gaze seemed far away as she said, "Someday, you'll understand."

"You keep saying that," I reminded her, "but someday never arrives." I gripped my glass tightly. "Are you ever going to tell me about him?"

"Holly," she said harshly, "there isn't anything to tell you."

"Bullshit." I didn't like swearing at my mother, but I was sick and tired of this wall she had erected around my father's identity. "I want to know his name. I want to know where he lives. I want to know what he does. I want to know why he didn't want us."

Her hard expression softened. "Holly, he wanted you."

"No, he didn't. He let you leave Russia pregnant with me, and he never even had the decency to visit me or write me a letter or call me on the phone."

"Holly, you don't know the price he paid to keep you safe. He risked *everything* for you."

My breath caught in my throat. It was the first time she had ever mentioned anything like that. "What does that mean?"

"Your father knew that you wouldn't be safe if he acknowledged you as his child. He did everything he could to make sure you would be safe and happy here in Houston with me."

"Why wouldn't I be safe with him?" I swallowed anxiously. "Is he...? Is he in the mafia or something?"

"Why would you ask about the mafia?" She seemed concerned. "Who gave you that idea?"

"No one," I answered quickly.

She narrowed her gaze. "Did Kostya say something?"

"No," I replied forcefully. Now, I was the one narrowing my eyes. "Why would you assume Kostya said something?"

"Holly, I'm not stupid. I know what that man does for a living."

I wasn't going to argue with her about his work. "What does Kostya have to do with my father?"

"Nothing," she said, hurriedly.

"You're lying," I insisted. "Mom, whatever he does, whoever he is, I don't care. I just want to know. I've always assumed he was married or maybe in the government or a criminal."

"He's not in the government." She turned away from the island and walked to the built-in refrigerator. "I thought we might do something simple. Eggs? Some turkey bacon? Fruit?"

Staring at her back, I tried to make sense of what she had

said. She had confirmed he wasn't in the government but the other two? "Are you saying my father is married *and* a criminal?"

She kept her gaze focused on the interior of her neatly arranged refrigerator. "He was married."

"Was?"

"His wife passed away more than ten years ago."

"And the other part? The criminal part? That he's part of the Moscow underworld?"

She unleashed a tight laugh. "I'm saying that he *is* the Moscow underworld."

Trying to process the confirmation of my worst fears, I reached for my glass of wine and finished it off in one long gulp before reaching for the bottle to refill it. "What's his name?"

"Leave it alone, Holly. This is a door you don't want to open."

"But—"

"Holly." She turned toward me in a huff of frustration. "Your father gave me very specific instructions when you were born. I've followed them, and it's kept you alive and safe. Your father isn't part of your life, but he's taken care of you. Anytime you needed something, he was the first to offer to help."

"What are you saying?"

"The money I used to buy your salon building? Your tuition to SMU, your sorority fees, your clothes, your cars, your vacations," she listed off all the privileges I had enjoyed. "I've always made a very good living, but your father paid every single penny of your upbringing. He was absent from your life, but he wasn't uninvolved. I sent him copies of your report cards. I sent him finger paintings and construction paper crafts. I made sure he had video of you cheering at football games and photos of you in the homecoming court and at graduation."

At a loss for words, I watched her crack eggs into a bowl. So much of what I had believed about my father had just been shattered. I had so many questions, but I sensed Mom was done talking for the night. Feeling confused and sad, I pulled out one of the tall barstools and slid onto it, silently nursing my glass of wine while she cooked.

When she presented me with my plate, she changed the subject to shopping, and I let her. Part of me understood that it was selfish and cruel to make her relive her memories of my father, especially now that I knew that she had been the other woman. Maybe that was why she had never married despite all the nice men she had dated. Maybe her heart was still back in Moscow...

"I don't think you should drive," she said, eyeing me over the two bottles of white wine we had polished off during dinner.

Feeling tipsy, I agreed with her. "Can I borrow your couch?"

She laughed and started to clear away the dishes. I joined her at the dishwasher and loaded the pieces she handed me into the racks. She engaged the alarm before grabbing her suitcase and hefting it upstairs to the third floor where the master suite was located. The townhouse had an elevator, but she never used it.

While she unpacked, I made use of her extensive range of beauty products to remove my makeup and wash my face. We both had expensive taste when it came to beauty, but she had me beat with her jars and bottles of La Prairie, Shiseido, Sisley and La Mer. I scrubbed and dabbed and rubbed in the various anti-aging potions she had on hand before finding an extra toothbrush in a cabinet and borrowing a nightgown from her enormous walk-in closet.

"You had better not hog all the covers," she warned as I face-planted onto her bed.

"*Mmmmph*," I groaned, my head starting to spin as that fifth glass of wine hit me. Having shared my mother's bed until I was almost ten, it felt familiar and right to be here again. Even after she had kicked me out permanently, I had still snuck into her room after bad dreams or during storms. In high school, I had often visited her bedroom for refuge and talk therapy about mean girls and boy drama.

A long time later, after I had started to doze in and out, Mom lifted the covers and slid into bed next to me. I felt her hand glide along the top of my head and over my hair, the gentle motion soothing and taking me right back to my childhood. No matter how many birthdays I celebrated, I would always be her baby.

It was also one of those moments where I realized how very few years she might have left with me. Twenty? Maybe thirty? It wasn't enough. It wasn't nearly enough.

As the pull of sleep dragged me down, I heard her say something. It might have been my woozy brain playing tricks on me, but it sounded as if she were speaking another language.

A language that sounded very much like Russian…

CHAPTER TWELVE

CHECKING HIS REAR-VIEW mirror, Kostya turned down a road lined with abandoned buildings and shuttered businesses. The maze of potholes was a hazard that he navigated from memory, not wanting to bottom out the borrowed sedan. Other than the occasional transient, he hardly ever saw anyone walking along the cracked sidewalks here.

The old medical waste disposal company compound was the kind of place few people ever gave more than a dismayed glance as they sped through the derelict block. With its sagging fence, rusted signs and boarded up windows, the place looked like the set of a post-apocalyptic horror film. The biohazard and radioactive waste warning signs were an effective deterrent to most visitors. Not even graffiti kids jumped the fences to tag the walls.

Once on the property, he entered the main office building and walked through it to a rear section of the abandoned processing factory. He had a locked and reinforced room hidden away on the main floor and let himself inside using the biometric keypad. After turning on the lights, he placed everything he had taken from Marco's hideout on the stainless-steel worktable in the center of the room.

While he waited for a pot of coffee to brew, he went into

the bathroom. When he was washing up at the sink, he splashed some cold water on his face and patted his tired, dry eyes. He wiped his face with a few paper towels from the stack by the sink and took a moment to study his haircut. He touched the ends and thought of Holly.

That one taste of her had ruined him. The days of lying to himself were gone. He couldn't pretend that he was perfectly happy living his solitary life. He couldn't pretend that he didn't need a partner in his life and a woman to love. He wanted what Nikolai had found in his wife. Vivian looked soft and sweet, but there was a ruthless streak in her. She would do anything to protect Nikolai and her baby and her family.

How far would Holly go for him?

How far would he let her go?

He cringed thinking of her face if she saw him now. If he had to tell her that he had robbed a bloody corpse, what would she say?

If he had to tell her that he had burned down a house and risked lighting up an entire trailer park, would she be disgusted? Horrified?

If she had to see him now, rifling through a dead man's belongings while trying to decide who would die next, would she want to see him again? Kiss him again? Let him make love to her?

Tortured by those thoughts, he left the bathroom and made a cup of coffee before moving to the table. He slipped on a pair of black nitrile gloves from the box he kept there and began to process the weapons and backpack he had taken from Marco's hideout.

The weapons were what he would expect someone like

Marco to keep on hand for protection. They were throwaway pieces, not too cheap, but not top of the line either. The handguns had black electrical tape wrapped around the grips. One had been fired recently and one smelled as if it had been recently cleaned.

The knife he had taken from the scene, the one Tiffany had stabbed her lover to death with, he decided to clean and destroy. There was no reason to keep it. She was just a kid who had panicked, and the sooner she could walk away from this whole mess, the better.

Searching her backpack, he found her wallet, powered down phone, a phone charger, a wadded-up change of clothing and some toiletries. He gave the backpack a more thorough check, running his hands along the seams and pockets. He felt something stiff along the bottom of the backpack and inspected it more closely. A tiny slit had been cut and then glued back together with something clear.

Curious, he sniffed the glued seam. Nail polish?

He ripped open the seam and discovered a folded manila envelope. Tossing aside the backpack, he unfolded and opened the envelope. Inside, he found a thick stack of cash and multiple sets of clean IDs for Marco. Birth certificates, Social Security cards, driver's licenses from multiple states and passports from three different countries. He examined each piece of identification, noting the high quality of the watermarks, font, inks and paper textures. These were much better than the average cobbler's work.

As he looked at each piece again, studying them even more closely, he accepted that Diego's suspicions were correct. The only way Marco could have gotten his hands on clean IDs and all the supporting documents with this kind of quality was if he was, in fact, an informant. Someone had given him a new life in exchange for information.

But why Marco? What the hell could he know about anything important? Was this just the case of an overeager Fed going after the low-hanging fruit?

Looking at the envelope and the hastily created hidden pocket, he started to form an idea about what Tiffany and Marco could have been arguing about that led to his death. There was nothing in the envelope for Tiffany. Was he planning to split and leave her behind? Did he have other plans for her? Had she found out he was planning to do something terrible? Was this her leverage? Had she tried to steal his ticket to freedom in exchange for her life or for something else?

Planning to get those answers in a few hours when he caught up with Sunny, he tossed aside the envelope and documents and picked up Marco's wallet. He removed everything inside the wallet and investigated each piece, right down to the last dollar bill.

Putting it down, he removed his gloves and reached for his coffee before picking up the bagged phone and finger. Taking both to the laptop station across the room, he plugged a USB cable into the phone and pressed the severed finger against the screen to unlock it. He added his own fingerprint to the system before opening the program Fox had created that would retrieve everything from the phone. Taking the finger to the small refrigerator, he placed the plastic bag holding it onto a shelf until he had decided whether to process or destroy it.

Sometime later, when the program had copied the entire

phone, he spent a few moments clicking through the photos and address book. At first glance, there was nothing on the phone that could help him. There were a couple of racy recordings and photos that compromised Tiffany. Disbelief at Marco's stupidity, he deleted them immediately, not even opening the videos beyond the first frame. The fuck kind of idiot recorded himself in bed with an underage girl?

A soft alarm alerted him to the arrival of another vehicle on the property, and he glanced at the security screens mounted on the far wall. Max's familiar face filled the screen as she punched in her code at the keypad. She drove onto the property and paused just inside the gate to make sure it closed completely before crossing the dimly lit lot to park next to him.

They had made up since their spat the morning after the thwarted hit at Holly's salon. Of all his little spiders, Max was always the one to call him on his bullshit. Sometimes she annoyed the ever-living-fuck out of him, but mostly, he was glad to have her as part of his secret crew. She was the one he could count on to always take care of the others and keep them safe.

Max was also the only person he could trust with the type of lab work he needed done. She was two years into her doctorate in nanotechnology after finishing a double bachelor's in biochemistry and nanoengineering. She was a genius who practically breathed chemistry, biology and physics. She had loved playing at forensics from an early age and had taken on creating and maintaining his little library of DNA samples and collected weapons while still in high school. She was going places—and he was going to miss her when she was too successful and busy to help him anymore.

The lock on the door popped as it disengaged. Max entered the hidden lab in a huff of attitude. She had a dark knit cap barely holding back the heavy waves of dark hair curling around her shoulders. A black pair of leggings and an oversized sweater with some geek reference he didn't understand camouflaged the body she deliberately tried to hide.

"You know, Big K, some of us have classes and jobs and research." She took off her hat and draped it on the hook next to the door. "This had better not keep me up all night." She stared at the pile of evidence on the table as she gathered her long hair into a coiled bun. "Do I even want to know where all this shit came from?"

"Marco's hideout," he answered truthfully.

She made a face. "Did you find the girl?"

He nodded.

"Alive?"

"Yes."

"Marco?"

"Dead."

"Oh." She held his gaze. "You?"

He shook his head. "Tiffany fixed the problem for me."

"Jesus," Max said softly. "She's, like, Lobo's age, right?"

"About," he replied. "Sunny took her to a safe house for the night."

"And then what?"

He shrugged. "I haven't gotten that far. I have to figure out some way to bring her back to Houston with a strong enough alibi that she won't be bothered."

"Good luck with that," she muttered and grabbed a disposable lab coat from the box on the counter. After slipping into the lab coat and some gloves, she approached the table and picked up the backpack. "What am I looking for? Anything in particular?"

"The backpack isn't my priority. It's belongs to the girl. But this," he gestured to the envelope. "I want whatever you get can off of this envelope and the contents."

"So, fingerprints, trace, DNA…" She picked up the envelope and studied it. "What am I running the results against? Do you have a suspect in mind? Other than Marco and Tiffany, what do you hope to find?"

"I think it came from a Fed."

She raised an eyebrow at that. "I'll need Fox's help to get into those databases."

"Wake her up. My payroll comes with strings."

"She won't be much help. She and Nate were heading out tonight. They're probably dabbing and playing video games at his place by now."

He grunted with annoyance at that piece of information. "She keeps telling me they aren't dating, but every time I turn around, they're together."

"They're definitely not dating," Max replied. "Or fucking in any sort of friends-with-benefits way."

"Women say that all the time when they want to hide something."

Max snorted. "She's hiding something, but it's not Nate."

"What is that supposed to mean?"

"That you need to open your eyes and pay more attention," she muttered rudely.

"Is there something I need to know? Something that affects all of us and our security?"

She rolled her eyes at him. "No. That's not what she's hiding. Whatever Fox's faults, she would never put any of us at risk." Sighing, she said, "It doesn't matter."

"If it doesn't matter, why did you bring it up?"

"Just forget about it."

Not wanting to argue with her any longer, he crossed the lab to the reinforced and securely sealed door along the back wall. He punched in the code at the keypad and scanned his thumb to unlock it. The lights turned on automatically, the fluorescent bulbs casting a pale blue sheen on the metallic walls, cabinets and countertops.

He snatched a pair of gloves from the box mounted on the wall and approached one of the ultra-low freezers where they kept samples. Inside this freezer, there were five shelves, each shelf divided into dozens of compartments. Max kept a detailed laminated map to identify the location of each sample referenced by a searchable database code.

His gaze moved to a sample that was slightly sticking out of its compartment. Glancing at the map, he found the correct slot. Calling out to Max, he asked, "Why were you looking at Lana's DNA?"

"Yeah, about that," she called back and walked into the storage room. Keeping her gloved hands at her sides, she explained, "I had a theory. I wanted to check it out before I said anything."

Closing the freezer door, he asked, "What theory?"

"Well," she said carefully, "you know the dossier that you got over the summer?"

"Yeah."

"And then the package you got last month?"

"Yeah."

"Well, I was going through the package after Fox handed it off to me, and I found a fingerprint."

"From?"

"It was really degraded, but it hit on Interpol. Like from way back," she clarified. "The name and all the information related to the print was redacted, but the owner of the print was from Russia."

"Well, we already knew that," he said, slightly deflated. "Is there any way to get the Interpol data?"

She shook her head. "I tried, but the records are gone."

"I bet they are," he grumbled, already sensing a pattern.

"I was irritated that the print ended there, but I started thinking about the age of the records and the photos. They belong to someone who was there when you were a kid. Maybe another operative? Someone who worked with your parents? Or," she added, "these records came from someone who knows things about you other people don't. Someone who was close to you. Someone who knows you get squirrely when your parents are mentioned."

"I don't get squirrely," he argued.

She ignored him with a wave of her hand and continued, "So, I started thinking about what kind of person would keep shit like this. I thought about the way you taught me to build my own little blackmail collections. I thought about your lessons on poison pills," she added, her words taking him back to the various times he'd instructed his little spiders on the finer points of extortion and securing their safety even if it meant hurting someone they cared for or respected.

"And you think the package I received is someone's poison pill? That the person who sent it is willing to take it in the neck if it means I get hurt too?"

"Yes."

"And what does that have to do with Lana?"

"Well, okay, this is where it gets a little Info Wars crazy." She glanced around the room and frowned. "We really need a whiteboard in here."

"Are you going to lecture me, Professor?"

"Not a professor until I finish my thesis," she reminded him. "And not a lecture," she clarified. "A walk down memory lane, if you will."

"I'd rather not. A walk through my memories is like a walk through a minefield."

"It's not much safer for me to go down it either. Poking around in your past is the fastest way to bite a bullet."

"Which is why I've always told you to stay out of my business."

"And yet," she gestured around them, "here we both are."

He exhaled roughly. "Well—go ahead. Tell me your theory."

"I was thinking about what you told me about the guy who burned you. Your old partner, you know?"

"No, I don't remember Borya," he said sarcastically.

He'd been on a long-term assignment with Borya, his mentor. When Borya got too close to one of their assets, the lines between reality and legend became blurred. It happened sometimes. Living your legend—your cover—was like breathing. Everything that was a lie became truth.

Tamara, the asset Borya had gotten too close with, eventually fell pregnant. When it was time to leave, to end the mission and extricate themselves, Borya had refused to leave her behind. He had gotten a taste of what a normal life could be like and wasn't going to walk away from her. They had ended up having to fight their way out, and Kostya had taken a bullet meant for Tamara.

Once they had gotten back to Moscow, they had been permanently separated as a team. He'd gone into solo operations, and Borya had married Tamara and moved to intel. He hadn't paid as much attention to Borya as he should have after their split, and it had cost his friend his integrity and his life. Tamara had been a double agent the whole time, a radical terrorist who had wanted access to the inner workings of the Russian government—and she had gotten them.

"Right," Max said, "but here's the thing. I was thinking about that story and how it ended."

"With everyone dead but me?"

"That's not true, though, is it?"

"I was there. I pulled the trigger."

"You killed the baby? Their kid?"

"The fuck kind of question is that, Max? No! I did not kill their daughter. She had been killed by the same people who tried to kill me when I got burned. They were using the baby as leverage after they kidnapped her. She was killed in a car wreck when they were fleeing their safe house."

"You're sure? You saw the body?"

"No, I didn't see the body."

"And, if the girl had lived, she would have been what? A little older than Lobo?"

"About, yes."

"Uh-huh," she said, holding his gaze. "About the same age as Lana?"

Like a fist to his gut, a sickening thought hit him. What if Lana was that little girl all grown up now? What if she hadn't been used as leverage against Borya and Tamara? What if she had been tucked away somewhere secret, trained and taught in the same way he had been. What if she had been placed here in Houston to get close to him? To get close to Holly? To get close enough to hurt him?

"Do you have the results yet?"

She shook her head. "I got started yesterday afternoon. I had some issues with the DNA sample for Borya because it was so old and degraded. I got that situation handled and started running them yesterday before going to work. You should have your answer in forty-eight hours at the most."

Tense with stress, Kostya said, "If this girl is who we think she is, she's here to kill. She's here for me and maybe Holly. She's become friendly with Lobo. She might hurt her to get to me."

"She won't get the chance." Max delivered her statement in that calm, cool way she had. "You Russians aren't the only ones who know how to use poisons."

"If she's here to hurt us, I'll take care of it."

"Someday, all that taking care of things for other people is going to catch up with you. Someday, you're going to need someone to take care of things for *you*."

Unable to get her words out of his head, he stood there as she returned to the main part of the lab and prepared her workspace. She was right. Someday, it was all going to catch up to him.

Maybe today. Maybe tomorrow. Soon, he felt for sure.

Wanting to make sure Max understood how much he appreciated the way she answered his call no matter how inconvenient, he said, "I'm sorry for dragging you out of bed and back into the lab."

"Eh," she said with a wave of her hand. "I was driving myself crazy with my research data and was about to lose my shit from anxiety." She shrugged. "If I hadn't come here, I probably would have tracked down Nate and Fox to get some of that Banana OG. Mellow my shit right out…"

"It's illegal, Max."

She looked around the room. "Uh, so is all of this. Like—way more illegal than a spliff."

"Okay," he conceded. "You have me there."

"Speaking of Fox," she said with a playful smile, "you should be prepared the next time you see her. She's going to savage you after what she saw on the security cameras earlier."

"What?" Kostya reacted in shock, more at his stupidity than anything else. *Shit. The cameras!*

"She says she didn't see anything X-rated. She killed the cameras when you two started making out like a pair of horny weasels."

"Weasels?" he repeated defensively.

"Yep. Dirty, horny weasels." Max laughed at him. "You know she's never going to let you live this down, right?"

He clapped his head in both hands and groaned. "You girls are going to be the death of me."

"Probably, Pops," she said with a laugh. "Probably."

CHAPTER THIRTEEN

YAWNING, KOSTYA PULLED into the private driveway along the rear of Nikolai's home and punched in the gate code. He parked in his usual space and killed the engine. Worn out and desperate for sleep, he polished off the last few gulps of lukewarm and too bitter coffee in his travel mug before grabbing his leather jacket to cover his sidearm. Nikolai's rule around the house was that all weapons had to be hidden. As far as he was concerned, it was a pointless stipulation, but he complied out of respect. Nikolai's castle, Nikolai's rules.

Stepping out of his car, he glanced at the gray sky and wondered if there might be rain. As he opened the wrought iron gate that separated the carriage house from the yard, he heard the unmistakable slap of paws against wet grass and cobblestones. It didn't take him long to spot the oversized and rambunctious puppy barreling toward him. Acting quickly, he closed the gate to keep the dog from escaping the yard.

While the dog ran circles around him, he stood still and let it get used to his scent. Seeing the puppy made him think of Holly's Christmas gift. She hadn't mentioned it again, but he knew he had hurt her feelings by not picking out a dog yet. He didn't like the feeling that gnawed at him for disappointing her.

Crouching down, he rubbed between the puppy's ears and scratched its chest. He guessed the dog was forty or forty-five pounds. The huge, muddy paws that slapped at his boots and jeans suggested this dog would grow to be very large and very loud. Judging by its happy temperament, this would be a good family dog, one that would keep prowlers and other miscreants away while also being gentle and playful with the dozen children he expected Vivian to give Nikolai.

"Come on." He whistled high and sharp at the dog to get its attention before leading it down the cobblestone path.

Nikolai waited on the back porch, leaning against a freshly painted white column in only his pajama bottoms. It was rare to see him like that, his dark tattoos stark against his paler skin. There were only a few inches of skin that lacked decoration. His body was a roadmap of misdeeds and glories, of regrets and successes, of blood and honor.

Here, in the comfort of his home, Nikolai didn't have to hide the truth emblazoned on his skin. But it was more than a man feeling comfortable in his own home. They never spoke of the trauma Nikolai had endured as a child. That was a dark, evil secret that Nikolai would kill to keep contained. Even before he had dredged up those old secrets and discovered what had happened to Nikolai as a little boy, Kostya had always wondered if he'd been hurt.

There had always been clues in the way he carried himself. Aloof, alone, cold, distant. Those expensive suits he wore were like his armor. The tattoos he had earned doing hateful, terrible things were like his spiritual shield. Put together, he presented himself as a man above feelings and emotions.

Until Vivian, of course. She had figured out what every

other woman who had vied for Nikolai's attention had failed to see. She hadn't tried to change him. She hadn't tried to break down the walls that he had built to protect himself. He was too scarred and traumatized for that. She had burrowed under that icy fence, using her warmth and love to melt it away until she was tucked away *inside* that walled off world with her husband.

Bit by bit, the boss was softening. Standing outside at dawn, his torso bare while he watched his wife's new puppy gallop around the yard was proof of that. There had been a time when Kostya had worried Vivian's influence might weaken Nikolai. He had been dead wrong to even consider it. She had awakened a protective beast inside her husband. The lengths to which Nikolai would go to keep his wife and unborn child safe were boundless.

"You're up early." Kostya joined him on the porch and leaned against the other column. He reached into the pocket of his jacket for his pack of smokes and lighter. It was a dick move, knowing the way Nikolai craved the nicotine when he was stressed, but this morning he needed it.

"I'd rather be out here than inside cleaning puddles off the hardwood." Nikolai leaned in as if to catch the first puff of smoke. "Giving Vee a dog might not have been my best idea. I've been up four times with him."

"Sounds like good practice for fatherhood," Kostya said in between drags. "And motherhood," he added.

Nikolai shot him a look. "She needs to rest, not go up and down the stairs all night."

He smiled knowingly and enjoyed that deep burn of smoke before exhaling. He wasn't about to remind Nikolai that his wife regularly ran five miles at a time. Climbing up and down the stairs to chase after a puppy was nothing she couldn't handle. Instead, he asked, "What are you calling it?"

"We haven't decided."

"You mean *she* hasn't decided?"

"No, she wants me to name it," he said as if he couldn't understand why. Pushing off the column, he retreated to one of the wicker chairs and sat on the thick cushion. Lifting his leg, he rested his left ankle on his right knee, freely showing the bells tattooed on the top of each foot. Never one to waste time with idle talk, he asked, "Did you find him?"

Kostya dropped onto the matching chair. "Yes."

"And?"

He gestured to his neck, silently signaling that Marco was dead.

Nikolai's mouth tightened to a grim line. "You?"

He shook his head. "The girl."

"The girl?"

"Yes."

It was a wrinkle neither had foreseen. "Was it clean?"

He shook his head again. "Not even close."

"And?"

"I took care of it." He gestured with his lighter before tucking it away in his pocket.

Nikolai frowned. He wasn't a fan of using fire to solve problems. "Was anyone else hurt?"

"As far as I know, no one was hurt."

"Where's the girl now?"

"A safe house with someone I trust," he answered carefully. "I'm going to see her later and get some answers."

"Was Diego right? Was Marco a mole?"

"It looks that way." He hesitated a moment before adding, "I wasn't the only one looking for Marco last night."

"Oh?"

"Spider beat me to the house."

"Spider? What did he want with Marco?"

"I don't know. We didn't have time to talk. I was more worried about getting the girl out, cleaning the scene and making it out of the city."

"When are you going to see him?"

"Later," he said.

"Take someone with you," Nikolai ordered. "I know you and Spider go way back, but he's not one of us. We can't trust him."

"I'll take the kid," he decided. "He needs to get some more real-world experience."

"Do you think it's possible Spider is bent? That he's working with Marco or the same Fed?"

"Anything is possible," he replied. "I used to be able to sit across from you and tell you without hesitation what I knew to be true. Lately? I don't fucking know. I'm losing my touch."

"You're stretched too thin. You're tired. And you're getting fucking old," Nikolai remarked. "You need to find someone to work with you. You need to train one of our men to do what you do."

"It's not that easy, Kolya. This is the kind of work that takes years to master."

"What about your little spiders?" Nikolai asked, holding his gaze for an uncomfortably long moment.

"What about them?" The boss knew that he had people he

trusted, silent partners who helped him with jobs, but he'd never asked for their names.

"I'm sure there's one or two of them that could be a good candidate for your apprentice."

"None of them are Russian."

Nikolai frowned. "That's a problem, but maybe we could get around it."

"I don't want any of my girls tied to the mob for the rest of their lives."

Nikolai reacted with surprise. "Girls?"

Fuck. He tossed down his cigarette and stubbed it out with the toe of his boot before rubbing his tired eyes.

"I won't say anything about them," Nikolai promised. "I won't put them at risk."

"I've already done that," he said, his voice haggard and drawn. "I never should have brought any of them into my life. None of them should be involved in this dark, dirty shit I do."

"Then why did you do it?"

"I don't know," he admitted softly. "There was just something in each of them that I recognized. Something that I knew I could use. I could mold them, teach them, turn them into something dangerous and useful."

"But?"

"But then I started to care about them," he confessed. Looking at Nikolai, he clarified, "Like a father. I'm the fucked-up father to a group of fucked-up orphan girls."

"I don't know what to say to that, Kostya."

"There's nothing you can say that I haven't said to myself."

They sat in silence for a few moments, the sound of the dog running around the garden and the hum of morning insects surrounding them. Eventually, Nikolai said, "I won't ask you their names or what they do for you, but you need to make sure there's some way for me to find them if something happens to you. To make sure they're safe and that they have money."

He shouldn't have been surprised by Nikolai's offer, but he was. "I've already taken care of them. They're all set up when I die—but I'll make sure they know to reach out to you and how to prove they worked for me."

"Hopefully, we won't need to worry about any of that for a long time."

"I've exceeded my shelf life," he replied darkly. "Men in my line of work rarely see their forties."

"You're one of the lucky ones, I guess."

Leaning forward to pick up the cigarette butt marring the otherwise spotless porch, he said, "I don't know about luck." He tossed the butt into the ceramic wastebasket tucked away under the patio table between their chairs. "What do you want me to do about Spider?"

"Depends on what he has to say." Nikolai scratched at the stubble on his chin. "I'd rather leave it to Romero. We don't need the added trouble. We still haven't found Lorenzo, and he's actively trying to kill my wife, my baby, my friends, my crews." He touched his chest with each word. "This shit with Marco and Tiffany was a distraction. Find out what Spider was doing there and let it go."

The back door opened, and Vivian stepped out onto the porch. Clearly not expecting to find anyone but Nikolai out here at this time of morning, she quickly grabbed the sides of her thin robe and drew them closed across her growing stomach, hiding the wide swath of skin peeking out between her tank top and pajama pants.

"Good morning," he greeted, keeping his gaze trained on her face to set her at ease.

"Morning." She gestured to the door. "I didn't realize you had company. Would either of you like some coffee?"

"No," Kostya said as Nikolai shook his head.

Lowering his foot, Nikolai patted his lap. Vivian smiled and accepted her husband's invitation, leaning into his embrace as he placed a lingering kiss on the side of her neck. His arm curved around her belly, his hand resting on the fullest part in a protective touch.

The achingly sweet and intimate moment did strange things to Kostya. It was painfully easy to imagine Holly like this, pregnant and happy and seeking the warmth and security of her husband. The acknowledgment that he would never be that man for her slashed at him like razor blades, leaving him bloody and weak.

Not wanting to intrude on Nikolai's home life any longer than necessary, he stood up. "I need to go, or I'll be late for my meetings."

"Don't forget to stop by the gym to talk to Vanya. He's leaving town with Sergei for the fights in Vegas. I told him we would look after things while they're gone."

"When are the boys from New York coming?" Mentally shuffling around all the available men he could assign to Bianca or Erin, he was reminded that they were running low on manpower. If a fight was coming, they needed every capable hand they could get.

"Soon. I'm working out the details."

"Before you go," Vivian interjected, an impish smile curving her mouth, and held out her hand. "Do you have something for me?"

"I do." Kostya retrieved the gold bracelet from his pocket and handed it to her.

She accepted it with a triumphant grin. "Tell Holly thank you for me."

"I will."

"When?"

He ignored Nikolai's intense stare. "Tonight. Probably."

Her smile grew even bigger. "Tonight is good."

The puppy began to bark, and the surprisingly loud sound drew Kostya's attention. He had been around full-grown Great Danes before but had no idea the puppies had such a powerful bark at such a young age. He stepped off the porch to get a better look at what had caused the dog to bark and spotted a neighbor's cat walking atop the fence. The puppy jumped at the fence and made a terrible racket trying to scare it away.

Nikolai whistled sharply, and the puppy scurried back toward the porch, its uncoordinated gallop making even Kostya chuckle. The dog paused to bark at him before trotting off to return to his master.

"Stasi," Kostya called out as he took the cobblestone path toward the garage. "Name it Stasi."

Nikolai's laugh echoed across the yard as Kostya let himself out and returned to his car. He doubted Vivian would care for the name, but Nikolai would probably insist on it now. After the way she had manipulated the situation with Holly, he didn't feel too bad about it.

CHAPTER FOURTEEN

THE THUDDING, THROBBING ache in my head was a fierce reminder of why I stayed away from sweet, dry wine. It was too enjoyable, too easy to over indulge, and I was an absolute baby when it came to hangovers.

Nauseated, I rolled over in bed, confused to see a ceiling that wasn't mine and to feel sheets that were too silky against my skin. It was the glass of water and the two aspirin on the bedside table that helped me remember where I was. Marshalling my energy, I sat up, swiped the two aspirin and swallowed them with long gulps of the still cold water.

Closing one eye, I managed to read the alarm clock on the bedside table. When I saw that it was only five o'clock, I groaned. Mom was probably downstairs in her gym, already sweating through an hour of cardio and weight training. The thought of exercising made my stomach lurch and my head swim. I dropped back to the pillow and draped my arm across my eyes while I waited for the aspirin to work.

My mind was a jumble of thoughts, words sliding around and bouncing off the walls of my brain as I tried to make sense of everything that had happened last night. I had more answers about my father, but I also had so many more questions.

What was his name?

What did he look like?

Did I have sisters? Brothers?

Could I meet him now that I was grown and things were different?

Would he even want to meet me?

That was the most troubling question. What if he didn't want to meet me? What if he was content with the current arrangement? Would I ever get to know about my ancestors, my history, my people?

"You're still in bed?" My mother came into her bedroom wiping sweat from her forehead with a towel. She seemed amused to see me so obviously hungover. "I have to shower and get to the office. Would you like me to make you breakfast?"

The thought of food made my stomach turn. "No, thank you."

"Should I call a driver for you?"

"No, I'll be fine." She gave me a look, and I said, "If I don't feel up to it, I'll get a Lyft or something."

She wrinkled her nose. "Just call for a car, Holly. I'll pick up the tab."

There was no use arguing with her about the cost of a private car and driver. "Okay."

"You can borrow some clothes from my closet." She bent down and kissed my forehead. Her warm fingertips brushed hair away from my face, and she smiled down at me. "I miss having you just down the hall."

I touched her hand. "I miss spending time with you, too."

"We should do something about that," she decided before

straightening up and heading to the bathroom. She lingered in the doorway. "Maybe you could move in with me."

"Mom, I have a house and a mortgage and—"

"Just think about it," she pressed. "Please?"

"All right. I'll think about it." As she disappeared behind a closed door, I couldn't help but wonder what in the world was going on with her. Last night with that comment about grandkids and now asking me to move in with her? She had insisted she wasn't sick, but now I was gripped by fear. What if she was lying?

Stop. She would tell me if she was sick. She wouldn't lie to me.

She lied about my dad...

Feeling lost, I hugged a pillow and closed my eyes. *I want Kostya.*

It was a strange feeling to acknowledge. I wanted him with me. I wanted to feel his arms holding me close. I wanted to hear his strong, calm voice as he told me everything would be okay. I wanted to hear him say that my mother was fine and that he would help me find my father.

But after my mother left, and I dragged myself into a shower, I decided that asking Kostya to get involved in my family drama was a bad idea. If my father had gone to such great lengths to keep me safe, he wasn't going to be happy if Kostya started poking around in my life. Considering my mother had confirmed my father was involved in the Russian criminal underworld, I had to be careful. For all I knew, my father might have bad blood with the mafia family Kostya served.

But how would I get the answers I wanted? I couldn't ask

my mother. I could try looking online to make a list of likely candidates—but then what? What would I do to narrow it down? To identify my father?

DNA.

It struck me suddenly. There were databases of criminal DNA, right? What if my father was in one of those? What if I had my own DNA profile? Could someone find my father by using the paternal half of my DNA? Was that even possible?

I didn't know anything about DNA really, just the things I had seen on television and in movies. I only had a vague idea of how paternity tests worked. My gaze settled on my mother's toothbrush and her hairbrush. It would be easy enough to get my mother's DNA if I needed it, but what about my father's?

If he wasn't in a database, how would I manage to put together a list of possibilities? If I had a list of possible fathers, how would I get their DNA? I couldn't exactly swan over to Russia and start asking random strangers for blood samples. Where would I even start?

Vivian. She had told me that I could come to her. She could help me.

But she's pregnant.

Not wanting to put any unnecessary stress on her, I decided I couldn't go to her. I wouldn't put her at risk or ask something like that of her.

But I could go to her husband. I could ask him for help. The worst he could was say no, right? He would be able to give me a list of names. He might even have contacts who might remembered my mother.

Wondering how to approach him about my problem, I finished dressing, texted my mother to let her know I was leaving, set the alarm and left her house. I hit up Starbucks for the biggest jolt of caffeine and sugar they offered and grabbed a pastry and breakfast sandwich to quell the gnawing hunger of my hangover.

When I arrived at the salon, Savannah had already opened the building and Billie was setting up the reception area for our first early guests of the day. Sunglasses still in place, I avoided their curious glances and waved silently before scurrying across the cutting floor.

Safe in my office, I opened my closet and removed the small luggage tote where I stored an extra set of necessities in case of salon accidents. I peeled out of the borrowed dress and draped it over my desk chair so I could change. Savannah walked into my office as I was shimmying back into the dress, covering up my pair of clean undies and bra that I'd fished out of my tote.

Savannah snorted with laughter before closing the door behind her and leaning against it. "Well, this looks like an interesting story."

"Not really," I replied, trying to smooth out the front of the dress. It was one size too big but the style and cut draped nicely.

"Let me decide. Spill it! Tell me all the delicious details."

"Well, there's not much to tell. I destroyed two bottles of wine with my mother as we had a lovely chat about my biological father who apparently is a widowed criminal kingpin back in Moscow and then I passed out in her bed and woke up with a hangover from hell."

"Jesus." Savannah seemed taken aback. "And I guess you borrowed that dress from your mom's closet," she remarked, gesturing to my back. "That still has the tags attached."

"What? Shit!" I craned my neck to see the tags dangling there.

She motioned toward the Starbucks on my desk. "Please tell me you used the drive-thru and did not embarrass our entire salon by walking through a Starbucks with wet hair, no makeup, no panties and Saks tags hanging off your ass."

"Drive-thru," I confirmed, reaching for the top drawer on my desk to get a pair of scissors. "Will you clip them for me?"

She took them but hesitated. "What if your mom wants to return it? They won't take it back without the tags."

"I'll tell her to take it out of my inheritance."

"You sass her like that and she'll take it out of your backside," Savannah warned.

"Mom never spanked me when I was little. I doubt she's going to start now."

"For nineteen-hundred bucks she might…" Savannah snipped the tag and then grabbed my Starbucks bag and drink. "Come on. Let's get you in a chair and make you pretty."

The salon wouldn't open to our earliest clients for another half hour so we had some time. Savannah plopped me down at my station and grabbed some styling products from the shelf on the nearest wall. While she dried and styled my hair, I gobbled down my breakfast and checked my email and social media. Knowing our clients would find this moment amusing, I snapped a pic with Savannah and posted it to our social media accounts with a fun caption.

"You want to talk about your father?" Savannah asked while handing me disposable applicators and brushes as I made use of the makeup counter.

"There's not much to say." I made a face while drawing on my eyeliner, and Savvy clicked her teeth next to me.

"Here, let me do it! You're going to end up looking like a hungover raccoon if you keep dragging that pen like that."

Grateful for her help, I sat down on the closest makeup chair and closed my eyes so she could work her magic.

"So…? About your dad?"

"Mom said that he was married. She told me that he *is* the Moscow underworld."

"So, what? He's a mafia boss? Like a godfather?"

"I don't know. Maybe? Probably. I mean—is that what they're called in Russian? Godfathers?"

"Hell if I know," Savannah said with a shrug. "He sounds dangerous, Holly."

"He must be. Mom warned me not go looking for trouble."

"Which means you're definitely not going to leave it alone," she said while expertly applying a nice winged line.

"No, I'm not."

She went quiet as she applied eyeliner to the other side. "Please be careful, Holly. You know that I understand what you feel more than anyone else. I've wanted to find my bio parents since I was, like, seven, but sometimes, I think, maybe it's better not to know. Maybe there's a reason why they left me in a backpack in a church pew."

I grabbed her hand and held her gaze. "Savannah, if you ever want to try to find them, I'll do whatever I can to help."

"I know you will, but I don't want to know. Not now, at least." She squeezed my hand. "Just make sure you consider all the ways this could go if you start knocking on doors back in

Russia. Once you open those doors, you can't control who or what comes through them."

Her warning remained in the back of my head as I greeted our first guests and styled clients. Mid-afternoon, I had a block of free time. After cleaning up my station and letting Savannah know where I was headed, I stopped by the front desk where I found Billie and Lana talking about the weekend.

"What are you doing on Friday?" Billie asked as she handed Lana a stack of matte black gift bags to open and fill with client freebies.

"I am doing nothing," Lana answered, her English greatly improved with the help of Billie's constant chattering. "It is my day off."

"You want to go see a movie? Have lunch?"

Lana beamed excitedly. "I would like this very much."

Glad to see Lana had found a real friend in Billie, I stepped forward and caught Billie's attention. "I need to run some errands."

Billie gestured toward the sleek computer screen displaying the day's appointments. "Your book is clear until six."

"I'll be back by five, maybe a little earlier. If you need me for anything, call and I'll hurry back."

After a quick detour into my office to get my handbag and sunglasses, I left the salon. Once in my car, I didn't give my destination a second thought. I drove straight to Samovar and slid into a parking spot just a block away. Feeling a bit nervous, I smoothed a hand down the front of my dress and removed my sunglasses, tucking them inside my purse.

When I entered the restaurant, I was taken aback by the rich colors and décor. It was like stepping inside a Faberge egg.

The lobby's ruby red walls and dark chestnut leather couches were inviting and warm. In the main dining area behind the hostess's podium, the walls were a deep emerald green. Shiny red booths lined each side, and square tables with crisp white tablecloths dotted the center of the large room. There were gilded doors along the left and rear of the room, probably leading to private dining areas.

As I stepped up to ask for a table, the hostess smiled apologetically. "I'm sorry, ma'am. We've stopped seating for lunch."

Feeling foolish for not checking the restaurant's hours, I murmured, "Oh."

"We open for dinner at six. Would you like me to reserve a table for you?"

"No, I came here to—"

"Miss Philips?"

Not used to being addressed so formally, I glanced behind me to see Vivian's husband just coming through the front door. Flanked by men in dark leather jackets and jeans, Nikolai cut an impressive figure in his bespoke steel gray suit and ice blue tie.

"Hello." I had only spoken to him two or three times at the salon so I wasn't quite sure how to address him. It was strange, though. When I was in his presence, I felt as if I had known him for years. There was something strangely familiar about him. Something about his eyes and his nose…

"Are you looking for Kostya?" he asked, stepping closer. He looked me up and down with one glance, as if trying to decide if I was in trouble. "I can call him if you need him."

"Um, no, I wasn't looking for him. I was actually looking

for you."

"For me?" he seemed surprised.

"Yes. I think I need your help," I admitted, holding my breath as soon as the words were out.

"My help?" he seemed taken aback. His expression turned dark with concern. "Is someone bothering you?"

"No." Surprised by his strong reaction, I quickly added, "It's a personal matter."

"I see." He studied me for a moment. "Have you eaten?"

"No. I was hoping to try the food here for a late lunch, but I didn't know that you're closed."

"You've never been here?"

"No."

"Kostya's been remiss. He should have brought you here on your first date."

So he knew we were together. "We haven't exactly had a first date yet."

"I see." His lips thinned, almost disapprovingly. Glancing away from me, he started speaking Russian to the tall man with the shaved head standing behind him. The man motioned with a wave of his hand—a hand that only had three fingers.

Gesturing toward the main dining room, Nikolai switched to English and said, "Walk with me."

Falling into step beside him, I allowed a few quick peeks at his profile. He was tall and lean, built more like Lena's husband than Erin's. The intimidating chill that seemed to follow and surround him was even colder standing this close to him. He wouldn't hurt me or be unkind, but there was something dangerous about him. It made his relationship with Vivian even more curious. She was so soft and sweet, all kindness and heart. Her husband was sharp and steely, aloof and restrained.

"We'll be in here." He opened one of the gilded doors at the rear of the restaurant. "We can speak without interruption."

"Your restaurant is incredible," I said as he walked me to the table in the center of the beautifully decorated room. The table wasn't your standard piece of restaurant furniture but an obvious antique with coordinating chairs upholstered in cream. The cozy space had warm lighting that highlighted the traditional Russian art hanging on the Prussian blue walls. "These colors are so intense."

"I'm sure that you understand the need to transport your guests to another place when they walk through the front doors," he said, holding out my chair.

"When Savvy and I went to the drawing board for the salon, we decided that was our focus. We wanted guests to step inside Allure and forget about everything except being pampered."

"It works. Vivian loves going there." After I took my seat, he walked around to the other side of the table and sat. "Thank you for keeping her bracelet safe and returning it to her."

Seemingly from nowhere, a waiter appeared from a side door and filled our glasses with water before picking up the artfully folded napkins from the table setting and draping them across our laps. Nikolai said something to the older man in Russian but paused with his hand held up. He turned his attention to me and asked, "Are you allergic to any foods? Fish?"

"No."

He finished giving instructions to the waiter who left the room with smooth strides and shut the door behind him. When we were alone, he reached for his water glass. "I hope you don't mind. I ordered lunch for us both."

"Well, if I did mind, it's a bit late to ask, isn't it?" A heartbeat after my admittedly sassy response, I regretted it. This man wasn't known for taking any bullshit from anyone.

Nikolai's face registered surprise—and then he laughed. It wasn't very loud or very long, but he seemed almost amused by my tart comeback. "I can see why Vivian likes you so much."

"I shouldn't have—"

"You should have," he replied matter-of-factly and sipped his water. He placed his glass back on the table and eyed me carefully. "This thing with you and Kostya—"

"Is my personal business," I interrupted without hesitation. I managed to hold his icy, piercing gaze as I set the parameters of the conversation. "I know that Kostya works for you." I chose my words carefully. "I'm not here to find out what that means or entails."

"Then why are you here?"

"I need help finding someone."

He frowned. "Are you missing an employee?"

"No." I touched the golden edge of the plate in front of me. "I'm looking for my father."

A few moments of tense silence stretched between us. "Your father."

"Yes."

"Surely your mother—"

"She's been very clear that she isn't going to tell me anything else about him."

Nikolai tapped the fingers of his right hand on the table. I noticed that he wore his wedding band on that hand. Vivian wore diamonds on both ring fingers, and it had only occurred to me just now that it was her right hand that held her wedding ring. "What do you know about your father?"

"Not much," I admitted. "I know that he's a Russian widower who is, um, in the same line of work as you."

His mouth twitched with a smile. "Well, there aren't many men in my line of work so it shouldn't be hard to find him."

A frisson of hope blossomed inside me. "So, you'll help me?"

"I can try." He held my gaze for a moment. "Do you understand what you're asking, Holly? Do you understand that once we start opening doors, they swing both ways? You walk in from the good side, and bad people walk out from the other side."

"My best friend told me the same thing this morning."

"She's smart. You should listen to her."

I swallowed nervously. "I understand that I might not like what I find."

"That's the least of your worries." His lips flattened together in a perturbed line. "You have a good life. You have a mother who loves you. You have friends. You have Kostya," he added quietly. "You have everything you need in your life. You don't need to go looking for trouble."

"You're right," I agreed softly. "I do have a wonderful life—but I need to know who I am. I need to know where I came from and who my people are. Can you understand that?"

Nikolai glanced away from me, his gaze falling to the table

for a moment. "I was an orphan. I don't remember my mother, and I didn't find my father until very recently. So, yes, Holly," he lifted his gaze to mine, "I do understand you."

"You'll help me?" I asked pleadingly.

He sighed and nodded. "I shouldn't, but I will."

The door opened before I could thank him, and the waiter returned with a gleaming silver rolling cart laden with appetizers. Spotting the caviar, I glanced at Nikolai with surprise. Caviar for lunch seemed a bit decadent, but he acted as if it were the most normal thing in the whole world.

"If you're going to have the caviar, you must have the vodka." He gestured to the incredible spread the waiter began placing on the table. "Or champagne," he offered an alternative. "It's truly the only way to enjoy it."

"I'm going to need an Uber," I murmured, watching the waiter fill shot glasses with vodka and wine glasses with something white and crisp.

Nikolai laughed. "I'm sure we can find someone to drive you back to the salon." He raised the tall, thin shot glass filled with vodka, and I mimicked the move. "*Za roditeli.*"

Certain there was no way I could attempt that without butchering it, I said, "Cheers."

Nikolai knocked back his shot, but I sipped mine, enjoying the cold, clear burn of the chilled vodka. "Wow," I said with a slow exhale. I felt like a dragon exhaling a breath of fire. "That stuff is potent."

"Only the best for new friends." He gestured toward the caviar. "Please."

"What did your toast mean?" I asked, leaning forward to inspect the delicacies before me.

"To our parents."

But there was something in his tone that said made me think I was missing the joke. He wasn't being cruel or poking fun at me, but it was as if he knew something that I didn't. Whatever it was, I had a feeling it was going to change my life forever.

CHAPTER FIFTEEN

"AM I IN trouble?" It was the first time Boychenko had spoken since Kostya had picked him up.

He glanced at the kid. "Guilty conscience?"

Boychenko shook his head. "No."

"Then why are you asking if you're in trouble?"

"Because the people you pick up and drive out of town don't ever come back!"

He laughed at the kid's obvious fear. "You're coming back to Houston with me so calm down and try not to piss your pants. I don't have time to take my car for a full detail."

"I'm not going to piss my pants!" Boychenko glared at him. "Where are we going anyway?"

"Galveston. I told you."

"Yes, I remember, but *where* are we going once we get to Galveston?"

"A beach."

"And then?"

"A bar."

"And then?" the kid asked, growing more exasperated with each question.

"And then I'm going to meet with Spider and you're going to watch my back."

"Why are we meeting Spider all the way out here? Why not just sit down with him back home?"

"Because neither one of us want to be seen together around Houston."

"Why not? Did something happen?"

"Jesus," he growled. "Do you always ask this many fucking questions?"

The kid shrank back into his seat. "Sorry."

Blowing out a tired breath, Kostya said, "It's fine. It's me. I'm tired as fuck."

"Do you want me to drive?"

He shook his head. "I'll fall asleep if I'm in the passenger seat."

"Yeah. That's the point."

"It's nothing against you, Boy, but I don't trust anyone in my driver's seat."

"Okay." Boychenko stretched out his legs and drummed his fingers on his knee. After a few miles of silence, he asked, "Does that Holly woman know what you do for Nikolai?"

He shot Boychenko a warning look. "What Holly knows or doesn't know is none of your business."

"That's what Vivian told the boss when they were arguing about it last night."

Shit. "They were arguing about me and Holly?"

"Yeah. Not like loud or angrily or anything. It was more of a tense discussion, I guess."

"And?"

Boychenko shrugged. "I didn't hear all of it. Only the part where Vivian told the boss to mind his business and let you two work things out."

"That's it?"

"That's it. But why does he care who you're dating? What's Holly to any of us?"

"It's not about Holly," he lied. "It's about me not getting distracted. Which is exactly what's happening now." He frowned at the kid. "Listen, this is how it's going to work when we get to the beach…"

SHORTLY AFTER DROPPING Boychenko a little farther down the beach, Kostya found himself staring at a biker bar. The throbbing knot of anxiety in his stomach wouldn't go away. In fact, it seemed to grow bigger and stronger as he walked into the rundown bar.

Before last night, before Holly made her move, he never would have hesitated to take a solo meeting. He had always been pragmatic about death. Sooner or later, it was coming for him. He had always accepted that a bullet with his name on it was waiting for the right moment to strike his skull.

But now he had a reason to keep breathing.

Mindful of his surroundings, he gave the bar a once-over as he stepped inside. There were no customers that he could see and only a handful of employees. If Spider had been working with Marco or if the people behind Marco knew that Spider had been in his house last night before the fire, any of the waitresses could be undercover cops. There could be bugs under any table or chair and video cameras behind any of those liquor bottles shelved behind the bar.

Three women in tight jeans and black cropped tees cleaned tables and set up chairs while two other women stood behind the counter, one of them counting her till for the start of the shift and the other setting up her bar. The one at the register noticed him just inside the doorway and motioned toward the rear of the seating area where Spider sat with a beer and a late breakfast. He held a wadded ball of napkins in his left hand and seemed to be clenching it rhythmically.

Without a word of greeting, Kostya settled into the seat across from him. Spider reached for his beer, his hands showing a slight tremor, and took a sip. "So how was the drive?"

"Short."

Spider gestured to his plate of half-eaten eggs, hash browns and greasy bacon. "You want breakfast? I can get Susie to fire up the grill for you."

"I'm fine." He doubted this place could even pass a health inspection. Eyeing the beer bottle, he remarked, "Bit early for a drink."

Spider grumbled before draining the last of his beer. "Is it time for our romantic walk on the beach?"

Kostya cracked a smile and reached for his wallet. "Let me buy your breakfast first."

After tossing down a couple of twenties, Kostya slipped his wallet into his back pocket and walked out of the bar with Spider a few steps behind him. They followed the cracked pavement along the side of the building toward the path that led down to the beach. Kostya waited until they were hidden by the building and a pair of dumpsters to launch his attack.

With speed that shocked Spider and left him defenseless, Kostya struck the other man across the front of his neck and chest, pinning him to the back wall of the building. With his forearm against Spider's throat, he gave a good push, showing Spider he meant business, and then quickly shoved aside the worn leather vest and patted him down for weapons and wires. The sweaty skin under Spider's shirt told him everything. This man was scared shitless.

After Kostya removed his forearm, Spider shoved with both hands and snarled, "What the fuck is wrong with you?"

He got up in Spider's face. "You're going to ask me that? After last night? What the fuck is going on, Spider?"

Wanting to throw this man a line and hoping he would take the chance to save himself, he said, "We have been friends since the first day I stepped foot in Houston. We've worked together for years. We've always been honest, and we've always done right by one another, even when it wasn't easy. Tell me what the fuck is happening here—and I'll do whatever I can to protect you if you're in trouble with Marco."

Spider pushed off the wall and ran his hand over the top of his head and down the length of his dark braid. He glanced at the bar and shook his head. "Not here."

His brisk strides carried him down the cracked path toward the beach and Kostya hastened to catch him. When they were a safe distance from the bar, Spider wordlessly offered him a cigarette. Kostya took it, leaning forward to light it on the matte black Zippo held out to him. After a slow inhale, he breathed out and asked, "Why were you at Marco's place last night?"

Spider flicked ash toward the ground. "I was following orders."

"Orders?" he repeated, taken aback. "Who gave you orders to kill Marco?"

Spider hesitated. "Your people."

"My people?"

"Your boss's boss."

"Maksim?" He didn't believe it. "Maksim gave you a job?"

"Romero gave me the job. Told me it had come from Moscow. Told me to get rid of Scorpion and Marco and to do it fast. I didn't ask any questions." Spider eyed him with suspicion. "You really didn't know?"

"I wouldn't be here asking stupid questions if I did." What Spider had just said bounced around in his head. "You said they told you to get rid of Scorpion. Did you?"

"I couldn't find him. I figured Scorpion would run off to his sister's place or that she might know where he was, but I only found Marco there. Made sense that he'd be there with the history between him and Scorpion's sister."

"What history?"

"They have a kid together. Marco and Scorpion's sister," he clarified. "It was a one-night stand years ago. If I knew where she was, I could probably track down Scorpion."

"She and the kid are in Arizona," he shared, putting together the pieces. "My skiptracer says that she and the kid left a few weeks ago."

"Convenient," Spider grumbled.

"Do you think Scorpion would go with her?'

"Maybe. She tried to stay away from trouble. Scorpion didn't talk about her or the kid much. He only talked about her to complain about Marco being late on his child support payments and having to track him down to get the money his sister needed."

"Did Romero give you any reason for the hits?"

"I assumed Marco and Scorpion were talking to the wrong people," Spider said. "Scorpion would fuck us all for a bag of silver. Fucking Judas," he spat angrily. "He and Romero have been on the outs for a long time, and when I got the top spot instead of him, he started to put some distance between himself and the rest of our club. I suspected then he was playing a different game, had a different long-term plan than the rest of us."

"He knows too much to be a loose end," Kostya warned, thinking of all the years Scorpion had been deep in the shit with the club, organizing drug and gun runs and worse. "What does he have on you personally?"

"Enough to put me away for the rest of my life." Spider dropped the cigarette and smashed it with his dirty, scuffed boot. "But that's not why I need to find him and kill him. I'll go to prison. I'm not afraid of doing my time. That's part of this life, and I accepted that when I signed on and took my first patch."

"But?"

"But she didn't. I won't let him ruin her life."

"She?"

"Marley." His stepdaughter.

"Is he threatening her? I can get someone to keep her safe."

"That's not the problem." Spider looked drawn and tired. "You ever tell a lie so big that it gets away from you? Twenty years later, you look up and you can't even begin to imagine how the fuck you make things right." He seemed broken and dejected as he said, "They're right, you know. It's not the lie that gets you. It's the cover up."

"I understand that better than anyone you'll ever meet."
He hesitated to ask, not sure he needed another secret to keep.
"What lie did you tell?"

"Marley's mother isn't her mother," Spider revealed in an
anguished rush. "It's all a lie. All of it. Everything about her
birth and her father and mother and me."

Taken aback, he asked, "Why did you lie?"

"Because her father, her *real* father, was a piece of shit
dirtbag who raped my baby sister," Spider explained with
barely contained rage. "She was just a kid. Not even sixteen
and he hurt her so bad…" His voice trailed off as the memories seemed to overwhelm him. "It was my fault. I should have
been watching her better. I shouldn't have let her have anything to do with the club or me."

Kostya stayed silent and let the man confess it all.

"When I found out what happened, I lost it. I found him,
and we hauled him out to the middle of nowhere and beat the
shit out of him. Then we handed him a shovel and told him to
start fucking digging. When it was deep enough, I killed him,
and we filled in the grave."

"We?"

"Romero and me and—"

"Scorpion," Kostya finished for him, already piecing it together. Spider wasn't Marley's stepfather. He was her uncle.
"What happened to your sister? Why did you need to lie about
the identity of her mother?"

He didn't answer at first. He swallowed a few times, as if
choking, and finally said, "Annie killed herself. Stuck a
goddamn hose in the tailpipe of her car and locked it in a
garage. I found her later that night. The baby, Marley, was

screeching her head off in her crib when I got there."

Spider glanced away, his gaze moving to the gentle roll of the ocean. "After the funeral, I made a decision. I didn't want that shit following Marley around for the rest of her life. So, I started looking for a mama to take care of her. I didn't have to look far. Kim had practically grown up with Annie. They'd been best friends since they were kids. She didn't have a family so I didn't have to worry about other people keeping our secret."

"So, you gave Marley to Kim?"

Spider nodded. "She loved Marley from the first time she held her, and I could tell that she just wanted to be a mother. She wanted a home and a family. Romero helped me get a forged birth certificate. Kim was young, maybe too young, but I didn't have the skills or the time to be a father. I was wrapped up in the club. Back then, I was an angry son of a bitch, and I had no business being a parent. We made up our story and started living it. Eventually, I married Kim because it made sense and kept Marley close to me. And we just—well—we've never told the truth."

"*Blyat.*"

"Now you understand why I have to find him."

"Even if you kill Scorpion, he's probably told that story to someone else by now. They'll use it to hurt you or blackmail you."

"I'll go to prison before I roll on my crew," Spider said resignedly. "But Marley…"

"I'll make sure she's taken care of," he promised. "It's the least I can do."

"I'd appreciate it. I've got her set up with life insurance

and some investments. She'll be all right when I'm gone, but if I'm just in the pen? She's going to struggle."

"From what I've heard, she's a very smart girl. She'll be fine."

"I hope so," Spider said with a sad smile. "I hope to God she'll forgive me when she finds out I've been lying all this time."

"I wish I could help you with that, but I can't." He held out his hand, and Spider shook it. "Good luck."

"Yeah," Spider clasped his hand tightly, "good luck to you, too, brother."

"Cut your fucking hair," he ordered, stepping back. "I recognized you in the dark because of that braid. You're going to want to blend in soon."

His advice given, he walked away from Spider. Feeling the cool sea breeze on his skin, he followed the worn wooden path back to the parking lot. When he was behind the wheel, he scanned his surroundings, looking for any sign of a tail, and left the lot. He found Boychenko at their meeting spot.

"Where are we headed now?" the kid asked as he fastened his seatbelt.

"Webster."

"The fuck is in Webster?"

"Two girls. One of them with a big fucking secret…"

CHAPTER SIXTEEN

"Now, listen," Kostya said as they idled in the drive-way, waiting for a garage door to open, "whatever you see or hear today, you take to the grave. If you don't think you can handle the secrecy, you stay in the car and wait for me."

"I can handle it," Boychenko assured him.

The garage door began to move, and he inched forward into the space. "Don't talk. Don't ask questions. Find a corner and stay in it. Listen. Watch. Learn."

Boychenko nodded studiously. "Got it."

When the garage door closed behind them, the side door into the house opened to reveal Sunny. Seeing that it was him, she visibly relaxed and stepped away from the door, disappearing back into the townhome. Getting out of the car, he noticed the sleek black SUV sitting in the space to the right and the neatly organized shelves lining the back wall of the garage. Apparently, Sunny spent more time here than he'd realized.

Boy trailed him into the house where they found Tiffany sitting at a dining table drinking a Sprite. The girl looked tired and sick, her skin pale and her eyes ringed with purple. Her wet hair hung limply around her face, and he was struck by how old she looked. The stress of what she had survived had aged her ten years in the span of a few days.

"Where'd you find this kid? Recess?" Sunny teased, eyeing Boychenko with some curiosity as she hopped up onto the counter and picked up her mug of hot tea. "This your first day playing Kostya's shadow?" When Boy nodded, she said, "Well, good luck, kid." Gesturing to the Keurig on the other counter, she asked, "You want some coffee, K?"

He started to turn down the offer but then decided he needed another jolt of caffeine. After fixing a cup, he sat down across from Tiffany and stretched out his legs. He sipped his drink, savoring the heat and bitterness, before saying, "You probably won't believe me, but I'm here to help you. My goal is to get you back into Houston, with your family, and without the police involved in any way."

A panicked expression crossed her face. "Please, I can't go home." She glanced at Sunny and pleaded, "You promised I wouldn't have to go back!"

"I did, and I mean it," Sunny assured her. Looking at him, she explained, "Once you hear what she has to say, you'll understand why she doesn't want to go home."

Certain he was about to uncover yet another layer of shit that would make his life even more difficult, he sat back in his chair. "Well...let's hear it."

Tiffany ran her thumb up and down the side of her Sprite can, moving the condensation around as her lower lip wobbled and her cheeks flexed rhythmically. "I don't know what I was thinking getting involved with that psycho. At first, it was exciting, you know? My heart was always racing when I was with him, and he was so different than all the other boys I'd dated." She closed her eyes. "And then he showed me what a monster he was."

"You slew that monster," he remarked. "He can't hurt you anymore."

"Oh, yes he can," she insisted. "He knows things about me and about my family. Things that are going to get us all killed!" She started to cry. "That's the only reason I agreed to meet him again after the way he beat me up the last time I saw him. He said that if I didn't come meet him he was going to call ICE and have my whole family picked up. He said my aunt and uncle would be deported, and my mom would go to prison for life."

He glanced at Sunny who sat stone-faced before asking Tiffany, "What did he tell you about your family?"

Tiffany wiped her eyes. "He had all of these pictures of my mom when she was younger. She was in, like, these army uniforms learning to use guns and knives. There were pics of my mom with dark hair and a headscarf. I swear to God it looked like she was in Afghanistan or Iran." She sniffed loudly and shook her head. "It didn't make any sense to me. My mom is the freaking president of the PTO! She was a homeroom mom when I was little. She made cupcakes and brought juice boxes and apple slices. We don't have guns in our house. We're just—we're normal people!"

Kostya's heartrate increased. Was Tiffany's mother the one who had brought the dossier on Nikolai and the others to Houston? Was she the one who had given it to Eric? Was she a former operative? KGB? FSB?

"What happened after he showed you the photos? Where were you?"

"I met him at Stripes. We were parked in the back where it was dark. After I threw the pictures at him, he freaking hit me and then handcuffed me. He had a gun! The psycho kept telling me he would shoot me if I made any noise or tried to get someone to help me. He took me to a couple of different places, a gross motel with stains all over the bed and carpet and then to that doublewide where he told me about his kid."

"What was his plan?"

"He was going to use me as bait to get you guys involved."

"Us? Me?" He touched his chest. "Or Nikolai?"

"All of you, I guess. He said that my mom would go to you guys for help, and they would send you to find me. He was going to kidnap you and take you to meet someone else. Some bug guy."

"Scorpion?" he guessed.

"Yeah. I guess." She wiped at her teary face. "He kept telling me how he had a deal worked out and showed me all of his fake IDs. I took them and put them in my bag when he was sleeping after he made me…" Her voice trailed off as she grimaced, and he understood what she didn't want to say. "That's how the fight started in the kitchen last night. He realized the envelope was missing. He hit me again, and I lost it. I grabbed that knife and, well, you know."

"I know," he murmured. "Did he say anything about the people who had given him a deal?"

"Just that she was some lady Fed," Tiffany sniffled and grabbed a paper napkin from the caddy in the middle of the table. She wiped her nose and said, "She apparently knows everything about all the criminals in the city. He said you were on the top of her list."

"I'm on the top of a lot of lists," he replied, not at all bothered by that threat. "Did he say anything else? Is there anything you learned from him that can help me find the people who want to hurt your family?"

She shook her head. "That's all he told me before..."

"Yeah," he said, knowing she meant before she killed him. "I took care of that. You don't need to worry about it. Sunny will help you come up with an alibi that works."

"We've been working on it," Sunny assured him. "You've got enough shit to deal with so let me handle all of this."

"Gladly." He finished his coffee in a long pull, stood up and carried the cup to the sink. "Whatever you have to spend, I'll reimburse you. Just keep her safe and hidden as long as you can."

"I will."

"Let's go, kid." He reached into his pocket and tossed his keys at Boychenko. "You're driving."

The kid seemed surprised but then grinned and hurried out the door. Sunny rolled her eyes at Boychenko's enthusiasm. "He's like a puppy."

"He's already housebroken," Kostya said with a smile. "He's a good kid," he added seriously. "We can trust him."

"I hope so." Sunny's voice had that warning lilt to it, the one that reminded him she wouldn't blink if she thought Boychenko was a risk to her own safety. "Listen," she said, touching his arm as she trailed him into the garage, "I have to get some freelance work done. I'm going to reach out to the Fence."

The Fence was one of the Professionals. He was their specialist in forgeries, selling and acquiring stolen goods and other similar jobs.

"For the girl?" he asked, certain that was the only reason

Sunny would reach out for help.

She nodded. "We have a problem we need to handle as soon as possible, but she's not old enough to get it done without her mom's signature. I need some fake ID for her. Just something to bump her age up to eighteen so they won't hassle us at the clinic."

"Clinic? Is she sick?"

Sunny shook her head. "Not that kind of clinic."

And then he understood. "Oh, I see."

The poor girl's appearance made sense now. Pregnant, kidnapped, raped, beaten—she had suffered too much. She wanted a clean break, wanted to get away from this horrible period of her life and start over again.

"If you can't get what you need from the Fence, let me know. There are other options in town. They're clean and safe," he added. "Not back-alley coat hanger horror shows."

"We'll get it figured out," she told him. "I just wanted you to know that I was reaching out to your competition. Didn't want you to get your feelings hurt."

"Funny," he grumbled and walked away from her. "Keep me updated. Let me know if you need help."

"Be careful, Kostya."

As he slid into the passenger seat, he glanced at Boychenko. "You wreck my car? You get pulled over? You do anything stupid? You're going to meet my graveyard. Understand?"

Boy swallowed and put the car into reverse as the garage door slowly opened. "Yep."

CHAPTER SEVENTEEN

AFTER DROPPING BOYCHENKO at Samovar with explicit instructions on what to tell Nikolai, Kostya drove straight to Tiffany's house. From the outside, nothing looked amiss. He tried the front door and found it unlocked. Cautiously, he entered the house, drawing his sidearm and listening carefully. If Tiffany's mother had been a covert operative, she was dangerous.

Inside the living room, it looked exactly as it had the last time he'd been here. There was a magazine on the coffee table, a half-filled cup of tea next to it on a coaster. The house felt empty and too quiet. He took a deliberate step forward and then another. He debated checking the bedrooms or the kitchen first before settling on the kitchen.

The instant his boot crossed the threshold of the kitchen, he felt and heard the unmistakable crinkle of plastic sheeting. It was taped to the floor, the ceiling and the walls. He had used the same setup on numerous occasions to make cleanup easier. It seemed someone had the same idea for cleaning up his death.

And that someone was Holly's mother.

Wearing all white trousers and a blazer, Frances looked like an ice queen sitting at the kitchen table. She seemed callously cold, her back stiff and straight and her displeased expression warned him not to fuck around with her. Gripping a pistol equipped with a silencer in white gloved hands, she was looking for a reason to pull that trigger.

"I've been waiting for you," she said in perfect Russian. Having only ever heard her speak English with that slight Texas twang, he was, frankly, impressed.

"I would have hurried back from Galveston if I'd known," he replied in their mother tongue, holstering his weapon and opening his jacket to show her that was the only firearm he had above the waist.

"Ankle?" she asked, keeping her gun trained on his chest.

He lifted his jeans to show her what he had strapped to each boot. She didn't ask him to remove the knives or guns. She only gestured to the chair across from her, and he took it.

"So," he said, stretching out his legs and reaching into his pocket for his cigarettes and lighter.

"So," Frances parroted, watching him light up. She sneered slightly. "Must you?"

"My last cigarette," he said, flicking the ash on the table and noticing the file folder in front of her. "I think that's traditional, isn't it? One last cigarette for the dead man?"

"I wouldn't know. My marks rarely get the chance to see my face let alone have time to reach for a cigarette."

"I believe that," he replied, exhaling a lungful of smoke. "How else could you have gone this long undetected?"

"I've survived this long undetected because I'm fucking good," Frances countered. "I wrote the book you used to become the man you are today. In some ways, I was more of a mother to you than Nina."

He stiffened at the mention of his mother. Her remark cut like a razor, slicing at the soft and vulnerable part of him. Not taking her bait, he asked, "Did you work together?"

She nodded. "Once or twice. Their turf was Europe, and mine was here."

"How long have you been here?"

"I came here as a child. It's the same story that most of us have. I was chosen from the orphanage and taken to a special training center. After a few years, they brought me here where I grew up as American as apple fucking pie."

"The perfect cover," he mused. "And after the KGB collapsed? You started working for FSK and FSB?"

"For a while," she admitted, "but then I got out on my own terms."

"Because of Holly?"

"Everything I do now is because of Holly," she answered truthfully.

"Including killing me?" he asked, his gaze settling on the menacing Grach pointed at his chest.

"I haven't decided yet." She eyed him suspiciously. "I'm not sure if you actually care about Holly or if you're using her to get back at Maksim."

"For what?" he asked, genuinely confused.

Her suspicious expression faltered. "You don't know?"

"About Holly being his daughter? Yes, I know that."

"No, not that," she said with a sigh. She pushed the folder toward him. "Read."

Wondering what he didn't know about Maksim, he picked up the folder and opened it. The stack of photos on top had his full attention. He flipped through them, each photo making his stomach twist harder and more painfully. Holly. Maksim. Nikolai. Vivian. Maksim's kids with his late wife. Yuri and Ivan with their wives. Dimitri holding his daughter. Artyom walking hand in hand with Chess's little girl through the zoo. A beautiful young blonde in '80s clothing. And then finally his own family. *My mother. My father. Me.*

Each photo had a number scribbled on it in red. The ones who were dead—his parents, the pretty blonde—had large red X marks drawn over their faces. The other photos were numbered. Vivian was six. Nikolai was five. Holly was four. Frances was three. Maksim was two. *And I'm number one.*

"Who does this hitlist belong to?" he asked, his gaze lingering on Holly's face.

"I thought you would have figured that out by now," Frances remarked with disappointment. "I did send you all the clues you needed."

Of course. "Were both files yours? The one that came to my house last month and the file Eric was given?"

She nodded. "The dossier that Rada gave Eric kept the detective busy chasing dead ends for a long time."

"So, Marco was right about Tiffany's parents," he said, flicking more ash onto the table. "Were they your agents?"

"I inherited them from a former colleague. They wanted out of the life, and I made it happen. Giving Eric that dossier was the last thing Rada ever did for me."

He seized on that detail. "For you? But is she working for someone else now?"

"Yes. Not by her own choice," she added. "She was being blackmailed."

"By?"

264 | ROXIE RIVERA

"The same person pulling Marco's strings."

"And who is that?"

"It's complicated."

"It always is in our line of work."

"Where is Marco? Do you have a location on him?"

"A morgue in College Station," he said, looking through the photos again. "Tiffany takes after her mother." He gestured to his neck. "Left a hell of a mess behind."

She narrowed her eyes. "The fire? That was you?"

He nodded. "You keep a very close eye on the news."

"Dead body? Arson?" She shrugged. "It made it onto my radar."

"The girl is safe, in case you were wondering."

"I was. Her mother is very worried."

"Did you move them?"

"I sent them to a safe house. I owed them that much, at least. Do you want to reunite Tiffany with her mother?"

"No," he answered firmly. "She was very clear that she doesn't want to see her family anytime soon."

"Do you blame her? It's always difficult for children when they learn scary things about their parents."

"Is that why you haven't told Holly who her father is? Who you are?"

Frances glanced away, her gaze settling on the floor as sadness darkened her face. "She would never forgive me, and I can't lose her."

"I don't want to lose her either," he admitted, "but she deserves to know what I am and what I've done."

"Not yet," Frances said, pinning him in place with her cold stare. "We have to get through this," she added, pointing to the folder, "before you tell her the truth. If you spring it on her, she'll run, and we'll have a harder time keeping her safe. If you care about her," she paused, "if you *love* her, you'll wait."

Not wanting to talk to Frances about his feelings for Holly, he simply nodded in agreement before returning his attention to the folder before him. "Who was pulling Marco's chain? Who did he think he was working for?"

"It was a fake DEA agent." She leaned forward and rifled through the pages and photos in the folder he still hadn't looked at yet. She found the photo she was looking for and slapped it down in front of him. "Slava Gruzin. She's been in Canada under a fake name—Sally Green—since the nineties."

"I know her," he said, taking a closer look. "She was younger, obviously, but I remember her coming to my dinner at our house when I was a kid." Feeling strangely homesick seeing a face tied to his childhood, he glanced up at Frances. "Is she still out there?"

She shook her head. "She was handled two nights ago."

"By you?"

She shook her head. "I'm too old for wetwork. I have a contractor I prefer for jobs like that."

"Local?" he asked, thinking she used one of the Professionals.

"He used to be," she replied, leaning back in her chair.

Picking up on her hint, he asked, "Gabe Reyes?"

Was that why Gabe had wanted to speak with him? Why he had asked Nate to give him those contact details? To give him a heads-up about the work he was going to be doing in their territory?

"Yes. His rates are higher than most, but he's worth it.

And he's clean about his work," she added, narrowing her gaze. "That fire was pathetic."

"You weren't there. I didn't have a lot of time to clean the scene. I had to make do." He waved his hand. "It worked out fine. Very little collateral damage."

"Your lack of planning is astounding."

Never one to take criticism gracefully, he retorted, "Your lack of transparency is going to get Holly killed."

She pursed her lips. "You don't get to sit there and tell me how to protect my daughter."

"You're not the only one who wants to protect her."

"I'm aware of that," she said, setting her pistol on the table. "Which is why you're still breathing."

He tossed down the folder. "I'm tired of these games. Just tell me what the fuck I need to know and let's figure out how we're going to protect Holly."

Frances inhaled sharply before exhaling slowly. She lowered her weapon to her lap, changing her aim from his chest to his dick. He wasn't thrilled about that, but he figured it was better than a bullet to the heart.

"You aren't going to like the story I'm going to tell," she began. "There's a very real chance that we're going to die. You and me," she clarified. "Me for something I did years ago, and you for the sins of your parents."

"Well, you'll have to be more specific because I've seen my parents' files and they committed a number of sins for the motherland."

"Yes, but this one, in particular, was the worst," she countered. "It's not in any of the files, but it started all of this." She pointed to the folder. "The girl. The blonde."

He took her picture from the folder. "What about her?"

"Look at her."

He did. He really looked at her. And then he knew. "Is this Holly's mother? Her birthmother?"

Frances nodded. "Kira Gurianova. She was a young agent. Brand new but very good. She had that natural talent for this kind of work. She would have been great someday."

"But?"

"But she made the mistake of falling in love with my brother."

"Your...brother?" Kostya finally made the connection. "You're Maksim's *sister*. You're Holly's aunt. Nikolai's aunt."

She nodded, her gaze taking on a faraway quality. "After our parents died, we were separated as children. Maks ended up in a boy's home, and I went to a girl's orphanage. I got plucked out very quickly and sent for training. He had a rougher start to life. Much like Nikolai," she added. "It's why they're so much alike. Not in their dealings with women, thankfully, but in all the other ways."

"Was Kira a honey trap for your brother?"

"It started that way. He was onto her in an instant. He's always been scarily good at ferreting out liars. He knew what she was and what she wanted from their first meeting. She got under his skin. Before they knew it, they were in love. *Real* love," she emphasized. "He loved her in a way he never cared for any of the others. I think he would have eventually divorced Galina for Kira. It was that serious."

"Which would have been a problem for her handlers," he murmured knowingly. "Why were they after Maksim? This was a wild time for our country. Politically," he clarified.

"From what I've read of the files back then, the mafia wasn't high on the list of priorities for our intelligence agencies."

"You're right. It wasn't. This wasn't about politics or national security. It was a vendetta, plain and simple."

"Between?"

"Maks and Igor Rybak."

He blinked. "The shadow head of KGB? The man who personally trained my parents?"

"And me," she said. "And Kira. And many others."

Realizing how deeply the connections between Maksim and his own family went, he felt suddenly off-kilter. "What was their vendetta about?"

"A woman," she answered sadly. "It seems to be the running theme in my brother's life. The details aren't important, but it was bad enough that Igor spent most of his life trying to hurt my brother."

Kostya was certain the details were important, but he would get those answers later. "But he didn't know you were Maksim's sister?"

She shook her head. "There weren't any files on us as children. After the war, there were more important things than getting paperwork done correctly. I didn't find Maks again until I was in my early twenties. By then, he had a bloody, violent history, and Igor was part of it. I kept my mouth shut and made sure we were never tied together as siblings. I did whatever I could to help Maks grow his empire, and he did whatever he could to help me when I needed it."

Going back to the picture of Kira, he said, "Igor knew that Maksim wouldn't be able to resist a beauty like this."

"Yes. She wasn't careful, though. She got pregnant, and

once her handlers realized her condition, they pulled her from the field. She was held in isolation and interrogation for a few weeks before they sent her out for an abortion."

"That obviously didn't happen," he remarked.

"She killed the agents who had escorted her and escaped. Maksim put her up in different safe houses, kept her happy and healthy while she carried his baby. I was working in Moscow at the time, doing energy contracts and negotiations between the Russian and American governments. I kept my ear to the ground and tried to keep Maksim apprised of any developments toward Kira."

"If Centre wanted her, they were going to find her eventually. You, of all people, should know that," he said.

"They sent their best team to find her—and they did."

Seeming anxious suddenly, she reached across the table for the pack of cigarettes he'd dropped there. He slid his lighter toward her, and she lit up, her thin, elegantly gloved fingers working the lighter with a kind of graceful elegance he had rarely seen.

She inhaled, her eyes closing briefly, and then blew out a long, slow breath. "I got a tip from a friend on the inside, and I left to go find and move her. Maksim was too far away so I knew that I had to be the one to get there first. But there was a storm," she explained. "A terrible blizzard. It slowed me down. When I got to the safe house, it was too late. Her guards were dead. The nurse and midwife staying with her were both dead."

"And Kira?"

"Shot in the heart and the head, dead on the floor by an empty bassinet." She closed her eyes and swallowed hard. "She had gone into labor earlier in the day. All the equipment and supplies for a delivery had been used. There was still a pile of bloody laundry in the corner of the room. She would have been too weak to fight or run."

"And Holly?" he asked, his heart in his throat.

"I heard a banging in the kitchen," Frances said, her eyes glistening with tears. "I followed it and found the back door open. It was banging against the frame because of the wind. There was snow building up on the kitchen floor. I went to close the door and then I heard this strange sound. It was…it was like a little kitten. Just soft and weak." Her hand was shaking as she brought the cigarette to her mouth for another draw. "And that's when I knew what they'd done. They had thrown the baby out into the cold to die."

"What?" he asked, aghast at the cruelty. "Just tossed her out in the snow?"

"They put her in the trashcan. Just dropped her in there like a piece of garbage." She flicked ash on the table. "I picked her up and put her inside my coat. I got in the car, put her inside my shirt against my skin and closed the coat over her, and I drove away as fast as I could. I took her to a hospital that I could trust, told them she was mine, and never left her side again. It was easy enough to get the papers I needed to bring her home as my daughter."

Kostya was at a loss for words. Their business was a messy one, and sometimes terrible things were done, but to torture a baby by throwing them out to die in the cold? It was something he couldn't fathom. It was a cruelty that he didn't understand.

"How did Maksim respond?" he asked.

"The same way he always does. Violence. Bloodshed." She put out her cigarette on the edge of the table and pocketed the butt. "It was a volatile time politically, and he used his contacts to make sure that Igor was done."

"He had him killed," Kostya said, trying to remember when, exactly, Igor had died. "It was February, wasn't it? When he died?"

She smiled wryly. "Do you really think my brother was going to let the man who killed his lover and tried to murder his baby just die? Do you think him that merciful?"

He went cold at the thought of how far Maksim would go for vengeance. "Torture?"

She nodded. "For a while."

"And then?"

"And then Maks sent him to a place where he would be forgotten."

He finally put together the clues she'd sent him. "The fingerprint!"

"I know one of your spiders hit the Interpol database. Igor was wiped off of the databases years ago. He's a ghost."

"But he's the prisoner in the Black Dolphin you wanted me to find."

"He *was* the prisoner in the Black Dolphin."

"Was?" he repeated, his heartbeat ticking up a few paces. "He's dead—or he escaped?"

"Escaped."

"How? That prison is inescapable."

"Not when you're dead," she replied. Reaching forward, she touched the photo of Slava. "She finally located him in the prison a few months ago. She found a doctor working in the facility that she could extort. She used him to have Igor declared dead after a heart attack that he probably induced with medication. Once Igor was in the prison morgue, it was easy enough for her to smuggle him out into the real world."

He looked at the photos and their numbers. "And this is *his* hitlist."

"Yes. He's killing everyone who betrayed or abandoned him."

Trying to think critically and logically, he said, "Igor is old now. He's been in a shithole for almost thirty years. He's broken down physically and mentally." He glanced at Slava's photo. "And his only ally is dead."

"No," she countered. "He's found other allies."

"Mexico," he said, feeling that cold chill ripple up his spine again. No wonder they hadn't been able to locate Lorenzo.

"The enemy of my enemy," she replied. "They're both men with nothing to lose."

Worrying about the mayhem Lorenzo and Igor could cause together, he stated the obvious. "We have to find them."

"I have Gabe working on it. He got some information from Slava, but I'm not sure how much of it was useful. I suspect he'll sniff out Lorenzo quicker than Igor."

"One will lead us to the other." He started piling everything back in the folder. "What are you planning to do?"

"Work my contacts. Convince my brother to stay in Moscow. Keep Holly safe."

"Maksim is wanting to come here?"

"Mexico," she answered with a shake of her head. "He wants to be the one that finally kills Igor."

"That's just what we need," he grumbled, thinking of the

trouble Maksim could cause down south. He was just as hardheaded as Nikolai, maybe even worse.

Just as he started to close the folder and slip it into his jacket, he caught sight of his mother. Remembering what Frances had said earlier about the sins of his parents, he slowly glanced up at her. She had a sad look on her face, her pale eyes darkened by regret. She shook her head, as if reading his mind. "You don't have to ask if you aren't ready to hear it."

His heart clamored in his chest, making it hard for him to breathe. Nevertheless, he asked, "What team did they send after Kira?"

"Your parents," she said after a second's pause. "Nina and Arkady."

Feeling lightheaded, he stood abruptly and pushed away from the table. He pocketed the folder, his cigarettes and lighter. His mouth dry, he said, "I'll be with Holly tonight if you need to find me."

Frances didn't try to stop him leaving or tell him that she didn't want him near Holly. Maybe she understood more than he had suspected. Maybe she saw him as a mother would see their child. He was suddenly a little boy whose life had been completely upended by the knowledge that his parents had tried to kill the baby who had grown up to be the woman he loved.

He needed to see Holly. He needed to hold her and love her. He needed to be with someone who cared about him, who had always been real and truthful.

Out in his car, he raked his shaky fingers through his hair. There was something else that Frances hadn't told him. It was an answer he hadn't been ready to hear.

If his parents had killed Kira, had Maksim killed his mother and father?

Glancing back the house, he felt a twisting punch in his gut. Or had he just been sitting across from the woman who had murdered his parents?

CHAPTER EIGHTEEN

"DID YOU SEE the ballroom mockup and cost estimate for the gala?" Savannah asked as she swanned into my office and dropped onto the sofa.

"I glanced at them," I said, my gaze fixed on the computer screen in front of me. While I had been out at Samovar, there had been a minor dustup between a client and one of our newest stylists. Gesturing to the screen, I asked, "Were you on the floor when this client complained?"

"Yes," she said with a roll of her eyes. "It was absolute bullshit. Nisha was supervising Katie. They talked to this girl at length about the color she wanted, and the reality of how many appointments it would take to get there. I heard Nisha and Katie both suggest a more natural peachy or caramel tone to the highlights, but the client insisted on silvery blonde!"

"Was it really as bad as her shit fit would have me believe?" Rereading the nasty comment that had been left on our social media account, I worried the client had been left with a dye job from hell.

She shook her head. "The highlights were beautiful. Katie did a really good job of giving the client what they wanted while also balancing the overall look of her hair. It's not Katie's fault that her client didn't listen to the advice she was given.

Here." She pulled her phone from the pocket of her skirt and tossed it at me. "Look at the photos I snapped of her hair. It looks perfectly fine."

And it did. It looked very nice, flattering even. It wasn't exactly silver, but it was close. With only one appointment, there was no way to take dark brown hair to silver even with a bucket of chemicals and heat.

"It looks very good," I agreed, trying to be as unbiased as possible. "What set off the client?"

"She said it wasn't the same color as the girl in her Instagram photo. I tried to explain that the girl in photo had a different starting hair color, and also, the girl in the photo had, like, seven filters layered together. Who the hell knows what the real color of those highlights were."

"Do you want to handle this?" I tossed her phone back at her. "Normally, I would, but you were on the floor when it happened."

"I'll handle it."

"Nicely," I urged, knowing how Savannah could get sometimes.

"Yes, mother," she replied sarcastically. "So—how did your little errand go?"

"Strangely," I admitted. "Vivian's husband was oddly welcoming, and he agreed to help me find my father."

"Well, I guess that's a good thing," she said uneasily.

"I think so."

"You're a big girl. I trust you to know if you need to pump the brakes," she said, rising from the sofa and shrugging. "You have any plans for tonight?"

"I've got to run a few errands and then I'm headed home

to do laundry and catch up on housework. You?"

"I've got a meeting for the gala to discuss the budget." She made a face. "And then, after that, a handful of Advil, a bottle of Moscato and whatever I can find on Netflix that I haven't seen yet." Smiling, she gestured to the door. "I'm heading out. The girls have all left, and the front of the shop is shut down."

"I'll be gone in a few minutes," I said, shutting down my computer.

"Okay. Good night."

"Night."

After closing my office and doing a final check of the salon, I set the alarm and left the building. Once I was in my car, I opened the Waze app on my phone and looked at the address I had found earlier. I debated a few seconds before tapping the screen and leaving the parking lot.

The app's voice guided me through my car speakers, telling me when and where to turn. I slowed down as I reached my destination and parked across from the darkened building in one of the few parallel spots available. I thought about getting out and investigating the building, maybe try the front door, but my better instincts warned me to stay put.

Sunrise Sunset was scrawled on the door's window in yellow. The logo of a rising sun reflected as a setting sun sat underneath it. There was no phone number. No website. The place had no social media presence whatsoever.

It was definitely a front, but for what? Something simple like laundering money or something worse? Did I even want to know?

What would Kostya say if he found out I'd come here tonight? That I'd spied on his phone call?

Startled by the sound of my phone, I damn near jumped through the windshield. Glancing down at the screen, I saw my mother's face and answered quickly. "Hey, Mom."

"Holly, where are you? I came by the salon, but it's already closed."

"Oh, I'm just out running some errands," I lied, putting my car in drive and merging back onto the road. "Why did you come by the salon? Do you need a trim?"

"No, no, no," she answered. "I thought I'd stop by and keep you company while you were closing up."

"Sorry! I would have stayed later if I'd known you were coming by to see me."

"Don't worry about it. I'm headed back to the house. If you need anything or if you want to come over, I'll be up for a while."

"Not tonight," I said, navigating through an intersection. "I have to catch up on laundry and some cleaning I've been putting off. My house is a mess."

"Well, if you change your mind…"

"I know where to go."

"All right. Let me know when you get home."

"I will. Goodnight, Mom."

"I love you, Holly."

"I love you, too."

After I hung up, I couldn't shake the thought that my mother wasn't telling me the truth about her health. Why else would she be acting so oddly? Worried that she was sick, I decided that I would spend the night with her tomorrow and try to get the truth out of her.

When I turned onto my street, I spotted Kostya's car in

my driveway. My stomach erupted with a swarm of butterflies at the sight of him leaning against his car, waiting for me. There was something in his stance that worried me. He seemed stiff, almost aggressive in the way he held his arms. He looked like a predator ready to pounce.

As I pulled into the garage, he got back into his car and drove into the empty space on the right side. When I got out of my car, he was waiting for me as the garage door slid closed behind us. The expression on his face concerned me. He looked so tired and broken, his eyes sad and his face lined with stress.

Touching his cheek, I asked, "Are you okay?"

He leaned into my hand. "I am now."

"Kostya." I caressed his face. "What's wrong?"

"Everything." He leaned down and nuzzled me. His mouth sought mine, and I rose up to meet him, pressing my lips to his. His hands fell to the roof of my car, and he boxed me in against the door, his hard, hot body feeling so damn good against mine.

I clutched at him, grabbing handfuls of his shirt and dragging him even closer. His wild kisses left me breathless as I wondered what in the world had happened to leave him so shaken.

"May I stay with you tonight?" he asked in between feverish kisses.

"Yes. *Please.*"

His hands slid down to cup my bottom. I shivered wickedly, my body pulsing with desire and need. "Can I use your shower?"

"Only if you let me join you..."

He followed me into the house, his hand in mine. The body heat radiating from him set my body on fire, igniting all my nerve-endings and making my heart race even faster. By the time we made it to the master bathroom, we had shed our shoes, and he'd tossed his jacket carelessly onto a chair in my room. I watched him take off his shoulder holster and stow his gun in the drawer next to mine. I was only a little surprised by the knives he had hidden away on his body.

For a moment, he just stood there, staring at me. There was something so vulnerable in his eyes tonight. He seemed wounded. If I asked, he wouldn't tell me what was bothering him. I knew him well enough to know that. So, I held out my hand and beckoned him to join me.

His fingers were strong around mine. With a smile, I tugged him into the bathroom. Dropping his hand, I started the shower, adjusting the temp the way I liked it, warm but not too hot. When I turned around, he had already taken off his shirt. I stepped forward and gripped his belt buckle, slowly unfastening it as I held his gaze. He leaned down and pressed his mouth against mine. His kiss was gentle, searching, and I melted into him.

In between fevered kisses, we undressed each other, laughing and smiling when he tumbled a bit from the jeans wrapped around his ankles. Eventually, we made it into the shower. The hot water and steam felt so good on my skin, but Kostya's arms wrapping around me and dragging me back against him felt even better. I shivered as he kissed a slow, meandering line down my neck.

"I missed you today," he said softly, his breath tickling my ear. "I wanted to see you so many times."

"You should have come to the salon or called me. I would have met you anywhere you wanted."

He kissed my temple before letting go of me. "I was in Galveston most of the day. That's a long way for you to drive just to see me."

"I would have done it."

"I know you would have." He lathered a bar of soap between his hands. "That's why I didn't call."

I frowned at him. "That's silly."

"No, it wasn't."

The way he said it made my stomach clench. Whatever he'd been up to since he left the salon last night had obviously been very dangerous. From his haggard expression, it had its toll on him. Touching his chest, I held his gaze. "I know you can't tell me what you were doing, but I need you to know that I would never break your confidence. I hope that someday we can get to a place where you can tell me the truth, where you can unburden yourself, and know that I'll never tell a living soul."

His expression softened. Leaning down, he kissed me tenderly. "Holly, I do trust you. If I thought telling you everything would make it easier for us, I would in a heartbeat."

"But?"

"But, right now, the only thing keeping us both safe is my silence."

"I understand," I whispered against his lips and kissed him again.

That seemed to be the end of his willingness to talk. His soapy hands started to roam my body, outlining the curves of my breasts and hips. I didn't want to talk anymore either.

Grasping at his shoulders, I closed my eyes and relished the feel of his hands gliding over my skin. Unlike last night, we were taking it slow now. Exploring. Feeling.

Taking the soap from him, I started to lather up his skin, moving my hands over his tattooed flesh. His lean body was so hard beneath my fingertips, every muscle, every sinew perfectly outlined. I studied the art decorating his skin, wondering if I would ever find out what each one of these pieces meant.

Sliding my hand down the flat plane of his stomach, I didn't waste time playing coy. I grasped his hard cock, stroking it from root to tip, and eliciting an animalistic groan from him. He thrust into my hand, and I smiled triumphantly, lifting up to nip at his bottom lip. He groaned again and inhaled a shaky breath as my other hand moved down his thigh and cupped his sac.

"Holly..."

"Relax," I urged, wanting to give him some relief from all the tension he carried. My hand stroked up and down his shaft, the slick soap easing the way. I stabbed my tongue against his, urging him to let go, and he did. He pressed my back against the tile and thrust into my hand while he devoured my mouth, leaving me breathless and panting. He gripped my ass in one palm and slapped the other against the tile behind me, bracing himself. Stroking faster and tighter, I urged him on with a whispered, "Come for me."

He growled my name before capturing my mouth in a kiss that left me dizzy. He jerked against my hand as I eased him down with gentle caresses. Wrapping his arms around me, he dragged me back under the water. His mouth found mine again as the water ran down our bodies, rinsing away the soap clinging to us.

We didn't bother with towels as we stepped out of the shower. In the back of my mind, I cringed at the thought of getting my duvet wet, but in the moment, I didn't really much care. All I wanted was Kostya. On top of me. In my bed.

His mouth was on mine as he guided me backwards across the room. When the backs of my thighs hit the edge of the bed, he gave me a little shove, and I ended up flat on my back. Giggling and reaching for him, I wiggled up higher on the bed. He came down on top of me, his lips crashing against mine before his tongue darted between them.

"Konstantin," I breathed out his name and arched into his touch. His hands were so strong and sure as they moved over my body, sliding along my curves and caressing me gently. He danced a line of soft, ticklish kisses along my throat and across my breasts. He lingered there, his lips on my nipples until they ached. I gripped his shoulders and dragged my fingers through his hair, scratching my nails over his scalp and making him groan.

"Open your legs," he ordered roughly. A shiver of anticipation coursed through my body as I followed his instruction, widening my thighs and planting my heels on the edge of the bed. He kissed a teasing line down the inside of each thigh before nuzzling his mouth against my heated sex. His fingers parted me, baring me to his hungry gaze.

At the first swipe of his tongue, I dropped my head back to the bed and closed my eyes. He was gentle at first, his tongue exploring and dipping into me. I tried to angle my hips and direct his attention to my clit, but he was having none of that. His strong hands held my legs open and my hips down, forcing to me be patient.

All the tension and worry I had been carrying for the last few days melted out of me. His mouth worked tenderly over the most sensitive part of me, licking and lapping until I was breathing shakily. When he settled his tongue over my clit, I cried out with relief. He chuckled dark and low against me, the rumbling sound adding a delicious twist to his flicking motions.

"I'm going to come," I whispered breathlessly, feeling that coil of pleasure building inside me. He groaned against my pussy, urging me to let go and feel. My climax started slowly, tendrils of ecstasy unfurling and spreading through my body. I rocked against his mouth, my hands in his hair as I cried out his name again and again.

When my orgasm started to fade, he turned his attention away from my clit. First one finger and then two found their way inside me. He thrust carefully, pushing and rubbing until he found that little spot that made my entire body jolt. I surged off the bed, my hips arching upward as my head fell back. "Kostya!"

He laughed at my predicament before dropping his mouth to my clit again. He worked his magic in a way no other man had with me. I'd had some damn good orgasms in my life— but holy fuck. The way Kostya thrust his fingers and lapped at me with his strong tongue left me screaming.

My climax hit me with a wild burst of pleasure that rocketed through me. My whole body tensed and jerked in time with his incessant licks. I clawed at the bed, grabbing handfuls of the covers and hanging on for dear life as he changed the angle of his fingers and the pressure of his mouth. The third orgasm was so quick and hard I saw stars and couldn't breathe, my mouth hanging open as I pressed into him, desperate to wring every last bit of stimulation I could from him.

"God! No more!" I tried to pull away from him, but he had grasped my hips in both hands now, his tongue languidly moving between my folds, teasing over my clit. "Please."

With a final soft kiss between my legs, he stopped. He caressed my lower belly and thighs while I tried to catch my breath. My arms and legs tingled, and I could feel the slick wet mess he had made of me on my inner thighs. I reached down to touch him, my fingers finding his damp hair. With a little tug, I urged him up on top of me.

"We don't have to—"

"Shut up and fuck me," I interrupted roughly, my voice hoarse from all that yelling. Locking my legs around his waist, I all but dared him to try to escape me. He grinned down at me before grabbing my ass in one hand and hitching my body up a little higher. He was rock-hard again, his cock nudging between my legs and making me pant with excitement.

"Oh," I drew out the word on a low moan as he slid deep on a smooth thrust. With a hand on my hip and another planted next to my head, Kostya dipped down to kiss me. The muscles in his neck were taut as he rocked into me, his pace slow and unhurried. Every stroke was like heaven, our bodies working perfectly together.

Unlike our rushed sex at the salon, this was different. Tender. Gentle. And oh so good. I clutched at his shoulders, burying my face in his neck. He smelled of my soap, floral and light, but also a hint of me still lingered on him. I kissed his throat and jaw before finally resting my lips against his ear. My hard breaths made him shiver, and he started driving into me harder and faster. I sensed he was trying to hold back long enough for me to come again, but my body was wrung out from the wicked things he'd done with his mouth.

I slid a hand down his back and over his hip before grabbing his ass. I pulled him hard into me, taking him deeper with his thrust and angling my hips to meet him. He looked down at me, his eyes questioning, and I nodded, silently communicating that I wanted him to let go. He dropped his forehead to mine, his hips snapping rapidly as he chased his climax.

"Holly," he groaned my name, his accent dragging out the first syllable in a way I had come to love. I embraced him tightly, not wanting to let him go. Here, in my bedroom, we were safe from all the mafia shit he was mired in for life. We were secure here, cocooned from everything and everyone who wanted to tear us apart.

When he slid off of me and fell onto his side, he draped his arm across my waist and dragged me against him. His arms encircled me, and I could tell he had the same thoughts I did. He didn't want to leave this bedroom. He didn't want to face the truth of our situation. He didn't want to acknowledge what neither of us were brave enough to say.

This won't last.

I blinked hard, refusing to cry or give into that feeling of sadness that had engulfed me at the ugly thought. More than anything, I wanted to make this work. He wanted the same thing. I could feel it in the way he touched me and the way he looked at me. We wanted the same thing—a life together.

But it wasn't up to us. His secrets and his ties to the mob

threatened this new, blossoming relationship. Were we strong enough to break those ties?

The thought rattled around in my head as I drifted off to sleep in his arms. When I woke a few hours later, my mouth dry and stomach growling, I gently shifted away from him. He was dead to the world. The dark circles under his eyes and the stress lines in his forehead saddened me. Wanting him to rest, I carefully moved away from him and off the bed.

Not bothering with clothes, I used the bathroom, wiped up the water droplets pooled on the tile and turned off the light. It was a bit muggy in the bedroom so I switched on the ceiling fan and killed the overhead lights we had left on after making love. Wanting it to be cozier for him so he would rest, I turned down the thermostat. As I made my way down the hall, I picked up the clothing that we had dropped earlier.

There was enough moonlight coming in from my kitchen windows that I didn't bother with the lights. Standing naked in front of the open refrigerator, I stared at the shelves for something to eat. Nothing looked particularly tasty so I closed the door and padded over to the cabinet by the sink for a glass. The sound of the clinking ice cubes smacking against the glass was so loud in the quiet house. I hoped it wouldn't wake Kostya since he seemed to sleep so light.

The cold water felt so good as I thirstily gulped it down. As I lowered the glass, I felt a strange shiver along my neck and back. It was odd feeling, almost as if someone were watching me. Turning around toward the arched doorway of the kitchen, I expected to see Kostya looming there in that quiet, serious way of his.

But the archway was empty.

Something sharp and cold pressed against my spine and a rough, stinking hand clasped over my mouth. The callused palm slapped hard against my lips, suppressing the scream of shock that erupted from my throat. Horrible, sour breath surrounded me as the intruder pressed his mouth close to my ear and hissed, "You fucking scream again, and I'll gut you like a deer."

Naked, alone, vulnerable—I prayed that Kostya would wake up.

Save me.

CHAPTER NINETEEN

A WAKENED BY HOLLY moving out of bed, he had been too tired to ask her where she was going. Eyes closed, he listened to her putter around in the bathroom. She turned on the ceiling fan and switched off the light, making the bedroom more comfortable. He considered getting up for a glass of water, but his whole body ached from lack of sleep. His fuzzy brain and dry eyes demanded he stay right where he was, dehydration be damned.

He had started to doze off again when he heard the sharp plink of ice cubes. It woke him up just enough that he became aware of something else. A smell that didn't belong in Holly's house. He sat up, suddenly alert, and breathed in deeply. Gasoline? Oil? Exhaust?

His stomach dropped. It was a smell he'd detected earlier that morning with Spider. It was the smell of a biker.

Fuck.

He jumped out of bed, not wasting time to reach for his clothes. He grabbed a thin gold belt Holly had left over a chair. He didn't dare fire a gun in her house. Not now. Not with all the complications swirling around the city. Police crawling over Holly's house and digging through their lives would be an absolute disaster.

With stealth, he moved down the hall, his bare feet noiseless on the tile. Holly's muffled scream hit his ears, twisting his gut and making his heart race. Adrenaline spiked his bloodstream. His muscles twitched. His jaw clenched. He was going to fucking kill someone.

He hesitated near the open doorway of the kitchen. She had kept the lights off, familiar enough with her house to not need them in the dark. He was glad for that. The shadows shielded him and gave him the element of surprise he needed.

The low hiss of a man's voice cut through the sound of Holly's panicked breathing. It occurred to him that she was naked, and a new burn of fury lit him up. Some piece of shit had their hands on her and was feeling the soft skin that belonged to him and only him.

"Where the fuck is that Russian?"

Holly yelped, and a moment later, the man snarled, "And don't fucking lie to me, you skinny bitch."

"Bed-bedroom," she stuttered out in a whine of pain.

"You're going to walk me to the bedroom. If you make a noise, I cut you. If you do anything to wake him up, I cut you. Now move!"

Kostya backed up, retreating to the darkness inside the guest bathroom. Grateful for the open door, he controlled his breathing, staying still and disappearing into the shadows. Holly's shuddery breaths filled the hallway, her fear palpable. Her attacker had a knife, of that much Kostya was sure. He had to be careful. He had to be precise.

Seemingly oblivious to his position in the bathroom, Holly walked by on shaky legs. He counted to three, watching the man behind her pass the doorway before stepping out in a silent flash of movement. He looped the thin belt around the man's neck, twisting the ends wrapped around his hands tight.

There was a rough choking sound and the clatter of a knife hitting the floor as Kostya lifted the man off his feet. Kicking and flailing, the attacker tried to free himself. Kostya pulled harder, crushing the man's throat and waiting for the telltale flop of a dead man.

Taking the man to the floor, he wrapped his legs around the attacker's waist and kept yanking on the belt, the pressure enough to crush the man's windpipe and starve his lungs and brain of oxygen. The lights came on suddenly, momentarily blinding him. Certain this asshole was dead, he let go of the belt.

Holly leaned against the wall at the far end of the hall, just next to her bedroom. Her hand rested on the light switch as she cried silently, tears running down her face. A trickle of blood followed the curve of her hip and trailed down her thigh.

"You're hurt!" He scrambled to his feet, but she stepped back as if afraid of him. Gutted by the sight of her fear, he stopped moving. It was normal for her to react that way. She had never been around violence. She had never seen the ugliness of life. But it still hurt him to see her fear. "Holly…"

"Is…is he dead?" Her eyes were fixed on the strangled body on her hallway floor.

"Yes." He stepped in front of her, blocking her view of the ghastly expression on the man's face.

"Who he is he?"

He glanced back at the body. Even without the leather vest and with his tattoos covered in long sleeves, he recognized the man. "His name is Scorpion. He rides with a biker gang."

"Why did he want to kill you?" she asked, her voice small and anxious.

He sighed and wiped his hands over his face. "It's a long, ugly story, Holly."

"That you're not going to tell me," she guessed correctly.

He shook his head. "Not now."

She didn't look happy about that but didn't argue with him. Trembling less, she asked, "How did he get in here?"

"I'm not sure." He tried to remember everything they had done and not done on the way into the house. "The door in the kitchen that leads to the garage."

"Shit," she swore softly. "I usually lock it, but…"

"I know. That's my fault. I should have made sure it was locked and that your alarm was set. I'm sorry, Holly. This shouldn't have happened."

"But it did," she said somberly. Nervous now, she asked, "What do we do? I mean, we can't call the police. Right? Like that would be really stupid?"

"It wouldn't be the smartest option for either of us," he agreed. Knowing what had to be done, he said, "Get dressed."

"What about you?"

"I have to wrap up this body before he makes a mess."

She frowned with confusion. "What do you mean?"

Not wanting to sicken her, he explained, "Strangulation causes a complete loss of muscle control."

Understanding filtered across her face. "Oh." She looked suddenly squeamish. "What do you need?"

"I can handle it. You just worry about yourself."

Glad that she hadn't completely lost her shit after being

attacked and watching him kill a man, he ducked into her guest bathroom and jerked the shower curtain off the rod. Shower curtain rings scattered and clanged as they fell into the tub. He snatched a couple of towels and a washcloth from the rack, too. Out in hallway, he placed the shower curtain down and gently rolled Scorpion's body onto it. He shoved a washcloth in his mouth and wrapped towels around his waist to catch any fluids that might escape.

Staring down at the man he had known for a decade, not well but as a moving part of the underworld machinery, he frowned. Though his face was slack now, almost peaceful, Scorpion had clearly been through hell. Greasy hair, thick stubble, the strong scent of sweat and dirt and oil wafting from his skin and clothing. Kostya's gaze settled on the smudges of Holly's blood on Scorpion's knife hand and forearm. Pale strands of hair glistened in the loosening grip of his other hand.

The sight of Holly's blood and hair struck him with the weight of a freight train. This piece of shit biker had gotten the drop on him in Holly's own house. He had been so wrapped up in her, in his needs and desires, that he had put her in danger. *Stupid fucking asshole.*

Silently berating himself, he rifled through Scorpion's clothing like a pickpocket. A powered down phone. A wallet. Some loose bills and change. A knife. A gun. Nothing useful. Setting aside the personal belongings, he tightly wrapped Scorpion in the shower curtain.

"Here."

He glanced up at Holly. Dressed in grey shorts and an oversized pink sweater, she held out a roll of duct tape. "Thank you."

He made quick work of sealing the wrapped body and stood up. Handing the tape back to her, he said, "I need to get dressed so I can handle this."

"Handle it how?" she asked, trailing him into her bedroom.

"Holly," he said in a warning tone. "You really don't want to know."

"But I fucking do!"

Her angry shout took him by surprise as he pulled on his boxer briefs. The fear that overtaken her earlier was gone. Now, she was seized by anger.

"Listen, some crazy person just broke into my house, put a knife on my spine and tried to kill us both. I just watched you strangle him with my belt. I think I deserve to know what the fuck is going on in my own damn house!"

And suddenly all the reasons he'd had for never crossing the line of their friendship to date her were blaring in his head. This was what he'd been trying to avoid. She didn't belong in his dirty, seedy underworld, but here she was, mired in a murder he had just committed in her house.

"I went looking for a girl was missing," he said, grabbing his jeans. "She was mixed up with a man—an older man—who was using her as bait."

"Bait? For what?"

"To get to her family," he said, reaching for his socks and deliberately not going into the details about Tiffany's mother. "The man she was with had a partnership with Scorpion." He gestured to the dead body out in the hall. "Scorpion came here to kill me tonight because I uncovered his secret plot against our bosses."

"Is he the only one coming after you?"

He laughed roughly. "Hardly."

"Is this...is this what it's like for you every night?" she asked, her voice filled with concern.

He shook his head. "You'd be surprised how rarely this kind of shit happens to me."

"Because you're usually the one sneaking into someone's house to deal with them first?"

He met her unwavering gaze. There was no point in lying to her now. "Yes."

She swallowed hard. "So, this is what you do? For Nikolai?"

"Mostly," he admitted. "It's my job to keep our family safe. Usually, it doesn't come to this, but if it does, I don't hesitate."

"How many?" she asked, her voice breaking. "How many have you...?"

"I don't keep track," he lied.

"That many?"

"Does it matter?"

"I don't know," she admitted, sounding so unsure. "It probably should."

"But," he asked, his heart in his throat.

"But I love you," she confessed with a sob. "I love you, and I don't care what you've done or what you're going to do."

His heart damn near exploded in his chest. He crossed the space between them with purposeful strides and wrapped his arms around her. Dragging her against his chest, he buried his face in her hair and held her as she cried. It killed him to know he'd done this to her. That he had earned her love and trust but had also made her feel this conflicted. *She loves a murderer.*

"Holly," he whispered against her hair, "I love you. I've never loved anyone like I do you. There's never been anyone like you and there never will be again. You're it for me."

"I don't want to lose this," she said, her voice muffled against his chest. "I don't want to lose *you*. I'm so afraid we aren't strong enough to make this work."

He cupped her face and tilted her head back so he could gaze down into her beautiful eyes. "If I were better man, I'd leave you right now. I'd walk out the door and never come back. I'd let you go. Let you find a man who deserves you. A good man. Someone who doesn't live in the shadows. Someone worthy of you." He pressed his lips to hers in a lingering kiss. "But I'm not a better man. I don't want to lose you. I don't want to let you go."

"Then don't," she said, clinging to his arms. "Don't let me go."

He brushed the soft strands of hair from her face. "Holly, there are so many horrible things happening right now. There are secrets I have that will hurt us both. There are terrible things in my past."

"We'll figure it out," she said matter-of-factly. "Somehow, some way, we'll figure it out, Kostya."

"I promise you, Holly, that I'll try my hardest." He kissed her again, not wanting it to ever end. "I'll try."

"I know you will."

Her unwavering faith in him shook him right to the core. He pressed his lips to her temple for a lingering moment before letting her go. Cupping her face, he said, "I need you to come with me. You're not safe here."

KOSTYA | 297

She nodded without hesitation. "Okay."

"Pack a bag with whatever you'll need for a few days—clothes, toiletries, your gun."

"Okay."

While she headed for her closet, he pulled on the rest of his clothes. He glanced at his watch. At least it was still early. Their neighborhood was filled with nine-to-fivers, and he doubted anyone would be out on the street at this hour.

"Do I need my passport?" She stood in the doorway of her closet, a leather weekend bag in hand. She'd changed into leggings and added a hoodie and sneakers. "Or cash?"

He hoped it wouldn't come to that, but it wasn't a bad idea to take both. "Yes."

"Okay." She walked to chest of drawers against the opposite wall of her bedroom, opened the bottom drawer and retrieved a locked box. She spun the numbers on the lock and popped the lid. Grabbing stacks of banded cash, she tossed them into her bag along with her passport and a few credit cards. "Mom," she said, as if sensing he would want an explanation. "She's got all these weird rules about always being ready to leave at a moment's notice. She had some close calls traveling for business, and it made her paranoid."

You don't know the half of it. He didn't say that, of course. He wasn't about to hint to Holly that her mother was so much more than she understood. Not now. Not tonight. Not after what had just happened to her.

"Sometimes paranoia keeps us safe."

She snorted softly. "I can just imagine what you keep in a safe."

"Crypto, diamonds, international currency, clean papers," he listed off the contents. "I like to keep things small and light, easy to carry."

"Crypto?" She zipped up her bag. "Like Bitcoin?"

He nodded. "I keep some of it in cold storage."

"I bought some a few years ago." She paused, as if trying to think. "More than a few years ago. It's just sitting in a wallet that Savvy helped me set up. I have no idea what it's worth."

"Probably a fucking fortune," he replied.

"You think?"

"I think."

"I'll check it out when I get back." She hefted her bag and hesitated before asking, "I am coming back, right?"

"In a few days," he said, stepping close and pulling her into his arms. He kissed her cheek and held her close. "I want to make sure everything has settled down and that nothing can tie Scorpion to this house. As soon as it's clear, you can come home."

She pulled back and smiled sadly. "I don't think this is home anymore."

Feeling like the biggest piece of shit for bringing violence and death into her home, he kissed her tenderly. "I'll help you find a new one. I'll buy this one from you so you can get out of here as quickly as possible."

"If any other guy said that to me, I'd know he was talking shit, but you? You'll walk in the door with a cashier's check."

"Market value," he teased. "We wouldn't want to raise any suspicions."

Stifling a laugh, she pressed her lips to his. When she ended the kiss, she turned serious. "What happens now?"

Somberly, he said, "The part I never wanted to share with you."

CHAPTER TWENTY

G RIPPING MY TRAVEL mug of sugary sweet coffee, I wondered how long my jitters would last. Next to me, Kostya navigated the dark city streets, occasionally reaching for his coffee from the center console. Black, of course. Like his car. Like his clothes. Like the shadows where he dwelled.

I almost died.

The thought kept tumbling around in my head. It was an incessant, annoying hum in the background. *I almost died.*

But I didn't.

All things considered, I had come out of my first brush with death with only a small cut. It still throbbed a little, but the scar would be small and unnoticeable.

Not to him. I glanced at Kostya. Every time he saw the scar from Scorpion's blade, he would blame himself for what had happened. He would feel guilty that he had exposed me to this horrible, ugly world he inhabited.

"I chose this."

"What?" Confused, he looked away from the windshield and frowned at me. "Chose what?"

"You," I explained. "I chose you with eyes wide open. I mean—I didn't know *exactly* what being with you would entail, but I had a good enough idea. What happened tonight at my house wasn't all your fault. I invited you into my life and into my home and trouble followed you. That's on me."

He didn't say anything at first. His jaw clenched and relaxed. Finally, he reached across the console to hold my hand. Lifting our entwined hands, he kissed the back of mine. "It doesn't make it easier for me."

"It will. Eventually," I added. "We're adults. We made adult decisions. Now, we're dealing with adult consequences."

He grunted in agreement, and we lapsed into silence. I wasn't sure where he was taking me, and I didn't care to ask. Just being with him, safe in his car, was enough. Before long, though, I realized where we were heading. "What's in Texas City?"

"A warehouse I own," he said, reaching for his coffee.

"Do you own a lot of warehouses?"

"Yes."

"And businesses other than your security gig?"

"Yes."

I swallowed anxiously before asking, "Like Sunrise Sunset Delivery?"

His gaze snapped to mine. "What?"

Playing with the zipper tab on my hoodie, I confessed, "The other night, when you used my office phone, I called the number. It went to a recording so I sort of...well...I went there."

"When?"

"Earlier tonight."

"Did you get out of the car?"

"No, I parked across the street. My mom called, and I got spooked and left."

He sighed. "It's not my business. A woman I helped a few years ago owns it. She handles deliveries of a sensitive nature."

"Is she a good friend?" I asked, trying to stop the jealousy sliding into my voice.

"Yes, but not in *that* way," he assured me. "I haven't had a friend like that since a few months after you moved in next door."

"Are you serious?" I turned in the seat to study him. "You haven't had any girlfriends in all this time?"

"Not one," he confirmed.

"Well, now I feel like shit." I tried not to think about all the dates I had gone on while he had been patiently waiting next door.

"For what? Enjoying your life? Don't be. I'm glad you were happy."

"I wasn't happy," I countered. "I had some good dates, but they always felt...wrong. There were only a couple I brought home—"

"I know," he interrupted, his voice darker and rough now.

I narrowed my eyes at him. "Exactly how close have you been watching me?"

"I don't have cameras in your house."

"But?"

"But I keep track of when you leave and come home," he admitted.

"Pervert," I teased, reaching over to pinch his leg.

"I didn't hear you complaining earlier." He snatched my hand and dragged me closer, half hauling me out of my seat so he could kiss me. It was a quick, hot touch of our lips together before he pulled away and turned his attention back to the traffic. "I only did it to keep you safe. I worried someone might hurt you to get to me."

"I know why you did it. If I'd found out a few months ago, I would have flipped out on you, but after tonight, I understand why you do the things you do. Even if they are kind of creepy," I added.

"I'll try to be less creepy in the future," he said with a smile.

I thought about our months and months of missed chances. "You know, Kostya, what we've had together the last few nights has been better than anything I've ever experienced with any other man."

"I don't need my ego stroked," he said, reaching over to squeeze my thigh, "but it's nice to hear."

I rolled my eyes. "What I'm trying to say is that—"

"I know what you're trying to say," he said seriously. His hand slid up my thigh to grasp mine. "I feel the same way. It's different with you."

Hand in hand, we drove the rest of the way without talking. There didn't seem to be anything else to say. The closer we got to Texas City, the more I could smell the sulfurous tang of the petrochemicals saturating the air. Eventually, the rows of neatly arranged houses gave way to massive industrial complexes filled with tank batteries, factories and tall smokestacks spewing God only knew what into the night air.

Kostya made a series of turns before sliding up to a locked gate around the ugliest building I had ever seen. It was rotted out in some spots, the rust eating through the metal roof and sides. A faded sign had fallen off the front of the building, and now sported graffiti tags. Three feral cats ran across the cracked pavement, ducking and hiding as the headlights of the car spooked them.

"Is this place safe?" I asked, my hand tightening around his.

"Not really," he admitted. "Don't touch anything when we get inside. You'll need a tetanus booster if you do."

I couldn't tell if he was teasing or serious. He leaned across me to open the glovebox and retrieved a pair of black leather gloves. After he tugged them on, he rolled down the window and punched the keypad to unlock the gate. He drove through, waiting for it to close and lock behind us before driving farther onto the property. He chose a spot behind the warehouse, shielded from the street and all the other rundown buildings around us.

"Let's go."

I followed him out of the car and into the building, trailing close behind him on the cracked sidewalk and stepping carefully. When we reached the heavy door, he unscrewed the cap on the end of the metal railing running along the sidewalk and withdrew a hidden key. He unlocked the door, pocketed the key and reached back for me, taking my hand in his leather clad one and tugging me into the dark building.

It smelled terrible inside. Dusty, dirty, dank—just awful. Unable to see in the blackness of the space, I clung to his hand and wondered how the hell he could navigate so easily. It seemed as if we had been walking forever when he slowed to a stop and unlocked another door. When we stepped across the threshold, he turned on a flickering fluorescent light. After a few seconds, it hummed to life, blazing brightly and illuminating the dingy old office.

"Sit here." He pointed to the leather and wood chair behind the desk. "I don't want you to leave this room."

"Where are you going?" I asked, apprehensive about being left alone.

"To another area of the factory," he said, trying to reassure me. He cupped the back of my head, his leather gloved fingers sliding over my hair as he pulled me close. "I need to take care of things."

"Things?" I grimaced. "The body?"

He nodded. "Your DNA and mine are all over him. I need to make sure he's clean before…"

"Before you dump him?" I guessed, thinking how close we were to Galveston Bay. "In the water?"

"Yes. The currents are usually favorable for this kind of disposal, but sometimes things don't work the way they should. If he gets fished out of the water too quickly, I want to make sure there's no trace of us left on him."

I wasn't sure I wanted to hear his answer, but I asked anyway. "Is this the best way to handle it? I mean," I sighed, "I know it's not like the movies, but what about, you know, a barrel of acid or fire or something like that? Like they do in TV shows and stuff?"

His expression turned from one of guilt at exposing me to this side of his life to one of shock. "Jesus Christ, Holly, what the fuck are you watching?" A second later, he added, "Yes, there are other ways, but this is the right one for this job. I need it to look like it has nothing to do with you or me. If he's found, it needs to look like some bikers got him. There are bars and clubhouses up and down the coast. If he washes up, that's where police will go first with their questions."

"What if—"

Kostya swooped in and silenced me with a kiss. "No more questions, Holly. Stay here. I'll come get you."

He left without another word, shutting me away in the windowless box that had once been an office. With an annoyed huff, I sat down on the squeaky chair. It was surprisingly comfy and well-built. I spun around in a slow circle and observed the shelves packed with yellowed manuals and cracked brown binders. There was an ancient dot matrix printer on the other wall and a fax machine that had to be older than me.

Bored and sure I was going to be stuck here for a while, I reached for one of the manuals. I blew the dust from it and cracked the spine. It was a manual for some sort of chemical process to clean metal. Hands-down, it was the most tedious thing I'd ever read, but I kept reading. I fought the urge to get up and open the door and look for Kostya. He had been very clear, and even though I wanted to know what he was doing, I trusted that he knew what was best for me right now.

Turning the page on the manual, I tried to imagine my mother in a place like this. She must have spent so many hours listening to operators and supervisors mansplain the petrochemical business to her in rooms just like this one. It couldn't have been easy climbing as high as she had in a field dominated by men.

If she could see me now, she would have blown a gasket. All the lessons she had taught me about staying away from men like Kostya—and here I was, hiding in an abandoned factory while the man I loved did unspeakable things to keep me safe. The fear of disappointing her made my stomach churn. She'd done everything for me, worked so hard to make sure I had the life she hadn't, and now I was risking it all for Kostya.

She'll never know. No one will ever know what happened tonight. It had to be that way. I had to keep this ugly secret forever.

Ninety-four pages into the manual, I heard a noise outside the door. I sat up straighter, closing the manual, and listened. Was it an animal? One of those cats I'd seen earlier? A rat? A racoon?

Footsteps.

It didn't sound like Kostya. He moved with stealth. These footsteps were loud and clumsy. I stood up carefully, holding my breath and praying the chair wouldn't squeak. Looking around, I searched frantically for a weapon. My gaze landed on a broom in the corner. I picked it up, gripping it like a bat, and got ready to swing as the door started to open inward.

I didn't hesitate. I swung as hard as I could, aiming for the dark hooded figure coming into the office. The intruder hissed and ducked, and I slammed the broom into the metal door, shattering the wood and crying out as the impact rattled my wrists.

"Holy shit, lady!" The intruder flung back her hoodie, revealing dark hair and electric blue cat-eye glasses. "I'm not your enemy, Holly!"

Still holding a large piece of the broom, I held it up, ready to swing at her again. "How do you know my name?"

"My company installed the security system at your salon, remember? Hen House Security? That's me." She touched her chest. "I'm Fox. Kostya is a friend of mine."

She was right. I finally recognized her. Realizing I'd almost knocked her head off, I dropped the broom. "Oh my god! I'm so sorry!"

"No, it's okay. I would have taken that swing, too." She looked me over and asked, "Are you okay? Did you get hurt?"

"I'm okay."

"And K? Is he okay?"

"I'm fine, Fox." He appeared behind her, startling us both. Scowling at Fox, he asked, "What are you doing here?"

"What do you think I'm doing here?" she retorted sarcastically. "Your perimeter cameras at the house went batshit. I caught someone sneaking into her house. I tried to call you, but you didn't answer. I managed to find Sunny and sent her to the house. You were gone when she got there, but Holly's car was still in the garage. She smelled bleach and figured you'd left to take care of a problem."

"Where's Sunny now?"

"She found a motorcycle a few blocks away. She ditched hers in Holly's garage and drove the other one to a chop shop."

"Devil?"

Fox nodded. "Sunny trusts him, and he hates those fucking bikers. He'll make that bike disappear by morning."

"And you came here because…?"

"Because I wasn't sure if you needed help," she said. "You weren't at the house. You weren't answering your phone. I checked all the security logs on your buildings, and this was the only place you'd visited."

"I appreciate you checking on us, but we're good."

"You're not," she argued. "Nate came to see me right before you got attacked at Holly's place."

"And?"

"And he was really adamant that you contact Gabe. Like tonight. Like now," she said, reaching into her hoodie and producing a cheap phone. "Nate gave me a number. It's fully charged and ready to go."

He took the phone from Fox and pocketed it. Looking at me, he said, "I need you to go with Fox now."

"What?" I shook my head. "No way! I don't want to be separated from you."

"It's safer this way." He stepped toward me, and Fox quietly left the office. "Holly," he cupped my face, "if Gabe is trying to reach me like this, it's urgent. It's the kind of urgent that means terrible things are coming. I need to handle it, and I need to know you're safe. Fox has places all over the city where you can hide. Stay with her, and you'll be safe. I'll come for you as soon as I can."

"Kostya, please," I begged, my eyes stinging with tears. "Let me come with you."

"Holly," he breathed my name and pressed his forehead to mine. "I need to handle some things so I *can* be with you in the future. I need to make sure all of this shit is *done*." He kissed me with so much love that I started to cry. "I want out, Holly. I want a real chance with you. I have to do this."

Sniffling, I kissed him, clinging to his shoulders as if he might disappear into thin air. "You better come back for me."

"I will, Holly." He crushed me in his arms, holding me so tight I couldn't breathe. I didn't care. I wanted to stay with him, just like this, forever. Letting go, he stepped back. "Stay with Fox. Call in sick to work. I'll contact you as soon as I can."

I nodded silently, wiping away the tears on my face. He turned his back on me and strode out of the office, stopping just long enough to give Fox instructions. And then he was gone.

CHAPTER TWENTY-ONE

"HOUSE OR APARTMENT?" Fox asked as she barreled down the highway in her black Jeep.

"What?"

"Do you want to lay low in a house or apartment? I have access to both."

"I'm fine with whatever," I decided. "It's my first time doing this safe house thing so I don't have a preference, I guess."

"Yeah, it's a bit of a mind-fuck the first time," she said, switching lanes. "Hopefully, you won't have to do this again."

"How many times have you had to run like this?"

"Twice." She sped up to pass a truck and switched lanes again. "You hungry?"

Surprisingly, I was. I had been queasy after being attacked and watching Kostya manhandle a dead body wrapped in a shower curtain. My stomach throbbed with emptiness now. "I wouldn't say no to breakfast."

"Tacos okay?"

"Sure."

"There's a taco truck that I really like. It rolls around town, usually near construction sites. It has the best breakfast tacos. Barbacoa that melts like butter in your mouth on these super soft corn tortillas..." She smiled excitedly. "It's a spiritual experience."

Recognizing the same quirks in her that had endeared me to Savvy, I asked, "You eat a lot of early morning breakfast tacos?"

"I have problems sleeping." Her playful smile faded, and her hands tightened on the steering wheel. "I'm trying to get a better handle on self-medicating so I drive a lot. I get hungry. I eat. It's a cycle."

"Have you thought about therapy? One of my friends had an issue with insomnia. She saw a counselor and sleeps like a baby now."

Fox snorted. "If I went to a therapist with my story, she'd either have me committed as a nutcase or call the police and have me picked up for murder."

"Oh," I said quietly, wondering just how safe I was with her.

"It was self-defense," she added quickly. "My boyfriend." She shifted uncomfortably in her seat. "He wasn't the guy I thought he was. He was a monster, and he did terrible shit. When I figured out what he'd been doing, I tried to leave, but he was bigger and stronger. Before I knew it, we were fighting to the death. Somehow, I won, and suddenly, I had a body at my feet."

"Kostya?" I asked, thinking how similar her tale was to mine.

She nodded. "He came over and handled it."

"Is that how you met?"

"No." Fox shook her head. "When I was in high school, I got into some trouble. Hacking and money laundering and illegal gambling," she explained with a wave of her hand. "I, uh, got on the wrong side of the Albanians that run most of that action here in the city. Kostya saw something in me, I guess. Something useful. He got me out of that mess and helped me get right."

"Are there others like you? Other people he's helped in his own strange way?"

"Yeah. Me and some other girls you'll probably meet soon," she said, turning into a parking lot with a brightly painted taco truck and a busy line of construction workers. She parked and reached over to tug on my hood. "Put this up, and stay here. Keep your head down and don't look around. There aren't any traffic or security cams high def enough to get a good shot of you, but I don't want to take any chances."

I covered my hair and ducked my face, staring at my lap. She wasn't gone long, giving me just enough time to start thinking about how I had lost complete control of my life. By the time she got back in the Jeep, handing me a paper bag filled with tacos, I had so many questions and wasn't sure if she had the answers. "What happens now, Fox?"

"We're going to a place I have on Capitol Street." She buckled her seatbelt and backed out of our makeshift parking space. "Once we get there, I'll set up a burner for you. It will ring out as your regular number so none of your friends or family will think anything of it. You'll let everyone know you're not feeling well. You'll eat breakfast and go to sleep."

"I don't know if I can sleep," I admitted, my head touching the window. "I'm so amped up."

"It will pass," she said matter-of-factly. "You'll drop like a rock. You aren't used to the adrenaline and cortisol spike. You'll crash for a few hours."

"Are you used to the spikes?"

She laughed. "Girl, I smoke so much fucking pot medicating my anxiety that my adrenal gland is saturated. I probably couldn't even manage a spike if someone held a gun to my head. And anyway," she continued, "I'm not really a hands-on kind of helper. That's more Sunny and Lobo. Max and I are the brains behind most of Kostya's more intricate jobs. I don't get my hands dirty or get exposed to much of the scary shit anymore."

"Who are Lobo and Max?"

"Two of the other spiders," she explained. "That's what he calls us. We're his little spiders crawling all over the city for him. I handle most of the tech. Sunny does the skiptracing. Max is our resident scientist, and Lobo is, like, his apprentice." She glanced at me and added, "That's about all you'll get out of me on that topic. Their stories are theirs to tell."

Suddenly feeling tired and cranky, I rubbed my forehead. "I understand."

"I know it's a lot, Holly." She reached across and squeezed my arm. "It's easy to accept that crazy shit like this happens to other people, but it's hard to take when it's happening to you."

Feeling as though I could trust her, I asked, "Do you think he'll ever be able to get out? To walk away from the mafia?"

She was quiet for a moment. "Others have done it. Ivan Markovic, Sergei Sakharov—they've both left."

"But?"

"Their cases were different than Kostya's. Ivan and Sergei were street soldiers. They were high up in the local hierarchy, but they weren't a huge threat to the original family back in Moscow."

"But Kostya is," I said quietly.

"Literally knows where the bodies are buried," she interjected. "And that doesn't even take into account the shit he did with FSB before he joined the mob."

"What's FSB? Is that a different mafia family?"

Eyes wide, Fox glanced at me. "Did he not tell you about FSB?"

"No. What is it?" I asked, dread creeping back into my chest.

"*Federal'naya sluzhba bezopasnosti Rossiyskoy Federatsii,*" she said in what sounded like perfect Russian. "Federal Security Service of the Russian Federation," she translated. "It's basically the modern version of the KGB. Technically, it was FSK when Kostya joined as a teenager and got renamed to FSB later."

I swallowed hard. "So, he was, like, Russian CIA?"

"Yeah, basically," she confirmed. "That's how he learned all the skills he uses now as a cleaner."

I felt my world tilting again. Kostya wasn't just in the mob. He had been a spy. A secret agent. "Is Konstantin Antonovich even his real name?"

"Konstantin is," she confirmed. "When he joined as a teenager, they gave him a clean name and papers. Konstantin died with his parents. When he got burned, he decided there was no reason to hide under an alias anymore. He went back to his birth name."

"Burned? I didn't see any scars on his body."

"Not that kind of burned," she said. "It's what they call it when a spy's cover gets blown and they lose the support of their government. It's why he had to leave FSB."

"Why was he burned?"

"Politics," she said matter-of-factly. "He needed to get out so he went to the big boss in Moscow, got put together with Nikolai and came here to Houston."

"But, I mean, like our government knows what he was, right?" I gripped my seatbelt tighter as I considered how many people might have me under surveillance.

"Sure, they know, but they also know that he knows the dirtiest shit about the things they were doing. There's a professional sort of courtesy they have when agents retire. As long as he doesn't meddle in government affairs here or try to support Russian government ops, they don't bother him."

"But he's in the mob here," I protested.

"You know that. I know that. Is there proof?" She looked at me and shrugged. "The police here know what goes on with Nikolai and the Albanians and Nickel Jackson and the Reyes brothers and the cartel and bikers—but if they could prove their crimes, they'd have them all in jail. These guys that run around in the underworld are fucking smart. They're careful. They're clean. They stay out of trouble."

"What if their luck doesn't hold? What if someone makes a mistake?"

"There are ways to handle that."

"Like?"

"Bribes. Blackmail."

"And if that doesn't work?"

"Exile."

"To where?"

She shrugged. "A country without extradition treaties, or a place where you have friends who can help you live under the radar."

"Where would you go?" I wondered, thinking how easily she took all of this in stride.

"Nepal," she answered without hesitation. "I'd embrace my inner Doctor Strange and find myself in a temple somewhere."

"Doctor Strange?"

"You know, Steven Strange?" She made bizarre movements with her hand almost as if she were performing a magic trick. "Brilliant, asshole surgeon who tears up his hands in a car wreck so he runs away to the Himalayas to find the Ancient One to heal him, but in the end, he becomes the Sorcerer Supreme."

Still confused, I asked, "Is this, like, a superhero thing?"

"Are you kidding me?"

"No."

"Jesus, okay, listen, after you take your nap, we're having a Marvel marathon."

"I don't know if that's something I—"

"Listen, you can sit in my safe house and worry about Kostya or you can kick back and let me distract you with sexy superheroes. This will all go a lot faster if you're keeping your mind occupied."

"Fine." Grudgingly, I nodded and accepted her advice. When we turned onto Sampson Street, I studied our surroundings. It was a mix of residential and commercial. It seemed as if there were attempts to gentrify the area. By the looks of it, the attempts weren't very successful.

"This is us," she said, turning onto Capitol and then into a private alley between rows of townhouses. The one car garages were hidden along the back of each unit. As she pulled into ours, I said, "This place looks new and really nice."

"The listing called it industrial chic or some realtor shit like that." She snorted. "I try not to think about the asbestos they probably tiled over and the lead paint they just covered with a few coats of primer." She killed the engine. "But I got a good deal on it. Most of the townhouses in this price point are absolute hell holes, you know?"

"Yeah." Unbuckling my seatbelt as our journey came to its end, I asked, "What do you think he's doing right now?"

"Who? Big K?"

"Yes."

"Plotting," she said seriously. "Trying to get a handle on his murder rabies."

"What the hell are murder rabies?"

"That's what Max calls it when one of his loved ones gets hurt," she explained. "The only cure is death—and he's the grim reaper."

CHAPTER TWENTY-TWO

"Y OU'RE A HARD man to reach," Gabe Reyes growled, his voice rough and deep.

"I've been busy," Kostya said, spraying an enzymatic cleaner into the trunk of his car.

"You and me both, asshole."

Kostya smirked at Gabe's rudeness. It wasn't anything personal. It was just his usual attitude toward everyone. "I'll show more professional courtesy next time."

"You better," Gabe snapped. "I don't have time to chase you down, man. I'm over here running down multiple leads, keeping tabs on the cartel and this psycho fucking old Russian and you can't even pick up the damn phone?"

"I apologize, Gabe," Kostya said, hoping that was enough to soothe the irritated mercenary.

"Yeah, man, what the fuck ever," he snarled. "Listen, you got problems, Kostya. Your city? It's about to get really loud and really bloody."

"Oh?" He moved the phone between his ear and shoulder and reached into his black bag for another bottle of solution that he used to saturate a few spots of the trunk upholstery.

"I've been keeping an eye on the cartel stragglers who haven't pledged loyalty to Hector. I figured there's a chance they'll lead me to Lorenzo or the escaped con the old lady has me chasing down. A Border Patrol agent I pay for intel let me know that the stragglers all crossed over yesterday evening," Gabe explained. "They came across at different points— Hidalgo, Laredo, Progreso, Brownsville. Some of them were in private vehicles. The others came in commercial trucks. It's a mix of Mexican nationals and Americans."

"How many?"

"Nineteen."

"Shit." He glanced at his watch and then did the mental math on how long it would have taken them to drive from the border to Houston. Glancing around the empty warehouse parking lot, he said, "They're here already."

"Yeah. I figured I'd let you know in case Hector wasn't aware of what was coming."

He hadn't heard from Hector in weeks. The new cartel kingpin was busy rebuilding his empire and swatting the last of Lorenzo's forces, but he should have been trading more information.

"Hit squad?"

"Some of them, yes. The rest aren't well trained. There will be collateral damage."

He winced, thinking of all the innocent lives that could be lost and all of the publicity and police that would bring. Nikolai was going to go ballistic. "Thanks for the heads up."

"Wish I could be more help, man. Call Diego and Nate. I sent them a list of the names. These guys will probably try to hide in their territory until they strike. My brothers might be able to give you some intel from the streets."

"I'll find them later."

"You get one of my brothers shot, and I'll shoot you, Kostya. You know that, right?"

"I know you will." From anyone else, he would have considered it an empty threat, but Gabe was fiercely protective of his family. He had done much worse than shoot someone to earn his exile.

"I'll be in touch if I have any other updates." Gabe seemed to hesitate before adding, "Watch your back. You've got an avalanche of shit coming at you."

"Duly noted."

"Get rid of the phone."

The call ended, and he broke down the phone. He finished detailing the trunk of his car, checked through his mental cleaning list to make sure he hadn't missed a step and finally got behind the wheel. The urge to call or message Holly was strong. He pushed it away, reminding himself that every second he wasted was a second that his enemies were plotting. Grabbing his work phone, he called Artyom.

"Yeah?" Artyom grumbled on the second ring, his voice groggy with sleep.

"It's me. I'm coming over." He hung up and called Sunny next.

"Did Fox find you?" Sunny asked, all business.

"She did."

"Are you guys okay?"

"We're fine. Fox has Holly."

"Safe house?"

"Yes."

"Do you know which one?"

"I didn't ask."

KOSTYA | 321

"Well, I'm almost done at Holly's house. You owe her some new cleaning supplies," Sunny warned. "I wasn't sure where I needed to clean so I've done the whole house."

"Thanks."

"You get rid of the trash?"

"Yes. Fox said you found a bike?"

"I handled it."

"Listen, we have another problem." He quickly filled her in on what Gabe had told him.

"What do you need me to do?" she asked, ready for her orders.

"Get with Fox. Have her open surveillance on all of our tier one and two locations. Put the word out on the street that we're paying for good information."

"Anything else?"

"Tell Max to take Lobo out of the city. I don't want either one of them here for the storm that's coming."

"I'll handle them first. I'll touch base later."

"Be careful."

"You first," she said and ended the call.

He tossed his phone into a cup holder in the center console and stretched his neck. As he idled at a red light, he tried to get into the mind of the Mexican kill squad that had been sent to Houston. They wouldn't try for big targets first. They would go lower down the food chain—street soldiers like Boychenko. Maybe hit a few captains like Artyom or Danny or the men who had gotten out like Ivan and Sergei.

Or, if they were looking to make a statement, they would go after the women and children. Vivian, Erin, Lena, Benny, Bianca, Holly—the women were the targets that would cause the most pain for Nikolai.

He wiped his face and hit the gas. Losing men was expected. A captain here, a few street soldiers there—it was just part of doing business. But families? Wives, girlfriends, kids—never. It would be the greatest failure of his life if one of them were hurt.

Yet, he couldn't deny that using them as bait was probably the easiest way to end this whole mess with the cartel once and for all. It was risky. It was dangerous. It could end badly, but the thought wouldn't leave him as he made the drive back into Houston.

He tried to remind himself that he had been planning for an event like this for years. There were layers of security. There were protocols in place. The men were trained. They knew what to look for and how to react. Drawing the hit squad into a trap using the wives and girlfriends would be relatively easy to plan.

When he pulled up to Artyom's townhouse, he turned off the engine and took a moment behind the wheel to gather his thoughts. Stepping out of the car, he glanced around the quiet neighborhood. Most of Artyom's neighbors were retirees or older singles. Anyone lurking around and hoping to make trouble would be spotted easily enough.

Glancing at the sky, he estimated how long they had until sunrise. Locking his car, he checked the street again before taking the sidewalk to the front door. Before he had even raised his hand to knock, the door opened and Artyom used it to shield his body. His gaze was narrowed with suspicion, and he had a gun in hand but pointed at the floor.

"Sorry to wake you so early." Kostya stepped inside and

waited for Artyom to lock the front door.

"I don't even want to fucking know," Artyom grumbled, his eyes still tired and his cheeks and head thick with stubble. He placed his loaded gun on the entryway table and scratched at his neck. His sweats hung low on his stomach. His bare chest and upper arms were a roadmap of dirty deeds and crimes, the dark tattoos covering almost every inch of skin. His forearms and hands were sparingly decorated, but there were more hidden under his pants.

"Scorpion broke into Holly's house, held a knife on her and tried to kill us both." There was no point in delivering the information in a nice way.

Artyom swore roughly in Russian before turning on his heel. "We need coffee."

"I'd prefer vodka."

Artyom pointed to the rolling bar cart in his kitchen as he continued to the coffee maker on the counter. "Scorpion?"

"Handled." He looked around the ultra-sleek and modern kitchen. It had been Artyom's last remodeling project in the townhouse. Soon, the street captain would put it up for sale, find a new property to flip on his downtime and settle in for a few months. Artyom had made a sizeable amount of money flipping properties around the city. It was part of his retirement plan. Every now and then, he would let another soldier in on the deals and share some of the profits and knowledge.

"Holly's safe?"

"Yes." He helped himself to a heavy splash of vodka and kicked it back in one swallow. He breathed out the fiery burn and then poured a little more. "I sent her to a safe house."

"One of ours?"

"No."

"Probably for the best," Artyom agreed. "If you sent her to one of ours, Nikolai would be beating down the door in half an hour." He glanced over his shoulder. "Does he know?"

"Not yet," Kostya murmured before downing the rest of the vodka.

"I'd rather not be there when he does."

"I don't want to be there either," he replied with a frown. "I promised him I'd keep her safe."

"Technically, you did." Artyom placed a mug of hot coffee on the center island for him.

"I don't think Kolya is going to be happy about technicalities. Do you want milk?"

"Yes. You know, if you have worse news than Holly and Scorpion, give it to him after. Make it quick," Artyom suggested. "He'll be so pissed off by the new information that he'll forget about the other mess you've made with his sister."

It wasn't the worst the plan he'd ever heard. Before he opened the refrigerator to grab Artyom's milk, he noticed the childish drawings and art hung on the stainless steel. His gaze drifted to the paper zebra frame around a photo of Artyom with Chess and her little girl at the zoo. Artyom looked good in the photo. Happy. Natural. He was the kind of man meant to be a father.

"So, you and Chess?" he asked, stooping low to get the milk carton from the refrigerator.

"Careful," Artyom warned, his voice deepening. "I'm not interested in any opinions on how I choose to spend my free time."

Kostya held up a hand as he brought the milk to the island.

"I don't have a problem with it. Neither does the boss."

"But you talked about it."

"We did," he confirmed. "I was told to leave you out of the dirtier work. Kolya doesn't want you getting in trouble."

"I appreciate the thought, but doing the dirty work is my job. It's the whole reason I came here with him." Artyom reached for the milk and poured in enough to turn his coffee a pale brown. "It's not that kind of relationship, though."

"What does that mean? You aren't fucking her?"

Artyom scowled at him. "Do you have to be so fucking crass?"

"I'm just asking." He shrugged and returned the milk to the refrigerator. "Is that a no?"

"It's complicated," Artyom finally said. "I care about Chess. I shouldn't have let myself get close to her, but it happened so slowly that I didn't even recognize what it was until—"

"Until you realized you loved her?"

"Yeah."

"Does she love you?"

"I don't know," Artyom admitted. "Sometimes, I think she's going to tell me that she cares about me. Sometimes, I think about finally asking her to go out on a date."

"You haven't even taken her out?"

"Have you taken out Holly?"

"No," he admitted bitterly.

"Then shut the fuck up about my relationship with Chess," Artyom snapped. "Worry about your own business."

"I forgot how pissed off you get in the morning," Kostya replied, not at all taken aback by Artyom's rudeness. "Listen, take it from the man who waited too long to make his move. Quit fucking around and make it happen with Chees. You're getting too old to play these fucking games. If you love her and you want to be that kid's dad, you better you make your move before someone else does. Someone who won't take care of them the way you will," he added pointedly.

"When the fuck did you become Dr. Phil?"

Kostya chortled and sipped his coffee. "I've had a lot of time to think the last few weeks. I'm feeling all the time I've wasted. All the time I've lost scuttling around in the dark. I'm tired of all of it."

Artyom's eyebrows rose. "You want out?"

Kostya exhaled a long, slow breath. "Yes."

"Nikolai would let you go tomorrow, but the old man..." Artyom shook his head. "I don't know, Kostya. It could get dangerous. Especially with the Holly problem," he commented worriedly. "You know how possessive the old man can be."

"I do." Knowing Artyom was trying to be a good friend, he said, "I'll be careful."

"What the hell are we going to do without you?"

"I have contingency plans in place," he promised. "Some of my spiders are more than capable of taking over for me, and we can always promote someone from within the ranks."

"Like?"

"Boychenko," he said.

"The kid?" Artyom asked incredulously. "He's not made for your kind of work."

"We don't what that Boy's capable of because he's never been given a chance," Kostya countered. "I think he could be taught to be a good cleaner. He's a blank slate. He has no bad habits to break. He's a sponge waiting to be filled with knowledge."

Artyom grumbled low and took a thoughtful drink of his coffee. "The boss won't like it."

"He doesn't have to like it. He just has to trust me."

"Good luck convincing him of that." Artyom swirled the coffee in his cup with a slight movement of his wrist. "You didn't wake me up to talk about Holly and Scorpion. Why are you really here?"

"Gabe Reyes called me. He's working with someone I trust, and he wanted me to know that a kill squad came across the border yesterday. They're headed here."

"It's finally happening, huh?"

"Yes. Today."

"Of all the fucking days! We're already stretched thin on the streets, and we've got two teams on Erin and Bianca."

"When do Ivan and Sergei get back?"

"Tonight. Should I call them back earlier?"

Kostya shook his head. "It might tip the cartel off that we know."

"What's your plan?"

"We bait a trap."

"With?" Artyom's face slackened as he seemed to put the pieces together. "You want to use the women as bait?"

"As much as it turns my stomach, using Vivian and the others is probably the easiest way to catch these assholes. They want to hurt Nikolai personally for the way he supported the coup against Lorenzo. Going after his wife or the wives of his friends is the way to do that." Worried Artyom might be badly distracted, he asked, "Chess?"

"She and Aly are in Los Angeles on business. They're staying at Disneyland for a few days."

"Good. We know they're safe."

"And the others? Are they going to be safe? What if we fuck up?"

"We won't." He tried to sound certain, but there was always a chance that things would go south.

Artyom blew out a noisy breath and wiped his hand across his face. "I'm going to need more coffee."

CHAPTER TWENTY-THREE

"YOU SURE YOU don't want me to bring you something? Maybe some soup?" Savannah offered, her voice filled with concern. "Or I can run you to urgent care if you think you need fluids or medicine."

I hated lying to my best friend. "No, I'm starting to feel better. I'm going to rest and focus on rehydrating myself."

"Seriously, though, how many times have I told you not to eat that garbage grocery store sushi?"

"I know. I'm paying for it now."

"Okay, well, if you change your mind about soup or a ride, call me. I'm staying late to get catch up on some paperwork and inventory and restocking."

"Be careful, Savvy. Those boxes are heavy, and unpacking them is a two-person job."

"Lana is staying late with me. I'm training her on our inventory systems. She's ready to take on more responsibility."

"Maybe talk to her a little bit about community college," I suggested. "She's so smart, Savvy, and I don't want her to miss out on opportunities."

"I'm right there with you on that, Holly. I'll talk to her. I'll ask her to look into HCC or Lone Star. The only hurdle will be her English fluency."

"She's really making a lot of headway. I'm sure there are classes she can take to help her become more fluent. We can call the admissions offices and see what they recommend. It can't hurt to ask."

"I agree." She paused, and I could hear her being paged by Billie. "They need me back on the floor. Call me if you need anything."

"I will."

"Take care, hon."

Hanging up the burner phone that Fox had given me, I settled back into the cozy couch and closed my eyes. I didn't like lying. It made me feel gross. Deep down, I knew that Savannah would understand why I was telling tales, but it didn't make me feel any better.

"You're protecting them by lying," Fox said from behind a massive bank of computer screens on the other side of the open living area. She had been monitoring different security feeds and traffic cameras all day. Her phone would ring every half hour or so and she'd give someone—Sunny, possibly—an update.

"I know," I replied glumly. Glancing at her surveillance setup, I asked, "How are things going?"

"Quiet, mostly," she said and pushed out of her chair. "I'm headed to the kitchen. You want anything?"

I shook my head and gestured to the leftover pizza on the table. "I'm still full."

"I'll stick the rest of this in the refrigerator." She snatched up the box on her way to the kitchen. "Do you want another drink?"

"I'm good."

"Did you get a hold of your mom yet?" she yelled over the sound of ice cubes blasting her cup.

"No," I called back. "That's not unusual, though. She's always in meetings and taking calls. I sent her a text, and it was read so she knows I'm taking a personal day to help a friend."

"You think she'll buy it?" Fox asked, coming back into the living area with three Dr. Pepper cans clamped between her left arm and her body and a full glass in the other. "Because if she goes by your house and you're not there and she starts poking around…"

"She won't go by the house without calling me first. She's always been very respectful about my privacy."

"Because she caught you *in flagrante delicto* once before?" she guessed with a teasing smile.

My face got hot just remembering the one and only time my mother had ever barged into my bedroom and found me flat on my back, legs in the air, with my then-boyfriend's head buried between my thighs. "I was twenty and home on summer break. It was super embarrassing."

Fox laughed. "That's one of the perks of not having family, I guess. Nobody ever bothered me about sneaking a little afternoon delight."

"No family? Did you grow up in foster care?"

She nodded. "Yeah. It wasn't horrible like a *Lifetime* movie or anything. I had some really nice foster parents. I was older when I went into system—seven—and I had some behavior issues so I wasn't ever top of the list for adoption." She shrugged. "I had a pretty good childhood all the same. I'd already finished high school at sixteen, and my last foster mom helped me get everything together so I could be emancipated at seventeen. Never really looked back after that."

"Do you keep in touch with any of the families that fostered you?"

"Sure. Christmas and birthday cards. That kind of thing."

A knock at the door interrupted us. Fox instantly produced a handgun from behind her desk and tapped on her keyboard. She relaxed after a few stiff, apprehensive moments and tucked the gun back away in her desk. "It's Sunny."

"I'll get it." I rose from the couch and answered the door, being careful not to show my face as I opened it. As soon as Sunny stepped through the door, I recognized her. The fuchsia and orchid mohawk she was sporting had been one of my most favorite styles to come out of our salon in the last few weeks. "You're one of Nisha's clients!"

"Yep," she said, shifting the white plastic shopping bag from one hand to the other. She shut and locked the door behind her. "Don't answer the door again."

Her strict tone took me by surprise. "Okay."

"Seriously, Kostya will have our asses if anything happens to you." Sunny's appraising gaze swept the townhouse. She frowned at the television screen. "Is she making you watch all her superhero movies?"

"They're fun," I said, feeling a little defensive of Fox. "I needed the mental escape."

"If she starts throwing comics at you, run. You'll end up listening to her argue about which comic storyline the MCU needs to adapt next. Secret Wars versus Secret Invasion versus Wang the Conqueror—"

"It's Kang the Conqueror," Fox corrected grumpily. "You go see Nate for info?"

"Yeah." Sunny held out the plastic shopping bag. "He sent you a gift from his grandma."

"Ooh!" Fox reacted with excitement and rushed away from her monitors. "Tamales! Gimme!"

Sunny held it away from her. "Promise me you will not eat the whole dozen tonight."

Fox rolled her eyes. "Stop policing my food intake."

"Don't call me whining for Tums at three in the morning." Sunny handed over the package.

"I'll call Max," Fox replied, taking the package in both hands and hugging it close. "She won't let me suffer."

"Max and Lobo are out of pocket."

"What? When?"

"Daddy's orders," Sunny said. "He wanted them out of town. Max took Lobo to IAH, picked a flight and they're on their way to New York."

"City? Or state?"

"Both, apparently. They're going to spend a couple of days doing the tourist thing in the city and then a couple of days at a B&B in Sleepy Hollow."

"What! That was my idea!" Fox pouted. "I was going to take Lobo to Sleepy Hollow and Salem! We were going to do the whole Sanderson Sisters thing!"

Sunny shrugged. "Take her again. Kid needs to get out more anyway. She spends too much time practicing her weapons drills and—"

"Kid?" I interrupted, trying to follow their conversation. "How old is Lobo?" Another thought struck me. "Is she his daughter?"

"No!" The both answered in unison before exchanging a

worried glance.

Fox eventually answered me. "He found Lobo when she was a little girl. He brought her back to Houston, and we sort of all adopted her."

"Technically, Max did adopt her," Sunny corrected. "She's Lobo's guardian until she turns eighteen."

"But she's a kid," I interjected, aghast at the idea of someone young being pulled into all this bullshit. "Why is a teenager being exposed to this?" My stomach dropped. "Is he...is he training her? To kill people? To clean up crime scenes?"

Sunny seemed uncomfortable. "Look, I think these are questions you should address to Kostya."

"You're damn right they are," I grumbled, getting to my feet and taking my new phone with me. Sunny and Fox started to argue in low voices as I marched into the bedroom I'd been given and closed the door. Feeling sick to my stomach at the idea of a little girl being taught to do the horrible things Kostya did, I angrily tapped a message to him.

Are you seriously training a teenager to do your job? WTF, Kostya!

I paced the room as I waited for his response. My stomach churned even more when I started to understand that I had no idea what other secrets he had. Until last night, I'd been able to convince myself that his mysterious, illegal work didn't affect me in any way. I hadn't been forced to confront the reality of what he did.

He kills people.

He killed for me.

I rubbed my face with both hands and wondered what it said about me that I wasn't as bothered about him killing Scorpion. The man had tried to kill us both. It was easier to excuse what he'd done because our lives had been in danger. I told myself it was different than if Kostya had just killed someone to protect the illicit business of the mafia.

But he's done that.

All of the news stories about gangland style murders and the street violence raced through my head. How many had he been involved in? How many other crimes had never been reported because he'd made them disappear like the body in my house?

It struck me then that the same hands that touched me so lovingly were the same hands that had done terrible, violent things. As much as it pained me to admit, I would welcome those hands back on me in a heartbeat. Love hadn't blinded me to his faults. It had only made it easier to accept them. I accepted Kostya for the man he was instead of the man I desperately wanted him to be.

A series of alarms interrupted my troubled thoughts. I hurried out of the bedroom and into the living area where Fox and Sunny were talking quickly and staring at the many computer monitors. Fox moved from station to station, tapping her keyboards and cursing up a storm.

"Shit." Sunny's brow furrowed. "That's the Markovic place, right?"

"Yeah."

"Do we have eyes on the wife?" she asked, leaning forward.

"Erin," I said, rushing to join them. "Her name is Erin."

There were multiple security system feeds on the monitors. My gaze moved to the monitor that had taken all of Sunny's focus. A brown delivery truck was parked in front of Erin's luxurious home. There were men in matching uniforms and guns standing on the porch and inside the entryway of the house. My heart skipped a beat at the sight of a bald man on the floor, face down and in a pool of blood. He looked familiar, like one of the guards that sometimes came to the salon with Vivian.

"K, you've got five assholes at the Markovic house," Sunny said into her phone. "Looks one of your men is down. It's Arty. I'm looking for Erin now—"

"There," Fox said, pointing at a monitor. "They've got her."

My attention jumped to the screen Fox indicated. Erin, her hands cuffed in front of her and some kind of fabric stuffed in her mouth, struggled with two men trying to drag her out of the house. I covered my mouth to stifle my shocked gasp. Both of her feet were off the ground as she kicked and twisted, throwing her elbows and even trying to headbutt the man who hoisted her up into the back of the truck. She was tossed into the back and the other man jumped in behind her. The door swung closed, and the vehicle sped out of the driveway.

"Fuck," Sunny swore sharply into the phone she held. "Looks like they've got Erin in a delivery truck. We've got 911 on the way. I'm heading after the truck. Better get eyes on Vivian. Call me when you get this."

"I need to get back to my building," Fox said as Sunny pocketed her phone. "I need access to the traffic cams and other shit."

"Go," Sunny ordered. "Find that truck." She looked at me

and frowned. "You stay here. Doors locked. Blinds closed. Lights off. You are a ghost here, understand?"

I nodded, my heart racing with anxiety. "I'll be fine. Go. Help your friends."

"Kostya or I will come back for you later," Sunny said as she strode to the door. "We'll move you to a different safe house as soon as we can."

Without a look back, Sunny was gone. Fox gathered up her things, gave me a quick and encouraging hug and ran to the garage entrance by the kitchen. As she slipped on a pair of sneakers left there, she said, "I've got security all over this place. You're safe here. Just don't leave."

Just like Sunny, she was gone without giving me time to reply. Talking to the closed door, I said, "But those were my shoes…"

CHAPTER TWENTY-FOUR

"WHAT A FUCKING shit show," Ilya snarled as he hustled a wounded Ten into a waiting SUV.

"I don't need your bullshit right now," Kostya snapped back. Fully aware that he'd fucked up and underestimated the crew sent from Mexico, he had already taken responsibility for the disaster unfolding before him. At this point, his focus was on fixing the fuck-up and getting everyone home safely.

Glaring daggers, Ilya slammed the door shut once Ten was in the backseat. "I can't believe Artyom agreed with this bullshit bait plan of yours. Now he's fucking shot and in the hospital. Foma and Mitya are dead in Vanya's house. Boss's wife almost got killed." He gestured to the warehouse art studio where Ten and Vivian had been ambushed. "We've got to get Ten fixed up before his PO catches him and tosses his ass back in prison. And now we've lost Ivan and Sergei's wives plus Danny and Boy!"

"We haven't lost them," Kostya remarked roughly. He was checking his phone for the hundredth time when Fox sent a message that she had found the delivery truck that had taken Erin and was running through traffic cams to track it to its final destination. "We'll have their location soon."

"Yeah? And if they've been hurt? You want to be the one

KOSTYA | 339

that tells Vanya that the only woman he's ever loved got taken? Got raped? Got killed?" Ilya shook his head. "You sure as shit are not delegating that job to me."

"They'll be fine," Kostya ground out, his voice calm while his stomach was a mess. Ilya was right about all of it. If anything happened to Erin, Ivan would go berserk. With Sergei at his side, the two men would rampage like wild beasts and the collateral damage would be impossible to contain.

"I hope you're right." Ilya jerked open the door on his SUV. "If you're not, I'll be the first one to volunteer to take you out on a boat and drop your body into the Gulf."

Like I'd give you a fucking chance...

His gaze moved away from Ilya's SUV to Vivian, her face and upper body covered by Nikolai's jacket as her husband bundled her away into her father's SUV. Romero's unexpected appearance a few hours earlier had been an unwelcome complication. Considering what had gone down with Scorpion, he hadn't been thrilled with the idea of telling Romero what had happened to his one-time close friend. Surprisingly, the ex-con had taken the news with little more than a shrug. Apparently, Romero had long suspected that Scorpion was bent.

"Where are they going?" Kostya asked as he joined Nikolai on the sidewalk outside the warehouse.

"As far away from here as possible." Nikolai's gaze was fixed to the rear of the SUV taking his wife and unborn baby away from the city. "She'll be safe with him."

He made a noncommittal sound. Once, years ago, Romero had left Vivian to die from a gunshot wound. Now, he was trying to prove himself as father of the year material. The world was a wild fucking place sometimes.

"You know Vanya is going to strangle you when he finds out that Erin is missing," Nikolai remarked. "If, by some miracle, he doesn't kill you, Sergei will."

"It's my fucking mess," he replied matter-of-factly. "I made the wrong decision this morning on undeveloped intel. Our women got hurt. I have to answer for that. If that means Ivan and Sergei are going to beat the shit out of me and put me in the ICU for a few weeks? So be it."

"You say that now," Nikolai grumbled. "You've never been hit by Vanya." Scratching his fingers through his hair, he asked, "Do you have any idea where they'd take Erin or Bianca? Do you think they're together? With Danny and Boy?"

"It's easier to guard four hostages at one location than separately."

"Do you think they're still in the city?"

He shook his head. "Probably close by, though. I'd take them somewhere rural. Somewhere they won't be heard easily. Somewhere that's easy to hide the delivery trucks and big rigs that carried this hit squad into the city."

"A barn?" Nikolai suggested. "A factory? A warehouse?"

"Something like that," Kostya agreed.

"How are we going to find them?"

"My spiders are working on it."

"And this mess?" Nikolai gestured to the warehouse behind him and the dead bodies inside.

"I've already made a call."

"The Professionals?"

"Yes."

"And Holly?" Nikolai asked, his jaw flexing with obvious

irritation. He'd been none too pleased when he'd learned that Holly had been held at knife point and had helped him dispose of the body.

"Safe," he assured him.

"Does her mother know?" Nikolai glanced at him. For someone who had only found out that morning that his aunt was living in Houston and had been a covert operative, the boss was taking it well. "We really don't need the complication of an ex-KGB agent breathing down our necks."

"I'm more worried about the fact that she's your aunt," Kostya replied. "Family is even more dangerous than spies."

"I suppose in my case that's true," Nikolai grumbled. He rubbed his hand over his jaw and exhaled loudly. "I can't even believe that my aunt and my sister have been living here all this time. I should have been looking after them both."

"I don't think Holly's mother needs to be looked after," Kostya remarked dryly. "If anything, we needed her more than she's ever needed us."

"I suppose Holly won't need my help finding her father anymore."

Kostya frowned at him. "What are you talking about?"

"She didn't tell you?" Nikolai seemed surprised. "She came to Samovar yesterday afternoon. We had a late lunch, and she asked me to help her find her father."

"Why would she come to you?" he asked, trying not to sound hurt.

"Her mother told her that her father was Russian mafia so she came to me for help finding him.

"For fuck's sake!" He closed his eyes and wondered how she could be so incredibly naïve as to walk into Nikolai's restaurant and ask for that kind of help.

"She's not going to let this go."

"I'll handle it."

"When?"

"Soon."

Nikolai's phone began to ring, and he stepped aside to answer it. Kostya grabbed his own and texted Fox for an update. She answered quickly.

Lost the truck on I-10W. Following another lead. Will text asap with updates if Sunny finds anything.

"Any news?" Nikolai asked, pocketing his phone.

"The truck with Erin was last seen on I-10W. My spiders are following other leads." He gestured with a lift of his head. "You?"

"Besian," Nikolai said. "He's loaning us enough men to cover our wounded and missing. They had an attempted hit at the garage, but Devil handled it."

"Any other problems?"

Nikolai shook his head. "Not like this."

"But?"

"He's worried about the other outfits in town trying to make trouble with Lalo's boys."

"That's not our problem tonight. Hector and Lalo should have had better control over their men. All this?" He motioned around them. "They're the ones who weren't sharing information and who didn't tell us that Lorenzo had enough men left to pull this kind of job. If shit goes sideways for them? Not our problem."

"I don't want the Reyes boys getting in the middle of it,"

Nikolai explained. "They're useful. They're the future."

"Don't say that loud enough for Lalo to hear you. He'll do something stupid."

"It would be an easy way to get rid of him," Nikolai reasoned.

"Let's clean up one coup completely before we start another, yeah?" He reached into his pocket to grab his vibrating cell phone and answered it. "Yes?"

"I think I've found them," Sunny said, her voice calm. "Fox ran the names from the list Gabe gave you. She found an old dairy farm out here that belonged to the grandfather of one of the guys on the list. It went into foreclosure a few years ago. Someone bought it at auction for a fucking steal. Fox dug deeper, and she tracked it through a few other sales until it ended up back in the hands of the grandson."

"That sounds like a good lead."

"It is," she confirmed. "I'm checking it out now. Binoculars," she added, letting him know that she was staying far away and hidden. "There's a huge building here. Probably where they did the milking? The doors are closed, but there are some big, deep tire tracks in the mud and caliche. I've seen six different guys so far. There must be more of them inside…"

"What are the approaches like? Any sort of security?"

"Fox is looking at maps for me right now. There are two different farm roads that head out this way, and one looks like it comes in from the rear of the dairy farm. Security is nonexistent by the looks of it. I'll scout some more and let you know."

"Be thorough."

"Yep."

He lowered his phone and met Nikolai's waiting gaze. "One of my girls thinks she's found their hideout."

"Where?"

"A dairy farm," he said, looking at the skyline. "It will be dark soon. That's the perfect cover for getting in and out without being seen."

Nikolai glanced at his watch. "Sergei and Ivan should be at the airport by now." He grimaced. "If we go meet them, all hell will break loose."

"Ilya already told me he's not going to tell Ivan what's happened."

Sighing, Nikolai picked up his phone and dialed a number. "Give the phone to Ten," he ordered. A moment later, he said, "I need you to find Vanya and Sergei. Tell them what's happened. We think we've found the women and our soldiers. I'll send you the details as soon as I have them."

After the boss hung up, Kostya asked, "Really? Sending Ten when he's already bleeding?"

"Neither Sergei nor Vanya are going to hit him looking like that. He's safer than either of us."

He couldn't argue with that logic. As they walked to his car, he took a moment to check his phone again and noticed the message he'd missed from Holly. *Shit.* He read it twice, wondering how the fuck the subject of Lobo and how she'd come into his life had possibly come up at Fox's safehouse. He didn't even want to think about what Holly was imagining right now.

His thumb hovered over the screen for a moment. Another message popped onto his screen, this one from Sunny. He hurriedly typed out a reply to Holly and hit send. She wasn't going to like it, but he didn't have time to get into it with her right now.

Sliding behind the wheel, he glanced at Nikolai before dropping his phone in a cup holder. "Sunny found a barn where we can gather…"

CHAPTER TWENTY-FIVE

N OT LONG AFTER Fox left with my shoes on her feet, I shook myself from the stupor that the anxiety inducing security footage had caused. Remembering what Sunny had said, I shut off all the lights and computer monitors and made sure all the windows had the blinds and curtains closed. I checked all the locks on each window and the two doors.

Satisfied I was secure, I curled up on the couch and tried not to think about what was happening to Erin. I kept seeing the bleeding man on her doorstep, and the way Erin struggled to free herself from the men kidnapping her. Were they hurting her? Was she suffering?

I tried to convince myself the men who had taken her wouldn't hurt her. Surely, she was worth more to them untouched and unharmed.

Unless...

No. I refused to think like that.

Feeling glum and overwhelmed, I closed my eyes and wished I could fall asleep for a little bit. I wanted to stop thinking about all the terrible things happening. I didn't want to worry about Kostya, Erin, Sunny, Fox or anyone else who had been dragged into this nightmare of violence. I wanted to go back to my easy, carefree life where my biggest worry was whether or not we were going to meet our client goals for the month.

Plagued by thoughts of what-if, I eventually drifted off to a fitful sleep. The distant sound of a phone ringing finally penetrated my vivid nightmare, and I jolted awake. It took me a moment to make sense of my strange surroundings. The room was pitch black and eerily quiet. It felt late, as if hours had passed since I'd fallen asleep.

Hearing the phone ringing again, I reached out for it, slapping the cushions around me. Remembering I'd left my new phone in the bedroom, I pushed off the couch and walked across the living area to find it. My steps were careful as I walked through the dark house, trying to remember the furniture placement.

Seeing the faint bluish glow of the phone, I grabbed it and sat down on the edge of the bed. I scrolled through the missed calls and texts. They were mostly from my mother, each one more upset and containing more capital letters than the last. Apparently, she had gone by my house and found it empty, my car in the garage and no sign of me anywhere. Now she was threatening to call the police if she didn't hear from me.

Checking the time, I realized it had been hours since she'd contacted me. I had been asleep longer than I had estimated. Knowing my mother was probably having a fit, I sent her a quick message, reminding her that I had called and messaged her earlier about helping a friend. Hoping to soothe her panic and keep her from causing a scene, I promised to call her in ten minutes.

Quickly, I read through the other messages, almost all of the remainder from Savannah about salon business. There was only one from Kostya, a rather curt reply to my message about Lobo.

We'll discuss Lobo later. Don't leave the safe house.

I frowned at the tone of his message but decided against replying with something equally as terse. I was too tired to get into a text message fight, and I really didn't want to have a conversation this important without being able to look him in the eye.

My thumb hovered over the screen when the phone rang again. I didn't recognize the number and decided not to answer. It was probably a robocall or some scam anyway. As soon as the call went to voicemail, I started to type out a message to Kostya, but then another message popped up on my screen from the number I didn't recognize.

Curious, I tapped the message to open it—and gasped. It was a photo of Savannah and Lana. Both were gagged and crying with blood on their faces, a trickle from Savannah's nose and a thick rivulet from Lana's mouth. Starting to panic, I zoomed in on the photo and realized they were in some kind of vehicle. A van? A delivery truck?

Thinking of Erin on the security footage earlier, I started to lose it. "Fuck! Fuck!"

What do I do?

Call Kostya. It was the only option.

Another message zoomed into view. This time, there were knives pressed to Savannah and Lana's necks. Both had their eyes shut. Both seemed to be praying.

Another message dinged. It contained an address and a threat.

Come alone. You have 30 minutes. Or we start cutting.

Shaking with adrenaline, I checked the address, and it was less than ten minutes from the safehouse. I had time to get there on foot, but I had to hurry.

Certain Kostya was going to go ballistic, I took a screenshot and sent the image to him with a short message.

I can't wait. I'm going. I'm sorry. Find us. Please.

Out in the living room, I grabbed the shoes Fox had left behind and jammed my feet into them. They were at least a size too big, but I didn't care. Knowing the silent safe house alarms would alert her to me leaving, I opened the front door, raced across the xeriscaping and jumped onto the sidewalk.

Glad that I had at least tried to keep up with my cardio and workouts, I fell into a steady rhythm. My gaze darted from the map on my phone screen to the dark streets surrounding me. As I ran, a million thoughts bombarded my brain. None of them were good.

I wasn't stupid. I knew what a colossal mistake I was making right now. I was racing straight into a trap, but I couldn't let my best friend die without trying to help her. If I got there in time, maybe I could stall until Kostya or Fox realized I had left. If I got there, maybe they would let Savannah and Lana go and just take me.

The hopeful part of me, the part that believed in Kostya and his abilities, knew he would find and save us all. There was no other option. It was him—or our deaths.

Out of breath and sucking air like a fish, I rounded a corner and slowed my pace. According to the map, I was close to my destination. I jogged cautiously forward, my gaze jumping between the dark warehouse storefronts and the eerily quiet and empty street. There was a large and empty space between a cabinet shop and a storage place that seemed to beckon me closer.

Realizing this was likely where I needed to go, I swallowed hard and turned on the flashlight on the phone. Holding it out in front of me, I swept the bright beam side to side. I stepped gingerly through the overgrown grass, my shoes crunching on broken glass. I avoided the discarded cans and other trash, worried I would fall or hurt myself.

The sound of an idling vehicle—a big rig—caught my attention. I came around the side of the woodworking shop and spotted a white 18-wheeler sitting in the empty parking lot behind the building. Before I could even get a glimpse of the license plate to snap a photo for Kostya, the hairs on the back of my neck stood on edge. I recognized the sensation as a warning that someone was close—too close.

But before I could even turn around, a gloved hand had clamped over my mouth, stifling my scream of fear. Something sharp pricked my neck and then stabbed deep. The phone fell from my hand. I tried to fight, to get away from the pain of the needle buried in my neck, but my head started to ache suddenly. My eyes crossed, and I had a hard time taking a full breath.

Sagging and barely conscious, I felt my body being hefted up high. My head dangled low, bouncing against the lower back of a man who smelled of stale cigarettes and greasy food. I tried to fight the sleep threatening to overwhelm me, but whatever I had been injected with was too strong. I barely registered being tossed into the back of the truck, my hip and shoulder slamming into the metal floor so hard I thought they might have broken.

Just as my eyes started to drift closed, the last shaft of light from the parking lot lamps illuminated Savannah and Lana slumped together nearby. My last thought was of the only man who could save us now.

Kostya.

CHAPTER TWENTY-SIX

"GOD ALMIGHTY, THIS thing is hot!" Spider grimaced as he tossed the body on the metal slab protruding from the open crematory furnace.

"That's the point," Kostya remarked, blinking his tired eyes as he shielded his face from the heat. Normally, he preferred to take bodies that needed disposal to the funeral home, but this old beast of a furnace he'd picked up a few years ago and hidden in a warehouse was less conspicuous and faster.

"How long does it take?" Spider wondered as he pushed the drawer forward and closed the heavy door.

"Two hours."

Spider glanced at the pile of bodies on the tarp near the furnace. "This is days of work, Kostya."

"No shit?" he deadpanned. "I won't do them all at once. It's too much work. Some will go into deep freeze. Some will go out to the Gulf. Others will go into the ground. I have to process them first."

Spider made a face. "How the fuck do you handle this kind of work? What the hell kind of nightmares do you have?"

"I don't," he lied. "I sleep like a baby."

"Spoken like a man who never had a baby," Spider retorted. "Babies don't sleep for shit, man. You're up and down all fucking night." Rubbing his jaw, Spider asked, "Do you want me to help you process these?"

"Do you have somewhere better to be?"

"Shit, I can think of a dozen different places I'd rather be than this nightmare factory."

But he didn't leave. Spider stayed and helped him with the ugly work of cleaning up the mess left over from their raid on the dairy farm where Erin, Bianca, Danny and Boy had been held. Considering the shitty luck they'd had all day, the recovery of the women and their soldiers had gone off without a hitch. Ivan and Sergei had their wives back, and Danny and Boy were recovering in the hospital. Ten had gotten patched up and sent home before his PO had gotten wise to the possibility Ten might be doing something illegal.

"What do you think the police will think" Spider asked as they stood at a sink washing their hands sometime later.

"Probably that it was a kidnapping and ransom gone wrong," Kostya reasoned. "They took Erin and Bianca. Both of their husbands work at the Warehouse. They were just in Vegas with their fighters competing for high dollar prizes. Ivan is known to be wealthy. Bianca has money."

"I guess that makes sense," Spider agreed. "Fuck, the cops are probably so tired of all of our bullshit they won't look very deep."

"If we're lucky," Kostya said, reaching for a roll of paper towels. As he dried his hands, he asked, "Did you talk to Romero? About this shit with Scorpion and Marco?"

"Yeah."

"And?"

"He's glad it's done. He was disappointed to find out Spider had turned on us, but it happens in this business all the time. I felt like he was expecting it."

"You tend to develop a sixth sense about betrayal." Remembering Spider's worries about being ratted out by Scorpion, he added, "I tracked down Spider and Marco's contact. She wasn't actually working with the government. She's dead now so she isn't a risk to any of us."

Spider narrowed his eyes. "If she wasn't working for the government, who was she working for?"

"Lorenzo and an old problem from back home," he answered. "Lorenzo will be handled tonight."

"You think Hector has good intel on Lorenzo's hideout?"

"I do." Hector had offered an address just before they had raided the abandoned farm to rescue Erin and Bianca. He'd checked the address with Fox before giving it to Nikolai and providing him with everything he needed to finally finish this.

"And the other problem? From back home?"

"I'm working on it."

"If you need help…"

"I know where to find you."

Spider looked around the warehouse, his gaze lingering on the now clear floor where the bodies had been piled earlier. Kostya sensed he'd had enough cleaning for one night. "Why don't you go home? I'm almost done here. I can handle the rest of it alone."

"You sure?"

He nodded, and Spider left without another word. Alone in the stillness of the warehouse, he took a moment to close his eyes and just breathe. Long, deep, slow breaths to relax the tight coil of anxiety in his chest. He was a stranger to failure. He didn't like it. Standing here, knowing that he'd made a bad call earlier that morning, cut deep. Bianca and Erin could have been killed. Danny, Boy, Ten and Artyom were all injured. He'd lost two men, both of them leaving behind girlfriends and kids.

Fucking disaster.

Leaning back against the sink, he kept thinking about what Spider had said. The toll all these years of wetwork had taken on him was starting to add up. There was a tiredness in his bones he couldn't shake. A fatigue that couldn't be fixed with sleep. He needed a break from all of this. A permanent one.

But those feelings of responsibility and loyalty to Nikolai were hard to shirk. He didn't want to leave his crime family in the lurch. He didn't want the soldiers and captains and their families to suffer because he wasn't here to clean up their messes and make all their mistakes disappear. He didn't want to lose the only real friends he'd ever had.

I don't want to lose Holly.

There was the crux of his problem. He would have to choose. He couldn't keep Holly in his life, be the man she needed him to be, and continue working as a cleaner. The two things were simply incompatible.

A buzzing sound infiltrated his thoughts. He patted his pockets but they were empty. Glancing across the warehouse, he spotted the worktable where he'd tossed his jacket earlier. He strode toward it and reached into the right pocket to retrieve his phone. Looking at the screen, it was blowing up with phone calls and messages from Fox and Sunny.

And Holly.

His heart stuttered in his chest as he tapped on her message and read it.

I can't wait. I'm going. I'm sorry. Find us. Please.

Mouth dry and stomach roiling, he swiped to answer the incoming call from Sunny. Before she could speak, he asked, "What happened?"

"I'm sorry, K. We fucked up! Big time," Sunny said in a panic.

"Tell me what happened!"

"I left the safe house to track down leads. Fox left the safe house to get to her control center so she would have access to traffic cams. We left Holly at the safe house and told her to stay put. Everything was fine until the alarms went off, and I got there as quickly as I could but she was already gone."

"Gone? Where?" He tried to calm his voice, but the fear of losing Holly had overwhelmed him.

"I found the phone in an empty lot behind a couple of businesses near the safe house. There were messages and photos from a burner phone. They used Savannah and Lana to lure Holly out of the safe house. She had a time limit—thirty minutes—or they were going to start torturing her friends."

"How long ago did she leave the safe house?"

"A little over an hour."

"Shit," he cursed, knowing only too well how far she could have been taken in that time. "Do you know where they took her? Can you track her?"

"They dropped her phone so the easiest possibility is out. Fox is digging through traffic and security cams trying to find vehicles driving into and leaving that area, but it's kind of a shithole down there so she isn't having much luck."

This is not happening. He had been so preoccupied that he had taken his eyes of Holly just long enough for someone to grab her.

"Do you have any ideas?" Sunny asked. "Any leads I can chase down?"

"I have to make a phone call," he said, already dreading it. "Tell Fox I'm coming to see her. Meet me there."

"Okay." Sunny hesitated. "Kostya, I'm so sorry."

"Don't apologize. This is on me." He hung up and tried to calm his racing thoughts. Visions of Holly being tortured with Savannah and Lana tormented him. Was she scared? Was she already hurt? Bleeding?

Swallowing hard, he dialed a number he'd only had for a day. There was only one ring before it was answered. Hissing like an angry cat, Frances asked, "Where is my daughter?"

"He took her. She's gone."

CHAPTER TWENTY-SEVEN

A PAINFUL SENSATION in my ears drew me out of my drug-induced sleep. Groggy and nauseated, I lifted my head and tried to focus. My eyes were dry, and my vision so blurry I couldn't figure out what I was seeing.

"*Shh*," Savannah's familiar voice urged in a gentle, mothering way. "If you make too much noise, they'll come back here and hit you with the drugs again."

More awake, I realized I had my head against her shoulder. I grimaced at the wetness on my chin. I had drooled all over her shirt, but she didn't seem to mind or even notice. Her gaze was focused on the platinum blonde hair in her lap. Wrists bound, she tenderly stroked Lana's hair, her face pinched with worry. "She woke up and started fighting with them so they hit her with another syringe." She lifted her gaze to mine. "She's so small, Holly. They're going to kill her with that shit."

Sharing her concern, I swiped at my chin with my bound wrists and finally managed to take in our surroundings and make sense of it all. We were in a plane. A large jet, by the looks of it. The three of us had been corralled in an area that was normally used as a galley. Our legs and wrists were bound with plastic ties. Savannah and Lana both had bruised and bloodied faces. I'd managed to avoid that fate so far, but I didn't hold out much hope that I would be lucky enough to stay that way.

Forcing a yawn, I popped my ears and relieved the pressure. "Are we descending or climbing?"

"Descending," Savannah said quietly.

"Do you know where we're going?"

"Mexico," she said, leaning forward to gaze toward the main cabin area. "There are five of them watching us. Two pilots. No attendants. One of our kidnappers went into the cockpit a while ago, and I heard them talking about landing. Something about the cargo in the back and the trucks they need to meet to keep the delivery schedule."

"Cargo? Us?"

She shook her head. "This is a delivery jet. Like FedEx but not."

"They had delivery trucks when they kidnapped Erin earlier."

"They kidnapped Erin?" she asked, aghast. "Is she okay?"

"I don't know." Glancing around nervously, I wondered aloud, "Why Mexico? Why did they want us?"

"You," Savannah corrected. "They wanted you." She gulped anxiously and looked down at Lana. "I have a feeling we aren't going to be around very long. After we hit the ground, they don't need us anymore."

My stomach dropped. It made me sick to even think about it, but she was right. They had been used as bait to lure me into a trap. They had done their part. What would happen to them now? Would they kill them? Would they rape them first? Sell them into sex slavery? How many horrible things would happen to them?

This is all my fault. All of it.

But why me? Why did these psychos want me?

Was it Kostya? Were they going to use me to get to him?

"Some of these guys are Russian, Holly." Savannah's expression showed confusion. "Lana was yelling at them in Russian, and they were just laughing at her in the most condescending way. The others are Mexican. I just—I don't know what to make of it."

"Maybe it's a gang thing," I guessed. "Like a different family in the Russian mafia and some cartel guys?" I shrugged hopelessly. "I don't know."

"Well, we need to figure it out if we have any chance of negotiating for our lives," she said seriously. After a few tense moments, she added, "I guess you weren't really sick, huh?"

Ashamed, I shook my head. "Someone broke into my house last night and tried to kill us. Kostya put me in a safe house."

Her eyes widened. "Are you okay? Did he hurt you? The guy who broke into your house?"

I shook my head. "He cut me a little, but it's fine."

"Is he...?"

I nodded. "He's dead."

"Jesus." A second later, she asked, "Why did you leave the safe house?"

"They sent me pictures of you and Lana. I couldn't wait. I just...I ran."

Savannah rolled her eyes. "I love you, but you are really dumb sometimes."

"Rude." I jostled her shoulder. "But, yeah, it was really

dumb."

"Well, did you at least have a good time with Kostya before all this shit went down?"

My face felt warm as I nodded. "We were naked and in bed when the break-in happened."

"He banged you like a screen door in a hurricane, huh?" Her mouth quirked with a playful smile.

Laughing and starting to cry at the same time, I nodded. "Yeah."

"Hey," she bumped me with her shoulder, "we're going to be okay."

"I don't know, Savvy," I said, tears running down my face. "This doesn't feel like something we're going to walk away from…"

"We have to try," she insisted. "Whatever this is— whatever they want—we have to do whatever it takes to stay alive until he finds us." She held my gaze. "Kostya *will* find us."

Sniffing, I wiped at my face with the backs of my bound hands. "You're right. We have to stay calm."

The plane started to drift lower, the pressure changing enough to make my ears hurt again. I reached out for Savannah's bound hands, grasping them as best I could. We shared a look, silently communicating what neither of us could say. There was no telling what waited for us on the ground, but we were going to fight to survive.

CHAPTER TWENTY-EIGHT

"WOULD YOU STOP breathing down my neck?" Fox snapped at Sunny as Kostya entered her private lair. She had taken the top floor of the building that held Hen House Security as her own personal space, outfitting it with the best electronics and technology money could buy. He had long ago given up trying to understand what all the different gadgets did or where all the wires went.

"I'm not breathing on you!"

"I can't think with you hovering over me!"

"Sorry." Sunny walked away from Fox's control center and started pacing the floor in the far corner of the room. She raised her head as she finally noticed Kostya and frowned. "We don't have anything yet."

"You're looking in the wrong place." He stepped behind Fox and scribbled a name on the notepad by her arm.

"Who the fuck is Igor?" she asked, brow furrowed.

"The man who took Holly and her friends," Frances interjected from the doorway. Dressed in all black, she cut an intimidating figure, her posture stiff and her gaze one of disdain. He could practically hear her thoughts as she glanced around the room, taking in Fox's messy space. She was probably cataloguing all the faults, the easy security breaches and the lack of exits in a crisis.

"Uh, K?" Fox looked up at him, her eyes wide with surprise. "Why is Holly's mom here?"

"I'm not her mother. Biologically," Frances corrected as she walked closer. "I'm her aunt. Maksim is my brother."

"Holy tangled web," Fox muttered. "And this Igor guy?"

"He used to be my boss," Frances explained. "Back when we were—"

"In the KGB," Fox interrupted, her hands flying to the bottom drawer of her desk. "I got the files last night," she rambled, hauling out a pile of moldering, yellowed paper crammed into disintegrating green folders. "From our contact in Russia," she added, flipping open the folders and flicking through the pages. "I'd planned to read them all today, but then I had to take Holly to the safe house and…"

"Focus," Kostya instructed gently. "Is there something in there that can help us?"

"There was a list of names. Aliases," she said, as she flicked through the papers. "One of them was Nicaraguan. Something Ortega."

"Mariano," Frances said. "I think it was Mariano. He was there with the Sandinistas."

"Marcelo," Fox declared, finding the correct page. "Yeah, Marcelo Ortega."

"His cover was running a coffee plantation," Kostya remarked, reading over her shoulder. Glancing up at Frances, he asked, "Do you think they would take the girls there?"

"I doubt that plantation is still in his control. It's been too long. The government would have taken it and privatized it by now," she guessed. "I don't know that he would be able to get the political cover he needs to fly into Nicaragua without raising alarm."

"But if he had one business in Central America, he probably had others," Sunny suggested. "Like, that's how y'all made money, right? The high-ranking government members and KGB agents? You laundered money through business interests in other countries."

"Yes," Frances agreed. "That was generally the way it was done. It would have been easier to do in places like Central America back then. There wasn't as much oversight. You could get away with a lot more."

"So maybe we start looking into the business ties he had back then," Sunny decided as she hurriedly moved to a computer and plopped down in a rolling chair. "We skiptrace his alias and his business ties to see if any of those old properties or accounts are still active. We dig down deep and look into his old partners and associates."

"He's working with Lorenzo Guzman," Kostya explained. "They have a common enemy."

"My brother," Frances clarified.

"I'm sure there's a long fucking list of people who consider him an enemy," Fox muttered under her breath. "Sunny, are you good to handle the skiptracing? I finally have access to the flight data I need."

"Flight data?" Kostya asked, leaning forward for a better look at what she was doing.

"The delivery trucks," she said, tapping away and scrolling quickly. "Sunny and I were talking about the trucks that were used to take Erin and haul the cartel crew around town. There was a delivery truck parked behind the salon when the kidnappers busted in and took Savannah and Lana. They got hustled into it."

"You think a similar sort of decoy cargo jet may have been used to get them out of the country," he said, following her reasonable assumptions. "What are you looking for now?"

"A list of all the flights that took off within, maybe, an hour or two of Holly going missing. I assume they'd want to move quickly."

"Yes. Ideally, they'd want to take the girls straight to the tarmac and load them in the jet. They'd head south after takeoff so filter out any other destinations."

"Yep." Fox winced with pain as she typed.

He frowned. "Are you okay?"

"My feet are killing me," she grumbled and shrugged. "I guess they're swollen or something."

"You sit too much," Frances interjected. "You're too young to be spending so much time in a chair. You need to switch to a walking desk."

"Not really a fan of exercise," Fox muttered as she scanned the departure data. "These look promising," she said, pointing at her screen. "And this one. Shit. These two also. We need a better way to narrow down our search."

"I'll call Gabe." Frances moved to a corner of the room for privacy. "He might be able to help us trim down the list of possibilities."

Fox glanced up at him with surprise. "She knows Gabe?"

"He does some freelancing for her."

"Freelancing," she grumbled, making a shooting gun motion with her left hand.

While Fox, Sunny and Frances worked, he moved to a

computer station a few feet away and cued up the security feeds from Allure. He skimmed through most of it, slowing down the fast-forward as he got closer to the abduction of Savannah and Lana. Both women were working in the supply closet. Savannah seemed to be teaching Lana her system for organizing and the digital inventory she had on a tablet. Lana took the tablet from Savannah and began inputting data while Savannah cut open boxes.

Suddenly, the view went black as the salon lost power. A few moments later, the faint glow of emergency lighting that Fox had convinced Holly to install began to illuminate the exit paths through the salon. His gaze moved back to the supply room where the blue glow of the battery powered LEDs lit up the space. Savannah had a calming hand on Lana's shoulder and neither were aware of the men coming into the salon through the back door.

These men were dressed differently than the ones who had attacked Erin and Bianca. These men moved with military stealth, their steps fluid, their weapons raised and at the ready. In the supply room, Savannah finally heard the noise of the team coming to kidnap them. She pushed Lana behind her and rushed to the door, closing and locking it quickly.

Holding the box cutter like a weapon, she walked backwards toward Lana and reached for her phone on the nearby shelf. The men were outside the door as Savannah tried to get a signal on her phone. She couldn't know it at the time, but the kidnappers had jammed all the cell phone signals and cut the phone lines in that area. She had no way to reach the outside world or call for help.

She shoved Lana into a small space between shelves and

moved boxes quickly in front of her, trying to hide her from what was coming. The door rattled on its hinges as one of the kidnappers slammed his boot against it. It didn't take long for the door to give.

The team was inside the room in seconds, overwhelming Savannah. She fought like a cat, swiping two of the men across the face and neck and their arms with the razor blade in the box cutter. She wasn't going to let them take her that easily.

But she didn't stand a chance. A backhanded slap knocked her to the ground, and she didn't move for a few moments. The other men on the team kicked aside the boxes and quickly discovered Lana, dragging her out by her arms and smacking her as she screamed with fear. In less than a minute, the men had both women tied up and hooded and carted them out of the salon like hogtied animals.

He swallowed hard at the thought of what Savannah and Lana might have suffered since being taken. Holly would likely escape any real violence because she was the high-value target, but her friends? They were expendable. Women who were expendable didn't fare well in situations like these.

Holly would never forgive herself if Lana or Savannah were beaten and raped or murdered. She would never forget. She would never move on from the guilt. It would consume and ruin her.

"Fuck!" Fox growled and shoved away from her desk. She jerked off one and then the other sneaker and tossed them across the room, throwing a tantrum like a toddler. She rubbed her aching feet and scowled while muttering the filthiest string of profanity.

"You almost knocked me out!" Sunny shouted with irritation, picking up the shoe that had landed on her desk. She was about to throw it back at Fox when she stopped and stared at the sneaker in her hand. "This isn't your shoe."

"No, it's Holly's," Frances said, snatching it out of Sunny's hand. "I have the same pair. We bought them on a shopping trip."

"Oh. My. God." Fox said each worth dramatically and covered her face with her hands. "I am so stupid. Stupid!" She scooted back to her keyboard and started typing furiously. "So dumb!"

"You were in a hurry," Frances reasoned. "I'm sure—"

"That's not why she's stupid," Sunny interrupted, standing from her chair. "She's stupid because if she took Holly's shoes then Holly is probably wearing hers."

"And?" Frances asked, brow furrowed.

"And Fox puts GPS trackers on all of her stuff," Sunny explained. "She's always losing things. Her phone, her shoes, her purse, her keys—she's like a child."

"I fucking heard that," Fox grumbled. "I can't help it. I have ADHD."

Sunny rolled her eyes. "Self-diagnosed."

Kostya raised his hand, silently telling Sunny to let it go. The two of them bickering wasn't helping.

"The shoes aren't reporting a signal right now," Fox said, "but they reported one at the airport."

"Which one?"

"Bush." Fox minimized and opened another screen. "If we use the time stamp and GPS location from the shoes," she murmured, while scrolling through the departure data of the cargo flights, "we can narrow it down to…" She trailed off and opened another window to get the GPS locations of the runways at the airport. Back at the departure screen, she scrolled and clicked. "This one! General Francisco Javier Mina International Airport."

"Tampico, right?" Sunny said, almost running back to the desk she'd been using.

"Yeah," Fox replied. "TAM is the code."

"What did you find?" Kostya asked, his heartbeat kicking up as he realized his spiders were solving the puzzle.

"This Igor guy? He used to run his coffee shipments through a port in Altamira which is right near Tampico. He had a bunch of warehouses in that area."

"Had?"

"It says they were all seized by the government, but that doesn't really mean shit does it?" She glanced back at him over her shoulder. "Lorenzo could have bought them back at some point. You never were able to find his stock piles in Mexico. We looked everywhere, but we never had this data point." She gestured to the pile of papers. "This might be where he's been keeping all of his extra guns and money and drugs. Maybe where he kept some of the men who came here to kill and kidnap tonight."

"How long is the flight from Houston to Tampico?" Frances asked, already on her phone.

"Two hours?" Fox said, reading the departure and arrival information on her screen.

"We can't just land there and expect them not to know," Kostya warned. "We need a better plan."

"And that's what I'm doing," Frances said, turning her back on him and striding away as she began to snap instructions at the person on the other end of the line.

Fox touched his arm and smiled encouragingly up at him. "You're going to find her and save her. We know what we're doing now, KGBeast."

The use of her nickname was a moment of levity he desperately needed. He reached out and tugged her ponytail in response.

"We're your team, Kostya." Sunny had joined them. "We're with you. Whatever you need, we'll find it. Whatever it takes, we'll get them back."

"You're handy with a gun," Frances addressed Sunny but it wasn't a question.

Sunny nodded. "Yeah."

"You're coming with us." Frances glanced at Fox. "You're staying here. We'll need your help once we get in country." Holding his gaze now, Frances said, "It's time to end this. All of it. I'm done looking over my shoulder."

"I don't think that ever goes away," Kostya remarked dryly. "Even if we kill them all."

"Maybe," Frances agreed. "Either way, it will feel good to finally cut Igor's throat."

That he believed wholeheartedly.

CHAPTER TWENTY-NINE

"SOMEONE IS COMING," Lana whispered, skittering away from the door where she had been listening carefully. She hurriedly moved back between us and hauled her knees to her chest, making herself the smallest target possible.

I swallowed anxiously and eyed the door. Once the plane had landed, we had been drugged again and brought to this strange, decrepit place. They had put us in a damp, dark room that smelled of mildew and had layers of dirt and grime all over the concrete floor. We had been released from our zipties, but they had taken our shoes and watches and jewelry, even Savannah's belt.

With only a single bottle of water to share and a filthy plastic bucket in the corner serving as our bathroom, we had been sitting here for hours. There was an old metal bench along one wall, but it was rickety and rusty and unsafe. We had already tried to look out the small window at the rear of the room, but the murky coating of mold and dirt made it impossible to see anything clearly. It was eerily still around the building so we reasoned we were in the middle of nowhere. No road noises, no cars, no airplanes overhead. Just the steady hum of insects.

"We need weapons," Savannah whispered, her gaze darting around the dim room. "We need a way to protect ourselves."

"They have guns," Lana replied matter-of-factly. "They're going to do what they want with us." She seemed suddenly older and wiser as she said, "When they take you, don't fight. They will hurt you more if you do. Close your eyes. Open your legs. Let them take what they want. It's easier that way. Better for you. Safer."

My heart ached for Lana as I fully realized what she had been through before she came into our lives. There were signs that she had been pimped out and used, but it was never a certainty. Not until now.

"Breathe deep," she added, her gaze haunted. "It hurts less if you relax." She gestured between her legs. "And if they want the other, use your mouth first. They won't last as long back there if you do. It's easier to take when it's quick."

My stomach tried to revolt, and I swallowed down the rush of bile that threatened to erupt. How many times had Lana been raped? How many times had she been sodomized? How long had she been used and abused by men? Weeks? Months? Years?

The lock on the door clanged, and the hinges squealed as it was pushed open. Lana grasped my hand and Savannah's, holding tight as we stared at one of our kidnappers. He looked us over, his gaze lingering on Savannah for a moment too long before it moved back to me. Pointing in my direction, he said something in Russian that I didn't understand.

"You have to go with him," Lana translated softly. "Their boss wants you first."

"No!" Savannah put her hand out to stop me, but I shook

it off, pinning her in place with a look. She silently pleaded with me not to go, but I made a gesture with my hand, telling her to stay with Lana.

Like a shark, the Russian kidnapper eyed me with a predatory glare. A shiver coursed down my spine as I walked by him and out of the room. The hallway was just as grimy and dark, and I fought the urge to hug myself and start crying. After he had secured the door, the Russian flicked his fingers at me. I fell into step beside him, struggling to keep up with his large strides.

With sneaky glances, I tried to make sense of him. His outfit—black tactical pants and shirt, heavy military style boots—warned me that he wasn't a man I could escape or evade. He seemed trained, and I didn't want to test his skills. I turned my attention to path we were taking, winding through a series of hallways before reaching the main floor of the warehouse.

There were crates stacked all over the place. They were huge towers of them, some wooden and others metal. The smell of rust and something else I couldn't place filled my nose. It was a strange, caustic smell, and I didn't want to breathe it in too deeply. Staying close to the Russian, I followed him through the warren of crates, each step filling me with dread.

He stopped, and I had to catch myself before I plowed into his back. He spoke to someone I couldn't see and then stepped aside. His meaty hand clamped my shoulder, and he roughly shoved me forward. I stumbled over my feet, dragging the bare toes of my left foot across the uneven concrete and skinning the tips.

Wincing, I swallowed my cry of pain. My gaze darted to the old man standing in front of crates moved together like a makeshift table. Tall and thin, he had stooped shoulders and only a few wisps of white hair on his bald head. There were dark spots on his yellowing skin, showing his age and poor health, and heavy lines of wrinkles along his neck.

When he turned to face me, I schooled my expression and didn't react to the absolute blackness of his eyes. They were devoid of emotion and chilled me right to the core. He smiled at me, his grin evil like a villain from a horror movie. His teeth were brown and brittle, and even from this distance, I could smell the horrendous stench coming from his mouth on every breath.

"You look just like her," he said, his voice gravelly and wet and his accent heavily Russian. He coughed into a stained handkerchief clenched in his bone thin right hand, his lungs sounding wet. "Just like her."

"Who?" I asked, afraid to get any closer and trying to buy some time. I noticed the blood specks on his ill-fitting white shirt and worried he had some kind of disease that was making him cough up bloody mucus.

He wiped at his mouth, clearing away the sputum on his lower lip, and stuffed the handkerchief into the pocket of his black slacks. "Kira."

Confused, I frowned. "Who is Kira?"

He laughed, his lungs protesting the effort as he wheezed and rattled. Taking the handkerchief out of his pocket again, he cleared his throat and dabbed at his mouth. "Your mother."

"My mother's name is Frances—"

"Your *real* mother," he interrupted.

I blinked. "I think you're confused—"

"I'm not confused. I know what I know. I know all the lies you've been told." He turned back to the makeshift table and picked up some photos. When he walked closer to me, I stepped back, not wanting to breathe in his air, but the Russian kidnapper was standing so close behind me that he reached out and put a hand between my shoulder blades, holding me in place. "Look."

Reluctantly, I took the photos from him. I didn't recognize the man, but there was something familiar about him. His eyes. His nose. I'd seen them somewhere before…

My gaze moved to the young woman he was with, his arm around her slim waist as he pulled her close. My stomach wobbled as I studied her face. It was like looking in the mirror. She reminded me of myself when I was in college.

I flipped to the next photo. It was my mother with the man from the first picture. They were smiling and laughing in the photo, but their closeness was different. It wasn't the closeness of two lovers. It felt more…familial.

"The woman you know as your mother was born in Leningrad. Her name was Ekaterina Prokhorovna when I found her in an orphanage. She was exactly what we needed. Clever. Moldable. Keen to survive. Ruthless." He suppressed a cough as he continued, "I handpicked her. I made her into the woman she is today. I sent her to America. I gave her the chance of a lifetime—and she betrayed me."

"I don't know who you think I am, but you're wrong. My mother was born in—"

"Longview? Yes? Her parents died when she was young. Her childhood home burned down so she doesn't have any photos of them or her original birth certificate. Does she?"

I hesitated. "Lots of people lose their parents young or have houses that burn down. It doesn't make my mother a liar or whatever you think she is."

He shook his head and spun back to his table. He picked up another stack of photos and thrust them at me. "Look."

I didn't want to look. I wanted to get the hell out of there. I wanted to run away from this crazy old man.

But I didn't. I took the photos. I looked.

They were stills of my mother, much younger, in a military style uniform. She was learning to fight and shoot. In other photos, she was being trained in some kind of academia, books open in front of her, a pencil in her hand.

Barely able to speak, I asked, "What is this?"

"Ekaterina at the institute. She was very motivated. I'd never met any young child with a drive as strong as hers. I didn't see it again until Kostya."

My head snapped up, and I narrowed my eyes. "What?"

"I never got to train him, but I had already picked him to be my next protégé. His parents had worked for me. I had found them the same way I had found Ekaterina. They were the perfect agents, and they'd been raising the perfect son. I was going to take him under my wing—and then *you* happened."

Taken aback, I asked, "Me?"

"Kira," he explained, pointing at the photo of the young woman who looked so much like me. "She was one of my agents. She was a honey trap for Maksim, but she broke all the rules. She fell in love with him," he said, his voice dripping with disdain. "And then she conceived you."

I looked at the photo of Kira and Maksim again. Was he right? Were these my biological parents? But how did my mother figure into all of this?

"Ekaterina helped Kira after she escaped my custody. She was in Russia at the time on a business trip, and once she found out that her brother was going to have a baby with one of my agents, she chose family over me and everything I'd given her."

"Her brother…?"

"Ekaterina and Maksim are brother and sister. The woman you think is your mother is actually your aunt. Your real mother, Kira, died the same day you were born. Well," he added with a vicious smile, "she didn't exactly die. She was murdered by Nina on my orders. Nina Antonovich," he clarified. "Kostya's mother."

I tried to take in everything he had just said, but it was a whirl of words and gut-wrenching emotions. Kostya's mother had murdered mine when I wasn't even a day old!

"Ekaterina took care of Nina. She caught up with her a few days later. She was quick about it. It was a clean death. Kostya's father, though…" His voice trailed off as he sighed dramatically and then started to cough. "Well, Maksim and his temper were infamous."

My stomach churned at the way he so casually discussed the murders of my mother and Kostya's parents. He acted as if they were just expendable chess pieces he had been pushing around the board for his own amusement and gains.

"Why are you telling me this? Why did you kidnap us?" I gestured around the warehouse. "What is the point of any of this?"

Shocking me with his swift movement and strength, he invaded my space and gripped my throat in his bony, hard hand. He squeezed so hard I couldn't breathe and started to feel my vision go fuzzy. "The point is that *you* are the reason I spent decades in prison. *You* are the reason I was tortured and starved and beaten. You and Ekaterina and Maksim ruined my life, and now I'm going to take yours."

His other hand had wrapped around my throat, increasing the pressure that was choking the life out of me. Feeling woozy and terrified to pass out, I marshalled the last of my energy and kicked the old bastard hard, right in the shin. His grip faltered as he cursed nastily at me, and I inhaled a deep, shaky breath before slamming my knee into his stomach as he bent forward in pain.

Strong hands gripped my shoulders, spinning me around with so much force that I practically flew through the air before slamming into the dirty concrete floor. My knees hit first, jarring my skull, before I flopped forward and smacked my chin. Dazed and bloodied now, I gasped for air and tried to stay conscious. My vision blurred, and I couldn't make sense of what was up or down. I clamped my eyes shut for a moment and fought the urge to vomit or pass out.

The old man snarled angrily. A moment later, the guard manhandled me off the floor and all but dragged me away. I managed to get my feet under me and stumbled forward, staying upright and close to him. I tried to fight with my captor, swinging my elbows and clawing at his arms, but he was so much taller and bigger. When I managed to strike his face, tearing into his cheek and neck with my fingernails, he shouted furiously and slapped me so hard I fell backward onto my ass.

Reaching down, he squeezed my forearms so tightly that I cried out in pain, his fingers burning and bruising my skin as he twisted my arms away from my body and lifted me to my feet again. Grabbing my wrists in one huge hand, he pinched my chin between his thumb and forefinger and forced me to look up at him. "I'm going to make you watch while my men fuck your friends. When they're done, you're going to get on your knees and lick every last man clean. Then? Your holes are mine."

Horrified by his threats, I didn't fight him as he dragged me to the room-turned-cell. He gripped the back of my neck, his fingers tangled in my hair and tugging at my scalp, while he unlocked the door. He pushed me forward into the room, and I hurried to get away from him and ran straight into Lana's arms.

At the same moment I realized Savannah was missing, he seemed to realize it as well. He stomped into the room, striding toward Lana to question her. I didn't even see Savannah until she had already struck. Using all her might and the years of charity softball games she had under her belt, she slammed a piece of metal into the back of his head, stunning him. She didn't hesitate before swinging again, this time cracking the side of his skull.

Blood sprayed everywhere as his scalp burst open. Lana and I both flinched at the sickening crunch of metal hitting bone. As he fell forward, Savannah swung again, hitting him between his shoulders to make sure he was going down. Terrified another guard had heard the fracas, I scrambled to the door, closing it quietly and pushing my back against it, desperate to keep it shut. Lana ripped off her dirty socks and shoved them in the guard's mouth, silencing the groaning sound he was making.

"Here." Savannah had taken off her shapewear, slipping it down her legs and out from under her skirt. "Tie his hands with this." She went for his bootlaces next, ripping them out quickly and using them to secure his ankles so he wouldn't be able to stand or walk.

"Help us," Savannah whispered hurriedly as she gestured for me to come closer.

Together, the three of us dragged and pushed the guard to the corner of the room. We rifled through his pockets, taking his phone, the Mexican pesos and American dollars in his wallet and the knife from his boot sheath.

"I thought he'd have a gun," Savannah admitted glumly. "We could have used a gun."

"We have a knife," I said encouragingly. "And you've got that."

She lifted the metal hunk that I finally recognized as a leg from the bench. "It's better than nothing."

"We really have to get out of here. Like now," I said, thinking of the guard's threats to rape us and the demented old man who had tried to strangle me. "The man who kidnapped us is a certifiable nutcase. And he's sick."

"Sick?" Savannah repeated. "What do you mean?"

"He was coughing. Like coughing up blood." I gestured to my face and shirt, both speckled with his spittle. "He's all thin and stooped, and I think he might have broken out of a prison or a mental hospital in Russia."

"Tuberculosis?" Lana suggested nervously. "It's common

back home, especially in places like prisons."

"Oh, that's fucking great," Savannah grumbled. "I'm leaving here with tetanus," she showed her cut hands and the rusty piece of metal, "and you're leaving with TB." Shaking her head, she said, "Well, come on, huckleberries, let's get out of here."

"What is huckleberries?" Lana asked with confusion.

"It's a movie thing," I said, grabbing her hand and dragging her behind me. "*Tombstone.* Doc Holliday has tuberculosis. We'll watch it when we get home."

"Do you think you can lead us out of here?" Savannah asked as she pried open the door a few inches and looked into the dimly lit hallway.

"It's like a maze out there, but I know which way we absolutely don't want to go."

"That's better than nothing, I guess," she murmured before stepping out into the hallway.

Following her, I motioned to the right, indicating we needed to go that way first. Behind me, Lana locked the door of the room where we'd been held so it would look as if we were still secured in there. Quietly but quickly, we moved down the hallway single file, pausing at corners and holding our collective breaths before picking a new direction.

Startled by the unexpected sound of gunfire, the three of us froze. We exchanged terrified glances and moved closer together, squeezing against a wall and sliding down lower as if to make ourselves smaller targets.

"Should we go or stay?" Savannah asked, her courage faltering the same time as mine.

"Go," Lana said forcefully. "We go. Now. Or we die."

Knowing she was correct, I stood up first and peeked around the corner closest to us. Listening to the gunfire, it seemed to be coming from far behind us, in the main area of the warehouse where I'd been shown the photos of my mother and Maksim and Kira. It seemed safest to keep moving forward so I tugged Lana behind me and ran.

When we reached the end of another hallway, Savannah inched forward and took the lead. She peered around the corner and snapped back quickly. She reached back and pushed me against the wall. I did the same to Lana. Savannah lifted the hunk of metal high in the air and prepared to smack the living shit out of someone.

"Fuck!" A man swore loudly as he blocked the metal bench leg with his forearm. Dark eyes narrowing and mouth slanted with irritation, he snatched it out of Savannah's hands and lowered the menacing barrel of the HK416. "Watch out, Slugger Barbie. I'm here to save you."

"Like shit you are," Savannah snapped back, not trusting him anymore than I did. "You probably work for these assholes who kidnapped us."

"Baby, if I was going to steal you and tie you up, it would be to keep you in my bed."

"Fuck off," she snarled as he looked her up and down.

His hard face softened with amusement. As more gunshots erupted, his playful expression turned serious. "I'm Gabe Reyes. I'm here to get you three to safety while Kostya creates a diversion. So, you can either come with me right now, or try to find your way out on your own."

The three of us exchanged nervous glances. I recognized his weapon as one used by American forces. My mother and I had shot one together at a women's shooting club so I was aware of its history and use. Back in the warehouse with the crazy old man, I had seen Russian rifles and guns, mostly AKs and cheap knockoffs like WASR-10s.

"We go with him," I decided. We didn't have any other choice. If he worked for the kidnappers, he would shoot us if we tried to escape him.

"Come on." He put down the piece of metal and turned back the way he'd come. With the measured movements of a military man, he led us down one hallway and then another. We stayed close together, afraid to get separated or left behind. He kept his weapon raised, ready to fire. We could only hope that he was aiming for our enemies.

He raised his closed fist to signal us to stop. We had reached a T intersection of hallways with an exit door straight ahead. Huddled together, we watched him clear the perpendicular hallway before opening the exit just a crack. The early morning sunlight filtered into the dark space, and the clean scent of fresh air filled the dank hall.

With his foot holding the door, he stood with his weapon raised to his shoulder, ready to fire as his head pivoted side to side in a search for trouble. "Go."

Savannah ran out first. I pushed Lana after her and brought up the rear. When we were outside the building, he shut the door carefully with his foot, not letting it slam or make any noise. He took the lead again, pushing by Savannah before reaching back to grab her hand and tug her along behind him. She reached back for Lana and Lana for me.

By now, my heart was beating so hard that the pounding pulse in my ears drowned out everything around us. I was only vaguely aware of the nonstop gunfire erupting in the abandoned warehouse. My legs were shaky, and my fingers trembled as the adrenaline spike overwhelmed me. Lana's hand was just as wobbly in mine, her fingers jittery and cold.

Relief overwhelmed me when I finally spotted Kostya. He was using the door of an SUV as cover while he rapidly fired into the warehouse. The black bulletproof vest over his tight gray t-shirt washed away the terror I felt at seeing him so exposed and at risk. Unable to look away from him, I didn't even hear Gabe's instructions to Savannah and Lana. Instead, I followed without blinking, my gaze fixed on Kostya.

I sucked in a sharp breath at the sight of my mother. She was on the other side of the SUV, firing just as rapidly as Kostya. She lowered her rifle, letting the shoulder strap hold it in place, and reached for another weapon inside the vehicle. When she lifted the massive weapon with such ease and comfort, I realized that everything I had been told in the warehouse was true. My mother wasn't my biological mother. She was my aunt, and she was a Russian spy.

The huge barreled weapon fired with a loud *thunk,* shooting a projectile into the warehouse. Before it even landed, she fired twice more, sending fat rounds into the windows. A trio of explosions sent me to the ground. I fell on top of Lana, shielding her with my body and covering her face and neck as the burst of heat and smoke flared out of the building.

The metal walls screeched as they tumbled down, and the warehouse belched flames high into the sky. I heard men shouting and then more firing as they raced out of the engulfed building. Inside the warehouse, the contents of those crates started to catch fire and detonate. Each new explosion shuddered through my body, jarring my head and punching my stomach.

"Get up!" Kostya's voice was right in my ear as he lifted me off the ground and gathered me close. "We have to go. Now!"

Sunny had taken Lana in hand, dragging her along toward the idling SUV. Gabe had already hustled Savannah to an open door and was forcing her inside.

"Holly!" Kostya shouted again, shaking me from my stupor. "We have to go!"

I touched his face, my hand on his jaw, and gazed up at him. In that moment, all I could think about was the horrible, terrible truth between us. Kira. My mother-slash-aunt. My father. His parents. All of these people who were supposed to love and protect us had ruined everything before we had even met.

"Kostya," I said with a sob. "My mom—"

"I know," he whispered hurriedly, gathering me close. "I know all about it."

I slumped against him, desperate for his heat and his security. "I'm sorry. For everything."

"No," he said, kissing my temple. "No apologies. You're safe. You're coming home. That's all that matters."

Staring up at him through my teary gaze, I lifted on tiptoes to kiss him. His hand cupped the back of my head as he crushed his mouth to mine. I gripped the straps of his vest, holding on for dear life and not ever wanting to let him go.

And then Kostya jerked. Once. Twice. Two more times.

His hold on me faltered just I became aware of a strange spreading pain in my side. He pulled back, his expression slack with shock. I felt it then—the bloody wetness on my skin.

Glancing down, I watched the red stains soaking through his shirt and mine. It didn't make sense at first. He was wearing a vest—but he was standing sideways, giving just enough of an opening for a handful of bullets to tear through him. Two had blasted out the other side and gone right through me.

We both staggered together, him a few steps back and me two steps forward. We were like drunken dancers, each holding on to the other for balance. He fell first, flat on his back, and I dropped down next to him. He was breathing hard, sucking air in frighteningly shallow gasps. Blood was pouring out of him now, soaking into the grass and dirt around us.

"Go!" He pushed at me, roughly and weakly. "Go, Holly."

"I'm not leaving you!" Ignoring my own wounds, I pushed on the bullet holes I could reach, shoving down hard to put pressure on him. "You'll be fine. We'll get you to a hospital."

A bullet whizzed by me, snapping as it hit the ground. I flattened myself on top of Kostya, desperate to guard him from any more injuries, and glanced toward the warehouse. The old man—that crazy son-of-a-bitch—limped out of the burning warehouse, coughing up blood as he raised his shaking arm to fire again.

But not at me or Kostya. His focus was fixed behind us. I glanced back and saw my mother rushing to help us. He fired a shot that barely missed her, and I realized she'd left her weapons at the SUV. That psycho was going to kill my mother and the man I loved unless I did something.

The hard dig of Kostya's sidearm bit into my thigh. I pulled it from the hip holster, flicked off the safety, and did what I had done thousands of times at the gun range with my mother. I controlled my breathing. I aimed for center mass. I squeezed the trigger.

My first shot hit him square in the chest. My second and third hit just below that. The fourth shot caught him in the cheek as he fell forward. Blood sprayed as he dropped forward onto his face, unmoving and still. He wasn't going to hurt anyone else ever again.

Hands trembling, I switched on the safety and set the gun aside. My whole attention was on Kostya now. His lips were pale. His eyes were wide with shock. A clammy slick of sweat coated his skin. *He's dying.*

"We have to move him," my mother said as she knelt down and picked up the weapon. After tucking it into her waistband, she touched my bleeding stomach. "You're hurt!"

"He's hurt worse." I shook off her hand and moved to his head. I slid my hands under his shoulders, and she moved to grab his legs. Pain tore through my stomach as I hefted him off the ground, but I ignored it, desperate to save the man I loved.

Sunny appeared suddenly and helped us carry him back to the SUV. Savannah and Lana had put the seats down, making a large space in the cargo area.

While we loaded Kostya into the back of the SUV, Savannah scrambled into the passenger seat to make more room for us. Sunny closed the rear door and started digging around in some black bags for medical supplies. I slumped down next to Kostya, my own wounds starting to make me dizzy.

"How much cash do you have?" Gabe asked from the driver's seat as he aggressively gunned the engine and left the burning warehouse behind us.

"Enough," my mother answered, jerking off her own bullet proof vest before tugging off Kostya's. "Go to the closest hospital with an emergency room. We'll move him to a private hospital once he's stabilized."

Kostya's cold hand closed around mine, but his grip was so weak I had to thread our fingers together. I leaned down, ignoring the pain in my abdomen and touched my forehead to his. He tried to lift his other hand to touch my face, but his arm shook and fell back to the floor. My mother and Sunny began to treat his injuries, slapping bandages on him and injecting him with pre-filled syringes.

"Look at me," he ordered forcefully. When I met his determined stare, he said, "Nothing that happened before we met matters. None of it." He smiled up at me and whispered, "I love you, Holly."

"I love you." I kissed him tenderly, wishing I could give him my strength. "I love you so much."

His gentle smile slackened, and his eyelids fluttered together. His hand relaxed completely and slipped from mine. It took me a second to realize that something was wrong. "He's not breathing!"

"What?" My mother moved toward his chest and checked his pulse. "Holly, do you remember your CPR class?"

I recertified every year for the salon. Without a second thought, I jumped into action with my mother. She planted her hands on his sternum and began to push hard, pumping blood through his body in place of his weakened heart. When she paused, I lifted his chin, pressed my mouth to his and delivered rescue breaths that forced his chest to rise.

Back and forth, we pumped blood and breathed for him.

Sunny kept pressure on his wounds, but the blood kept pouring out of him, seeping into the upholstery and our clothing. Gabe and Sunny shouted back and forth. He drove fast but controlled, keeping the SUV safely on the road without swerving or flinging us around despite the high speed.

After another round of rescue breaths, I lifted my head and felt unbearably woozy. My body listed to the side, and my mother yell my name. Lana caught me, guiding me down onto the folded seat. She spoke to my mother in Russian, her voice calm and steady. A few seconds later, she was pressing a bandage into my side.

My eyesight began to fade out, growing fuzzy on the edges. I stared at Kostya's motionless body, his arms jerking with each push of my mother's hands and his chest rising with Sunny's shared breaths.

Please don't die.

CHAPTER THIRTY

MOUTH DRY AND head aching, I woke up from the strangest sleep. My arms and legs felt weirdly numb, but my throat and nose were sore. My head ached, and my stomach felt uncomfortably full and heavy. I blinked a few times, hoping to clear my fuzzy vision. The sounds of beeping machines filtered into my consciousness as I tried to make sense of my surroundings.

"You're in a hospital, Holly," my mother's gentle voice drew my attention. She had a bedside chair pulled close and held my left hand. Her clothes were wrinkled. Her hair seemed flat and dull. She looked so tired and old. "Do you want some water?"

I nodded and gratefully sipped from the straw she plopped into a cold bottle. The water washed down my throat and soothed the burning ache. Memories of the kidnapping and shooting raced before me. I glanced down at my side and tried to lift my gown to see the damage.

"Careful," my mother chided softly as she set aside the water bottle. "The scarring is minimal." She helped me lift the sheet and gown to reveal the dressing that stretched from my hip to navel. "You got lucky, Holly. They thought it was your intestines that had been hit by the rounds that came out of

Kostya, but it was mostly your ovary and fallopian tube. Your other ovary is perfectly safe and healthy. You'll be able to have children," she assured me.

Relieved the damage wasn't worse, I croaked, "How long?"

"Have you been out?"

I nodded slowly.

"This is the fourth day. You had an infection. You've been in and out since surgery. Your fever broke overnight, and your bloodwork came back much improved this morning." She looked as if she might start crying. Clearing her throat, she added, "They also started treating you for TB exposure. Lana told me you were worried so I mentioned it to the doctors. You'll need to take medicine for a while to make sure you don't get sick."

"Kostya?"

"He's alive." She squeezed my hand. "I won't lie to you. It was touch and go for the first two days, but he fought hard to get back to you." She smoothed hair from my cheek and tucked it behind my ears. "He's still in a medically induced coma. There was a lot of damage and blood loss. His body needs time to heal, but the doctors here are optimistic."

My eyes started to sting as my emotions overwhelmed me. My mother cooed softly and climbed onto the bed with me, moving to my uninjured side and wrapping her arms around me. She brushed her fingers through my hair and kissed my temple. "Holly, you were so brave. I've always been so proud of you, but you were so courageous. You saved yourself, Kostya and me."

Wanting to stay courageous, I asked, "Who was the man who kidnapped us?"

She sighed but didn't hesitate to answer me. "His name was Igor. He was a top official in the KGB. He was my—"

"Handler?" I interrupted, forcing her to meet my curious stare.

"Yes."

"He showed me pictures of you. Back when you were Ekaterina," I explained. "I didn't want to believe it, but then I saw you outside the warehouse…"

"I haven't done that type of work in a long time, Holly. I quit when you were born. I walked away from that life." She wiped the tears from my face with her thumbs. "I still occasionally do some freelance intelligence work for the CIA but nothing violent."

"So, all those business trips…?"

"Not all of them, but many."

"And your consulting business now?"

"Provides me some cover if I need to go into places that aren't very safe," she admitted. "I'm retiring at the end of December," she added. "It's time. I've been preparing for a while. With Igor gone, I don't have anything to fear anymore."

"What about Kostya?" I wondered worriedly. "What about everything that happened back at that warehouse?"

"It's been handled, Holly. When you're more clearheaded, I'll tell you the cover story. It's simple enough. Lana and Savannah had no trouble with it. Frankly, the police here have enough problems to handle. They were happy to close the case as quickly as possible."

Worried about Lana and Savannah, I asked, "Are they okay? Savvy and Lana? Where are they?"

"They're in the resort a few blocks away. This private hospital and the resort are in a kind of compound that caters to medical tourists. We're sending them home tomorrow."

I closed my eyes, thinking of the mess Savannah would have to handle when she got home. "I need to talk to Savannah before she leaves."

"She won't leave without seeing you. I'll bring her up later so you two can discuss things." My mother pressed her lips together. "You have to remember to be patient with her, Holly. She's been through so much, and she may be a little upset."

"Because of the way I dragged her into this?"

She nodded. "She's your best friend, and she'll come around, but you have to give her some space."

"I will."

"As far as Kostya is concerned, he'll be here for a while. Weeks. He has to recover, and it's not going to be easy. His work back in Houston," she shot me a look, "will have to be handled by someone else. Hopefully, while he's on sabbatical, Nikolai will realize that Kostya's time as his cleaner has ended."

"And then what? He just walks away from the mafia?" I frowned at her. "I don't think it works that way, Mom."

"It doesn't," she agreed. "But there are ways for him to be *in* without doing the wetwork." She settled into the pillow and smiled at me. "You called me, 'Mom.'"

I made a face. "What else would I call you?"

"Ekaterina? Aunt? Not-My-Mom-And-I-Hate-You?"

"I don't hate you." I touched my head to hers. "I'm not happy that everyone lied to me my whole life, but after meeting Igor and surviving the break-in at my house the other night, I understand why you did it. I don't like it, but I get it."

"Holly, everything I've ever done has been to protect you. Everything I'll ever do in the future, will be to keep you safe."

"I know, Mom." I blinked away tears. "I love you."

"I love you, Holly."

There were so many other questions I wanted to ask, but I was so tired. I didn't think my mother was up to an interrogation either. Some part of me didn't want to know anyway. I worried that I was opening Pandora's Box. Maybe some things were better left unsaid.

"YOU UP FOR some visitors?" Savannah asked from the doorway of my hospital room later that evening.

Nodding, I smiled encouragingly. Savannah and Lana's smiles faltered as they reached my bedside. Soon, the three of us were crying and hugging. The shared trauma we had survived was overwhelming, but it felt good to be together again, to know we had made it out alive.

"We brought you some things," Lana said, wiping her eyes and putting three shopping bags on the small couch on the other side of the room. "Clothes, toiletries, some magazines," she explained. "To make it more comfortable for you here."

"Thank you. I really appreciate that." My skin and hair felt so grimy. I needed a shower and wanted to wear something other than this thin hospital gown. "I can't wait to feel clean again."

"If the nurses will let you shower now, I'll help you," Savannah offered. "It's not like I haven't seen your little chicken butt naked."

I scowled at her. "I do not have a chicken butt!"

Savannah glanced at Lana. "She does. Cute little chicken butt."

Lana laughed and settled into the chair by my bed. "I do not think I should comment on this. I want to keep my job."

"After what we've been through, you have a job at the salon for as long as you want it," I assured her. "And if this was too much, I'll help you find a job somewhere else. I understand if you can't handle going back to the salon."

"It was not too much," Lana replied in that calm way of hers. "I am glad we were together. We make a good team."

"We do," Savannah agreed. She sat on the edge of my bed and adjusted the coverlet. "Nisha and Billie have been holding the salon together. A lot of our clients were worried about us. Our social media pages blew up so Billie has been handling them. There are reporters who want to interview us about our '*kidnapping and ransom*,' but I'm really not interested."

"Neither am I," I concurred. "The last thing I want is any more attention on my private life."

"I agree. I think it's best if we make a statement and then let that be the end of it," Savannah suggested. "If you want, I'll write it tomorrow. I can email it to you or your mom, and you can give me an okay or suggestions to change it."

I shook my head. "I trust you, Savannah. You know what needs to be said."

"Speaking of things that need to be said…" She glanced at Lana who stood and gave me a careful hug before wishing me well and leaving. Once the door shut behind her, Savannah sighed. "I know this isn't the time to get into a huge back-and-forth about what happened, but I need you to know that I'm not okay with being pulled into this mobster bullshit. We could have died, Holly! We could have been raped or sold. We are so fucking lucky that we are walking out of this unscathed."

"I know."

"Do you?" She tilted her head. "Do you understand what loving Kostya almost cost us?"

"It wasn't Kostya's fault."

Savannah scoffed. "Don't make excuses for him!"

"It wasn't his fault," I repeated forcefully. "Not this time. This was about me. About who I am. About my biological parents."

"What do you mean? Biological? But your mom—"

"She's my aunt. My dad is her brother. My mother, the woman who gave birth to me, was a Russian spy. The man who took us? He was in the KGB. My father was one of his targets, and my mother—Kira—was one of his agents. She fell in love with my dad, and they killed her for it. So, Mom took me from Russia and brought me home to Houston and raised me as her own child."

Savannah sagged with shock. "Holy shit, Holly."

"Yeah. It's…it's a lot."

"Yeah, it is." She gave me a quizzical look. "I cannot believe you're Russian!"

I rolled my eyes. "We always knew I was half-Russian."

"Yeah, but now you're like full-blooded Russian!" Lowering her voice, she asked, "Are you a legal citizen? Like are we going to have ICE beating down our doors and taking you to one of those concentration camps on the border?"

"As far as I know, I'm legal." I didn't really know. I was almost afraid to find out, but I would have to ask my mother soon.

"Jesus, Holly, your life is like a soap opera!" She bit her lower lip before asking, "Does your mom know that your birth mom was a spy? That her brother was a target?"

I nodded. "Yes, she knows everything."

"This is so screwed up, Holly." She hesitated. "How are you taking it? I mean, I guess now you know about your dad."

"It's what I wanted to know," I agreed. "I wanted to find out who I am and where I came from and I did."

"But it's not the story you were wanting to hear, is it?"

"Not even close," I admitted, feeling guilty for not telling her the truth about my mom's part in the tale. There were some secrets I wasn't going to share.

"Holly," she took my hand, "I really think you need to take some time off work. Like—way more time than it takes to heal from your injuries. Maybe get some counseling. You've been through so much, and now you're learning all this shit about your family? I don't want you to come back to work too soon. The stress of running the business and keeping your clients happy and dealing with the fallout from all of this might break you."

I started to argue with her. I wanted to tell her that I was perfectly fine and could go back to work soon. I wanted to tell her that getting back into my normal routine of work would be good for me.

But I didn't because she was right. I needed to get my head straight.

"Let Nisha split up my clients among the other girls," I instructed. "She has a good eye for matching stylists with clients. She'll keep them all happy until I come back."

"I was planning to do that anyway," Savannah said.

"We should tell Nisha that we're giving her part of the business," I decided. "It's not right to ask her to do all the extra work without giving her what she deserves."

"She's going to fight us on it."

"She will, but you won't take no for an answer."

"I won't," Savannah promised. Bending down, she drew me into a sisterly hug. "Don't worry about the salon or Lana. I'll take care of everything while you're recuperating."

"I know you will." I hugged her as tightly as I could manage. "I really am sorry about everything, Savvy. I never wanted anything like this to happen."

"I know you didn't." She released me. "I meant what I said about Kostya, Holly. I know you love him, but maybe taking a break from him would be a good idea, too. Our kidnapping wasn't his fault, but the break-in? The murder in your house? That's on him. You really need to figure out if you want to sign up for a life like this for the next fifty years."

I didn't want to think about breaking up with Kostya or not seeing him as soon as I was able to get out of this bed. I didn't want to fight with Savannah either. Not now when she was leaving. "I'll think about it."

She didn't believe me. Exhaling, she said, "Okay."

I watched her leave the room through the long window by the door. She met up with Lana, and they left together. Closing my eyes, I rested my head back against the pillow and thought about everything Savannah had said. As I fell back asleep, I was tormented by dreams of Kostya walking away from me forever.

CHAPTER THIRTY-ONE

THE MORNING AFTER Savannah and Lana returned to Houston, I was given the green light to get out of bed and shower. My mother helped me, not once making any remarks about my supposed chicken butt, and then encouraged me to stay out of bed and walk if I could. The first trip up and down the hall was excruciating. After a nap, I tried again and made three trips before I needed to sit down again.

By the end of the day, I felt strong enough to make the trek up to the ICU to visit Kostya. Mom went with me, standing close to me, but making me bear my own weight and drag my own IV pole. It annoyed me at first that she wasn't helping more, but deep down, I knew that she was doing it for my own good. She wanted me to get better and coddling me wasn't going to achieve that goal.

When we made it to Kostya's ICU room, we found Gabe sitting and sketching in the only chair in the room. He seemed nicer in this setting, less menacing and deadly in his jeans and black Henley. He was just as tall and solidly built as I remembered, and his eyes were still just as dark, like the blackest coffee. His nose had obviously been broken a time or two and not set very well. There were small scars on his face and larger ones on his forearms, most of those hidden by his tattooed sleeves.

"I'll get out of your way," he said gruffly, gathering up his sketchbook and pencils and jacket. "Go get some dinner, I think." He stopped as he neared the doorway. "You want anything?"

I shook my head. "I'm good, but thanks."

He nodded and left, closing the glass sliding door halfway to give me some privacy. He chatted briefly with my mother before walking away and disappearing down the hall.

Pushing the chair closer to Kostya's bedside, I sat down in it and rearranged my IV lines and the pole holding up the bags of fluid I still needed. Taking in the hospital bed and all the machines and tubes, I was shaken by how pale and sick Kostya looked. To me, he had always seemed so strong and powerful, so in control. Now he looked weak and vulnerable. It hurt to see him like this. It hurt me to know that he was here like this because of me.

There were incisions on his chest and stomach, all of them covered with bandages. Some of them had fluid or blood seeping into them. A white sheet covered him from the waist down. His chest rose and fell in time with the machine breathing for him. I found comfort in the rhythmic beep of his heartbeat on the monitor and the slow hiss of the ventilator. He was alive. He was fighting. He would wake up soon, and we could start over, wipe the slate clean and try to build a relationship based on truth.

"Holly?" A little over an hour later, Mom called my name from the doorway. "The nurses said it's time for you to go back to your room."

"Do I have to go?" I sounded like a petulant child, but I

couldn't help it. "I want to stay."

"I know you do, but you're still recovering. You won't be any use to him if you get sick."

Motioning for her help, I waited until she was standing front of me to take her hands and let her steady me as I stood. The pain along my incisions was intense, and I worried my stitches were going to open and my insides were going to fall out like a scene in a horror movie.

"You need your pain meds," my mother scolded. "Let's get you back in bed."

"What about Kostya? Is anyone going to stay with him?" I didn't like the idea of him being alone, especially when he was so vulnerable.

"I'm here," Gabe announced from the doorway. "I'm not going anywhere until he's out of that bed."

I squeezed his arm. "Thank you."

With a lingering glance over my shoulder, I left the ICU floor and made it back to my room. My mother helped me into the bathroom and back into bed. The kind nurses brought me a warm meal and pain medicine that I gratefully swallowed. By the time I'd finished my soup, I was drowsy again.

My head fell back against the pillow as my mother cleared away my tray. She opened the bag of toiletries that Lana and Savannah had brought me. Taking out a facial cloth from a travel package, she gently cleaned my face and neck before dotting on a little moisturizer from a tiny tube. A quick sweep of lip balm soothed my chapped mouth.

"There," she said, taking a step back. "It's not your normal beauty routine, but it will do."

"Thanks, Mom."

She kissed the top of my head. "Get some rest. You need it."

I didn't argue. I closed my eyes and dreamed of Kostya.

SOMETIME IN THE middle of the night, I woke up desperate to use the bathroom and thirsty as hell. Clearing my throat, I blinked a few times and let my vision adjust to the dim lighting. "Mom? Can you help me?"

"Your mother isn't here. I sent her to the hotel to rest."

Startled, I damn near bolted out of the bed when I realized there was a man sitting in the chair next to me. "Who the hell are you?"

"Careful," he scolded gently, raising his hands in front of him. "You'll hurt yourself."

His thick Russian accent registered finally. He sat forward, letting me see him better in the dim light. His hair was white, and his face was older and wrinkled, but I recognized him from the photos. "Maksim?"

"Yes." Sadly, he gestured toward the hospital bed. "This isn't how I wanted us to meet."

"No. Me either."

We stared at each other for a long moment before he asked, "Do you need a nurse?"

I shook my head. "Can you just help me get out of bed?"

"Of course." He rose from his chair, his movement swift and smooth. He was old, but he seemed fit and strong. "Take my hands."

They were warm and much larger than mine. Cautiously, he helped me out of the bed and put a hand between my shoulder blades. "Do you need help walking?"

"No. I've got it." I nervously smiled up at him before grabbing my IV pole and shuffling toward the bathroom. Once locked inside, I stared at myself in the mirror. Was this really happening? Was my father finally making an appearance in my life? In a hospital room in Mexico?

All these years, I had imagined that meeting my father would be something magical and beautiful. In reality, it felt awkward and strange.

Feeling out of sorts and confused, I used the restroom and washed my hands. When I emerged from the bathroom, Maksim was standing in front of the oversized windows overlooking the resort. I noticed there was a new bottle of water and a juice box on the tray next to my bed.

"I wasn't sure what you might like," he said, his back still toward me. "I can get something else from the nurses."

"Water is fine." I reached my bed and climbed back onto it without help.

He had moved closer, ready to steady me if I lost my balance. He reached for the pillows and fluffed them up behind me, making it easier for me to sit up and drink. He settled onto the end of the bed, his left leg bent so he could face me. "How are you feeling?"

"Tired. Sore." I drank some more water. "But I'll recover soon."

"Your mother will be glad to get you back to Houston. I suspect she's already hired someone to pack up all of your things and move them into her house. She's always struggled with your independence from her."

"She never showed it," I replied, surprised by how much

he understood of my mother's emotional state. "She always encouraged me to go out and live my life, to be a strong, independent woman."

"Yes," he agreed, "but she feared being away from you. She worried all the time about not being there to protect you."

"She raised me to be able to protect myself. She did everything right. I'm lucky to have her as my mom."

"We're both lucky to have her in our family," Maksim decided. "She's done more to help me than any other person in my life. She's kept two of my children safe in Houston all these years."

"Two children?" I asked with surprise. "I have a sibling in Houston?"

"You have a brother in Houston. You have a sister-in-law now. Soon, you'll have a nephew." His wary face seemed to soften at the mention of a grandbaby.

"Do you think...? I mean, would my brother want to meet me? Does he know about you? About me?"

"He knows about you, and you've already met him and his wife." He smiled almost mischievously. "She's one of your clients."

"What? Seriously? Who?"

"Vivian."

Taken aback, I sank into my pillows. "Vivian is my sister-in-law? So that means...? Oh my God." I covered my face with my hands. "I feel so stupid."

"Why?" Maksim wondered curiously.

"I went to Nikolai and asked him for help finding you—my father—in Russia. He was so helpful and kind." I rolled my eyes. "Which, of course, makes sense now because he knew the whole time!"

Maksim chuckled softly. "Yes, that does sound like a joke he would enjoy."

"He doesn't seem like the sort of man who jokes much."

"He had a hard life. Most of it was my fault," he admitted. "I've never been a very good father. Not to Nikolai or you or my other children. It never felt natural to me, and I never truly tried to be a better parent. My late wife took care of raising our children, and I was happy to leave it to her. Katya took you to Houston."

It was strange to hear my mother called Katya, but I thought it suited her much more than Frances ever would. "What about Nikolai? Who took care of him?"

"He took care of himself. His mother died when he was very young, and I let him go into the orphanage. When he was old enough, I pulled him into my world and made him the man he is today."

Frowning, I fought the urge to criticize his parenting of Nikolai. It was long done and couldn't be changed, but it was cold and cruel to send a little boy to an orphanage when he clearly had the means to raise him properly.

"You think I was wrong to send Nikolai to the orphanage," he guessed correctly.

"You *were* wrong."

The corner of his mouth lifted with a smile. "You have so much of your mothers in you. Neither of them—Katya or Kira—ever hesitated to tell me I was wrong."

"What was she like?" I asked carefully. "She looked very beautiful in the photos Igor showed me."

His face darkened at the mention of Igor. "I should have

killed him the night I caught him. Kira would never forgive me if she knew that I'd let him get to you."

I wasn't sure what to say to that so I didn't say anything at all.

"Your mother…," he started. "Kira was unlike anyone I'd ever met. She had a wild sense of humor. Irreverent," he added. "She wasn't afraid to make fun of me. She wasn't afraid to poke at me or tease me. She had a raucous laugh, and she loved life. She didn't fear what tomorrow would bring. She was living in the moment right up until they killed her."

"I'm sorry that I never got to know her," I said quietly, my eyes stinging with tears.

"She would have loved you so much," he assured me, taking my hand in his. "You would have been the absolute light of her life. But," he said, clearing his throat, "your life with my sister is the life you were meant to have. You can't dwell on what could have or should have been, Holly."

"I know," I whispered.

"I have her things. When I get back to Moscow, I'll send them to you. Books, journals, some of her clothing, photos, her papers—I've kept them all this time for you."

"I can't read Russian," I admitted, feeling strangely guilty about that. "I never had a reason to learn."

"Well, maybe Kostya can read them to you."

My gaze jumped to his. I couldn't read his face. "Does that make you upset? That I want to be with someone in your line of work?"

"Of course, it does. You were meant for a doctor or a lawyer or a CEO."

"I've dated those types of men. Lots of them. They weren't

for me."

"Yes, you got that affliction from Kira," he grumbled. "She always had an eye for men like me. I had hoped you wouldn't inherit that gene."

"The heart wants what the heart wants."

"Yes, I suppose it does." He pursed his lips together rather grumpily. "He can't leave my organization, Holly. For men like Kostya, men who know too much, leaving isn't an option."

"I know," I answered honestly. "I've figured that out for myself."

"And you still want him?"

"If he'll have me? Yes."

"You're too good for him. He'll never deserve you."

"That's your opinion."

He narrowed his eyes. "I'll talk to Nikolai. We'll figure something out for him. But you?" He pinned me in place with a serious look. "You will stay out of this life. You would do well to follow Vivian's lead. She knows how to walk the line."

"Then I guess I'll have to ask her to lunch so she can school me on being a perfect mob moll," I replied archly.

His mouth slanted with a smile again. "You'll be a good aunt to Nikolai's boy, and Vivian could use a friend like you, I think. You'll be good for each other."

"Are you matchmaking my friends now?"

"My choice of friends for you is better than that girl Lana you've taken under your wing," he said with a grimace of distaste. "She's not worthy of your time, Holly. Her mother was a terrorist, and her father betrayed Kostya, almost got him killed."

Although that bit of information about Lana shocked me,

I wasn't going to let him try to make decisions for me or boss me around like he must have done everyone else in his life.

"Okay, *Dad*," I said with irritated emphasis, "this is the point where I tell you that you can't just swan into my life after, like, thirty years and start telling me how to live. I like Lana. She's sweet. I know what she's been through, and she's amazing to have survived it. And that's all there is to it."

His unhappy stare faded slowly. "There's that backbone you got from Katya. She told me the same thing once, a long time ago. She was right, too." He lowered both feet to the floor and stood. "But don't tell her I told you that."

"No promises," I said, smiling as he gathered up his things. "Are you leaving?"

"I have a flight to catch." Gesturing toward the door, he added, "You're perfectly safe here. My people are watching over you. No one will dare hurt you here."

I didn't doubt him. He didn't seem like the kind of man people wanted to cross.

"When you're feeling up to it, I want you to come visit me. I want you to learn about your heritage and your family." He shrugged into his jacket. "I'm tired of my family being separated. We're stronger together, and it's time for me to make amends. I want you to meet your other siblings."

"I'd like that very much."

"Your mother and I can work out the details. It might be easier for you to come in the summer the first time. The cold can be very jarring for foreigners." He made a strange face. "Although, in a way, you're not really a foreigner at all. In fact, you're more Russian than Kostya!"

"How so?"

"He was born in East Germany."

"Was he?"

"His parents were stationed there under German covers. So, technically, he's a German."

"I don't think he'd take kindly to being told he's not Russian," I decided.

"No, he wouldn't." Maksim came close to my bed and awkwardly hugged me. "I'm glad we finally got to meet, Holly."

"So am I," I said, hugging him back. We weren't going to be the family I had always dreamed of having, but this was a good start.

"Give Kostya my best when he wakes," Maksim said, walking toward the door.

"Is that a threat?" I wondered aloud.

Maksim laughed. "Not really."

"Wait!" I called out, stopping him before he could disappear from my life again.

He stepped back into the room and looked at me questioningly. "Yes?"

"What was my name? What did Kira name me?"

His swallowed hard, his eyes suddenly glistening. "Polina. She wanted to call you Polina."

Leaning back against my pillows, I watched my father leave and dragged the covers up to my chin. I didn't even try to fight the sobs that tore from my throat. I thought about the woman who had given birth to me. She had loved me and protected me inside her. She must have had dreams for me. What did she hope I would become? Would she have been proud of me?

Those were questions I would never have answered. My father was right. I couldn't dwell on what could or should have been. My life was my life. There was no changing the direction it had taken to this point.

I was never going to be Polina Prokhorovna, born and raised in Russia with all the hopes and dreams of her mother, Kira.

I'm Holly Phillips—and I'm right where I am supposed to be.

CHAPTER THIRTY-TWO

"**Y**OU FINALLY AWAKE?"

Kostya grunted with discomfort. Pain radiated throughout his chest and stomach with every single breath he inhaled. His joints ached and felt uncomfortably stiff. His throat burned, and a gnawing hunger throbbed in the pit of his belly.

"You've been in and out the last couple of days. You wake up for ten or twenty minutes and then you drop off again."

Wincing at the bright sunlight filtering through the hospital room windows, he glanced at Gabe who had kicked back in a reclining chair near the bed. He sketched quietly, his pencil moving over the paper in rhythmic swipes.

Where was Holly? Was she still in the hospital? Had she gone home to Houston?

"Your girl is with her mama," Gabe said as if reading his mind. "They went to get lunch. She's been sitting with you since she woke up from her surgery. Stays here all day. Waiting for you."

Flashes of memories danced before him. Holly in the chair. Holly standing next to him, wiping his face. Holly reading a magazine article to him. "Is she okay?"

Gabe nodded. "As far as I can tell, physically, yeah. She

was discharged two days ago. She and Frances are staying at the resort next door. Holly's refusing to leave until you're healthy enough to get out of that bed."

Warmth spread through him at that bit of information. He remembered professing his love for her as he bled out in the back of the SUV. She had answered him without hesitation. She loved him, wholly and without reservation. She loved him enough to sit by his side, day after day, while nursing her own wounds. She wasn't going to leave him when he has wounded and vulnerable. She was making it clear that she was with him, from now until the end.

But, as quickly as that wonderful feeling of love and contentment filled him, another feeling replaced it. Dread. Fear. She had almost been killed twice in two days. First, Scorpion and then Igor. If she stayed with him, she would be just as vulnerable as Vivian, Bianca and Erin. She would be a target for people who wanted to hurt him.

Remembering the blood on her shirt and the terror in her gaze as she'd stared down at him, scrambling to help, tormented him. She had shot and killed a man to save him. She had lost that innocence.

I made her into a killer.

His heart stuttered painfully, the wild beating catching Gabe's attention as it blipped across the monitor. "You okay, man?"

"I'm fine." The punishing guilt of knowing that he had changed Holly's life for the worse left him feeling irritable. He glanced down at the tubes and wires coming off of his body and running to IV stands and machines. "Can I get out of this bed? Shower?"

Gabe set aside his sketchpad and pencil. "Let me get a nurse."

An hour later and after a lot bitching and complaining on his part, Kostya had finally negotiated the removal of his catheter and permission to shower. Hidden behind a curtain while a nurse did what needed to be done, he heard Holly return with her mother.

"He's awake? Like fully awake?" she asked, her voice filled with relief and excitement.

"Seems so," Gabe answered. "He's harassing the nurses to let him up to shower."

"He'll need help," Holly said. "I was only out for a few days, and I was so weak I needed Mom to steady me."

"I'll take him in," Gabe offered with amusement. "I'm sure he'll enjoy that."

"I can hear you!" Kostya called out, ignoring the nurse laughing at his predicament.

When the nurse was done, she gathered up the used supplies and opened the curtain around his bed. "Five minutes in the shower. You either have one of your friends help you, or we'll get one of our nurses."

"Yeah. Fine," he grumbled, shoving aside the sheet and swinging his legs over the edge of the bed.

"Slow down!" Holly rushed into the room and slid in front of him, her hands flying to his shoulders to hold him upright in bed as he swayed dangerously. "You're going to fall and knock yourself out!" She shook her head and frowned up at him. "Let us help you."

Pride was a damnable thing. He didn't want to look weak and sick in front of her. He wanted to be the strong, capable man she had always been able to count on for help. With their roles reversed, he felt off-kilter. "You don't have the upper body strength to catch me if I fall."

She rolled her eyes. "That's the first thing you've said to me since you told me you loved me."

Shit.

Leaning down to touch his forehead to hers, he whispered, "I still love you."

"You better," she teased with one of her playful smiles. "And, yes, you're right. I can't catch you if you fall. I'm on lift restrictions for a few more days." She glanced toward the doorway. "Gabe?"

"I'll drag his grumpy ass to the bathroom, but you'll have to do the hands-on work unless your mom has another suitcase full of cash for me."

"You're terrible," Holly said, wrinkling her dainty little nose.

Kostya reluctantly relied on Gabe's help to the bathroom. He tried to protest when Holly followed him inside and began to strip him of the hospital gown. Ignoring him, she untied the back of the gown and tossed it into the laundry hamper in the corner of the oversized bathroom. After turning on the water, she motioned toward the plastic and metal shower chair. "Come on."

"I'm not sitting on that," he refused stubbornly.

"Yes, you are."

"Holly, I can stand."

"No, you can't. You're about to fall over right now."

She was right, and it irritated him.

"Fine," he growled and shuffled to the chair. "Happy?"

"The last time I washed your hair while you sat in a chair, you were much nicer."

"If that's an option right now, I'll start smiling." He reached for her hip, but she evaded him.

"Stop! You're going to get me all wet!"

"That's the idea, *milaya*."

"You're incorrigible. And don't think you can start with all the Russian pet names now," she warned. "Now, hold still."

Closing his eyes, he decided to stop being an asshole and enjoy her mothering ministrations. She used the handheld shower head to rinse his body, starting at his hair and moving down carefully. The smell of dried blood and sweat and dirt filled the bathroom as the warm water amplified the scents.

He almost groaned when her small, soft hands began to massage his scalp with the citrus shampoo provided by the hospital. She had those magic fingers that set his whole body on fire as they scratched his scalp and tugged on his hair. Her hands moved down to his aching neck and massaged gently, easing the tension as she continued on to his shoulders.

When she began to wash his body, lathering her hands with the small bar of soap and wiping them along his skin, he watched her. Flashbacks of their shower and the incredible sex that followed made his groin ache. There were too many painkillers in his system to allow him to get fully hard, but his cock tried nevertheless.

She held his gaze as she stroked her soapy hand up and down his shaft and over his balls. "When they finally let you out of here, I intend to finish this."

"You keep that up, and you'll have to finish it right now."

She leaned in and kissed him tenderly. "Sorry, but our five

minutes are up."

He groaned with frustration as she washed his legs and feet. After rinsing him, she turned off the water and reached for a towel. She dried most of his body while he sat and then cautiously helped him stand so she could finish the job. She took a clean gown from the shelves near the hamper and helped him into it.

"Do you want to brush your teeth?" she asked, gesturing toward the unopened hospital toiletries.

"Please," he said, desperate to feel human again.

She opened a toothbrush and tiny box of toothpaste. "Do you want me to brush or steady you?"

"I can brush my own teeth," he replied, harsher than he had intended.

She rolled her eyes and handed it over. "Fine, but you are *not* shaving your own face. I'll do that for you."

"You took a straight razor to my hair. I'm perfectly comfortable with you shaving my face with a safety razor." He leaned against the sink and brushed his teeth. Behind him, Holly kept her hands on his waist and her body against his, bracing him just in case he got dizzy or weak.

When he was done brushing and rinsing, he lifted his gown for a better look at his chest and stomach. There would be a lot of scarring, some of it distorting his tattoos. If he were a vain man, he would have them touched up, but they weren't tattoos he had chosen for aesthetic reasons. They were business.

"Do you want me to shave you now or later?"

"Later," he said, leaning into her touch as she wrapped her arms around his waist, gingerly avoiding his injuries.

Her plump pout pressed tender kisses to his back. "I'm really happy that you're awake."

He closed his eyes, reveling in her touch and hating himself for what he would have to do soon. "I'm happy you're here with me."

"Always," she promised. "I'll always be here with you."

No, he thought sadly. *No, you won't.*

"WHY DO YOU get fish tacos and I have to settle for soup?" Kostya asked, dramatically scooping it up with spoon and letting it pour back into his bowl.

I fought the urge to sigh or roll my eyes. Ever since he had woken up two days ago, he had been grumpy and difficult. He was acting like a child about things, and as much as I wanted to call him on his ridiculous behavior, I understood that he was struggling with his recovery.

Calmly, I explained, "I'm not the one with eating restrictions. You are. So, either you eat the delicious *caldo de res* I brought from the restaurant or you can have salty vegetable soup the hospital is serving tonight."

He frowned but accepted his fate, taking a taste of the hearty soup. He didn't complain again after that first spoonful.

Hoping to steer him away from his moodiness, I said, "Savannah sent me the mock-ups for the Denim and Diamonds gala. They're outrageously shiny. I can't even imagine what the postage is going to be like on them with all of the rhinestones and glitter!"

"That's your sorority's charity thing on New Year's Eve?"

"Yep." I eyed him and tried to decide his jeans size. "We'll have to take you to Cavender's for some jeans and boots. Maybe Republic Boot Co.," I added, thinking how much fun I could have getting him a pair of custom cowboy boots.

"I'm not wearing cowboy boots," he grumbled sourly.

"You have to," I insisted. "It's the theme for the gala. How else are you supposed to two-step if you don't have boots?"

"I don't dance."

I rolled my eyes. "Everyone dances."

"Not me," he retorted. "Definitely not two-step."

"It's the easiest one to learn," I assured him. "As soon as you're out of bed, I'll teach you. We might not be the best dancers there, but we'll have a good time."

He made an unhappy noise. "You should take someone else. I'll be a terrible date for a party like that."

Pushing aside the tray holding my takeout, I sat forward on the chair. "I'm not taking someone else to my sorority's biggest charity night. You're the only one I want with me."

He put down his spoon with a noisy clink. "And what about what I want?"

Taken aback by his rude question, I asked, "Are you in pain? Is that why you're being such a jerk? Because if you're hurting, I can get a nurse in here to give you something so you'll feel better."

"Yes, I'm in pain, Holly. These doctors gutted me like deer and sewed me back together like a Frankenstein monster." He grabbed his cup of water and tossed it back angrily. "That's not why I'm acting like a jerk, as you put it."

"What's wrong? Why are you trying to pick fights with me?" I narrowed my eyes at him. "Are you trying to run me off? Because that's not how this works, Kostya. I'm not going to run away just because you're in here growling like a bear."

"Then maybe I need to be blunt," he snapped. "I want you to pack your things and go back to Houston with your mother. As soon as possible," he added meanly.

"I'm not leaving. I don't care how much you yell and complain. I'm staying here to help you recover."

"I don't want your help, Holly!"

I jerked back at his outburst. He had never raised his voice with me, and the thunderous sound of it made my stomach clench. "Don't yell at me like that. I'm not one of your street soldiers. You don't scare me."

He inhaled roughly and looked away from me. The muscles in his neck tensed, and his hands were tightening into fists. "I'm sorry I yelled at you," he said finally, "but that doesn't change what I want."

"You want me to leave?" I asked, dumbfounded. "You want me to pack my shit and go?"

He met my confused stare. "Yes. I want you to go."

"Why?"

"Because I realized something when I woke up, Holly."

"And what's that?"

"You're not the right girl for me."

His words stung worse than any slap. "How can you say that to me? After everything we've been through—"

"That's right, Holly. We've been through too much. It was selfish of me to ever think I could have you. We can't do this anymore. I won't put you and the people you love in danger."

"You don't get to make that decision unilaterally," I argued, desperate to make him understand. "I'm not a child, Kostya. I understand the risks. I love you, and I want to be with you even if—"

"I drugged you," he interrupted loudly.

Shocked by his statement, I blinked. "What?"

"That first night we stayed together at your place," he said, never dropping his gaze and forcing me to look at him and see that he was telling the truth. "When I came to the salon and found you and took you home?" He shook his head. "It was all a setup. You were on a hit list. Someone found out you were Maksim's daughter, and they were coming after you. Lana was a decoy—"

I stiffened as if someone had just thrown cold water on me. "What do you mean? Lana was a decoy? How?"

"I found her in a hotel room a few weeks before that night," he explained. "She had been bought and sold and then left behind. A colleague of mine found her and wanted me to look after her."

"You didn't recognize her?" I asked, thinking of what Maksim had said.

"What do you mean?" he asked, his brow furrowed.

"Maksim told me that her mother was a terrorist and her father betrayed you. Is that why your colleague wanted you to look after her?"

"I didn't know," he said quietly. "I suspected, but I hadn't confirmed. When I took her in, I was only thinking of her as being useful."

"Useful? She's a fucking person, Kostya! Not a tool!"

"She was the tool I needed to keep you safe that night," he countered. "She went into the salon with the rest of the women from the shelter, and no one noticed she didn't belong there. I told her to get the same haircut and dye job as yours. I wanted her to look like you from afar."

My stomach pitched violently as he spoke. "And then what?"

"I had her drug you. Your drink," he clarified. "She hid in the salon, and after Savannah left, she kept an eye on you until it was safe for me to come inside. I took you into the supply room at the salon and left you with Lana and Lobo while I took care of business."

"Took care of business," I repeated. "How?"

"How do you think?"

I closed my eyes as a wave of revulsion overwhelmed me. "You killed people in my salon while I was passed out in the supply room."

"I did."

"And then?" I didn't want to hear the rest of his horrible tale, but I needed to know.

"And then I had the girls clean up and get rid of the bodies while I took you home," he answered matter-of-factly.

"What is wrong with you?" I asked, suddenly furious. "Why didn't you just come to me and tell me I was on a hit list? Why didn't you ask me to let you into the salon while I hid in the supply closet? Why the hell did you just jump straight to drugging me?"

He didn't seem to have an answer. Not at first. Eventually, he said, "It was cleaner that way. The secret of your parentage stayed buried. You weren't a part of the killings. You got to sleep through the whole ugly thing and wake up the next morning without any awareness of what had happened."

Rubbing my face, I asked, "Is that why you wanted me to take a month to think about us? That next morning over breakfast? Because you were feeling guilty?"

"Yes. Partially."

A troubling thought hit me. "Were you ever going to tell me?"

"That I drugged you? Or that I killed people in your salon?"

"Both!" I exclaimed with exasperation.

"I'm telling you now."

"That's not what I asked."

"I don't know," he admitted. "I wanted to come clean so many times, but I couldn't do it."

"Why not?"

"I'm a coward when it comes to you," he confessed. "I didn't want to lose you."

"Until today," I said, starting to cry. "Now you're trying to push me away."

"I'm not a good man, Holly," he replied, his own eyes glittering and dark. "I'll ruin you."

"You already have," I whispered, wiping at my cheeks. "I love you. Just you. If you don't want me, that's fine. I'm not afraid to be alone."

His harsh expression slackened. "Holly, that's not what I want for you. I want you to be happy."

"You make me happy. Faults and fuck-ups and all," I added seriously. "I love you, Kostya." Picking up the tote bag I had been using as a purse, I slung it over my shoulder and wiped the tears from my face again. "But I'll go. If that's what you want, I'll do it. I'll go back to Houston and leave you here to wallow in your bitterness and bullshit."

He stiffened as I came close to the bed and leaned across

to kiss him, maybe for the last time. I pressed my lips to his, lingering for a few seconds while I fought the urge to weep. When I pulled back, he had his eyes closed, his jaw set as he breathed heavily. He was just as upset as I was, but he seemed determined to run me off.

"You know where to find me if you change your mind."

Barely holding it together, I left his hospital room without a backward glance. In the hallway, I ran into Gabe. He took one look at me, at my crestfallen face and the tears shining in my eyes, and drew me into a bear hug. "That stupid asshole," he muttered against my hair. "He's determined to be miserable."

"He's hurting," I said, trying to make sense of the man I loved. "Physically, emotionally—he's wounded. He doesn't mean what he's saying. Not really."

"He feels vulnerable," Gabe explained. "Having you here makes him feel weak. He feels guilty about everything he's done. It's hard to have all that terrible shit deep inside you when the woman you love is so clean and good."

"I'm not perfect, Gabe."

"Compared to him? You're a damn saint, Holly." He squeezed my shoulder. "I'll keep an eye on him. He'll be safe with me."

"Thank you, Gabe."

"You leaving soon?"

"Probably in the morning," I decided, certain there were flights we could take then. "Why?"

"I have something I wanted you to take back to Houston," he said, avoiding my gaze as if shy.

I suspected it was something for Savannah. He seemed

smitten with her, but I wasn't sure there was a future there. After Savannah shared her opinion on Kostya and his history, I couldn't imagine she would be accepting of someone like Gabe who seemed to have secrets of his own.

"Just send it to the hotel," I said. "I'll make sure I ask at the front desk before we go."

"Thanks." He patted my back. "You should get some rest. Don't worry about your old man. I'll handle him."

"Not too roughly," I insisted.

"No promises," Gabe said, backing away from me.

Alone in the elevator a few moments later, I closed my eyes and leaned back against the wall. I wanted to breakdown and start crying hysterically. I wanted to crawl in bed with my mom and drink wine until I forgot about the nasty fight I'd just had with Kostya. I wanted to run back to his hospital room and demand he let me stay and take care of him.

Somehow, I found the strength and willpower to leave the hospital and make the short walk to the resort. I crossed the lobby, got into the elevator and made my way up to the spacious suite I was sharing with my mother. When I entered the room, she was on the couch, sipping something white and crisp while reading on her tablet.

"You're back earlier than I'd expected," she said, setting aside her wine glass and tablet. She took one look at me and sighed, taking off her reading glasses and dropping them on her tablet. "Come here, Holly. Tell me what he said."

Crying, I dropped down next to her on the couch and melted into her motherly hug. It was just too much. Everything that had happened to me bubbled to the surface and erupted out of me like a volcano of sadness. The break-in,

Scorpion, being kidnapped, finding out about my biological parents, shooting Igor, being shot, watching Kostya almost die, finding out he had drugged me and killed people in my salon…

I sobbed and wept until I couldn't see straight or breathe. I let it all out and let it all go.

No more secrets, I promised myself. *No. More. Secrets.*

CHAPTER THIRTY-THREE

"DID YOU WANT to borrow this necklace?" My mother asked as she came into my bedroom with diamonds dangling from her finger. She looked stunning in the midnight blue gown she'd chosen during our Saks shopping trip. The halter style highlighted her toned arms and shoulders in a way that made me outrageously jealous. She had chosen flashy diamond earrings and a bracelet instead of going for an eye-catching necklace. "I have the other one, the teardrop, if you'd rather wear it instead."

"I definitely want that one," I said, greedily eyeing the glitzy piece. "I have to dazzle with my jewelry so people won't ask me where my non-existent date is…"

Mom smiled sadly. "I'm sorry he isn't coming."

"So am I." I lifted the ends of my hair while she draped the necklace in place and secured it. The necklace was heavy and cold, reminding me of ice crystals. As an accent to my silvery white column gown, it worked perfectly. My simpler bracelet and earrings were the perfect balance.

"Did you talk to him today?" Surprisingly, my mother had been supportive of me communicating with Kostya over text and email and the occasional phone call. He had caved first, texting me not even a week after I'd left Mexico to apologize and ask me to give him some time to get his head straight.

"Briefly," I answered truthfully. "He called this morning to wish me a happy new year since he knew that I'd be at the gala at midnight."

"Did you tell him you have a date?" She had a mischievous glint in her eyes.

"No! I don't want to make him jealous over an imaginary date. I want him to come back to me because he wants to, not because he's afraid someone else will snap me up first."

"If he keeps hiding in Mexico, someone else will snap you up first," she replied knowingly. "Look at you." She rested her hands on my shoulders and smiled at my reflection in the mirror. "What man tonight isn't going to want to take you home?"

"Mom!" I made a face at the idea of being picked up at the gala. "I'm really not in the mood for casual sex."

"Well, I am," she said with a naughty smile. "In fact, I intend to bring home my latest conquest so don't try crawling into bed with me later to sleep off your hangover."

"Mom! Please!" I didn't know whether to laugh or act grossed out by her oversharing. "I don't know why I let you convince me to move back in with you. You are almost as bad as my roommate sophomore year at SMU. I never knew what I was going to walk into when I opened the door on a Saturday night."

"I'll hang a tie on the door," she offered with a laugh as she swanned out of my room. "I'm leaving now to meet my date. Your car will be here in half an hour," she called out as she headed down the hall. "Lock up on your way out, please."

"I will." When she was out of earshot, I made a dramatic

gagging sound. My mother had a hotter sex life than I did these days. Maybe she'd always had one that was busier than mine, but I hadn't noticed it until moving back in with her. "I have to get a new place," I muttered to myself while touching up my makeup.

My house was supposed to close in a few days. Once I had my cash in hand, I planned to start looking for something new. I couldn't decide if I wanted another house or something more upscale like a luxury condo or apartment. Whatever I picked had to be pet friendly.

One of my resolutions for the coming year was to get a pet. I was leaning toward a cat, but a small dog, maybe a Pug or Pom, were on my list, too. There were a handful of rescues in the area that handled certain breeds so I had no doubt I could find the perfect companion.

I definitely didn't want a massive beast like Vivian and Nikolai had. Stasi was a wonderful and well-behaved dog, but I couldn't handle the noise, slobber or food bills. The dog definitely kept the house safe. Even friendly faces earned an eardrum blasting bark. I couldn't even imagine what kind of a clatter that dog would make if someone tried to threaten the family.

Knowing I would see Vivian and Nikolai tonight at the gala, I practiced the Russian phrases she had taught me so far. She was a very good teacher. If she hadn't been so happy as an artist-slash-housewife, she could have had a very successful career as an educator. She never made me feel dumb or slow when I struggled with the strange alphabet or the awkward pronunciations that felt alien to my tongue. I envied her patience and calmness and felt certain she was going to be an incredible mom.

The doorbell rang unexpectedly. I glanced at the clock on my nightstand. The car wasn't due to pick me up for another ten minutes or so, but maybe they were early because of a heavy workload. Grabbing my clutch, I dropped my lipstick inside, checked my reflection one more time in the full-length mirror and left my room. I descended the stairs carefully, not wanting to trip or slip, and hurried to the door. Even with heels, I had to lift up on my tiptoes to see out of the peephole.

My heart stuttered. *What is he doing here?*

Shaking with excitement, I opened the door and smiled at Kostya. He looked adorably uncomfortable in his starched jeans, white button-down, black jacket and bolo tie. Someone had helped him pick out the perfect boots and Stetson to complete his look. He cleared his throat and fidgeted with the skinny tie at his neck. "Your mom picked it out for me."

I laughed, finally realizing why she had left so early. "Of course, she did."

"May I come in?" He seemed nervous, as if he expected me to slam the door in his face.

"Please." I stepped aside and closed the door after he was safely in the foyer. Leaning back against the door, I studied him for a long moment. "You look good."

"You look beautiful," he said, almost breathless. "You always look beautiful, but tonight? You look amazing, Holly."

"Thanks." I shyly smoothed my hand down the front of my gown. "I usually wear black to this gala, but I wanted to try something different this year."

"I like it. The white," he clarified. "It reminds me of Christmas."

"Oh!" His comment reminded me of the present I had for him. "I've got your present in here—"

"Holly." He grasped my wrist as I tried to rush by him into the living room where our Christmas tree still twinkled. "I didn't come here for a gift."

Biting my lip, I stared up at him anxiously and asked, "Why did you come here?"

"To apologize," he said, cupping my face with his other hand. "To beg you to take me back. To get down on my knees and plead if I have to," he continued, his thumb gently stroking over my lower lip. "I was a fucking idiot to send you away like that. I know I've apologized before in our texts and phone calls, but I wanted to do it properly. Here. Standing in front of you."

"You don't have to keep apologizing for what happened in Mexico." I touched his jaw and breathed in his cologne, the scent comforting and sexy at the same time. "You were in a lot of pain, and you were scared. You were a real asshole, but I understand why."

"You don't have to forgive me for what I did in your salon, Holly." He seemed to be the most bothered by that. "You were right. I had other options. I could have come clean to you about the hit list. I could have made different decisions. I was arrogant and stupid to think that drugging you and getting you out of the way was the best choice that night."

"Yes, you were." I ran my fingertips over his chin and jaw. "You made a lot of mistakes. A *lot* of them," I emphasized, "but we can't move forward together if we're both mired in the past."

"Can we start over, Holly? I don't expect us to pick up

where we left off," he promised. "We can take it slow. We can do it the right way, the way you deserve."

"Yes, we can start over. I'd like that very much." I tried to blink away my tears, suddenly glad I had used my waterproof mascara. Holding out my hand, I said, "I'm Holly Phillips. I think you work for my dad."

He smiled at that and clasped my hand. "Kostya Antonovich. Former spy. Former mob cleaner. Current underboss and employee of your father."

"It's nice to meet you, Kostya." I gestured toward the door. "I'm on my way to a party. Would you like to come?"

"As your friend?"

"Or my date," I said with a shrug. "We can see how the night goes."

He tugged me close, pulling me into his arms and burying his face in my neck. "God, Holly, I have missed you so much. I was fucking lost without you."

Closing my eyes, I held tight to his shoulders, desperate for him to never let go. "You found your way back to me. That's all that matters."

He touched his forehead to mine. "I love you, Holly. I know we're taking it slow, but I need you to know that I never stopped loving you. I didn't think it was possible, but I love you even more now. Every day, it's like my heart is growing bigger and bigger for you."

Lifting up, I kissed him tenderly. "I love you, too. So much."

"Good," he said, sliding one arm around my waist and taking my hand with the other. "I love you so much that I let Gabe fucking Reyes teach me how to two-step."

Laughing, I let him guide me around the foyer of my mother's house, my heels and his boots shuffling in time to an imaginary country song. Eventually, I rested my face against his chest and enjoyed the gentle motion of his body leading mine. I could hear his heartbeat thudding through his chest, and it reminded me of all I could have lost.

It wasn't going to be easy. Moving forward, we still had a lot of issues to work out, and I was sure there would be disagreements. We had made it this far. Together, hand in hand, there was nothing we couldn't face.

"Happy New Year, Holly." He nuzzled my face. "I hope the coming year brings everything you want."

I pressed my lips to his in a sweet kiss. "It already has."

The End.

For Free Reads that continue each couple's story and for new release announcements, please sign up for my newsletter.
http://eepurl.com/sX-z1

Also by Roxie Rivera

Her Russian Protector
Ivan
Dimitri
Yuri
Nikolai
Sergei
Sergei 2
Nikolai 2
Alexei
Kostya

Fighting Connollys
In Kelly's Corner
In Jack's Arms
In Finn's Heart

Debt Collection
Collateral

About the Author

A *New York Times* and *USA Today* bestselling author, I like to write super sexy romances and scorching hot erotica. I live in Texas on five acres with my Viking husband, daughters, two loveably goofy Great Danes and two mischievous cats.

You can find me online at www.roxierivera.com.

Printed in the USA
CPSIA information can be obtained
at www.ICGtesting.com
LVHW041140051023
760079LV00001B/56